PART I

Praise for *LAST STAR BURNING*

"A rich and timely tale that twists
and turns so quickly, you might get whiplash."
—Aprilynne Pike, #1 *New York Times* bestselling author

★"A richly imagined dystopia
that brings new life to familiar tropes."
—*BCCB*, starred review

"Incredibly immersive and tightly plotted."
—*Kirkus Reviews*

"A gripping tale of trust, class struggle, and betrayal."
—*Booklist*

"Sangster does a masterful job of world-building, and
takes the time to develop characters and a plot that twists
in on itself multiple times."
—*SLJ*

"Deep world-building continues throughout the
entire story, rewarding attention and unspooling new
information right up to the breathless ending."
—*VOYA*

ALSO BY CAITLIN SANGSTER

Last Star Burning
Dead Moon Rising

SHATTER
THE
SUNS

a LAST STAR BURNING *novel*

CAITLIN SANGSTER

SIMON PULSE
New York   London   Toronto   Sydney   New Delhi

> *To Allen. Again.*
> *It's only fitting because without you,*
> *I never would have been able to do this.*

SIMON PULSE

An imprint of Simon & Schuster Children's Publishing Division

1230 Avenue of the Americas, New York, New York 10020

First Simon Pulse paperback edition November 2019

Text copyright © 2018 by Caitlin Sangster

Cover illustration copyright © 2018 by Aaron Limonick and David Field

Also available in a Simon Pulse hardcover edition.

For information about special discounts for bulk purchases, please contact Simon & Schuster Special Sales at 1-866-506-1949 or business@simonandschuster.com.

The Simon & Schuster Speakers Bureau can bring authors to your live event.

For more information or to book an event contact the Simon & Schuster Speakers Bureau at 1-866-248-3049 or visit our website at www.simonspeakers.com.

Cover designed by Jessica Handelman

Interior designed by Mike Rosamilia

The text of this book was set in Venetian 301 BT Std.

Manufactured in the United States of America

2 4 6 8 10 9 7 5 3 1

The Library of Congress has cataloged the hardcover edition as follows:

Names: Sangster, Caitlin, author.

Title: Shatter the suns / by Caitlin Sangster.

Description: First Simon Pulse hardcover edition. | New York : Simon Pulse, 2018. | Series: Last star burning ; [2] | Summary: "Sev must decode her mother's last words to find the cure to Sleeping Sickness before Dr. Yang can use it to blackmail people into submitting to his rule"— Provided by publisher.

Identifiers: LCCN 2018007370 (print) | LCCN 2018014769 (eBook) | ISBN 9781481486187 (eBook) | ISBN 9781481486163 (hardcover)

Subjects: | CYAC: Epidemics—Fiction. | Fugitives from justice—Fiction. | Survival—Fiction. | Fantasy.

Classification: LCC PZ7.1.S263 (eBook) | LCC PZ7.1.S263 Sh 2018 (print) | DDC [Fic]—dc23

LC record available at https://lccn.loc.gov/2018007370

ISBN 9781481486170 (paperback)

CHAPTER 1

POWER GROWS FROM THE BARREL OF A GUN. I DON'T care if it is in politics, if it's between two people who think they are friends or two people who have been enemies since the day they were born. Guns hone who you are and what you believe to one black-and-white plane, one purpose. When it comes to power, guns are too dangerous. Not only because they kill, but because if you're the one holding the weapon, you don't have to listen.

That is why I prefer games to assert my dominance. No one is dead at the end of a good round of Find the Bean.

Unfortunately, I'm not doing so well at the moment.

June's eyes meet mine from across the table, blank as the icy blue sky above us. Tai-ge raises an eyebrow as he looks over, sandwiched between two trading post roughers. His hands line up with the others, a long procession of palms on the table. I blink as another set creeps up onto the table next to mine, tiny fingers spread wide. Lihua smiles up at me, then turns to glare at Tai-ge as if he's the only reason I haven't won the game yet.

"You've got it." I point to him. He can't keep a straight face. Never could.

Tai-ge shows me both of his hands. Nothing but dirty calluses.

The wind blows through the pine needles, a frozen whistle that swirls around us up so high in the trees. An Outsider trading post, hidden from Reds and Menghu alike. Cai Ayi, the proprietor, laughs, the sound bubbling out and washing over all of us at the table. "Look at their eyes, Jiang Sev. You can see it in their eyes." Her double chin jiggles as she piles odds and ends from an earlier trade into a wooden box, too interested in our game to really pay attention. "Look at Loss. He's ready to explode."

"You can't help her, Cai Ayi!" Loss complains. One of the five roughers that work for Cai Ayi, he's a craggy mountain towering over me from across the table. Lihua wrinkles her nose at him, and he gives her a slow wink.

"What do you think, Lihua?" I ask, bending to whisper in her ear. The little girl just smiles and looks at her hands palm down on the table, delighted to be playing a game with big kids. After everything she went through to get here, I'm proud of her smile, proud she doesn't think all adults are waiting to stick her with needles like they did back in the Sanatorium. She nestles in close to me, the first prickles of hair growing on her head poking into my arm. She's the only one of the kids down here with us. Peishan, my old friend who we managed to extract from the City along with the kids, keeps them away when we're here if she can manage it.

Pulling at the fringe of hair that falls unevenly past my chin, I squint at Loss. He smiles.

I transfer my gaze to the other rougher at the table, Ze-ming. "It's there," I say, pointing to his right hand.

Ze-ming grins, flicking the white bean that was hidden under his palm at me. "Got me. Good thing, too. You were running out of tries before it got embarrassing."

I flip the bean into my palm and tilt my head toward him. "Does winning mean I get a discount?"

Ze-ming rolls his eyes and points to the bean. "For your superior powers of observation, that one is half off. Beyond that, you'd have to take it up with Cai Ayi."

Cai Ayi laughs again, shaking her head as she carefully closes the crate. "This game isn't smart enough for that, honey. You beat Loss at weiqi and we'll talk."

June sits a little straighter, though she doesn't look up from the table. She probably could beat Loss and all his ancestors seven generations back, but she won't speak up to challenge him. I grin at Loss, meaning to ask for her, but he's too busy making faces at Lihua to pay attention.

Cai Ayi's establishment is almost big enough to be a housing unit from the City, lights dancing so high in the leaves that it's hard to believe they belong to people when you're looking up from the ground. A single rope ladder is the only way to get up to the first platform, a patchwork of rough-hewn logs wedged between the large branches of the tree. Roughers stand watch over the ropes that fan out from there, a tightrope walk to the storehouse, or the canteen where Cai Ayi makes flower teas. Up a little higher, wooden plank bridges line the branches to form living quarters. A good step closer to civilization than I would have thought possible Outside a few months ago. Cai Ayi and her roughers are all well fed, easy to talk to, and ready to sell anything not nailed down. Quicklights. Food. The two canisters of inhibitor spray I have tucked snugly in my pocket. All honestly acquired, so they say, but I've seen the City seal stamped on more than one item here, and I'm pretty sure Chairman Sun doesn't come out this far to get his slippers.

I give Lihua an extra hug before I stand up. Cai Ayi may have agreed to board the children that June, Tai-ge, and I pulled out of the ashes of the Sanatorium, but I doubt the deal will hold if she finds out Lihua has a little help from a hidden Mantis bottle. The Sanatorium gave orphans a medicine that caused compulsions just like SS does in order to isolate them from the rest of the City and experiment on them. It wasn't just fake cases of SS in the Sanatorium, though. Luckily, out of all the kids we stole away from the City, Lihua is the only one legitimately infected.

Cai Ayi made it quite clear that infected are not allowed at her establishment. It feels almost irresponsible keeping Lihua's affliction to ourselves, but she can't come with us where we're going. And we can't tell, because I've seen what happens when you disobey Post rules. Loss threw one Wood Rat right off a platform for noncompliance, and it wasn't even a level close to the ground.

I can understand why infected aren't allowed, since compulsing Post patrons could end with a decision between fighting a Seph who means to cut off your toes to the tune of a nursery song or falling from the topmost platform. I'm not sure what she'll do if she finds out about Lihua. Interacting with Cai Ayi and the roughers is like eating a peach. Soft and sweet on the outside, but I'm afraid that if I take many more bites I'll break my teeth on a hard, bitter core.

I follow June with my eyes as she hops down from her seat at the table and walks over to Cai Ayi. Bareheaded, as if her golden curls don't matter. This far out, they don't.

Cai Ayi smiles at her, pulling out the bag of items we asked for, but June shakes her head, stonily silent until Cai Ayi fizzes over with laughter, adding an extra packet of dried pears.

Tai-ge puts down the set of kitchen knives that is going to pay for our supplies this week: the pears and a backpack for each of us. I pick up the closest pack, fingers skimming the clean fabric, though it shows obvious signs of previous ownership. Red ownership. Unit numbers are stamped in sharp, blocky numbers on the underside of each pack.

"What's that?" Tai-ge asks, peering over the edge of the box Cai Ayi has just pried open with a metal screech.

"Some minor growth regulators." She looks up with a grin, dropping the hammer she used to prize the box open. "I have a buyer for this batch due here in a few minutes, but if you're interested in starting a garden wherever it is June has you two stashed, I may be able to help."

"Minor growth regulators?"

"Not the kind that's going to put up a gas cloud. I don't deal in weapons, whatever their primary purpose is supposed to be. Not good for business. All my customers would be picking one another off. Or attacking the Post."

Tai-ge stares down at the growth regulators, the City seal stamped in red on the paper sacks. "What would you want for one of these?"

Cai Ayi harrumphs. "Leave your bargaining to June, boy, or you'll end up walking home stark naked. I've taken a shine to your fancy boots."

June steps forward to touch the bag of growth regulators and pulls something from her pocket. A book. She holds it up, sunlight catching gilt-edged pages.

"No! No, not that." I intervene, holding my hand out for the book. It's silly—a fairy tale that somehow followed me out of the Mountain—but I don't want to give it up just yet. June shrugs and hands it over. She pulls the knives back toward her, then unstraps a pair of binoculars from around her neck and points to the bag of pears, the packs, and the growth regulators.

Cai Ayi nods slowly. "You sure, June?" Binoculars are one of those things you can't find out here easily, I'd guess. We took these from the Chairman's house, but we found another pair that were in the supplies on board the heli we stole. Cai Ayi's shrug is just a little too pleased. She's getting a good trade here. "All right."

She pulls out the top bag of growth regulator and hands it over to Tai-ge, then pushes the package of kitchen knives back to June, who shakes her head. She points to Lihua and then the binoculars.

The pleased look on Cai Ayi's face falls a little slack. But she nods. "I suppose that's a slightly fairer trade. I can board your friends for another month. For the binoculars *and* the knives."

June shakes her head, handing the knives to me and holding out the binoculars.

Cai Ayi stares at her, but then the grin crinkles back up on her face. "Fine, fine, fine. I'll keep your bald little rats for another three weeks, shall we say? Plus the bags, the pears . . ." She ticks them off on her fingers.

Taking the knives back from me, June looks top-heavy, as if she's about to keel over under the weight of the binoculars and knives combined. She snakes one arm out and points to Lihua, then puts up two fingers.

Cai Ayi laughs. "Two months? All for some kitchen knives? You drive a hard bargain, my girl." But she smiles and takes the binoculars and knives both, setting the latter down on the now-half-empty crate to eye the binocular's glassy lenses. "Sky above knows what you want with growth regulators anyway. Aren't you folk just running through? If you were planning to stay, you'd have already set up a real camp instead of paying my exorbitant boarding fees."

"Never know when you need to plant some tarot." Tai-ge hefts the bag over his shoulder and we move to the ladder that leads to the ground.

I give Lihua one last hug and pull the straps of my pack over my shoulders, gritting my teeth at the prospect of climbing down the rope ladder. The City seal sitting between my shoulder blades feels odd, like if I don't keep an eye on it, the falcon and beaker will burn through my coat and brand me between the shoulder blades.

"Sure you don't want an escort back to your camp?" Ze-ming calls after us as we start down the ladder. Amusement curls in his voice.

They've offered every time we come. Ze-ming's grin wards off June's murderous glare in response to the question. Scavengers supposedly prey on Post customers, though we've yet to stumble into a nest of Wood Rats. I get the feeling that the roughers do a fair amount of scavenging themselves.

At least they're like me, for the most part. Playing games and telling jokes, even if they do have a darker streak. Mother played games, and I'm now wondering if her last words were another one, a riddle only I could solve to confuse the people she worried might be listening.

Except I have no idea what the words "Port North" could mean.

What I do know, though, is she told me to find my family in Port North. My *family*. Could that mean that I am not as alone as I'd thought? I shoot Tai-ge a smile and am rewarded when his cheeks dimple and he grins back. June's on my other side, her hand companionably on my arm. The sky might be icy, the ground cracked with cold, but I feel the fire of hope inside my chest as we go down the ladder.

My mother hid the cure to SS with my family. June, Tai-ge, and I are going to find them.

CHAPTER 2

TAI-GE'S EYES SCAN THE ICED-OVER BRANCHES AND bushes as we start the trek back toward the heli, his hand on the knife in his jacket pocket. He flinches as the pack rubs against his shoulders, and though his sleeves hide it, I know it must be irritating the long, scabby lines running up and down his arms. Scratches drawn by infected fingernails and teeth, attempting to keep us on the ground or come with us as we escaped the City. I'll have to check them over when we get back, make sure they're still healing properly. Not that my barefoot doctor qualifications will do much to help if Tai-ge has any real problems.

June's head is completely hidden by her pack, bobbing along in front of me as if it's walking by itself. "Do Cai Ayi and the roughers know?" I ask. "I mean, about contagious SS and Menghu invading the City?" I shiver, thinking of the tiger insignia snarling from Menghu collars. A more accurate depiction of the people inside those uniforms than I realized, back when I first met Helix, Cale, and Mei. Before I watched them kill people with no more thought than they took stirring sauce into their noodles.

Before they all tried to kill me.

June glances back at me around the edge of the pack and shrugs. "They'll find our camp soon if we don't move."

I shift my pack, the frame rubbing against my shoulder blades, the flickering hope inside me dimming a degree or two. I'm all for leaving, but it's getting to Port North that's the problem. No one seems to have heard of it. Not Tai-ge with all his Red connections. Not June, though she's spent her whole life Outside. Not Cai Ayi or the Roughers, either, Loss going so far as to ask what a Port was exactly.

A question I'd like to know the answer to as well.

It's been two weeks since I left Mother at the peak of Traitor's Arch. Two weeks since we escaped the burning City. My insides squirm at the thought of the people we deserted there, crying to be let on the heli, fighting with one another, shooting at one another. . . .

Howl falling to the ground, Tai-ge's bullets in his chest.

I shake my head, shoving the image away. It feels as if we've been playing Cai Ayi's Find the Bean game since the moment Mother gave me her instructions. Pointing and slapping at hands instead of placing our stones with the care and attention of a weiqi master.

Well, no more waiting. We don't have time to hope our ancestors or fate or luck throw something our way. If we don't move, it won't be the roughers we have to worry about. Mother was right to worry about who was listening when she told me to go to Port North. Dr. Yang was there, and if he gets to the cure first, then there won't be much left to hope for.

I touch the inhibitor spray in my pocket—the reassuring weight a promise no one else will be able to hold me at gunpoint so easily ever again—and twist to look back at Tai-ge. "What did you want with growth regulators? As far as I know, it's the wrong season for growing onions." The skies have been clear, turning the banks of snow around us rock-hard. We're lucky there are lots of paths cut through this area already, so following us isn't so easy as watching for footprints.

"Weak growth regulators can be used as an explosive if you add the right ingredients." Tai-ge answers. "If I siphon off some of our fuel, we could potentially use it."

"Siphon off heli fuel? Do we have enough to spare?"

"The heli mostly runs on solar. Fuel's for takeoff." Tai-ge grunts, pain pinching one eye shut as he readjusts the bag over his hurt shoulders. "You still set on breaking into Dazhai?"

Dazhai. The farm to which the Firsts fled, taking their Mantis and most of the City's Outside patrollers with them, if the radio transmissions are to be believed.

We disconnected the heli positioning device so no one will be able to follow its signature back to us. Unfortunately, it also left us blind until Tai-ge tweaked the radio so it would intercept transmissions. It's hard to glean much, just positions and reports and requests. Nothing to tell us who else survived the Menghu invasion of the City, or where Dr. Yang is, or whether the contagious strain of SS he set loose on the City is raging in this direction yet. But we have listened enough to know that if there's a map out there with Port North on it, it's probably at Dazhai.

"Yes." I keep my voice chipper. "I'm still set on breaking into Dazhai. You think we should use the growth regulators to blow something up? That sounds a little dramatic."

Tai-ge grimaces. "I'd say 'desperate' is a bit more accurate." A pause, and I know what's coming—an argument we've already had several times. "Sev, we don't have to break into a camp full of our own people. We could just . . . walk in. Find the highest-ranking Red and tell them we know where to find a cure to SS."

I can almost feel June scowling in front of me, as if she's calling down her own personal storm cloud. She knows what will happen if we go to anyone from the City. It's hard to forget after seeing Lihua, her hair still growing out from being shaved. She had a death date affixed to her name back in the City. All the kids we flew out of there did.

At least, it's hard for *me* to forget.

Tai-ge's spent his whole life with everything wrapped up and sealed like a red envelope at New Year's. I think sometimes he wishes he could forget that it wasn't just Peishan and Lihua who had expiration dates while they were still inside City walls. I was on the City's lung-stopping assembly line too, with every possible stamp of approval just waiting to clear the paperwork.

Tai-ge saw firsthand what happens when you try to go against the City.

I swallow, trying not to push away the memory as I would have a few months ago. Face it head-on, or the memories will congeal inside me. Tai-ge's father, the general of the Liberation army, about to shoot me. Tai-ge trying to explain to him Dr. Yang's connection to the Menghu as they poured into the City. The explosion. The blood, the screams, my eardrums shattered by the bomb. Little pieces of jade raining down on us as we ran.

We can't ever go back. "No one is going to listen to us, Tai-ge. And if they find June, they'll kill her."

"If I'm there, they can't . . . I didn't mean . . ." Tai-ge bites back the rest of his answer, looking at his feet instead of June's hunched shoulders. "Fine. We can talk about this back at camp."

There isn't anything to talk about that we haven't already said. The cure can't go to the City, or the Chairman will use it the same way he did Mantis: to control people. We still don't know how deep Dr. Yang's hooks were in the City. Walking back into rows of tents stamped with the City's falcon-and-beaker seal might lead us straight back to him. But as I search for new words that will convince Tai-ge of this, June stops, her chin raised toward the treetops. She breathes in deep, then lets it out.

"What is it?" I look out into the snow-silent forest, goose bumps erupting down my arms as the shadowy trees peer back at me.

She takes another deep breath, so much air it must be filling her to the toes. When she lets it out, the air clouds above her in an icy mist.

My voice lodges in my throat. "Did you hear something?"

"Maybe." She rubs her nose, then starts down the path.

"Is it not enough that I'm here?" Tai-ge whispers, continuing our conversation as if June hadn't stopped.

My stomach clenches. He thought I was a traitor but came for me down in the Hole anyway. I've always been the one flaw in his devotion to the City. Still, Tai-ge made the choice. He chose *me*. It's like the second half of a dream—the half I never let myself imagine before, when we were in the City. Tai-ge sitting next to me, planning with me, wanting to be with me, all without the barrier of stars sharp between us.

"I'm glad you're here." I stop and turn to meet his eyes, trying to inject the weight and importance I feel attached to those words. I know how much Tai-ge gave up to be here. His family, or what's left of it. His convictions about life and how the world should work. He came because he trusts me, because he missed me when I was gone from the City. Because they lied about where I was, about *what* I was. I give him a slow smile, waiting until I know he's truly listening. "I wouldn't trade you for anyone, Tai-ge. Of course it's enough."

He nods, the side of his mouth curling to match mine. We might not agree about everything, but we'll figure it out.

No one speaks for the rest of the walk, and the silence stretches tight across my shoulders, making me want to shrug it away. Our camp was June's idea, a casual suggestion to put the heli down in a wide clearing shielded from the wind by a set of rocky cliffs on one side, tall trees on the other. She didn't tell us about the Post until we'd landed. She constantly surprises me, though I don't know why. She's lived out here long enough to know where to find food and supplies. I guess I assumed she didn't because *I* didn't. A dangerous way to think.

It's twilight by the time we get back to the camp, a breeze stealing the ice's foggy breath and ruffling the shrouded hulk of the heli where it sits against the cliffs. We pass a metal column as we enter the clearing. A similar column perches at the top of the rocky outcropping towering over the heli, thick cables trailing to the ground where a metal bench sits, half covered by dirt and ice. Ruins from before the Influenza War. Though why anyone would ride a slick metal bench up a mountain, completely exposed to the frigid air, is beyond me.

Tai-ge holds the heli's canvas cover up for June to go in first, waiting for me to follow before ducking under himself. The two of us climb up the ladder after June, waiting for her to open the hatch.

"Prison," June says, her cool whisper sinking into the voice lock and flinging it open.

A joke, I think. Her only voiced complaint. Even I feel a little cramped in the heli cockpit after sleeping under the stars. But it isn't safe out there. I shiver, giving one last look to the trees. Anyone could be in these mountains. And if people weren't enough, the gores would be.

Just inside the hatch, I have to climb over June's sleeping bag and skip to avoid landing my wet boots on Tai-ge's sleeping bag. Still, it's much roomier than it was before we extracted all but the pilot and copilot chairs to make space for us to sleep. We unlace our boots and throw them next to the supplies piled by the cargo bay door. Tai-ge flicks on the radio to eavesdrop on Red transmissions, and June goes to the bags of food, placing the new bag of dried pears on top of the other supplies like a crown.

The wind sneaks through the heli, rattling the cargo bay door. We chose to steal this particular aircraft, meant for troop transport, because of the extra room. We had ten Sanatorium victims with us, their heads shaved clean. As we took off, a grenade hit us from underneath, leaving long tears in the heli's underbelly. Not an ideal place for Peishan, Lihua, and the others, since it wasn't just the cold we were worried about coming through the long gashes in the metal. It was a relief when Cai Ayi agreed to take them on. Even Lihua, who wasn't keen to leave June or the heli at first, seems to have settled a bit.

"Let's eat outside tonight." I grab a bag of rice, hefting it in my hand. It should last us another week or so. After that we won't have much more to trade if we want to keep eating. "I can't stand sitting in here." The forest outside might be troubling, but sitting inside feels too much like hiding. "We'll stay close to the ladder. Then tomorrow morning we'll get our things ready for Dazhai and let Peishan know we'll be gone for a bit."

Tai-ge hesitates, but June is down the ladder before he can say anything. Together, June and I gather Junis wood and build a fire, then the three of us slump in our sleeping bags around the smokeless flames, telling stories and jokes. Tai-ge even sings a Red drinking song, the departure from his straight-backed, buttoned-up state making me clap along, laughing at the rhymes. Even June smiles.

When the last flames die, leaving only char and ash in our fire ring, Tai-ge pulls me up to go back inside where it's safe. I pause to look up at the stars. Thousands of stitches in a quilted sky. It brings to mind the story Howl told me that first night after we left the City, a ridiculous fairy tale of a star falling in love with a peasant, only to be separated forever on opposite sides of the sky.

It wasn't only Tai-ge's world that gave one last shuddering breath during that invasion. I lost things that day too. My eyes catch on Zhinu, the daughter of the sun. She's alone up there in the sky. She always will be.

"What are you looking for?" Tai-ge's hand bumps mine as we look up into the night.

I grab his hand and squeeze it. I want to believe there's something more waiting for me at Port North than the dark empty ring surrounding Zhinu's lonely spot in the stars. That maybe it's a place I could belong instead of a fairy tale waiting to uncurl into yet another bad dream. But some hopes are too fragile to speak out loud, so I stand there with my hand in Tai-ge's, the silence between us too big to fill.

CHAPTER 3

THAT NIGHT, THE DREAMS COME. NOT THE ONES I used to have of being trapped inside my own body, paralyzed by SS. Now Cale visits me, a pile of Red corpses under her feet and her gun pointed at my head. June's old clan—Tian, Cas, Parhat, and Liu—lying in pools of their own blood. A gore's black eyes watch me from behind a curtain of vines, and Cale's dead weight on my shoulders pins me to the ground when the monster charges. Mother. Her papery skin tearing under my fingers, her eyes vacant.

I wake in a sweat, fear wrapped tight around my ribs. Rolling over, I go through a calming ritual of finding June's corn silk hair snarled across the rucksack she's using for a pillow. Safe. Next, Tai-ge, the shadows sinking deeper into the creases in his face that I don't remember being there before. Still alive. My breath catches at the blank space where Peishan and the kids are supposed to be, but then I remember: They're up in the trees with Cai Ayi. Before, when we all squeezed together in the cockpit, they snuggled together in the corner, arms and hands and tear-smudged cheeks sprouting from the muddled pile of humans.

I force my eyes to close again, but I can't stand the thought of sleep. Can't let the dead creep into my head again. I'm so tired, though, my body won't comply. Just as dreams start to twist my thoughts into stories, a noise scrapes my eyes back open. The whisper of metal brushing metal. Screwing my eyes shut, I wrap my fingers tight around the inhibitor spray.

I don't hear the sound again. But that doesn't stop me lying awake, waiting.

I must have fallen asleep, because I wake to Tai-ge at the control panel, the buzz of static in my ears. An echoing fear lances through me before I can brush it down as my brain tries to sort through the sounds that must have woken me. Voices squeezed through the tiny holes in the radio, Tai-ge whispering into the microphone . . .

I rub my eyes. Nightmares trying to claw their way into daylight. Tai-ge's not talking to anyone over the radio. He's listening to more reports. "Anything new?" I ask.

He shakes his head.

"Sleep okay?" I ask.

Tai-ge's hands drag down his cheeks, as though pulling them off might wake him up. "Like a chicken waiting for his turn to be fried."

"Let's not wait any longer, then. We'll eat, get our packs together." I pull myself up from the sleeping bag. "Choose a landing spot far enough away from Dazhai that we'll be able to get away before the Seconds can come find the heli. . . ."

June bolts up from her sleeping bag, almost like a bird diving for safety in the face of a predator. She grabs from our pile of potatoes, has the hatch open, and is down the ladder before I can finish my sentence. I glance back at Tai-ge, his mouth hanging open. He still isn't used to June.

"Shall we continue this conversation outside?" I ask, pulling the sleeping bag down and extracting my legs.

He nods. "Yeah. Let me find Dazhai on the downloaded maps and plot a course first. I'll be down in a sec. Throw a potato on the fire for me, would you?"

"Yes, sir." I give him a mock salute and am gratified when it teases an almost-smile from my friend instead of festering at the back of his expression like an unwelcome memory. He's going to be okay. All of this is going to be okay.

June glances up from kicking at the ashes of our fire ring when I come down, the Junis residue catching in the morning breeze adding a burned tinge to the air. I help her arrange wood from what we gathered the night before into something that might catch fire, though I suspect my presence is being tolerated rather than actually helping. By the time we have flames leaping between us, Tai-ge slides down the ladder. He rubs his eyes as he walks toward us, stomach audibly rumbling.

"Find what we need?" I ask.

"I think so." He fiddles with the zip to his coat before looking back up. "I still feel like we're doing this the hard way."

June stands up, a potato in each hand. "Leftover rice up in the heli," she informs me.

I blink at her, waiting for her to continue, but instead she turns around to start poking at the edge of the fire. Though I'm still not adept at interpreting June's lack of words, I think that might have been a request for me to *get* the leftover rice.

As I pull myself through the hatch, a dull thud sounds from deep inside the heli, the sound of metal on glass making my skin crawl. Rodents? Rats lived in the walls back at the orphanage. They would come out at night, looking for bits of contraband food smuggled up to the rooms. I hate rats. More than spiders or mosquitoes or . . .

How could rats have found their way up the heli ladder?

I hear another thud, something moving around in the aircraft's bulbous stomach, just behind the cargo bay's barricaded doors— where I heard the sound last night. And then, quiet. I close my eyes, trying to rein in my imagination. Maybe rats *can* get up here. Really large . . . person-size rats.

Did Loss and Ze-ming follow us? Or could it be Menghu, tiger snarls on their faces to match the slavering insignia on their collars? Wood Rats, ready to strip the heli down? Dr. Yang, planning to slit our throats before we realize he's here? Gores tearing through the broken metal? Or, worst of all, swarms and swarms of infected, crying for help beneath us, just waiting to break our bones and bite our fingers off one by one . . . I shake my head, trying to end the images, each more preposterous than the last.

June, too tired to climb up through the metal tears below like she usually does, pushed all the boxes away from the cargo bay doors before we went to sleep yesterday to check that nothing had snuck in. She's inspected the empty space every day we've been out here, the threat of stowaways or hijackers much more likely this close to the Post. We've been so careful. There couldn't be anyone back there. It must just be rats.

I reach for the chain that hooks over the handle to keep the door shut just to prove my fears wrong. As my hand touches the chain, something falls on the other side of the door, metal clattering as it hits. Accompanied by a hushed exclamation involving Yuan Zhiwei's underclothing.

City rats? Who can swear.

I jerk back from the door, almost falling over as my foot catches in the folds of Tai-ge's sleeping bag. Trying to be quiet, I slide through the hatch and back down the ladder, one hand clamped tight over my mouth. Tai-ge stands up when I get to the bottom, alarm twisting his eyebrows in a knot. June is nowhere to be seen, her leaf-wrapped potatoes left to cook at the base of our fire.

"Are you okay?" Tai-ge asks, looking me over as if there should be blood. "What's wrong?"

I put a finger to my lips to shush him. "Did June climb up into the cargo bay?" I whisper, hoping against hope that it was her I heard.

Tai-ge shakes his head. "Why are we whispering?"

"There's someone up there."

His hand slips down to his side where a gun would normally hang, and he looks a little lost when there's nothing to grab. We don't have any more ammunition, so the guns are stashed up in the cockpit. "June ran off into the forest to . . ." Tai-ge stops. "Actually, I don't know why she ran off into the forest. June doesn't usually talk to me directly. How many people?"

I shrug. "I don't know. One? Probably?"

"Did they hear you?"

"I . . . don't think so." It's almost more disconcerting to see Tai-ge turn his calculating gaze toward the heli's torn undersides than it is to see the longing in his eyes as he listens to Reds talk back and forth on the radio. We used to do tutoring sessions when his family was still in charge of brainwashing me back into City graces, but it was all history and ideology. I don't like to think of Tai-ge as someone who knows how to mark a target.

"You make some noise up front with the door." Tai-ge jumps up. "I'll come in from underneath and take them by surprise."

"You're not trained for one-on-one fighting, are you? You were supposed to have some cushy job behind a desk."

"I'll be just fine, Sev. Even I had to work my way through normal combat training. 'Believe you can conquer, and the world will bend.'"

"Is that a quote from Chairman Sun's book of sayings . . . ?"

Tai-ge ducks under the heli instead of answering. I hop on the ladder's bottom rung, watching until he's ready to climb up into the tears in the heli's belly before scrambling through the hatch. He doesn't seem flustered or worried that someone has invaded the closest thing we have to a home. I feel violated, as though something sacred is broken.

Once inside, I'm so distracted by the sound of my own heartbeat thumping in my chest that I don't notice the chain lock hanging limp against the cargo bay door until my hand is on the knob. Did June leave it loose last night? As I push the door open, it yanks out from under my hand, sending me stumbling into the cargo bay. Arms grab hold of me as I fall, pinning my arms to my sides.

The prick of a knife lights a line of fire under my chin. "Don't move. Don't yell." The voice is male. Whispering, but calm. "Wait until your friend gets up here."

That voice. Like the sting of alcohol on a cut as my brain tries to tell me I recognize it. Someone I heard speak in a dream, now come to life. I pull against him, curve around the arm pressing into my ribs so I can bite him, stomp on his feet, elbow his stomach. Anything to get away or warn Tai-ge. But jerking my head to the side only brings the knife closer, my breath drawing out in a gasp as the blade digs against my windpipe. Out of the corner of my eye, I can see scarring against the tan of my attacker's hand. A First mark.

It can't be. My brain refuses to process it. . . . I try to cry out a warning, but before I can make a sound, Tai-ge's head pops up through the jagged metal hole. When he spots me, the color drains from his face.

"Sevvy!" He scrambles up, eyes wide. "Let her go. You can have whatever you want. Just leave her alone."

"Everyone. Calm. Down." I can feel the man's heartbeat through his coat, pumping fast. A metallic thud echoes through the room, and the man's arms loosen. I push out of the circle of his grip, half running, half falling toward Tai-ge. He grabs me, and I spin around in time to see June hit my attacker again, the medikit sounding hollow as it strikes his head.

But the man still doesn't fall, hood shadowing his face as he stumbles forward, barely catching himself on unsteady feet. Just in time to catch a full blast of my inhibitor spray to his face. The knife falls to the ground, hood pulling back an inch or two as the rest of him goes down.

Which is when I start to scream. Because all the disbelief and horror attempting to shield me from the truth fall away. Of course I know his voice.

It's Howl.

CHAPTER 4

DEAD. HOWL WAS SUPPOSED TO BE DEAD.

And dead people can't hurt you.

"What is he doing here? How did he find us?" I grip my head, trying to control the chaos of my thoughts. My stomach fills with bile as I try to look anywhere but the slow rise and fall of his chest. June still holds the medikit outstretched in her hand as if she can't quite believe what she's done. Her mouth is open, trying to find words, and there's a tear on her cheek.

I crouch on the floor next to him, betrayal a smoky haze that curls around my throat.

Howl can't be alive. When I last saw him, he was twitching on a hangar floor, Tai-ge's and June's bullets in his chest, infected streaming across the floor, explosions, fire . . . Even after everything that happened between us, after running away from the Mountain in the middle of the night to get away from him and Dr. Yang's knives . . . some small part of me hoped I'd been wrong. That Howl had followed me so he could explain.

It's easy to absolve the dead. To allow them to squeeze back into the dreams they spun around you like a web because there's something pitiful and small about a body left to go cold. But regretting those bullets was just making up fairy tales, coming up with excuses for why I let Howl lie to me without tasting the deception in every word.

I wanted to believe.

It's just like that ridiculous book he gave me, the lure of a happy ending blinding the reader to reality even when it's rotting right in front of them. I should have let June give the book, gilded cover and all, to Cai Ayi.

"He . . ." June's voice brings my head up. She gulps and tries again. "He said . . ."

"You *knew* he was here?" The words come out in a blazing rush, and June shrinks back. "How long has he been back here?"

"Just last night." Her eyes barely make it up from the floor, connecting with mine for less than a second before dropping back down. "He said he wasn't going to hurt you."

"Yuan's bloody ax!" Tai-ge bursts in, voice too loud as he paces. "They're going to come for us. They're going to find us and kill us. Slowly."

June's horror dulls to confusion. "Menghu?"

"The *Menghu*? What in Yuan's name is wrong with you?" Tai-ge rants, falling to the floor beside Howl, pulling his hood back the rest of the way. "The Chairman's son has been missing for months now. Of all the places he could crop up . . . and we come at him with a rusty medikit and inhibitor spray."

My brain can't quite put Tai-ge's words together, each of them crumbling to nonsense inside my head. "You shot him." My voice tears at the edges. "Back in the City. When we were running." Turning back to June, I try to ignore my hands shaking.

"You both shot him. I saw him on the ground. He was dead."

"I *never*—!" Tai-ge swears again. "I wouldn't have shot at a First. I would have recognized him."

June pulls something out from under the bench screwed into the wall. A padded vest with two tears puncturing the front flaps. I've heard of these. Leftover from Before. Bulletproof.

"Maybe he won't remember." Tai-ge's voice drips with desperation as he crouches next to Howl's limp form, easing his head up from the floor. "If we figure out where he came from and fix him up, then the Chairman could—"

"Tai-ge!" I'm surprised by the acid corroding my voice. "*Get away from him. He's not who you think it is.*" June and Tai-ge both stare at me, Tai-ge taking a second before he carefully lowers Howl's head back to the floor. "June." I soften my voice. "Find some rope. Tape. Anything."

"I'm sorry . . ." June's mouth screws shut over the words. She drops the medikit and backs toward the cockpit doors. "You two were so . . ." She won't look at me, her eyes nailed to the floor. "I thought . . . he promised."

"Howl lies, June. You aren't the first to believe him." I turn to Tai-ge, his hands wringing together until the skin is bloodless and pale. "Find whatever he's using to communicate." I think back to the link Howl gave me in the Mountain, hidden inside his dead brother's gore-tooth necklace. "Jewelry, maybe? Something small."

Tai-ge stares at me as if I'm about to commit an unpardonable crime. I pick up the medikit, blood smearing across my fingers as I open it. There's some blue reinforced tape inside.

I pull a strip of the tape loose and take a deep breath. Start with Howl's feet. Focus on the pull of the tape, the muddy flecks littered across Howl's Menghu-issue boots as I bind them together. Shoelaces that look waxy and new. A frayed spot in the leather by his big toe. Anything but the memories flooding back. Of Sole, a medic who used to partner with him on bloody patrols, telling me stories of Howl killing every City-born he could find, children included. Of Howl showing me his forged City stars and promising to help me find a place I could belong.

I thought I could let myself regret the questions I didn't get to ask. The ones that would have settled what Howl was after once and for all. My shoulder scrunches around the tender line burning down the curve of my neck where Howl held his blade.

Those questions have firm answers now. Howl came after me, and he came with a knife.

"Tai-ge?" I insert some steel into my voice, trying not to hold my breath as I wind the tape again around Howl's ankles. "A link? Weapons?"

The floor creaks behind me as Tai-ge finally moves, extracting a pack from under the bench bolted to the metal. He undoes the top clasps and loses his grip on the muddy canvas, accidentally upending it to let Howl's things scatter across the floor. Tai-ge stares down at the mess of compressed crackers, water purifiers, and clothing, taking several deep breaths before kneeling to spread the things out into straight lines, flinching every time he touches something, as if each contact is leaving some kind of mark on his skin. Mostly there are long tubes of paper that roll free from Howl's things. They go every which way across the heli's uneven floor, getting caught under the benches and in the far corner, one wobbling right up to the lip of the corrugated tear in our heli's belly.

My arms and hands tingle, and I look away, focusing on Howl's sleeves, the frayed edge to the cuff of his coat. Pull the bulky jacket back from his wrists to press his palms together, trying to decide if I should tape over the long-sleeved shirt underneath or pull it back too. I don't want to touch his skin, don't want to look at his hands and remember the last time he touched my cheek or slipped an arm around my waist. The lines on his knuckles and palms are scrubbed over with grime, but his clothes somehow smell like spicy Mountain soap instead of dirt and campfire. There's a single red star at his collar, as if he's gone back to pretending his bloodline goes straight to Yuan Zhiwei.

His fingers start to twitch.

"I don't see anything he could communicate with in here." Tai-ge's voice is quiet behind me. "There's a gun. Some ammunition. And over by you there's the knife he . . . the knife."

"The one he almost cut me open with?" I kick the weapon back toward Tai-ge and tape over the sleeves, unwinding the tape as fast as it will go, then over the exposed skin at his wrists. "Get rid of it. The gun too." Nervous energy crawls down from my chest to my stomach, as Howl's eyelids begin to flutter, an army of ants looking for a good place to tunnel through. The inhibitor spray doesn't knock people out for long. It gives you enough time to run.

This time, I can't run.

Howl's eyelids scrunch down as if he knows pain is coming, but it hasn't quite settled yet. I wind the tape faster and faster, trying to win the race before Howl can open his eyes. One eye cracks, and then the other, deep brown irises glazed as they try to focus on my face. "Sev?"

I throw his hands away from me, off the floor and running before he can say anything else. When I get to the cockpit, I pull the door shut behind me, air squeezing out of my lungs in rapid-fire bursts I can't control. Cracking the door back open, I call to Tai-ge, "Just . . . push him out the hole in the floor and we'll take off.

We don't need to tell Peishan we're leaving. We have to get to . . . where we're going." I can't even say the name Dazhai out loud now, because then Howl would know where to follow us.

Why did he follow us?

"Sevvy." Tai-ge's voice is only inches away, on the other side of the door.

"Please, Tai-ge."

He sighs, the sound tinny and shallow. "If we let him go, he could ID our heli. And we talked enough about Dazhai that I'm guessing he knows we're headed there. Maybe he was hoping to stow away. Get back to where he belongs."

"Howl is *not the Chairman's son*."

Nothing from the other side of the door. Then, "Okay. That doesn't change the fact that he found us and we don't know how. Or why. If he's in contact with Firsts or Seconds or anyone else. If he does have some way to communicate, he could radio in the moment we take off. Tell them we're coming. We wouldn't even make it past the outer guard."

Fear trills through me. How *did* Howl find us? I know *why* Howl is here. The ticket that he thinks gets him out of jail slipped from his pocket and ran back to the City by herself, then destroyed the only other chance he had at avoiding Dr. Yang's scalpel. Wasn't that what he said right before Sole told me who he really was, that waking Mother up was my only way out of being cut open?

He was wrong. Dr. Yang could never have found the cure in our brains or blood. He was just manipulating both of us, trying to get us to run back to the City to wake Mother up so she'd tell me where she'd hidden her papers. Howl probably doesn't know that, though. So here we are again, Howl wanting to go home, and determined to take me with him as a human shield.

I lean against the door, hand clenched over my mouth. What if it isn't just Howl? Everyone in the Mountain thought we were the only cure to SS. Me and Howl. Are there more Menghu crawling in now, while we're distracted? "Okay. We can't leave him here. We need to move right now, though."

"We're not ready to move. We're already on risky ground hoping to abandon the heli at Dazhai before Seconds can get to us. We need time to scout where their lookouts are, to stash our packs and to make sure we have a way *out*. If we fly now, in broad daylight and without our supplies ready to go—"

Swallow. Deep breath. "Just . . . move us to somewhere in the middle, so Howl won't know where we are. We'll make sure he didn't tell anyone about us, take anything that could be a link to the Menghu, and leave him far away from any of the camps. Then we'd be safe to go to Dazhai."

Tai-ge's silence feels too loud. When he finally speaks, the sound makes me flinch. "Okay. Give me a second. I'll make sure he can't move. Check through his things again to see if I can find a communication device, and then we'll be off."

I nod, a jerky movement that feels unnatural. Tai-ge can't even see me, so I don't know why I'm doing it, but there's no way I'm going back into the cargo bay. No way I'm even speaking again, because Howl is in there and speaking where he'll be able to hear me feels untenable.

I turn to the controls, wishing I knew which buttons to push to get us started, so the moment Tai-ge walks in here we can take off. Once we're high enough, I'll . . . send June back to roll Howl out through the hole in the cargo bay floor when Tai-ge can't protest. Or something.

June. I blink, looking around the empty cockpit and my eyes

catch on the door, still gawping open like a starving fish from when I climbed in. It isn't just June I'm missing, though. It takes a few seconds before the uncluttered space next to the hatch registers, spots of rough carpeting showing through where all there used to be was mess.

June's sleeping bag and rucksack are gone.

CHAPTER 5

I SLIDE DOWN THE HELI LADDER AND STARE OUT AT the trees. "June!" I try to yell, but the sound comes out in a gasp. "June, where are you?"

The forest stares back at me, snowy white and needled green.

Tai-ge hops down next to me. "I thought we were taking off."

I breathe in deep, willing the forest to tell me which way to go, marking each leaf, each needle drooping down from the pines. June ran away from me once. From us. Me and Howl. There were Reds after us, and maybe she thought she could get away faster by herself.

But she wanted us to find her then. Now, I'm not so sure.

June's best at running, hiding. Making herself small where the danger won't think to pick her out. If Howl appearing seemed like a danger flag to her, maybe she thinks her chances are better with the trees.

"Sevvy." Tai-ge kneels next to me. "Maybe this is a good thing."

"A good . . ." I can't even choke the words out. "June took her stuff. She *ran*. We have to get out of here. And that *thing* in the cargo bay. . ." I can't force my mind back up there. The place I thought of as home is suddenly nothing but a broken lock with monsters peering out through the cracks.

"If we take him back to Dazhai, the Chairman will come out to welcome us himself. He'll have to listen to us. About the cure . . . about all of it. Sevvy, they've been looking for Sun Yi-lai for *months*. We'd be heroes."

"Sun . . ." I close my eyes, anger boiling deep inside me. "Tai-ge, I don't know how many more times I can say this before I break something. Howl isn't even from the City."

Tai-ge waits for a moment, as if there should be more. When nothing comes, he shakes his head, that steely set to his jaw that I've only recently come to notice flavoring every word. "I know you've been through a lot over the last months, Sevvy, but you're wrong about this. Whoever you think he is . . . I knew Sun Yi-lai back when we were in the City. I mean, as much as you can know any of the Chairman's family when you're outside the Circle. No one even knew his wife was dead until they put up the monument." Tai-ge scratches a hand through his hair. "I've talked to the Chairman's son before. More than once." He glances back up the ladder. "And that's him. He's tied up in our storage closet, and I'm officially a traitor. Unless we can convince him to go back . . ."

I shake my head, the movement growing larger as he keeps talking until I'm practically wagging my head trying to get Tai-ge to stop. What he's saying isn't possible. Not about Howl or about trying to contact the Chairman. It's as if Howl's lies somehow seeped into my friend, into the world all around me, one inky handprint that stained everything close enough to rub against me. "I told you about him before, Tai-ge." I told him some of it. Just that he helped me out of the City. Took me to the Mountain. Not that he lied about being a First or that he . . .

That he kissed me. That we were going to run off into the forest and pretend the world didn't exist. He made me like him. Love him, even, if that's possible in less than two months' time. My stomach churns, bile rising in my throat until I bend over, sure my stomach is going to expel everything I've ever eaten.

"Maybe this is some kind of misunderstanding." Tai-ge squeezes my arm, as if he thinks when I calm down, I'll see reason and believe him instead of my own eyes. "If it was him who took you out of the City, he must have gotten involved in something too big for him to understand. . . . It's hard to believe a First would go traitor, but it is possible."

I flick Tai-ge's hand away from me and stand. Hard to believe a First would go traitor? Does he even remember who he's talking to? I force down a bitter laugh. If that's what Howl was—a traitor First—I'd probably still be sitting next to him in the Core, eating from the Mountain's cafeteria, happily traitorous myself.

Tai-ge's voice is soft, the opening line in a negotiation. "You know, he was probably just scared. We surprised him, and—"

"No, Tai-ge. He wasn't scared. He wasn't surprised. And if I were you, I'd worry a lot more about how long we have before his friends get here than having your name carved into Traitor's Arch." I start walking, lines of pain starting at my eyes and etching through my head.

"Where are you going?" Tai-ge calls after me.

"I'm going to find June so we can get out of here." Not even Howl and his finger-bone-bracelet-wearing friends can make me take off without her. "Maybe she ran to the Post for help. Lock everything down. Seal off the cargo bay doors if you can. It might just be Howl, but I don't want to take any chances."

"If there could be more, then how does you going off into the trees alone make sense, Sevvy?"

I turn back to Tai-ge in disbelief and tamp down a spark of annoyance. "I'm *not* leaving without June."

I line my thoughts into tidy rows as I walk, attempting to give them some kind of meaning. Howl lived through the invasion. He came after me. We've been so careful, even though it seemed almost silly, because the Mountain no longer needs my skull, and the City is probably too preoccupied with not dying to care much about where we are. Kicking a pinecone out of my path, I bite back a swear word when my boot catches in the crusty ice and I land sideways on my ankle and fall onto the hard-packed snow. Sitting there with icy wetness seeping through my pants, an even darker thought occurs to me.

Dr. Yang might not tell anyone about the cure and Port North. He was so preoccupied with telling me how smart he is, how successful . . . It wouldn't be easy to cast himself the hero of a story where he put the person who cured SS to sleep so he could steal her research but then lost it instead—not unless the story ends with him having found the papers again. Dr. Yang isn't impatient. He spent eight years feeding the Mountain lies about needing me and Howl to reconstitute the cure, as if it would be his own special discovery, all while leading me closer and closer to his web until he could bite. He may have an idea about where the papers are now, but I can't see him sharing that information, not until Mother's test tubes are in his sweaty hands.

If Howl is working for Dr. Yang . . . what if he's here to wipe the slate clean? Get rid of the only other people who know what he is and what he's after? The only other people who could potentially take the cure out of his hands once and for all.

The line of pain at my throat where Howl's knife slid against my skin twinges.

I grit my teeth, dodging through the trees toward the Post, watching my footing so I don't end up rolling headfirst down a slope. It doesn't matter what Howl wants, because we're going to find a lonely, snow-covered mountain and leave him there so he can't creep back into my life ever again. All I need is June and we can take off. Slip right through Dr. Yang's fingers and find the cure first.

But the snow-laden trees are silent all around me. Not a hint of gold in all the white.

When I draw near to the Post's ladder, a foreign sound cuts through the frigid air, and I stutter to a stop, holding my breath, waiting to see if it's some kind of attack.

The sound isn't the threatening slicker of boots on ice, though, or the heavy, metallic sound of a gun being pulled from its holster. It's a note, high and lilting. The tone slides to another note and another, the haunting melody echoing inside of me as it slips ghostlike through the trees.

The hollow tune grows louder as I approach the Post's entrance, a tree with a platform lower than the rest. Loss grins at me from above.

"What'll you give me to let you up?" he calls.

"Is June up there?" I shout.

He gives the bundled-up rope ladder a kick and I have to jump aside to keep from being hit. "Most girls will at least offer me a kiss."

"Most girls who come would probably promise a kiss, then stick a knife in you when they got close enough." I start up the ladder, trying not to think about how high the platform is. The ropes bend and twist as I climb, make my stomach ball up inside me.

When I get to the last splintery rung, Loss extends a hand, helping me up onto the platform. "Should I turn you upside down to look for knives, then? I try to avoid offending longtime customers."

"I'm in a hurry. And since when do I count as a longtime customer?" I put my hands on my hips, trying to stop them from shaking.

"Not you. June's been coming through here for the better part of five years. Wouldn't want to scare her off."

"She's here?" I ask, trying not to sound desperate. Desperation is probably the first signal for roughers to take everything you have. I don't want to inspire any scavenging. Or kissing. Either one.

"Not that I know of, though I just started my watch." Loss glances toward the rope bridge that leads to the next platform over. "She could be up there now. It's been so good to see her smiling and . . . normalish. Never would have pegged little June as a mother hen, but the way she is with Lihua and the others warms this old rougher's heart."

"We have to leave *now*, and . . ." The music starts again, cutting me off short as it falls down through the trees around us like tears. "What *is* that?"

"Strangers." Loss points up to where a pair of bare feet hang over the edge of a platform. "I don't like it, them drawing attention to us with that racket. Your little ones are a bit keener, though. Wouldn't be surprised if they were shirking their cleaning duties to listen."

If June's anywhere, it would be with the kids. Winding my courage tight like a spring, I walk toward the precarious bridge that leads to the next platform over.

"If you're leaving, Cai Ayi'll be asking about a down payment on permanent boarding." Loss calls after me. He smiles when I turn back to him. "In case you don't come back? If June isn't negotiating for you . . ." His voice trails off when he notices my shaking hands. "What's wrong?"

"Nothing. I'm fine. We're fine."

He looks at me, unblinking, as if he can peel away the layers of words and find truth somewhere at its core. "If you say so. Things can be rough out there if you aren't used to it." Loss closes the distance between us, a concerned look furrowing his brow when I flinch away from him. He puts one of his oversize hands on my shoulder, the weight pulling me crooked. "I can help you with Cai Ayi. Go on up. I'll find someone to cover the ladder."

I grab hold of the rope that makes the bridge to the next plat-form, staring at my hands as I slide along instead of down at the ground. It's not a real bridge, just two ropes, one for your hands and one for your feet. Easy to cut down if people Cai Ayi doesn't like make it past the roughers watching the ground.

Once I'm across, I climb the rickety ladder that leads up to where the music sings out, boards embedded in the trunk so the tree's growth bows and slumps over each rung like a stomach bulg-ing over a belt. At the top, I find Lihua and Peishan, sitting with their legs pulled up to their chins, eyes wide on a man with a two-stringed instrument, a bow strung through them.

He's dark-haired and olive-skinned like City-folk so far as I can see, but the wide sleeves of his tunic cover his hands, so I can't check for City hash marks.

Lihua twirls her fingers along with the tune he's playing, as if she wishes she could dance but doesn't quite have the cour-age. Two other men stand on either side of the stranger with the instrument. One has skin as cracked as old leather and a dusting of gray hair around the back of his head. The other is much younger, his eyes a surprising green when they find mine. Both go back to watching the musician when it's obvious I'm not armed.

"Peishan?" I don't have time to care about the way she rolls her eyes when I kneel down next to her, and try not to push Lihua away when she leans against me. There's a panic in my blood, an energy that tells me if I stop moving, I'll die. Or maybe everyone else will. "Have you seen June?"

"Nope. Going to be quiet so we can listen?" Her whisper is sharp. It's hard to believe we used to share a room, staying up late to gossip about the nuns or for her to make up stories about me kissing Tai-ge to see if she could make me blush. (Only to be countered by me making up stories about her kissing the red-nosed foreman at the cannery. It wasn't always enough to get her to stop, but usually a good sexy description of his perpetually running nose was enough for her to throw a blanket over her head.) Things have changed, though. No more stories about Tai-ge's lips, though she's seen them much closer now than she ever did in the City. According to Peishan, everything—the Menghu invasion, contagious SS, and the fact that she's stuck up in these trees Outside with no walls to hide behind—is my fault.

I keep my voice calm. "We have to leave. I need you to make sure Lihua gets . . ." I glance over at her, not wanting to say anything about Mantis out loud. Not where one of the roughers or Cai Ayi might overhear. No infected allowed in these trees. "You have enough for a few weeks, right?"

"You're leaving?" Peishan's head whips around, but it only takes a split second before the surprise and fear harden into a frown. "Of course you are. Don't worry. It's not like you were doing much to take care of us anyway."

"Don't . . ." I look down at Lihua, her chin now tipped up to look at us instead of the man with the instrument, a wary expression on her four-year-old face. "We'll be back soon. Hopefully with more answers. And . . . more medicine." I can't tell her about the potential cure. I have to make sure it's real first.

"Fine." Peishan turns back to the music, pulling Lihua away from me and into her lap.

Irritation bubbles up inside me. I know Peishan has been through worse than I have. Just walking through the Sanatorium where they put all the patients Firsts were experimenting on made me want to scream. She was there for months. But Tai-ge and I were the ones who flew her out of the City, the ones who brought her here, where no one's allowed to have a gun. It's just easier to lay the blame at my feet. The City always did. I guess I'd hoped Peishan would be able to see through that.

I was wrong.

The music stops. I open my eyes to see the musician twisted around, looking at me.

"You feel this." He points to his chest, the words sounding clipped at odd angles and then sewn back together. His face is impossible to put an age to, creases decorating the edges of his charcoal-dark eyes. A face young enough to be born in my same decade, but only just.

I get up from my crouch by Peishan, walking back toward the ladder, my mind already threading through the trees, looking for a single golden glimmer. Worried I'll find something else instead. "Sorry. It's beautiful, but I have to go."

"The erhu digs deep inside you. It tells a story that connects with who you are." The musician swings his legs up from the edge of the platform and tucks his bow into a notch at the top of the instrument, where the strings are connected to carved knobs. His dark yellow tunic flows loose from shoulder to hip as he stands and loops the erhu's strap over his chest so the tall neck sticks out over his shoulder. The other two men tense as he moves toward me, their hands flat against their sides as if they're waiting for something important to happen.

Nothing does, though. He cocks his head to one side, waiting for me to answer his question. I shrug, not really wanting to find the words, thinking of the way the notes seemed to fill the hollow spaces inside me and carve them out at once.

"We are seekers, you and I." He reaches back to touch the erhu's neck. "Perhaps she called you to me because we seek the same thing."

I try a smile, setting my hands on the ladder's first rung. "At the moment I'm seeking a girl named June. Blond hair? Very quiet."

He shakes his head. "I seek a young man. About your age. It's the only place left he could be, here in your mountains."

"You're not from the mountains?" I turn back toward him, my heart twisting in my chest. "Have you heard of a place called—"

"Jiang Sev!" Cai Ayi's voice cuts me off, coming from above us. I look up to see her portly form scuttling down a ladder above me. "You need to leave."

A shot rings out. A *gunshot*, the sound piercing my eardrums. My feet freeze to the platform's planks, and I'm afraid to look down. Afraid a bullet just found me and that I'll see my own life streaming down my front in red.

Instead, the musician scuttles to the edge of the platform to look over. Lihua grabs me around the hips, Peishan only a step behind her as if she can somehow hide behind me when we don't know which direction the shot came from.

There's another shot as Cai Ayi jumps down onto the platform, her bulk making the wooden beams bounce. She levels a finger with my jaw. "They must have seen you come up. Not an hour ago, they came with a description of you and that *Red*. I knew I should have told June to keep you on the ground. Reds start burning trees before I've had time to answer their questions. They knew you well enough to ID you by describing *that*." She points to the patch of dark skin curling out from behind my ear, hidden beneath the fringes of hair that are too short now to pull back into a braid.

My hand slides up over the mark, my cheek cold. I'm afraid to touch it, to even acknowledge what she's saying.

Loss climbs onto the platform behind me. "Ze-ming's on the ground, Cai Ayi! We need Rash, Eriz, and Yi-ran *now*, and they're all two levels up. . . ."

Cai Ayi grabs hold of my arm and thrusts me toward the ladder. "Just go, honey. Before they kill all my boys. They probably won't shoot you if you come easy."

I stumble toward the wide boards, my heart feeling as if it's already given up. Peishan gathers Lihua against her, watching. "You want her to go down there?" she asks, a new vulnerability to her voice.

A low whistle jerks my attention up, and I catch a glint of gold up against the leaves. It's June peering down at me, two levels up and across a rope excuse for a bridge.

Elbowing Cai Ayi in the gut, I push past her to the ladder she just came down, scrambling up the fat rungs, Loss and Cai Ayi both only a breath behind me, swearing enough to make the evergreen needles wilt. The ground, at least thirty feet below, feels as if it's calling to me as I pull myself up, kicking at Cai Ayi's hands when they grab at my ankles.

Up to the next platform and then the next, I close my eyes and force myself out onto the bridge.

"Just shake her off! They can collect her body!" Cai Ayi cries, and the two lines jerk wildly under my feet and hands, all signs of Loss's goodwill from before vanished.

Only another two feet. One. And June's hand is around my wrist, wrenching me off the ropes and cutting them behind me.

I curl up on the boards, but only until another gunshot erupts in the still air. June's hand on my wrist helps me up from the self-protective crouch to look back at Cai Ayi and Loss on the other side.

"Tell them we escaped," June calls. "To follow the zip."

"June, my roughers, my *business!*" Cai Ayi snarls.

"You keep our kids safe. We'll lead them off. Tell them where we're headed."

Cai Ayi's mouth is a lemon and vinegar in the same glass. But she nods. "Get out of here."

June pulls me back without answering, only dropping my hand when we get to the ladder at the other end of this platform, snow speckled here and there as if no one has come up this high in a long time. So high the boards seem to sway under our feet, and the needles bite at us as if they're hungry. Even June goes slowly on this last ladder, only looking back once to check that I'm following.

The rungs are gray and cracked, and when we finally get to the platform above, I can hardly bring myself to stand. The ground below seems to chant for me to fall. Our tree sticks up above the others, a lookout tower over a flat plain of softly swaying needles. I try to imagine that the treetops skimming and rolling beneath the loose boards are solid ground just a few feet below us, but the argument feels stale in my head.

A cable is tethered to the tree trunk above us, the length of it diving deep into the trees in the heli's direction. Ten or more short lengths of rope hang from the line, clipped to the platform to keep them from slipping. June pulls two free, handing one to me before slashing through the others with her knife.

"Jump." She makes sure I have a good grip on the rope. "Don't think."

With that, she shoves her foot into the loop at the bottom of her rope, and hops off the platform, the pulley buzzing against the cable as her golden hair disappears into the trees. The rope she left for me is heavy in my palm, the rough fibers stinging new scrapes and splinters I received in the rush to get up here. I force myself to breathe out, letting go of all the air trapped inside me. I step into the loop, experimentally tugging at the cable over my head, waves of nausea and fear teasing my heart into a canter. The pulley starts to slip down the cable as soon as I put weight on it, and I dance back.

Another gunshot rings out, closer now, as if the Reds have made it up onto the Post's lower platforms. I close my eyes, lock my fingers around the rope, and jump. My stomach drops straight to the forest floor a hundred or more feet below. The pulley whirs above me as I start to fall faster, branches swatting at me as I slide.

My eyes pop open as I start to rise again, the rope scooping up and connecting to a massive tree trunk looming ahead of me. I wait for impact, imagining the rough bark slamming into my head and shoulders, but I slow to a stop before hitting, then slide back the way I came. The pulley screeches a complaint as my weight slows my momentum and stops me once again, sending me back down the rope until I come to a full stop. Stranded in midair.

A whistle trills through the air, and I catch a glimpse of gold hair on the far side of a tree trunk off to my left, the cable coming within a few feet of its gnarled branches. There's a rope almost within reach hanging from the closest branch. I shift my weight toward it and just manage to grab hold. From there, my heart fluttering like the last twitches of a dying butterfly, I transfer to the new rope and swing until I can latch on to one of the main branches and crawl into the crutch of the old tree. There are boards embedded in the trunk, just like the Post's awful ladders.

June stands at the bottom, her face upturned and impatient. She starts to walk away from the tree before I even hit the ground. Her feet hardly snap a twig, though a startled bird does streak up through the trees as she stalks by. She only turns once to check that I'm following, pausing to whisper so quietly I'm almost sure I misheard, "Good job not screaming."

CHAPTER 6

WHEN WE GET BACK TO THE PATH THAT LEADS TO the heli, we take it at a run. Every step sucks at my feet, as if the ground is trying to open and swallow me down into this trap. How would Reds have known to come asking for us here, and what could they want? There's no reason to go after the little Fourth traitor anymore, not with the City burning.

First Howl, then Reds. It can't be a coincidence. But why would Howl be working with anyone from the City?

I put a hand to my cheek as I run, the skin cold where my birthmark peeks out from under my ear. Cai Ayi pointed to it as if it were proof of something inherently wrong. My mother had the same mark. It linked us together, made us both into traitors, as if a spot of pigmentation on our skin could dictate our hearts.

I slow down to a jerky walk as the path steepens, my chest aching with cold. June is just a glimmer in the foliage ahead. Every sound, every birdsong, every flutter of pine needles has me on my toes, looking for the glint of gunmetal in the shadows. I alternate running and walking, only letting my lungs slow me down when they start choking off any chance of breath. It isn't until I get to the outcropping of rocks that protect the heli from sight that I realize June isn't in front of me anymore.

I trip, falling to my knees and trying very hard not to swear. "June?" I whisper. "*June?*" Louder this time. "We have to take off. Now!"

A ripple in the branches catches my eye, and from behind one of the rocks, June's face appears, half of it now hidden beneath the curls of a gas mask. "Go," she rasps.

"I'm not going anywhere without you. Come on." I pull myself up from the ground and start toward the heli again, stopping when she doesn't follow. "Why did you run away?"

She picks something up from the ground. Her rucksack, the old straps worn down to threads.

"Please, June. What did we do? I can't . . ." I take a step closer, surprised when she skitters away, maintaining the distance between us.

"No! Don't run away." I put my hands up, as if showing her I don't have any weapons will convince her not to go. "I can't do this by myself, June. Please."

June's eyebrows quirk at that, watching silently as I stumble through the icy rocks toward her.

"Were you worried about Menghu coming after us?" I ask, eyes caught on the awful rubber tubes of her gas mask. "Is it because you want to stay at the Post? If those Reds go away, I suppose it might be safer. You'd take better care of Lihua and the others than Cai Ayi ever could. But I . . . please don't leave me, June. I need you."

An image of my sister, Aya, ghosts up in my head, but now she wears June's face. I suddenly realize I can't even remember Aya's features, the same way I can't remember my father's. I blink the image away, knowing I can't substitute June in for Aya, no matter how much I want to take care of her. Still, I've already lost one sister. I can't stand to lose another.

June frowns. "I thought you'd . . ."

"You thought I'd what?"

She bites her lips, hands rubbing against her arms. "I messed up." One of the sleeves pulls up, a white line against her pink skin peeking out from under the fabric.

Scars. I've seen them before but hadn't really thought about it. I knew when we found June that her time with her "family"—or whatever the clan of infected scavengers she traveled with had called themselves—had been difficult. Only her father had been actually related to her, but even he . . . I shiver as I recall one of the first things June had ever told me about him. That her father wasn't hard like the others. That he was always *sorry*.

At the time, I thought it was just compulsions to be sorry for. But perhaps Tian and Cas—the leaders of the band—had been less forgiving of a young girl learning to live Outside even when compulsions weren't fogging their brains. Her father had sent her off with Howl and me on the sliver of hope that we could do better for her than he could.

How could June have thought *I* would hurt her, though? That running was a better idea than staying to face a mistake that wasn't even her fault? "June," I finally manage to say, "I'd be dead if not for you. Also, a lot hungrier."

"You could have been dead today *because* of me."

I take a deep breath and sit down on a rock, letting her keep the distance between us. Hurrying through this isn't going to work, no matter how close the Reds are behind us. "I didn't tell you about Howl. Didn't think it mattered anymore, because he was dead."

She waits.

The air seems to freeze in my lungs, Howl's presence a thundercloud behind us. Hiding what happened between us didn't seem to matter one way or another before, but I see now how dangerous it was not to tell June. "I was infected. When I was younger. And my mother . . . did something to fix it. I'm immune to SS now, to compulsions. All of it. I didn't know."

June bites her lip, eyebrows furrowing.

I stand, unable to hold still as I try to find the words to tell her. My hands search for the necklace with my four red stars, the shard of jade my mother gave me, and the rusty ring I picked up all those weeks ago when I first left the City. Instead, I find the red line scratched across my neck from Howl's knife. "I didn't know I was immune, but Howl did. He knew before we even left the City, and he didn't tell me. He took me to the Mountain so they could open me up and figure out what Mother did to fix me, and he lied to me so I would go without a fight."

"But you and him . . ." The words come out slower than a drip of honey, as if she has to search to find so many at once. "Before, it seemed like . . ."

I know what it seemed like. It seemed that way to me, too. "If there were any other explanation, Howl wouldn't have hidden in the heli. He would have just come out and talked to me."

Her forehead creases. "He said it was complicated."

"Unfortunately, it isn't all that complicated." I try to smile, to ignore the hurricane inside me at the thought of going back to the heli. Of having to face him. He knew that I liked him. He might have even . . . But I close that thought down before it can fully form. If Howl felt anything real for me, he wouldn't have led me straight into the gore's mouth. "Now you know. And I hope you also know I would never, *ever* hurt you. Please don't leave me."

June brushes her arm again, the scars standing out bone white.

"With friends, you're entitled to a few mistakes." I try to catch her eye, but she won't meet me halfway. "At least, I think so. It's been a while since I've had more than just Tai-ge. Can we please go now?"

June nods slowly, but she doesn't move. "And this Port North place . . . we're going there so no one will hurt you? Not for some kind of medicine to help SS?" She looks at my forehead, as if she can see the lines where the medics in the Mountain would have cut. Not judging, just asking.

"Dr. Yang—the person who was going to cut me open—knew he wasn't really going to find anything inside me to help. He needed me to wake up my mother so she'd tell me where her notes on the SS cure were hidden. We're going to Port North to get those notes before he does. He's going to use the cure to hurt people."

"Why?" She raises her eyebrows, expectant. As if this is a story I can tell her from start to finish.

"That's a good question, June."

"Is he going to try to stop us?"

Us. Hope is a fragile thing. "That might be why Howl's here. I'm not sure how much he knows."

June shrinks an inch, running a hand over her scar-lined arm, pulling her sleeve down so it hangs past her wrist. "Can't get infected like Dad. I *won't* be a Seph."

"That's exactly what we want to stop. Anyone having to live like that." I reach out to her, meaning to pull her into a hug. She watches my arm, her eyes narrowed as if she isn't quite sure what I'm trying to accomplish, so I let my arms fall. "I'll protect you, June. I'll keep you safe."

Tapping the side of her mask, her brow furrows once again. "I . . . I want to stay with you." Then she points to the heli without looking, her eyes going hard. "But I won't kill him."

"You won't kill . . ." My mind goes blank, following her finger to the sharp flare of sunlight reflecting off the heli's glass cockpit. Tai-ge has pulled the tarp back, the silvered metal gleaming in the icy winter sun. "You mean Howl?"

She nods. "He hurt you. But he saved my life before. I owe him."

I start toward the heli. "No one is going to kill anyone."

June still doesn't follow me. "Things are different when someone's running at you with a gun. I knew it was Howl back in the City. Didn't like to shoot at him, but he was with people who were shooting at us. This is different."

I turn to face her, and she finally meets my gaze, her green eyes looking too large for her face over the black curls of her mask. "No one is going to hurt Howl."

It isn't difficult to say. I *don't* want to hurt anyone. The relief in her eyes feels heavy, though, as if I've promised more than I realize.

CHAPTER 7

JUNE AND I CLIMB THOUGH THE HATCH AT THE SAME time, her rucksack and sleeping bag squishing against my side as we squeeze through. "Get us off the ground!" I call, looking around for Tai-ge. "It's not just Menghu we have to worry about. There are Reds at the Post. With guns."

In the two seconds of silence that follow—the time it takes June and me and her miles of sleeping bag to spill onto the heli floor—my heart goes still. Tai-ge isn't answering. I left him alone with Howl. What if . . .

But then the heli control chair swings around, Tai-ge's face twisted into a scowl, the faint light from the heli's control screens throwing shadows under his eyes. "I can't get the maps to work. When we disconnected from the network, everything went haywire."

"Come on, Tai-ge," I say. "We just have to *move.*"

Where *is* Howl? The cargo bay door is sealed, the boxes once again stacked in front of it. Everything is back where it's supposed to go, but the chilling undercurrent inside me still sets my teeth on edge.

And then I see it. The storage closet door is open a crack. There's a light on inside and a shadow of someone moving. My stomach clenches.

Tai-ge goes back to the screen set into the console, sliding his fingers across the map displayed. "I've been messing with it since you took off, and I still don't have it figured out. I don't know where to go, or exactly where we are. I'm not trained to draft flight plans, just follow routine courses. I thought I had a good route to Dazhai, but when I tried to find an isolated place to drop Sun Yi-lai, I got all turned around. . . ."

"Well, the *Reds* will know exactly where we are if we're not in the air in about five seconds. Didn't you hear me? They were *shooting people at the Post.*"

Tai-ge looks up from the screen, his hands freezing. "What?"

June goes up to the screen, brushing Tai-ge's hovering fingers away from the dim glow. Her finger stabs a spot of green nestled next to a dark ring of rocky-looking bits.

Tai-ge glares at the spot, blinking with a fierce sort of focus that makes me think he's trying to light the contraption on fire with mere force of will. "Are you sure? I thought we were down . . ."

June gives a dismissive shake of her head, batting his hand away again as it touches a meadow farther down on the map. She drags her finger across the screen so it shows a different place, a green field in summer that's incongruous with the frozen mountains outside.

"We can't go there, June. It looks like a farm." Tai-ge looks to me in appeal. "We don't know where all the survivors from the invasion went, but as far as I can tell, most of them ended up on farms closest to the City that produce food. I do not want to end this little adventure by being shot out of the sky. Unless you've rethought my plan to contact the Reds and—"

"No," I cut in, and catch myself looking at the storage closet door, Howl's shadow still beyond it. Listening. "And keep your voice down."

June points to the field again, then throws her rucksack on top of the boxes blocking the cargo bay door. She drops onto the floor next to them and braces herself against the cold metal, pinching her eyes shut. June doesn't like taking off.

"You're sure, June?" I ask. She nods without opening her eyes. "Let's do it, then."

Tai-ge peers out into the forest, then nods and begins fiddling with the instruments decorating the console. The heli engines shudder to life underneath us, the propellers filling the air with a dull roar as they begin to spin.

"Do I get a vote?" I barely hear Howl's voice over the propellers' thunder. Walking toward the cell door feels like wading through tar, every bit of me screaming in protest. Just as the heli makes its shivery departure from the ground, I slam Howl's door shut.

CHAPTER 8

THE LAND LOOKS BRUISED AND PURPLE UNDER THE
sun-killing clouds by the time we set down in the field June pointed
to on the map. Buildings stare at us from across the wide expanse,
blank-eyed and dark. Their rooftops bow under the weight of years,
jagged holes in their walls where the bricks have been stolen.

Abandoned. That's what this farm is.

What looked like fields on the map is a clogged mess of low
shrubs and grass. The City hasn't been here for years, by the look
of it. I glance over at the buildings, the thought of eyes watching
us from inside shivering through me.

Tai-ge pulls open the heli's hatch, but June puts a hand on
his arm to stop him from going out. "How likely are there to be
people here we should be worried about?" Tai-ge asks. "Scavengers? Sephs taking shelter? We already have to keep an eye on the
sky to make sure no one followed us."

June grabs the binoculars and a flashlight for an answer and
heads toward the hatch. She's never used the flashlight as a light
source while scouting; I think she just likes how heavy it is, as if in

a past life it was a bludgeon. A featherlight gust of wind wisps up through the hatch when she pulls it open.

"What if there are gores?" I dart to the ladder, about to climb down after her, but she waves me off. I know we can't risk *not* scouting, and she's made it clear on several occasions that my help is a hindrance, but it's hard to stand here doing nothing. I move to the console, where I'll be able to see her through the front windows, as if watching June will somehow keep her safe.

"I don't know why you keep talking about gores like they're going to pop up and tear us all to shreds." Tai-ge's eyes follow June as she makes a round of the field, then peeks into the buildings one by one. "Those stories that Outside patrollers tell are ridiculous."

"Gores are not made up, Tai-ge." June disappears into another of the dilapidated buildings, flashes of gold hair and pale skin showing through the holes marking the walls. "I might have spent half my time Outside hallucinating, but—"

"That's my guess about what you saw. Hallucinations would make anything seem worse. I've been Outside for weeks now. Wouldn't we have seen evidence of huge savage creatures that like to snack on fingers and toes?" Tai-ge leans against the console next to me and puts a hand on my shoulder when I don't respond. "Are you okay, Sevvy?"

I look away from the window as June trots off into the trees, her little frame lost in the darkness. "What?"

"Are you okay?" Tai-ge lets his hand drop down my arm, settling it on the console right next to mine. He feels warm standing so close. "I mean, none of us are okay, exactly. But you seem even less okay than you did before."

I look down at our hands, the traitor star burned between my pointer finger and thumb a horror next to the two smooth scars marking him a Second. A line of brown scabs pokes out from his sleeve, a crescent shape that looks suspiciously like a bite.

"I'm fine, Tai-ge. Take off your coat. We'll put some more anmicro on your arms."

"Don't worry about it. The scabs pull, but I think we've kept up on them enough that they're not infected." He pulls me away from the console, waiting until I have no choice but to meet his eyes. "I'm worried about you, Sev."

"I said I'm *fine*." Taking a step away from him, I turn to the problem I wish I could ignore. The storage closet almost seems to smolder and distort at the edges, as if it's a door into the eighteen levels of hell instead of the only barrier between me and the boy I didn't ever want to see again. "I mean . . . I will be once we decide what we're going to do with *that*." I point to the door. "Once we've got maps. And when we get to Port North before Dr. Yang does."

Tai-ge nudges my shoulder, narrowing the space I put between us. "You know the tubes that were in Sun Yi-lai's things? I thought at first they were some kid of weapon, or hiding something inside, but they're just rolls of paper. Shall we have a look? Maybe it will give us a better idea of what he was trying to accomplish."

"You know, I *am* sitting right here." I flinch, Howl's voice muffled from inside the closet. So he can hear us. "Just open the door. I'll tell you what they are."

"It's fine." Tai-ge lowers his voice, as if speaking too loud would shatter me into a million pieces. "He can't get out of there." He crouches by the console, opening the small compartment where we found the binoculars and a few other odds and ends. Now there are five tightly rolled papers, each a crisp white, about as long as my arm, and sealed with City wax. Carefully extracting the one on top, Tai-ge runs his hands down the length of the tube, fingers stalling on the falcon-and-beaker seal. "Do you remember the time we snuck into the market square with some of Mother's saved ration cards? It was the year those red beetles came out of the walls of the orphanage. You wanted a scarf, but they wouldn't give you enough cards to get one."

I blink, the change of subject whistling through me like vertigo. "Yeah . . . I guess. But . . ."

He peels the wax back carefully, using only his fingertips, playing with it as it goes soft in his hand. "You were going to cut the ends off so you could hide little bits in Sister Lei's bed so she'd think the beetles were living in her sheets. It took all afternoon to convince you to get a black one instead and to leave that poor old lady alone." He smiles. "Black looked better on you, anyway."

It didn't take all afternoon. Since when did I ever have an afternoon to argue over scarves in the marketplace? I brush the annoyed thought away. "What you don't know is that I *did* cut off the ends of the black one. She thought they were spiders, and it was even better," I retort. "And you're lucky I didn't do it to you too."

"You would have put real spiders in my bed." His smile almost erases the statue-like lines in his expression. Tai-ge never was one to laugh out loud. He hoarded his smiles almost as carefully as June holds on to her words, and the moments he chose to share one have always made me stop and pay attention, as if he's entrusting me with part of his soul. I lower myself to the floor next to him. "Did Sister Lei ever figure it out?" Tai-ge asks, batting my arm with the paper tube. "She couldn't have, or I would have heard about it in . . ."

And just like that, the memory sours. I reach for the tube, peeling up the last of the wax and smoothing the paper across the floor. Tai-ge would have known because it would have been in my reeducation reports. The Hongs knew everything about me. They probably knew the weight of my bowel movements and how many times a day I brushed my hair.

I wrinkle my nose. Hopefully not the bowel movements.

"I just . . ." Tai-ge smiles *again*, and there's a trace of my old friend somewhere deep inside him. The one who didn't clench his jaw so hard. The one who didn't see his dad torn to pieces two weeks ago. "I just wish things were less . . . not okay. Do you remember before?" The smile thins to a line, an uncommitted lack of expression too complete to be natural. "Do you remember how nothing used to matter? The most exciting thing that happened would be finding you'd dyed my face soap green, or the two of us hiding from the nuns to sneak in an extra game of weiqi." Tai-ge puts his hands down on the paper to smooth it out, deliberately brushing his palm across the back of my hand as he does so, and letting it rest there. "I miss us from before."

It's like a jolt of electricity shooting up my arm, and I've jerked away and folded my arms tight around my middle before I can properly think it through. Tai-ge crouches so close to me I can feel his body heat through my coat where our shoulders touch. He doesn't move, staring down at the paper on the ground as if I didn't just pull away from him like a little girl stung by a bee.

What's wrong with me? It's not like I've never touched Tai-ge before. It's just that there was always a wall there, a bright red wall with a general's title hammered into the bricks. Every time he looked at me, I felt as though our friendship was an impossible conundrum of sunlight shining through broken glass. The light was there, glittering, warm, *inviting*, but reaching out to touch it would have left both of us with cuts.

I'd still wanted to.

I'd wanted to more than I could stand, back when all we did was play practical jokes and illicit games of weiqi. Tai-ge was one of the few people who seemed to remember I was a person, no matter how many times his mother told him I was too damaged to be fixed.

It was Tai-ge's name that convinced me to leave the City with Howl, running from the executioner's ax because it might have sliced through my friend too. I did miss Tai-ge when we were apart, but I don't miss living under the shadow of Traitor's Arch, waiting for the day it would take me. I don't miss anything about the City, and the very idea of going back to the way things were before feels like trying to cram myself into a box that's too small.

But that's not where we're going. Tai-ge is here now. With me. He chose me.

He takes his time looking up, and when he meets my eyes, he doesn't blink. The rebellion of sitting so close to Hong Tai-ge, General Hong's son, thrills me. Looking back at him straight on, not moving away . . . it's a *challenge* to what we were, what the City said could and couldn't happen between us. The silence in the cockpit is heavy between us, a breath before something happens.

"Sevvy . . ." He's leaning toward me now. The air is honey, stuck in my throat, choking me.

The door to Howl's prison creaks, as if he's leaning up against the wood. The sound releases all the air in my lungs in a huff, and I jerk back.

Before I can say anything, June's light footsteps ping up the ladder, and her head appears through the hatch. "No one here. Not for a week at least," she says, glancing from me to Tai-ge, squinting.

"Good. Thank you for checking, June." I fill the awkward silence.

She nods, then walks to her rucksack to pull out her waterskin. I can't look at Tai-ge as he gathers himself together, letting my eyes fall back to the paper instead. It's waxy, sticking to my fingers as I smooth it out, the edges protesting after being rolled so tightly. The lines waving over the paper in tight swirls and circles don't make much sense.

Tai-ge leans closer to the paper, and the air still feels tight in my lungs, everything stretched until it's about to snap. I keep my eyes on his fingers as they follow the ebb and flow of the lines. "I think they're maps."

I glance toward Howl's closet when the door creaks again. "Why would he have brought maps with him?"

"I don't know. You said he spent time with the rebels." Tai-ge pulls up a corner of the heavy paper, examining the lines and numbers splattered across its face. "Could this be some kind of rebel notation of the area?"

"They all have a City seal on them." I draw another of the paper tubes out from under the control panel, fingers finding the red wax already pried up.

June rustles through one of the food bags and then sidles over, a slice of dried pear in her hand. She squints at the wavy lines on the paper spread across the floor. Setting her pear down, she takes the paper in my hands and unwinds it on the floor in front of her.

"Why do you think they are maps, Tai-ge?" I ask.

"I don't know. They sort of look like the encryptions of routes we flew back when I was finishing my pilot training. They kept all the big maps—the complete pictures—locked away in the City. You only saw those if you needed to." Tai-ge slides over to examine the second paper, similarly covered in dots, lines, and numbers, though the flow is different from the first one we unrolled. "These lines are almost definitely topographical, and maybe the numbers give coordinates? Specific sites? I don't know." He looks toward Howl's room.

I push off from the desk, moving between Tai-ge and the storage closet. "No."

June looks up, startled by my quick movement. Tai-ge's hands scrub across his mouth, and he goes back to staring down at the nonsensical mess of numbers and lines. "He could tell us, Sevvy."

"No."

"*No?*" Tai-ge stands up, facing me, his voice soft. "What's our plan? To sneak into Dazhai and hope we stumble on something with 'Port North' starred in bold and step-by-step directions how to get there? He came straight to us, and I'm almost sure they *are* maps. . . ."

"Would you trust a gore if it told you it could lead you across the forest?" I counter. "Or do you really believe it wouldn't take you straight back to its hutch?"

"More gores, Sevvy?" Tai-ge's voice rises a fraction. "We have very important information about countering SS when everyone we know is living in fear under a mask. You won't go to the Seconds. Now you won't even look at the information dumped in our lap. Were you hoping we could just keep flying until the sky opens and points out where to land? We need help." He points to the closed storage closet. "He would have had access to the bigger maps back in the City." He turns to June, who shrinks back a fraction, even though he isn't yelling. "How long was Sun Yi-lai in the cargo bay?"

June's eyes stay down. "A day."

"So he might have even seen maps from the camps after the invasion. . . ."

"No, he wouldn't have, because *he's not the Chairman's son*, Tai-ge! What's it going to take for you to listen to me?" Heat seeps into my cheeks, my voice coming out in a whispered rasp, as if I can keep Howl from hearing what I'm saying.

But Howl answers me anyway, each word an icy blade down my back. "I brought you the information you need, Sev."

Fear trickles down my neck. How did Howl know we were looking for anything?

"I want to *help*," he continues. "Open the door. You know I don't bite."

"Stabbing and shooting are not preferable to biting," I yell back, pacing the length of the heli. There's nowhere to go in this tiny space.

"Last I checked, it was you guys who were trying to shoot *me*." Something thuds against his door as if he hit the back of his head against it for emphasis.

"We should at least see what he has to say." Tai-ge's voice is too calm, a mediator trying to soothe me down. "Unless you'd rather radio in and try to get some information from the Seconds. We might be able to do it without giving up who we are—" Tai-ge breaks off as one of the smaller packs of rice hits him in the shoulder. June startles back, looking between me and the bag as if she can't believe I threw it.

"Bloody dismembering *Sephs*, Tai-ge, *we cannot talk to the Reds*. We can't listen to *anything* Howl says. That's how he got me to . . ." I stutter to a stop, the heli suddenly feeling very, very quiet. Tai-ge stares at me, his mouth open. I don't think I've ever yelled at him before. I've definitely never thrown anything at him before.

I clear my throat. "We don't know how Howl found us. What if those Reds after us at the Post were because of him? Maybe they weren't Reds. Menghu can change clothes just as well as you or I can." I gesture to my threadbare Liberation Army jerkin. Only weeks ago I was wearing Menghu green. "You don't understand. There are only two reasons he would come after us. . . ."

A loud thud echoes from Howl's door, as if he hit it again. "What is *wrong* with you, Sev? What do you think changed? When did I magically turn into a killer?"

"You lied about *everything!*" I scream.

"You're the one who just *left!*" he yells back.

"I'm not doing this." I go to the hatch, hardly waiting for it to hiss open before I start down the ladder. "I can't do this. Good luck to you all; I'm sleeping outside."

"With the *gores*? Come on, Sev. Just sit down, I'll make you some tea." Tai-ge almost looks as if he's about to laugh, half of it reserved for the gores he can't quite believe in because he hasn't seen them with his own eyes. How could he see anything in Howl but what he thinks he knows? Howl looks just like the City's imperial family, down to the portrait hanging in the City Center. It's not in Tai-ge to see anything but test tubes, tassels, and a golden soul from someone he thinks is a First. Before he could believe, he'd probably have to see Howl in a tiger-snarled coat, dancing with the other Menghu across the Mountain's sunken amphitheater floor like a prince from the dead pages of a book.

That's what it took for me to truly see it. That Howl wasn't any of the things he'd told me.

"I don't want tea." I stomp down the ladder, the rungs shaking with each step. "I'm sleeping outside. Better to be with the gores, the ghosts, and the Sephs than in here wondering whether or not Howl is going to slit my throat. I'll see you in the morning."

CHAPTER 9

MY EYES CRACK OPEN TO THE EARLY LIGHT OF DAWN,
the icy air cold and clear in my lungs. June's sleeping bag is tangled
behind me, though I don't remember her coming out to sleep next
to me. The girl herself seems to have disappeared.

It's the first time I've slept all the way through the night since
we left the City smoldering.

There's already a fire crackling just outside the heli tarp,
tangy whiffs of Junis wafting in. June must have slept out here
with me, then woken early enough to get breakfast started. Keeping my sleeping bag close around me, I wiggle out from under
the tarp, the bitter air biting at the exposed skin on my face and
neck. The cold air is a drink of clarity, distilling three things in
my brain.

First, I'm done arguing with Tai-ge about going back to the
Reds. If he doesn't trust me enough to stop pushing in that direction, then maybe it's better for him to go back himself.

It's a stark sort of revelation. The thought of him gone hollows me out, leaving me brittle as fine china. Last night, sitting

with him less than a breath away was an experiment I wanted to try, but it's not one I want to hang my life on. Tai-ge came for me during the invasion. He listened to me, he followed me, but reality isn't doused with adrenaline and wishful thinking. We're here in the middle of nowhere, not sure where we are going, and no matter how much I wish both of us could forget the City, I'll never be able to scrub away the brand melted into my skin. It was a nice story while it lasted, but Tai-ge coming this far with me—away from his parents' expectations, away from the rules and regulations that have been carved into his bones—is too much of a fairy tale to believe. He'll probably end up contacting them without asking, assuming it's a kindness. Intervening because the poor Fourth and the Wood Rat don't have the capacity to understand what is best for them.

Even if the thought feels hot and oppressive, I know that it's right. After so many explanations—graphic ones, in some cases—of what would happen to me and June if we set foot inside a Red perimeter, Tai-ge is still holding the party line. He may have good intentions, but if the path he's willing to walk to get to our end goal isn't the same as mine, he's just as much a danger as Howl is.

And, regarding Howl, the second thing I've realized is that Tai-ge is right about the papers. If they're maps that might help us, we have to do everything we can to use them.

Finding Port North and Mother's papers before Dr. Yang does was already an impossible mission. Dr. Yang knew what Mother was talking about when she told me to go to Port North. He could already *be* there. . . .

I clench my eyes shut, my heart sinking. We can't let Dr. Yang use the cure to control whatever is left of the City. I don't know why Howl is here, and I don't intend to listen to anything he has to say—but if he did bring us maps, and those maps give us a fraction of a chance at getting Mother's papers, we have to take it.

Howl said he wanted to help. How he knew what kind of help we needed or where to find us is beyond me, but we have to try. If he is here to keep us away from Port North or for some other reason I don't understand, we'll be ready.

And the last of my revelations: I know what Howl is now. He manipulated me before by convincing me we fit together somehow, but that won't work again. He's here, he's alive, he has papers that are supposed to help us, but I'm the one in control. June and I won't underestimate him no matter how much Tai-ge wants to kowtow.

It was Howl's mask that was dangerous, but now that I've seen his true face, there's no way for him to hurt me anymore.

The air freezes in my lungs. *We can do this.*

We'll find Mother's papers. We'll get them before Dr. Yang and . . . what will we do with them? Set up medic stations in Cai Ayi's trading post and stick infected when they aren't looking? Will we even understand the notes? Will we get there before Lihua's Mantis runs out? Before every inch of the City is burned and every person infected during the invasion is dead?

Breathe, Sevvy. One problem at a time.

"Sevvy?"

I jerk up from the ground, the voice shattering my creeping panic. It's Tai-ge, climbing down the ladder in a puff of frosty air that streams from the heli's paunch.

He crouches on the tarp next to me as I rub the sleep from my eyes and sternly instruct my heart to stop racing. But it immediately starts up again when he grabs hold of my shoulders and makes me look at him.

"What?" I demand. "Did you hear Reds on the radio? Did Howl get out?"

"I'm sorry." He doesn't blink as he speaks, as if he can somehow project whatever it is he's feeling directly into my brain. "I've been so stupid."

There are shadows lurking under Tai-ge's eyes, his face harder than I've ever seen it. My friend is slowly turning to stone. "Tai-ge . . . what?"

"Last night, I couldn't stop thinking." He takes a deep breath and holds on to it for a bit longer than is comfortable before letting it out. "Back in the City, I saw the Watch spit in your face, the nuns talk down to you. Heard my own family tell you there would always be something wrong with you. That deep down, you weren't made right and there was nothing you or any of us could do about it."

"If you're trying to cheer me up somehow . . ." I start to pull away, not wanting to remember any of what he was saying. I was okay back then, able to laugh about silly things people said. But that doesn't mean I want to hear them directly from Tai-ge's mouth.

"No!" His eyes pinch shut as if he can't even look at me, but his grip on my shoulders tightens. "No, Sevvy. I didn't realize this was different. I've never seen you this upset, even back in the City, where everyone was *horrible* to you. I didn't consider what that meant. I've been so wrapped up in . . . in the things we've lost. My father . . . he was there, and then he was *gone*. Everything was gone. The City, the people I knew. I kept thinking that if we just went back, things could somehow revert to the way they were supposed to be." Tai-ge's eyelashes are dark against his cheeks. "I don't even know who of the Seconds I know are left, and I'm not . . . I can't do this."

"You want to go back," I whisper. Thinking about it made my head hurt, but now that he's sitting here in front of me, it feels as if my heart is going to rip free from my chest.

"No." He lets go of me, taking long, measured breaths. Ever in control. "I came out to say that I'm sorry for the way I've been acting. And for things with the Chairman's son. I didn't listen to you and . . . are you okay?"

"What do you mean?" I clench my jaw, wondering how long before my newly acquired temper tears free. One more mention of Howl as the Chairman's son? Two?

Tai-ge's hands come down over his face, muffling his words. "I couldn't sleep last night. You and June were out here, and even though his door was shut, I started worrying that if I closed my eyes I'd wake up with my hands around his throat."

"Tai-ge." I lick my lips, "You're not making sense."

"He hurt you, didn't he? He did . . . something. To you." Tai-ge finally looks at me. "I should have been listening. And the way you flinched away from me yesterday, I just realized that you were out here with him for so long, and anything could have happened—"

"No!" I shrink down in my sleeping bag. "No, it wasn't like that." Of all the monsters I met Outside, that is one outline into which Howl does not fit.

Tai-ge's iron frame collapses in relief, and he nods slowly. "I was just in there to check on him, and he wouldn't talk to me. He keeps saying he won't talk to anyone but you. And the more he says, the more I realized that he's an entitled, controlling gore hole."

I press my lips together to keep from smiling. It isn't funny, really, but hearing Tai-ge talk so disrespectfully about someone he was scared to touch only a day ago strikes me as an improvement. "You expect less than a gore hole from the Chairman's own fake family, Tai-ge?"

"What happened?" he asks, not willing to share the joke. "I still don't know how it's possible that he's not the Chairman's son. We didn't run in the same social circles, exactly, but unless he's somehow very, very good with makeup . . ."

"A lot happened." I clasp my hands together for warmth, cold enough two of my fingers have started to go numb. "And I don't know why he looks so much like the real Chairman's son. It doesn't matter, because that's not who he is. There is one other thing we need to talk about, though." I press a hand to my cheek, not quite sure how to say it. "You are having a hard time out here."

His brows pinch together. "Yes."

"I want you to stay with us. But we are not going back to the Reds. You need to decide where you want to be."

He blinks once. "I'm here. With you." His arms wrap around me, the squishy sleeping bag fabric slipping as he pulls me close. "Yuan's ax, Sevvy. I'm not going anywhere. I spent years taking you for granted in the City. When you left, everything went dark. The whole City was gray and angry, and you weren't there to make me laugh about it."

He smells like sweaty clothes and dirt, but also the comforting scent that's all his own. Pulling my arms free from the sleeping bag, I hug him back as tight as I can.

It's the safest I've felt in weeks. Just us, together, as if there never were walls between us in the first place. Maybe when you have no future, it's easy to put things that used to be non-negotiable aside.

I force myself to shrug away the cynicism of that thought.

"I've changed my mind about Howl." I say it into his coat, my breath catching on the tightly knit fibers and melting the frost crystallizing across the fabric. "If he can help us somehow and he'll only talk to me . . . then I'll talk to him. I'll find out what he knows, what he wants. Then we'll leave him here."

"You don't have to." His voice is muffled against my hair. "We could always try torture."

I stifle a laugh, knowing Tai-ge doesn't mean it. "It's nice to have options."

CHAPTER 10

I CLIMB THROUGH THE HATCH, AND JUNE HOPS UP from her spot by the storage closet's closed door. She looks me directly in the eye for once. "His head is infected."

"You've been in there?"

June nods, pushing the medikit into my hands. "We can't keep him," she whispers.

"Why not?" I smile.

June doesn't, her gaze rock hard. "I said I wouldn't help you kill him."

The nuns had a bird they kept in a cage. A soldier brought it from Outside, its bright yellow feathers shining and opalescent when the sun hit them. I used to look at him where he hung in the cafeteria, one small mark of color in the gray, orphaned world. He started out singing, but as the weeks went by, his song faded to a single sad note, until one day we found him in a heap of broken feathers at the bottom of his cage. A wild thing shut up inside, taking everything the bird must have loved and replacing it with gawking orphans who shoved bits of bread between the cage's bars.

June's arms fold in front of her, and she stands between me and the storage closet as if Howl is the victim and I'm the monster. As if shutting him—a wild thing—away would kill him just as it did the bird. I reach out to her, letting my hands fold over her bony shoulders. "I'll look at his head, and if he has information to help us get to Port North, we'll take it. If not, then we'll head toward Dazhai."

She narrows her eyes.

"And we won't leave him in there to die of blood poisoning. Or boredom. We just have to decide when and where to let him out."

June gives me a curt nod, then goes to the hatch and jumps down without looking back. She wants this to be right, and I don't blame her. But I worry that she's not as wary of Howl as she should be.

The medikit lid screeches as I open it to check for anmicro ointment, finding it wrapped in a bandage under a spool of adhesive for closing wounds. Hopefully it isn't that bad or Howl will just have to die, promise or no promise. I wouldn't know how to use military-grade wound adhesive to save my own life, much less his.

When I've got what I need, I close the box, my hands shying away from the stain of dried blood caked across the corner. Squaring my shoulders, I push Howl's cell door open.

For some reason, I expected him to be sitting there waiting for me. Calculating his next move, deciding which words will make me feel the worst or which nudge will set me in the direction he wants me to go. Instead I find him curled up in the tiny space, asleep, his tethered hands awkwardly twisted under his head to make a pillow.

He looks so calm and quiet, sleep ironing the curves and lines from his face. Even after everything that has happened, it's hard not to think he's handsome. A face you can trust.

It makes me want to scream.

Howl cracks one eye open, the other quickly following when he sees me framed in the doorway. He sits up, stretching a little before leaning against the wall. He can't move very far because Tai-ge threaded a length of cord between Howl's bound hands and tied it to one of the bolted-in shelves. The cut at Howl's temple is crusted over with black, splatters of it down his neck and on his shoulder. The skin around the wound is red, and he flinches as he looks up at me, the skin puckering with the movement. There's a book next to him, a gold-leaf stencil of a sleeping woman on the cover. My book. The one Howl gave me back in the Mountain.

It's a story they told us even in the City, a girl condemned to sleep forever for her crimes. The City's version is so close to Mother's own story that it made my insides knot up every time I heard it. This version from the Mountain has her wake up instead, her whole family safe. Howl told me that if the girl in the story had a happy ending, then everyone else had a chance of one too. That was before Sole filled me in on who he really was, before Mother woke from her cursed sleep and then died. Happy endings all around.

Tai-ge must have given it to him.

I don't even know why I brought it with us. It's a fairy tale, like Zhinu and Niulang up in the sky. In real life, stars don't cry. Bloodthirsty creatures don't stand down when you sing to them. And I'm not going to be swayed into thinking I'm safe when the gores are slavering at my toes ever again.

Howl's eyes are bleary as if he can't quite focus on me. He looks over my shoulder, taking in the empty cabin behind me, then meets my eyes and waits expectantly.

"I don't want to talk to you," I say quietly.

"Yeah, I got that." He adjusts his bound hands with a cringe, then moves the book aside with his foot. There are still remnants of adhesive stuck to his pants where I taped his ankles together, but Tai-ge or June must have cut the rest of it off. "What happened? One second we were going to find the cure together and the next June and your Red friend were shooting at me." He looks down at his chest, a shadow of a smile curving one side of his mouth. "*Did* shoot me, actually. If I hadn't been wearing protective gear, I'd be dead."

Keep calm, I tell myself. If Howl wants to pretend he's guiltless, fine. I just need to know about the papers—and whether anyone else plans to sneak into our cargo bay. "How did you find us, Howl?"

"Why didn't you come talk to me before haring off into the forest?" He looks down at the tape twisting around his wrists. "Sole told me what happened, but it didn't seem like you to leave without even talking to me."

"You don't like it when people think for themselves instead of asking you what they should do?"

Howl shakes his head. "I thought she had to be lying, that Dr. Yang had some hold on her and they'd found you. That you were on some table in Yizhi—"

A chill runs through me. "Is Sole okay?"

He blinks. "I think so. She didn't come with us to the City."

I let out a breath, though the trill of fear stays, burrowing deep inside me despite my resolve not to be afraid. When I ran, I hadn't thought about it being Sole who would have to explain it to him.

Howl's eyes narrow. "How can you think *I* would have hurt Sole? She's the closest thing I have to a . . . a mother, or an older sister."

There it is. At least he's not going to pretend that First mark on his hand is anything but a scar. I want him to look me in the eyes. To admit it. "I don't think it's too far-fetched a thing to worry about, Howl."

"You don't think . . ." Howl clenches his eyes shut a moment before focusing back on me. "And you look like you're about to hyperventilate." He laughs, the hopeless, black sort of sound ringing in my ears. "After everything you lived through in the City, everything *we* went through, you're scared of *me?* We had a plan. You left without me."

My anger explodes. "I was scared of Helix! And Cale! At least they were straightforward. You knew they were going to kill me, and you led me to the slaughter like a piglet to gores in a feeding frenzy."

"A piglet? Of all the animals you could choose—" Howl starts, but I keep talking, not letting him interject any justification for what he's done.

"Sole is the one who warned me not to trust you."

"She told you about where I came from, but not—"

"No. She said that if it came to a choice between your life and mine, I'd be dead." My hand goes to my throat, the red line still twinging. "And she must have been right, considering that the last time we were in the same room together, you had a knife against my neck. I'm only in here to . . ." I look down at the tube of anmicro, realizing my grip on the ointment has squeezed it into a sticky mess all over my palm. "I promised June I would look at your head. If it's too hard for you to tell me how in Yuan's name you found us, I would appreciate it if you would tell me how to read those papers you brought, and then you can go back after whoever it is the Menghu are chasing this week."

I kneel down, my fingers shaking as I pull the bandage from the medikit out of its packaging.

Howl's stare is heavy. "There's nothing I can say to convince you to listen to me, is there? How could you think . . . does it not matter to you that—?" He cuts off, not a word of denial or explanation, just ashy silence. When he finally speaks, it's quiet. Strained. "It wasn't that hard to find you. I was reading the scout reports. One said you were fishing around at an Outsider trading post for northern maps. So I came."

The bandage's packaging won't open, and every time I pull at it, it makes me angrier, until finally I tear it open with my teeth. "Why were they looking for us?"

"The Reds? I'm not sure."

"Reds?" I look up in surprise. "How did you manage to get your hands on City reports?"

"I was at a City evacuation camp. Hopped on a heli that was headed in your direction and—"

"You were in a *City* evacuation camp?" I stand, going back out into the cockpit for my waterskin to wash off the blood caked on his forehead. We've been away from the river for a while now, and the waterskin is almost flat. I breathe easier out in the open space, as if there's a toxic cloud trapped inside the storage room, every moment spent inside making me choke.

"Yes. I was in a City evacuation camp," he replies. "The report mentioned you by name. Gave coordinates for where to find you and General Hong's son, with instructions to send in support forces and provide transport back."

"Transport . . . ? *Support?*" The words come out unbidden. "Like Tai-ge and I were on a sanctioned mission—?" I look toward the hatch, fiddling with the length of bandage. Tai-ge is down on the ground somewhere. If he somehow contacted Reds without telling me—

"Don't get all upset. None of the higher-ups are going to admit on open channels that Hong Tai-ge deserted. Morale's bad enough as it is. I don't know how they found you." I turn to find Howl awkwardly maneuvering a hand up to scratch at one of the dried tracks of blood, the tape binding his wrists together creaking. His voice softens. "But I wanted to get to you before they did. I wanted to make sure you were okay—"

"No." I go back into the cell, kneeling just out of arm's reach, the waterskin clutched in my hand. "No City reports, no First marks . . . no more vomiting lies all over me."

"Vomiting?" He considers. "I'd go for a less sanitized word if you're trying to be offensive. 'Upchuck' is a favorite of mine."

"You aren't the Chairman's son, and you're not going to get anywhere feeding that line to me anymore."

He smiles, but his eyes look flat and dead. "Hong Tai-ge is swallowing every word."

"Tai-ge just watched your buddies from the Mountain blow his father to pieces, so I'm going to give him a pass for not thinking straight."

Howl presses his lips together. I busy myself with tearing off the extra length of bandage. The familiar expression jars, as if now that I know who he really is, he should look different too.

"I'm sorry," he finally says. "Can't say I ever liked the General, but that's not something anyone should have to see."

"Seems like you've seen enough that it shouldn't bother you anymore." I pretend not to see the heavy look on his face as I unscrew the waterskin's cap and wet the folded bandage.

Extra bandage scrunched in my hand, I will myself to go near enough to clean off Howl's forehead. It feels like if I step into the no-man's-land between us, something will break. But then Howl leans forward, holding his hands out for the makeshift washcloth. Relieved, I give it to him, letting him wipe at the blood himself, no matter how much it bends his arms.

"I'm not the Chairman's son, you're right." Howl's eyes pinch shut as he swabs closer to the actual wound. "I've just been subbing in for the last two years."

CHAPTER 11

"SUBBING IN?" I TWIST THE BANDAGE MEANT FOR his head between my fingers. "You expect me to believe the Chairman didn't notice his son was replaced by a Menghu?"

Howl laughs—almost barks—sharp and abrupt. "The Circle has been telling you you're at war with a fake army for the last eight years, Sev. What do *you* know about the Chairman or his family?"

It sounds like a challenge, as if somehow Howl is looking askance at the star branded into my hand when he never seemed to notice it before. "What is that supposed to mean?" I ask.

"No need to look so offended. What does anyone in the City know about him? The Chairman might as well be a ghost. I lived in the same house with him for two years, and I still don't know much about him. He's a face on a poster, a voice over the speakers to everyone except the First Circle. I was just his very competent, *very* patriotic, shiny new son."

I pluck the cloth from Howl's fingers, slosh some water over it again, shuddering when it squeezes out brown. My skin crawls at having to come closer, but I make myself scrub at the bits of blood

Howl couldn't see to wipe away. Howl's words sound like another lie. A lie that would be easy to believe because it would explain so much. How sure Tai-ge is about Howl being Sun Yi-lai. The portrait that looks just like Howl in the City Center. Premier Sutan calling to Howl in the street using Sun Yi-lai's name. "How is that possible? Why would anyone believe—"

"The Chairman believed it. There wasn't anything else to believe. And before you blame me for 'disappearing' his real son, I don't know what happened to Sun Yi-lai," Howl continues, not quite looking at me as the cloth touches his forehead. "Dr. Yang didn't even know where he was, just that he'd been out of the City. Hasn't been seen in more than ten years. Dr. Yang fed the Circle some information about Sun Yi-lai being spotted with a Menghu escort outside the Mountain. They sent out a mission and came back with me."

Ten years? But if Howl was roughly the same age as the Chairman's son, that means the boy would have had to leave the City when he was seven or eight. Younger, even, if it's been longer than a decade. That doesn't make sense. We would have heard if the Chairman's son was missing for that long. I pull out the now-squashed tube of anmicro and slather it on across the cut. Howl flinches away from me, and I let the distance sit. The cut is long and ugly, but doesn't look so bad now that it's clean. The skin does look red, but it isn't hot to the touch and there's nothing disgusting seeping out of it, so unless June knows something I don't, there's not much to fuss over. I pocket the unused length of bandage and hold the bit I used as a washcloth tightly in my hand, wondering if we can boil it clean. We might need it again.

"I don't even know what Sun Yi-lai looks like. If we're the same age. I don't know if the Chairman cared." Howl blinks tiredly,

pressing the back of one hand to his forehead as if it itches. I bat
his hand away from the still goopy mess of anmicro, and he raises
an eyebrow at me but quickly gives it up when the movement pulls
at the wound. "I thought I was going to have to pretend to be
traumatized and refuse to talk about my time Outside when I first
got to the City. Dr. Yang made sure I had the bruises to make that
plausible." Howl settles back against the wall. "It never came up,
though. I hardly ever saw the Chairman, and no one else was brave
enough to ask. I was the heir, I was back, and that's all that mattered."

"They just let you walk in? Without blood tests or anything?"

Howl shrugs. "Dr. Yang said it wouldn't be a problem. And
he was right. He was there when they did all those tests, and they
mysteriously matched up the way they were supposed to."

"And no one noticed you were gone for those months we were
at the Mountain? Or questioned you when you reappeared during
the invasion? I thought all the Firsts were airlifted out before the
real fighting began."

A smile I recognize begins on his face, but I'm still surprised
when his voice warms up. "Maybe I'm so beautiful they couldn't
bear to think of me as a traitor."

My throat closes around what should have been a laugh but
is more horror than anything else. Howl notices and looks at the
wall behind me, the expression on his face turning sour.

I don't want the boy I remember from the woods—the one
who made me laugh while he boiled potatoes and sat with me until
I fell back asleep after nightmares—to show his face now. That
boy is dead.

No, that boy was never real in the first place.

I stand up, grabbing the waterskin with thoughts of pouring

the whole of it directly on top of his head. But I refrain. "Tai-ge says the papers you brought look like maps."

"Isn't that what you were looking for? I can be very accommodating. It's almost magical."

"You know where Port North is?"

"No."

"Would you have known ten minutes ago before I started yelling at you?"

Howl looks sharply at me, a ghost of a real smile parting his lips. "No, Sev."

"How do we read the maps, then?"

"You'll have to get the encryption key."

"You brought maps, but no key?"

"I didn't realize they were encrypted until after I left. I do know where we are most likely to find the key to read them, though. And it sounds like you were headed in that direction anyway: the camp at Dazhai. The Chairman is touring the other camps trying to keep up morale right now, so it might be a good time to go after it. Take me with you, and I'll find it for you."

I shake my head, not willing to entertain the offer. I've filled my follow-Howl-blindly quota. Enough for more than one person. "Why did you come find me?"

"I want you to take me with you wherever you're going."

"That sounds familiar. Let's fly off into the sunset together, Howl. We'll be a team."

"Don't accept an offer *less* than the original one proffered, Sev. Last time we talked about this, I offered to build you a tree house." Howl's half-real smile opens into the awful gore-toothed grin that's spoiled all the memories I have of him. Every joke, every moment I felt comfortable or happy with him, all replaced by this . . . creature. "I guess you should keep your options open, though. How was I supposed to know Tai-ge had a *heli*?"

"Okay." I stand up, dusting off my knees. "I think we can be done now."

"It's just as much in my interest as it is in yours to stay away from Dr. Yang at the moment, Sev." Howl leans forward. "Him and anyone else who knows how hard it would be for me to catch SS. You're running away, and you've got better transport than I do." He twists his wrists, pulling at the tape. "Even if it isn't exactly comfortable. I can help you, if you help me."

My jaw tightens, the words barely squeezing out between my teeth. "You really don't know." I don't know why I thought he might.

"Unfortunately, that is true about a lot of things." Howl wrinkles his nose, as if he's about to sneeze, twitching uncomfortably when it doesn't come. "What particular point of ignorance did you have in mind?"

"I doubt Dr. Yang cares where either of us are. Unless you're here to clean up last witnesses to what he did during the invasion, neither of us are much use to him." It comes out almost like a taunt. "He wasn't ever going to kill either of us. Not for a cure, anyway. It's safe for you to go back to shooting Reds with your friends."

"What do you mean?"

"Dr. Yang can't use us to make a cure, Howl. If he could have, he wouldn't have asked so nicely to cut you open all those years ago. He just wanted me to wake Mother up. She wouldn't have told anyone else where to find the cure."

Howl stares at me, and for a second it seems as if his composure will crack, his expression porcelain and hammer. "Wait . . . there's no way—"

"It's true." I wipe my hands on my pants, cringing when anmicro smears in a greasy arc across the rough fabric.

It's almost painful to watch the thoughts running rampant across Howl's face, but after a moment they clear, leaving nothing but blank. Howl looks up at me, and I can see the calculations forming, the mask pulling down tight. "So you woke her up. You know where the cure is. That's why you needed maps. Why you need to go to Port North."

My hackles rise. Why did I say that? One more piece of information for Howl to play with.

Howl smiles, and it's too white and clean. As if he has to work to bleach away the inky black lurking inside him and just took it a little too far. "Well, this will be a fun trip, then. Are you going to be able to sleep tonight, what with a gore lodging on the heli with you? I promise not to get my rabies all over you." He shrugs a little. "I'll try, anyway."

I slide the door open with one hand. "You won't be with us long enough to spread it around. You can go back to doing whatever you want with no fear of repercussions."

Howl starts to laugh. "I want . . ." His voice cracks, and he looks down, what I think was meant to be lighthearted suddenly heavy as lead. "I want to live through this, just like everyone else."

CHAPTER 12

WHEN I WALK OUT OF HOWL'S CELL, I CLOSE THE
door behind me but don't get much farther. The icy sheen of calm
coating my heart and mind have long since gone up in flames, but I
don't disintegrate into a pile of ash like I thought I might. Taking
deep breaths doesn't help slow my racing heart or the little burrowing spirals of disappointment digging deep into my chest.

What was I hoping for when I went in there? That despite the
lies, the *knife*, that Howl would somehow be able to explain everything, and we could go back to being friends?

He really did say he'd build me a tree house. It was a joke.
Something to lighten the idea of running away from the Mountain
when we were sitting Outside, listening to the gores sing their
terrible lullabies in the forest below us, trying to imagine what it
would be like to survive out there. Something that seemed to be
an impossible risk, a show of bravery on Howl's part, because I
still thought SS was gnawing at my brain, waiting to take control.
He would have been the one who had to wake up to my empty
shell, the darkness of compulsions peering out through my pupils.

Only, that isn't what would have happened at all, because I didn't have SS, and Howl knew it.

I take a deep breath, and then another, wrenching my brain back into the heli, to *now* and what has to come next. The bits and pieces of information that Howl so easily handed over gum together in my head, one congealed and quivering mess.

He really was the Chairman's son, or a slightly rabid stand-in, anyway. At least that means I wasn't so gullible as I'd thought. He and Dr. Yang managed to dupe the whole Circle—even General Hong—into believing. The things he told me when we met weren't that far from the truth. Running intelligence and Mantis out of the City as best he could and hating every moment.

Wishing he could put a bullet in the Chairman's head, no doubt.

It's the last bit he said that hurts the most, an echo of what Sole told me the night I ran away. Howl is a survivor. His life will always come first. Hearing him say it out loud stings, both because I wish dying wasn't one of the options all of us are facing, and because I know Howl chose his outcome long before he ever met me. No matter the consequences, he plans to be the last one standing.

My hand strays to my throat, wishing I could somehow rub away the red line made by his knife. If Howl really didn't know about the cure, then the knife was the opening move in a strategy that would have landed me back at Dr. Yang's feet.

I wrinkle my nose, wishing I could take back all of those quiet moments we had together. What was he thinking as we sat in June's family tent, waiting to see if one of her infected clan members decided to kill us? When I told him about my nightmares, or when he took me outside and kissed me? It couldn't *all* have been calculation, or he wouldn't have tried to keep me away from Dr. Yang and Yizhi. He wouldn't have planned an escape with me.

The heli floor jiggles under my feet as someone comes up the ladder, and Tai-ge's head pops into view. He takes in the closed door, climbs the rest of the way in, and folds his arms tightly around me. "What's he got for us?"

I push away, attempting a less-than-serious tone as I head for the ladder. "He's probably going to kill us while we're asleep."

"I'll leave Tai-ge out of any murder sprees if it makes you feel better!" Howl calls through the door. "I don't know how to fly the heli."

Tai-ge's abashed expression would have made me laugh, except for the fact that Howl's joke, however ridiculous it's meant to sound, might hold more truth than lie.

"He was masquerading as Sun Yi-lai?" Tai-ge asks once we're outside and I've had a chance to tell his version of things. June looks up from her spot on the ground next to the little fire, potatoes wrapped in wet leaves steaming in the coals at her feet. Tai-ge's face pales—and then goes very, very red. "It's true that Yi-lai hadn't been seen much until two years ago, but that doesn't seem possible."

"Hasn't been seen *much*?" I ask, sitting across from June.

"I was just a Red, Sevvy. The Chairman keeps to himself." Tai-ge lowers himself next to me, grimacing at the frozen ground. His hand comes down on top of mine, and I move over a few inches to give him room, folding my arms across my lap. He hesitates, then folds his arms too, as if that wasn't quite the reaction he expected. I blink, staring down at my hands. I wasn't trying to push him off me; it just didn't occur to me that him touching me was intentional until I'd already moved. Adjusting my legs so they cross, I decide to let it go. After talking to Howl, I need my own space.

"What do you think about the maps?" Tai-ge asks. "Wherever he takes us to get an encryption key could be a trap."

"He says it's at Dazhai, where we're going anyway," I reply. "The trick is whether we can get it without him getting us tangled into something." I touch the leather cord around my neck, pulling the four metal stars out from under my coat. Mother's jade shard and the rusty ring dangle next to the old pin I had to wear when I lived in the City, making it easy for anyone to see who I was. Tai-ge had two, and Howl only one. When I catch Tai-ge squinting at the ring, I shove the necklace back under my shirt. "If Menghu happened upon us, they probably would take us straight back to Dr. Yang, thinking I'm the answer to all their problems. It's a City camp. There's no reason for them to come after me, but they used *my* name and description at the Post."

"What reasons could Yi-lai—sorry, I mean *Howl*—have to take us to a City camp?" Tai-ge interjects. "The whole upset here is that his City ties aren't genuine, right?"

"Apparently, the report was pretty specific. That we were there, looking for maps. Maybe they wanted to take back the heli or—"

June flicks a bit of charred wood at the side of Tai-ge's head then looks at me, ignoring him when he looks around to see what hit him.

I hide a smile, the wood probably as close to an accusation as June is willing to make. "Howl said they might have been looking for Tai-ge. But they asked for me, too, and why mention *maps* specifically? It still bothers me not knowing *how* they knew we were there." Reaching out to touch one of the leaf-wrapped potatoes, I hiss when it singes my fingers. "I mean, Cai Ayi was just as upset as I was to find Reds barking up her trees, so it doesn't seem like she or the roughers would have reported us. Peishan, maybe? She didn't have any way to communicate."

Tai-ge shrugs, rubbing his temple where the wood hit, still trying to figure out what struck him. "We just don't know enough. Our plan to sneak into Dazhai was risky at best, but with Howl *telling* us we need to go . . ." He shakes his head. "There are too many players, and we don't even know where half the pieces are."

June blinks, hand going to her pocket. She pulls two bags out, dumping the first next to her knee. A pile of dark stones. The other bag she tosses to me, and I don't quite catch it, spilling white stones on the ground and across my lap. "You want to play weiqi?" I ask.

She draws a grid on the ground with the tip of her finger, a beginner's board only nine by nine squares. She places her stones across the joined points between squares without waiting for me to play, until there's an impenetrable black wall blocking off one side of the board. Then she takes one white stone and places it in the middle. "Too many people playing." She looks up at me.

"You mean we don't really know who is playing," Tai-ge interjects.

"Reds, Menghu. Howl." She waves at the board. "All packed together in one space. They're all in one another's way." She points to the unoccupied half of the board. "Dr. Yang wants Port North and the papers. Menghu want Sev. Firsts want the cure back. Reds want their city, more Mantis. Howl wants—"

"To be safe," I say. "He wants to live."

June nods. "Their pieces are messy. It might be a trap. So don't have just one plan. If we can advance"—she puts more white

pieces along the blank side of the board, barring off territory—
"we advance. If it goes bad, we run. Move in a different direction. There are only three of us, and we know more about all of
them than they know about the others. They'll just trip over one
another."

The point of weiqi is to occupy territory, not fill it square
after square with stones. It's like a real battle: Placing one soldier
every square mile over a grid wouldn't do much to help you win.
The point is to block your opponent off from large chunks of the
board, placing your stones so they create fortresses of space that
may as well be inaccessible to the other player. It's true that Dr.
Yang is holding his plans close. No one knew he couldn't come up
with a cure using the resources he had, that he needed Mother's
data. No one in the limited pool of people we've talked to seem to
even know where Port North is or what that means. The Reds are
just trying to regroup, so far as radio chatter tells. But it's impossible to know what the Menghu are doing. If Dr. Yang has control
over all of them, if he's still telling them he needs me to create a
cure . . . if he's taken them all to Port North and they're killing
the occupants one by one until they hand over Mother's papers.
Howl might know, but Howl lies. Howl doesn't care who dies, so
long as his head remains attached to his shoulders.

Our plan was to go to Dazhai. Howl is telling us to go to
Dazhai. His maps might be fake. But they also might be real. I rub
a hand across my forehead, the skin feeling hot.

Tai-ge looks at me. "Sev?"

"We should . . . do what we planned. Go to Dazhai. We'll look
for the key, but we'll look for maps, too, just in case what he's got
is a false trail. We just need to be flexible."

Tai-ge and June both nod in agreement.

"So, our original plan, but with extra ideas for if Menghu appear at the heli door when we land?" Tai-ge asks. "We set down before dawn, somewhere close enough to hike in, but far enough they won't jump right onto us. Abandon the heli because there's not much chance lookouts will miss us landing." He looks at me. "We'll . . . mine any information we can from Howl, including where the encryption key is and what it looks like. Sneak into the camp, leaving June outside, of course."

I glance over at June, her snarl of golden curls bright. No amount of mud or dirt can hide her Outsider features. The word makes me smile a little. Outsiders. All of us are Outsiders now, including the Chairman, at least until they figure out how to frighten away all the Sephs spreading SS inside City walls.

"After an hour or so, June sets off a distraction." Tai-ge points to the heli, the growth regulators he bought from Cai Ayi inside just waiting to be ignited. "We run away with maps, or the key, whichever we find, and head toward Port North on foot."

I sit forward, looking at June. "You really think we can dance around whatever Howl flies us into? Menghu with their guns drawn? The bloody-handed Chairman himself looking for his son? Can we plan for all of those without letting Howl know, so he can't trap us somehow?"

June's teeth show in her smile, plucking white stones from the ground and cradling them in her hand as she looks the makeshift board over. "We can do anything."

CHAPTER 13

I TAKE TAI-GE INTO THE STORAGE CLOSET, AND Howl only hedges a moment before agreeing to share what he knows about Dazhai with my friend, though I can feel his eyes on my back the whole way to the hatch. Outside, I walk until their voices are only a prickly whisper, busying myself stacking extra Junis branches to keep the fire going. June heads into the heli and comes back again after a moment, holding one of the two wintermelons we got from Cai Ayi, the weight knocking each step she takes sideways.

"Even one of those things is bigger than you." I smile at her, trying to drown out the cadence of Howl speaking, the words and expressions all sanded away just to leave the shape of his voice. "A whole gore could fit inside it. Wait, is that what you're cooking? Gore?"

June's smile is almost jovial, showing teeth and everything. "We can't carry these with us when we leave. So I'm going to make some real food."

"I remember what Outsider food tastes like from when we first met you, thank you very much. I think I'll pass."

June mimes throwing the wintermelon at me, but it's so heavy it just falls to the ground with a *thud*. She thuds down next to it and pulls out her knife. "You don't know what real food tastes like. Wood Rat special."

"I've never tried rat." I give her a delicate bow, reveling in each word from June's mouth as if it's a gift. She's opening up, blossoming into someone with opinions and stories, even if she doesn't always share out loud. "We City-folk only eat canned applesauce and small children."

"That's because you can't cook." She points to the Junis I piled. "Build the fire up."

By the time June has soupy vegetables bubbling inside the wintermelon rind, Tai-ge finally climbs down the ladder. "What have we got?" I ask, stretching my legs out next to the low flames, the fire's warmth sinking through my outer layers.

"About what I expected." He settles next to me, sniffing experimentally. "What is that? It smells wonderful." The rich smell of fresh vegetables and meat from our dried rations makes my mouth water so much it hurts. June doesn't acknowledge Tai-ge's compliment, concentrating on stirring the soup. Tai-ge shrugs, turning back to me. "Howl says only four members of the Circle survived, and they're all at Dazhai."

"Only four survived?" I frown. "Didn't most of the Firsts evacuate right when the invasion started?"

Tai-ge shrugs. "According to Howl, the rest of the First Quarter *is* there, like we thought. Aside from that, most of the eastern and northern garrisons are camped there, along with the Mantis stockpiles airlifted out of the City and enough food to feed the whole army for a few months. There should be more than one encryption key, but Howl says they're keeping a close eye on the maps and keys in the Second tents. He managed to lift the ones he brought to us because of his First mark and because the Chairman can afford to be careless inside his own tent." Tai-ge holds out bowls and spoons he brought from above to June, who takes them. "Howl says we won't get anywhere close. Not without him. We need his status."

"That's not an option." When a bowl thrusts itself into my vision, I look up to find June standing over me. I take it, relishing the steam as it warms my face. "Thanks, June."

Tai-ge watches as June dishes up another bowl and brings it to him. "What if he's right, Sev? What if we need First marks to get close?"

"Then we'll storm over the top of the camp in the heli. Or paint our faces with mud and wriggle through like snakes. We'll pretend to be Thirds and pour wine down scouts' throats until they ride us in on their shoulders."

"You've got a bottle of wine stashed somewhere?"

I roll my eyes. "Things are so messy right now, what are the odds that they check under everyone's masks and count the marks? The risk of contagion is too high. Howl is a bigger risk than wearing gloves to hide my brand and hoping for the best."

Tai-ge sighs. "So do we try for the ones locked in with the Chairman's things or do we break into the new General's tent?"

I don't miss the way his voice wavers over the mention of a new General. "How are you holding up, Tai-ge?"

He shakes his head, leaning over the bowl of soup and breathing in deep before looking out past the broken buildings into the trees beyond—and freezes. "Someone's watching us out there."

"There's . . . ?" My heart pauses, and I stare at the shadowed tree trunks, twilight purpling the air around us. I pull myself into a crouch, setting my bowl down. "Let's get inside, get your masks."

"Only one person." June looks up from dishing up another portion of soup. "Someone like me."

Like June? A Wood Rat? June stands and goes to the ladder, precariously balancing the bowl as she climbs up. She looks back when I stand to follow her. "No. Stay. If they'd wanted to, they would have come at us a long time ago."

"Are you going to eat inside?" Tai-ge calls after her.

June shakes her head without looking back and pulls herself through the hatch. The bowl must be for Howl. Tai-ge doesn't seem concerned about whoever it is out there watching us, so I let myself slide back to the ground.

I put a hand on Tai-ge's arm. "It's got to be difficult, listening to Howl talk about the camps. After your dad . . ."

"We can't waste time getting upset about anything right now, Sevvy." Tai-ge inches closer, and I'm glad for the extra warmth when his side brushes up against mine. "Your mother died too."

"She might as well have been dead for years. It was just a chance to say good-bye for me." I try not to think of the blood, of how frail she felt. "Or it was a release, anyway. For both of us. I don't know how you feel, but I have lost . . . so much. I even lost *you*, my best friend, for a while. All of us here have lost somebody to bullets. June's dad was shot right in front of her only a few months ago."

"We're all alone now," Tai-ge whispers, as if June's father being dead is no more or less than he expected. "Even if my father had survived, he'd probably be lost along with everyone else who was trapped inside the City. I'd probably be there too." He looks down. "I can't think about it now. When this is over, we can . . ."

Tai-ge licks his lips, staring hard at his hands, still and useless in his lap. "We'll be able to feel again."

I pinch my lips together, the sharp prick of tears needling my eyes. "I used to feel that way. I still catch myself pushing it all aside. You have to sometimes." It's dangerous to let yourself be flooded by your anger, sorrow, hatred, or worst of all, uselessness. They wash away anything that's left inside you that can act. But pretending it isn't there, that you're fine, isn't healthy either. How many years did I spend imagining Mother was a doll, dressed up and posed inside her glass cage in the City Center, as though she had nothing to do with me? How long did it take before I could let myself think of Aya, my own sister, as anything other than an empty space in my heart?

It was Aya—missing Aya, and wishing I somehow could have saved her—that made me want to help June when we first met her.

"If you don't let yourself feel any of it, then it weighs you down, Tai-ge." I allowed my family to be a weight on my shoulders instead of a memory of where I came from. It's not as if everything's fine now that I'm staring those memories in the face, trying to make sense of them, to let some of them go. But it's a little better. "Pushing it back makes it so you can't feel anything at all, good or bad."

Tai-ge looks at me, an almost-smile on his face. "You wouldn't even talk about your family back in the City. Not your sister, your father, your mother."

He reaches out to brush a strand of hair away from my face just as I pull away to brush it aside myself. "I couldn't. Mourning traitors? It probably would have gotten me a nice bed in the Hole." I bite my lip, thinking of Howl and how he did exactly what I'm trying to do for Tai-ge now. He opened the door. Let all the things burning up my insides explode out, or they would have turned me to cinders eventually. It wasn't saying things out loud that helped so much as knowing he was listening, knowing he was there. On my side. "I guess if you don't want to talk, that's okay. I just want you to know that I'm here and I care about you. If you want to talk, I'll listen. If you want to sit, I'll sit by you. Anything you need."

Tai-ge's so still for a second. But then he leans over an inch, shoulder heavy against mine. We watch the fire's embers crack and spit until the hatch hisses open and something thuds to the ground, heavy enough to be a broken body. I'm halfway to my feet, panic roaring in my ears, when June's boots appear at the top of the ladder, unharmed. She climbs down one-handed, her face now covered by a gas mask, two more empty bowls clutched against her.

"Do you think Howl can eat without help?" Tai-ge asks tiredly as June drops a second mask in his lap. He fingers the plastic curls, then fits it over his nose and mouth, turning his attention back toward the black of the forest. "His hands are tied."

June nods in response, ladling stew into a bowl, then setting it carefully just beyond the fire circle. She goes back to the ladder, heaving the thing she threw to the ground up against her hip. The other wintermelon. She waddles by, scoops up the bowl of soup, then walks out of the circle of our firelight, disappearing into darkness.

She comes back empty-handed.

I stare into the darkness as if I'll see the bowl of soup where June left it, tracing silver curls of heat up into the frozen night.

How do June and Tai-ge know there's only one person out there, eyes catching the light of our fire? Hungry. Cold. Watching, waiting. Hoping we'll leave something, or planning to take it.

How many left in the City, SS burning inside them? My days as a Seph were broken up by green pills in a little cup. An assurance I'd keep walking in a straight line, even as the hallucinations pulling at my brain tried to convince me otherwise. The people we left in the City don't even have that. Compartmentalizing their days and nights between moments of sick and moments of well, no one even trying to divide the one from the other.

SS doesn't turn you into something too far gone to save. Lihua isn't a monster any more than I ever was. That's why we're going to Port North. It's time for SS to stop twisting us to its will. And for the people with Mantis to stop twisting us along with it.

A bird calls out over the darkness, a hollow sort of *hu, huuuuu*. Bumps prickle across my arms. Thirds used to whisper old legends over their evening meals when electricity was being rationed. They'd say that if an owl lights in the tree outside your house, someone inside will die. Every sound that comes from its beak, the long *hu, huuuu* a command to start digging. Of course, we don't bury our dead anymore. And owls can't change the sound they make to tell people to start a bonfire, so maybe the bad luck doesn't apply.

I shrug off the long, lonely sound. Across the fire, June pulls her mask away from her face just enough to admit a quick sip of soup, the steam wafting in pearly trails around her face.

A smile finds its way to my mouth, a warm feeling in my chest as I think of that bowl of soup waiting out in the dark. After everything, I'm glad to see something being given rather than taken.

CHAPTER 14

GET UP HIGH. RUNNING IN WILL JUST MEAN BOTH *of our heads on the Chairman's desk.* I can't shoot someone, not even Reds who would happily tear me apart. I won't. I'm better than that, better than my mother. I just have to scare them off. *I can do this. This is Kasim's life.*

But then I see it below me. A single black eye winking up at me, the only point of light in the giant, muddled shadow lurking beneath my tree. Everything inside me screams for the Reds to run, to get away before the gore comes for them, but my voice is melted glass, ablaze in my throat. I watch, every move painfully slow and inevitable as the creature charges, jagged teeth finding flesh and bone. Screams. Kasim with a blood-smeared arc carved into his chest. Cale, her gun pointed at me.

It's a dream. I know it's a dream. But no matter how I twist and turn, the gun doesn't move, the gore doesn't sleep. I'm trapped in the tar of my own memories until I can force myself to wake. Nightmares don't retract their claws no matter how much you struggle, bringing you to the very edge before letting you fall.

Cale's finger squeezes her trigger, and the sound fills my whole world.

My eyes tear open. Sweat streams down my temples, my sleeping bag wet under my cheek. I roll to my back and stare up into the dark, hands clasped over my mouth to quiet the sounds of my gasps.

"Sev?" It's a whisper from where Tai-ge is keeping watch over the cargo bay door, the only way into the heli when the hatch is locked. "What's the matter?" the voice asks.

I sit up, inching closer to where Tai-ge sits slumped against the doors, his breaths rasping long and slow out of that monster mask. He's asleep. Not in a state to whisper anything.

And then my eyes find Howl's door next to Tai-ge's still form. Open.

Panic rushes over me in a swell, choking my lungs, and for a moment I can't speak. How did Howl get the door open? Is Tai-ge really asleep? Or did Howl get to him somehow?

Howl eases himself backward into the doorway, his hands extended into the room where they're tethered to the shelves inside. He can't get any farther, craning his neck over his shoulder to look at me.

"I heard you wake up. Are you okay?" he asks, the whisper hoarse. Whispers are tricky, scrubbing the owner's voice to a tattered remnant of the truth. "Dreams?"

I lie down, not willing to go close enough to shut the door. Howl can't get out. He can't reach Tai-ge. If he wants to pull against the shelves all night and bruise his wrists, it's not my problem.

"Sometimes, if you've been through hard things . . ." He stops, the silence heavy with indecision. "When I was with the Menghu, it would happen to some of them. The worst moments assaulting you when your guard is down and you can't make yourself forget."

I'm millimeters from saying something about Howl being the cause of my bad dreams, the catalyst that started the war in my head, but I shut my mouth instead. It's not fair to say that leaving the City was the beginning of sleepless nights, of wishing I could forget everything that came before this moment. Dead men and guns have just come to replace the dreams I had before. Of Father burning, Aya falling in the street, blood spattering the concrete. Of Mother's voice, crying, telling me she was sorry. Of darkness. Of Sleep.

"I just . . . understand," Howl whispers. "If you're scared. If you don't want to sit there alone, wondering if you'll ever be able to sleep again."

I roll over, facing the blur of darkness in his direction. "You have bad dreams too?"

He doesn't answer for a moment, but when he does, it's so quiet I can hardly hear him. As if it's a confession he's not quite comfortable airing. "No."

I turn away. Swallow. Force my eyes to close. Even if I wish the dead would leave me alone, I'm glad I'm human enough to remember them.

Before light creeps in through the seams in the heli's tarp over the cockpit window, a hand grabs my shoulder, jerking me out of my half sleep. I roll over to find a writhing mass of rubber tentacles and mesh filter in my face. Fear knifes through my heart, but before I can scream, the thing pulls the filters down, and my brain haltingly recognizes Tai-ge's face underneath.

"We need to get in the air if we want to make Dazhai before

dawn." He pulls the mask back over his nose and mouth. "Come help me pull back the tarp?"

My breath shivers from my lungs in reluctant streams, but I nod and follow him out. Outside, the night sky is clouded over, blocking all but a few silvery wisps of moonlight. Tai-ge pulls open the first set of controls, then goes still, staring out into the trees. I follow his gaze, my heart racing when it lands on . . . something.

It's too dark to make out anything, but it's more a feeling, like the scrape of a blade against my bare skin, the itch of knowing it's about to stab you straight through. There's something out there watching us. Both of us can feel it.

"Get the back side, Sevvy." Tai-ge hits the control to unlock the tarp from its anchoring points and runs to unlatch it from the cockpit's great glass eye and front propellers. I run around the back of the heli, my hands fumbling to pull the plastic covering free from the belly of the cargo bay and the four propellers jutting out on either side of it. By the time the plastic is slowly feeding itself back into its housing, I'm already at the ladder, trying not to think of what will happen if it jams.

Just as Tai-ge comes running, a dark smudge detaches from the edge of the forest, skittering toward us as if the shadows themselves are reaching out to drag us into the gloom. Then another shape, and another. I push him onto the ladder, worming my way up next to him so we both squeeze into the cockpit at the same time. Tai-ge slams his hand across the control to lock the hatch and runs for the captain's chair. I wait for the *thunk* that will mean the ladder has pulled all the way up, a shudder rippling through me when the mechanism whines instead.

The propellers ignite, filling the air with a steely roar. Finally, the ladder mechanism gives one last protest, and the ladder clicks into place. Our craft shivers into the air with an extra swing as if it is shaking something off.

I perch on the copilot's chair next to Tai-ge, breathing long and slow, as if I can exhale the adrenaline buzzing through me. Was it the watcher from last night, with friends to help? Made bold by a bowl of soup and the promises of an owl's call?

Looking through the cockpit windows, I can't see anything but the glare of the heli's underlights against the ragged field below us. Whatever—whoever—was out there, it doesn't matter. We're in the air. We're safe. But even though my view of the ground looks empty, it feels as if something is watching us.

The feeling solidifies inside me, prickled and sharp. We can't fail. The people in these mountains won't survive much longer if something doesn't change. None of us will. We have to find the cure. It won't change the Wood Rats who live alone and prey on others because it's all they know. But it will at least give more options to everyone else stuck out in the cold. I grit my teeth. We need a kiss to wake up the sleeping princess, one that isn't doled out by someone based on what they can take from you. We'll find a happy ending, because I won't stop until we do.

And that resolve, that feeling of control, banishes some of the fear boiling in my head. Fear that's been there my whole life, laughing at me. But no more. I am not helpless. I'm not a victim. I won't be.

CHAPTER 15

JUNE TAKES MY PLACE IN THE CHAIR BY TAI-GE WHEN she wakes up, letting me follow the growl of my stomach to our supplies. The storage closet door is still open as I walk by, Howl a shadowy smudge that takes up most of the floor inside. His arms are wrapped around his head, dead asleep as if our conversation last night never happened. Maybe it didn't. Maybe it was just another dream of the dark things inside me, wishing Howl would be the one to wake up because I did, that he'd care whether or not I could sleep.

I push the door closed, full import of finding it propped open in the middle of the night shuddering through me. "June?" She swivels the chair in my direction, gas mask sucked tight over her nose and mouth like a gargantuan caterpillar. "Did you open Howl's door last night?"

She gives a slow nod. "Stuffy in there."

I close my eyes for a second, not sure if I'm more glad Howl didn't magically unlock it from the inside or upset that June would open it for him and give him one less obstacle to hurting us.

Tai-ge fights with the controls, the mask cockeyed on his face as the heli wobbles from side to side. I grab a spear of dried meat and join them at the controls, nothing but darkness to tell me how high we are. Howl and Tai-ge plotted a course that would take us between a series of mountains, keeping the heli from being easily spotted. Everything that might alert Reds to our presence has been turned off, and I can see the strain of flying without the extra help from the heli's instruments in Tai-ge's shoulders.

June leans in to stare at the controls, shifting her balance along with the heli to keep herself from falling every time we wobble to the side. She points toward a dark outline that suddenly looms up in front of us, then to the base of the one just beyond, and finally to the glint of river mirror-bright even under the clouds that have rolled in during the night. Tai-ge nods as if this is some kind of plan, June pointing out the landmarks he knew were coming but couldn't find for himself. It seems to help, and when we finally set back down on the ground in one of the abrupt hills populating the mountain range's feet, Tai-ge sags back against his chair, sweat streaming down his temples.

"Let's never do that again," he says, voice exhausted as he pulls the gas mask over his head, rubbing at the spot where it dug into on his cheek. "June, if you hadn't come with us, we'd be skewered on the branches of a tree somewhere like a downed kite after the sweeping festival."

June hops down from the chair without responding. She goes to the boxes of supplies to rummage until she comes up with some dried pear slices. Tai-ge slowly kicks his chair around to face me, his almost-smile making his dimples stand out in each cheek. "She really likes those," he whispers, as if it's a joke just between us.

June stuffs the pears under her shirt, hugging them close. She steps sideways, keeping Tai-ge and me in her peripheral vision.

"Sorry, I didn't mean you *shouldn't* like them." Tai-ge puts his hands up to stop her running away. "Eat them. I still can't make myself stomach fruit that isn't canned anyway." He trails off as she pushes the boxes blocking the cargo bay door aside, wrenches it open, then stalks through.

"Does she hate everyone, or is it just me?" Tai-ge asks.

"I don't think she hates you any more than she hates anyone else she doesn't know very well." I smile to make it a joke, but he doesn't seem to notice. "Just give her some time to warm up."

I follow June's rat's nest of curls into the cargo bay and find her sitting on one of the benches, chewing methodically on a bit of pear. She doesn't move when I sit next to her.

"They taste so good," she says quietly.

"And they're all yours." I shiver as a rush of frozen air blows up through the holes in the floor. "Tai-ge didn't mean anything by it."

"He doesn't understand."

About to ask what he doesn't understand exactly, I stop myself. Tai-ge doesn't understand a lot of things about being Outside. He still doesn't believe in gores, for Yuan's sake. But there are things I don't understand either. What it means to glean and pick at the forest until you squeeze out enough food to keep the flesh from falling off your bones. Living under Cas, Tian, Parhat, and Liu, all sick with SS and perhaps not interested in eating food or sharing it.

"No one understands completely. Not about anyone else," I finally answer. "We all come from a place no one else has walked exactly. Fought fights and learned lessons other people didn't have to. But Tai-ge knows that. I just think he was happy to see someone so excited to eat dried pears when he'd rather be eating steak noodles flown in from one of the farms."

June's brow furrows. "Steak noodles?"

I shrug. "Fresh meat? From cows? Not dried. Cut up raw and cooked over a grill, then you put it with noodles in soup . . . ?"

The look on her face is enough to know I'm doing Tai-ge no favors by continuing this conversation, so I nudge her instead. "I'll write your name on the bag of pears. Every last one can be yours."

June rolls her eyes, but she pulls the bag of pears out from under her shirt. Together, we go back into the cockpit and prop up June's rucksack and the two packs from the Post by the wall, putting waterskins, food, and basic medical supplies in each. I stuff my sleeping bag into its sack, the slippery fabric already cold under my fingers as I cinch it tight to my pack. Tai-ge kneels next to me, arms full of Howl's maps. He slides them into the pack's side pocket, all five tubes sticking out from the top like stalks of bone-white bamboo. Stage one of our plan not to die.

"I've been wanting to ask, what are those?" Tai-ge points to my neck before zipping the top his pack closed.

I look down, finding my four traitor stars caught on the neckline of my shirt. Confused, I tug them free, wincing when one of the points pricks my finger. "You know what these are."

"I meant these." Tai-ge reaches out to touch the bit of red jade strung on the leather and the rusted metal ring next to it.

"This?" I touch the jade, Tai-ge's fingers so close they almost brush my jaw. I move back an inch, looking down at the necklace. "My mother gave it to me when I was little. Dr. Yang had it. Having it back and the stars . . . they felt important. Like things I wanted to remember about who I was and where I came from. Things I used to believe, and what has changed."

"And the ring?"

"The ring . . ." I bite my lip, willing my cheeks not to turn ruddy, but I can feel them heating up. "I found it Outside. You used to wear a ring like it, and it reminded me of you."

Tai-ge looks at it for a second, then back at me. He smiles. A real smile, dimples and all.

I look down, tucking the necklace away out of sight. After that weird moment between us in the heli earlier, Tai-ge and me staring at each other as if something was about to happen between us . . . it was exciting and felt like spitting in the faces of all those people who spit in mine back in the City.

But I haven't thought much about it since.

June walks by, handing me a gas mask—a disguise I wish I didn't have to wear since SS can't hurt me anymore. I turn toward the hatch as I pull it over my mouth and nose, my breath dank as it wheezes through the filter. I wore that ring every day I was out in the forest. Every day until . . . Howl. It represented something from my past I never wanted to forget, but it was a past I hadn't thought I could ever go back to, so I took the ring off.

Now it almost feels heavy around my neck.

Extracting my coat from the pile of boxes where I threw it last night, I nod to June. "You ready to go find Dazhai?"

She nods, sticking another pear slice in her mouth before stuffing the bag into her pocket and adjusting her mask so it's leech-tight against her face.

"You look nice today." Tai-ge flinches when I look at him, as if even he can hear how ridiculous he sounds. "Your hair looks less crazy with your mask on. I mean, it isn't ugly or anything."

I glance down at the mess of tubes dribbling down from my chin, as if a dead centipede decided to take a nap on my face. "Thanks, Tai-ge. I'll wear it more often."

Tai-ge nods and busies himself with strapping on his own

mask, either taking me seriously or pretending that wasn't the most awkward thing he's ever said to me. When the mask is fitted over his nose and mouth, Tai-ge checks that Howl's cell is locked. It isn't easy to play a game of weiqi when you aren't sure where all the other pieces are. Everyone agreed that Howl's stone was better contained where it couldn't sneak onto the board when we weren't looking.

Outside, the morning's earliest light is muted by a bank of clouds. The air frosts with our breath as we walk, and it's hard not to think of it as evidence of our passing, fogging around us every time June stops to listen. The sound of our boots crunching through the ice is loud in my ears, the tracks we leave behind an unavoidable clue that we've been here. There's not much chance we can come back to the heli. Even if no one at the camp noticed the scream of our propellers, our tracks will lead straight to it. So we're abandoning it for the Reds to take back, Howl trapped inside it with enough food and water to last a week or so.

Tai-ge doesn't say it, but I can see the relief in his face that Howl is going back to City people. Regardless of who Howl really is, he's glad to be returning the Chairman's proxy son, as if it's the titles that matter, not the truth of the thing.

My own feelings seem to spark as we walk away, a chapter of my life closed with a slam. I'll never see Howl again. I take a deep breath, considering. Does it feel good to be leaving him behind again, this time fairly certain he and his gore claws are locked away where they won't be able to come after me?

Reds won't kill him. He's still the Chairman's son to them. And by the time they find him, June, Tai-ge, and I will be well away. The awful uncertainty that came with leaving Howl bleeding on the hangar floor back in the City, wondering if I'd made a mistake, is gone. But as my boots punch through the crusty snow, iced-over pines reaching out to hurry me into their embrace where the Reds won't see our approach on Dazhai, it takes every string of self-control I can claim to keep myself from looking back.

PART II

CHAPTER 16

WHEN THE SUN IS FULLY UP, WE REACH THE RIVER WE saw from up in the heli. Snowflakes float down to us like a light sprinkling of ash. We walk along the bank of the river until June veers up the mountainside to a cluster of boulders. They lie just under the swell of a hill, a tree growing almost directly on top of them. June points up into the tortured twists of its branches, a snowcapped bundle of something stuck near the top, as if a giant took off his threadbare coat and left it there.

They're sticks and strings of dried grass. A bird's nest.

June pulls her rucksack off, then creeps up over one of the boulders, dragging the bag behind her. I follow her up, stowing my pack next to hers in the open chink of space between the ground and the stone. Tai-ge opens his pack, pulling something from inside before he shoves it under the rock next to mine. The ground is dry where the tree and the hill's curve protect the spot from the snow, though there's a littering of odd black clumps in the tree's twisted roots. I pick one up, turning it over in my hand.

The clump isn't dirt. It's soft, with bone-hard bits of white. . . . I drop it with a curse as it begins to come apart in my hands, and wipe my fingers on my pants. The white things *are* bone. Owl pellets.

"What's the matter?" Tai-ge asks, his chin folding awkwardly as he tries to look down his own shirtfront. He has a pair of red stars in his hand, jabbing them awkwardly into his collar.

I look away, pointing up at the nest precariously perched in the tree above us. "There's an owl."

Tai-ge takes a careful step back, smoothing his collar down, the pin like drops of blood against his neck. I don't like the way it looks so suited to his collar, almost as if putting it on made my friend complete. He looks up at the jumble of weeds and branches above us, ignoring June as she shoots us both annoyed looks before hoisting herself over the rock to wait for us on the other side.

It *would* be an owl's nest standing watch over our packs. Owls and their ghostly calls in the night, a warning that death is coming.

"It looks abandoned, Sevvy." Tai-ge pulls the growth regulator pack we bought from Cai Ayi and sticks it in a small bag looped over his shoulder. He climbs up and holds a hand out for me. "And owls are just birds. We can't put stock in silly superstitions from Before. Come on."

June points to the mess of twigs and grass once we're over. "You can find your way back?"

"In the dark? When it's snowing?" I shrug off a shudder, fiddling with the zipper of my coat instead. "I hope so. Let's try not to get separated, though. Just in case."

June cocks her eyebrow, and for some reason I think she must be smiling under her gas mask. "Snow'll hide our tracks. At least it'll help." She leads us around the curve of the hill and back to the river, the icy bits of snow making it hard to see much but her small, hunched shoulders as we walk. After a while we get to where the ground drops out beneath us, ancient canals meant to divert river water. We're close.

Now the real plan starts. We left Howl. Stashed the packs. Now we need to find a way in and leave June out here, where, after a decent amount of time, she can set off an explosion with the growth regulators and the tiny can of heli fuel we extracted from the tanks. We'll find the maps or the encryption key, then run out with the Reds who rush to investigate the explosion. Should go like clockwork.

Should. I hate the questions running through my head. What if we don't find the key or maps? What if the explosion goes off before we have a chance to find anything? What if someone recognizes us? What if sneaking in just gets one or all of us shot? What if—

Tai-ge nudges my arm, jostling me from my thoughts. "This is going to work, Sevvy. We're going to be fine. We'll find the key, we'll be able to read the maps, and we'll get the cure."

"Right. We'll be fine." I wish I believed that. Even if we do find the key and escape minus extra flesh wounds, what then? If we find the cure tied up with a bow, where do we take it? How do we make it? How do we give it out?

And does it even matter? Dr. Yang has had so much time, so many more resources than we could even hope for. What if the cure is already in his sweaty fist back at the Mountain, held high for people to worship?

I set my jaw, shaking off the frantic flares of doubt in my mind. This is going to work. There aren't any other options.

Glimpses of open space beyond the clutter of trees make me feel shaky, though we aren't exposed. Before we're close enough to the camp to be easily seen, June leads us up one of the taller trees and pulls out the pair of binoculars we found on the heli.

She takes the first turn with them, though it only lasts a moment before she shakes her head in disgust and hands them to me. The snow is getting heavier, filling the air between us and the camp with white. All I can see are little flares of orange dotting the cleared space sheltered by the mountain below us. Hundreds of green and brown bumps that must be tents, but it's difficult see much more about them. Then I catch sight of something just over the center of the tents. Black, with the City's beaker and falcon stamped into the fabric. The Chairman's own flag.

I hand the binoculars to Tai-ge on the tree branch below me, carefully not looking down. Even if trees are sturdier than those cursed ladders at the Post, the height still feels unstable. My feet belong on the ground.

"Howl wasn't lying about the Chairman being based here," I say when Tai-ge's had a chance to look. "Now that we're actually looking at it, do you think our chances of getting in are good?"

June nods, pointing to the opposite side of the camp. The sheltering hills below us are a series of snow-laden cuts making a giant's staircase down to the tents. Tiers of rice paddies, the river water diverted to leave them dry during the winter months. Across from us and below the terracing sit long, squat structures made from something that catches the light, plastic or glass. Greenhouses? And past that there are short, flat buildings with utilitarian lines and infrequent windows. Around the curve of the hills, I catch a glimpse of several rusted silos holding last season's harvest of rice, and snow-covered fields beyond.

It's a working farm. Like the place Mei must have picked peaches before she learned killing from Cale and the other

Menghu. Fields of people the City claimed without giving them stars, slaves instead of citizens. Fourths, like me, I thought. But there aren't that many traitors in the City. Where did the Chairman find all the people who worked these fields, who mined our iron and picked our apples?

June shifts next to me, holding her hand out to Tai-ge for the binoculars. When he hands them up, she squints through the glass at the wavy folds marching down the mountainside below us, as if she can see well enough through the storm to plot our approach.

"Guards down along the paddies," Tai-ge says. "But Howl was right about them not being all the way up here. Looks like they're just walking the perimeter of the camp and keeping watch over those silos."

"No reason," June says.

She's right. The fields are open on the other side of the camp, with no way to approach from that direction without being seen by guards on the tiers of rice paddies on our side. There's a section of ground staked out beyond the camp, the stubby forms of helis lying like corpses under their tarps. As we watch, the fluid sound of heli propellers whoosh overhead, the craft moving in to land.

"You didn't spend time in one of these farms, did you, June?" I ask, looking up into the swirl of flakes, then wish I hadn't when the white deluge makes my mind tip sideways with vertigo.

June shakes her head.

"Do you know anyone who was taken to one? Or people who went willingly?"

"Shh." June lowers the binoculars and hoists herself down from the branch we're sitting on, hissing under her breath when the movement sends a cascade of snow sliding from the branches to clump in the drifts below.

The cold nips at my ears as Tai-ge and I follow her down the trunk to a stand of trees scrabbling for purchase in the rocky ground, a spot mostly sheltered from the snow to assemble the growth regulator bomb. I pull my hood up over my head for warmth, listening to the air rasping in and out of my mask as Tai-ge carefully begins to combine the bomb elements. Every breath freezes in my hair, leaving the chopped-off strands white with frost, as if I've started to mold.

"You been to a farm?" June's whisper startles me against the snow's insulating quiet. She sits with her arms wrapped around her legs, chin perched on her knees. Her green eyes look like old jade, scratched and battered.

"No." I think back to Mei. According to her, the farms made City life for a Fourth sound like a dream. "I met a Menghu who grew up in one, though. Why do you ask?"

She shrugs.

"There are hundreds of farms and other outposts," Tai-ge says, pausing for a moment while he pours something into the growth regulator bag. "That's how we had fish, vegetables, rice. Mines and mills for steel. Cotton. Knowing where they were was privileged information." He sits back, looking up from the makeshift bomb. "Well, 'privileged' might be the wrong word. You knew where a farm was if you had to go there. Moving goods, Outside patrol duty. As a worker."

"But workers couldn't have all come from the City. And it seems that if there were hundreds of work-ready Outsiders waiting to be snapped up out here, we would have met more of them," I reply.

Tai-ge adjusts his coat, the City's beaker and falcon embroidered across the back. "Your guess is as good as mine." He stands, carefully holding the bomb at his side. "Let's get this thing in position and get this over with."

CHAPTER 17

WE DON'T START DOWN UNTIL THE LIGHT HAS BEGUN to leak out of the sky, night's blood swirling to fill the void. The guard walking along the topmost tier of the rice paddies has only been here a few minutes, fresh after a guard change. He doesn't have time to yell before Tai-ge's arm is around his throat, pulling him down into the dry trough. I take his position, trying not to listen as the man grunts, the air slowly choking out of him. The inhibitor spray feels hot where it sits in my pocket.

There's still one in my pack, but we can't afford to use it if we don't have to.

Trying not to listen, I walk along the thin wall of the paddy, attempting to mimic the guard's confident gait, but feeling more as if I'm tiptoeing along the spine of a sleeping beast. No one below us shouts. No soldiers flood up the pathway winding along the tiers, guns drawn. Another guard appears from around the bend of the contoured paddies three tiers down. And then another, and another. They form a clump around something set up on the edge of their trough like ants converging on a newly found treat, disassembling it to bring it back to their queen. Only instead of taking this thing apart, whatever it is, they're putting it together, one metal piece at a time. One of the soldiers detaches from the group, prowling along the edge of the paddy, his chin pointing down toward the camp just as much as it does toward the mountaintop above us, as if it's equally likely for danger to come from either direction.

Perhaps, if contagion is here already, it *is* just as dangerous either way. The guard looks up in my direction and gives a nod, which I return.

June crouches in the shallow trough behind me, taking the guard's gun when his body has gone slack under Tai-ge's grip. Tai-ge ties the man's hands and feet, then pulls a sock he brought from the heli and shoves it in the Red's mouth. He won't be yelling for help even after he wakes up. We'll have until the next guard change—four hours, if our observations from today are right—before anyone finds him.

June's hands flit over her hat and hood, pulled tight over her hair. She can't come into the camp. Even with a hood to cover her golden snarls and a mask to cover her face, we can't risk a single person looking her straight into those green eyes before she sneaks away to ignite the growth regulators.

"Ready?" I ask her without looking back.

Before I can take her silence as assent, something hard taps the side of my leg. I look down to find the guard's red enameled two-star pin in June's hand. I take it and pin it to my collar, the sharp points pressing uncomfortably against my neck.

Waiting until the man below us walks back to the cluster of soldiers, I hop down into the trench and duck behind the wall. June climbs up, adopting a wide-legged stance and peering down at the camp as if she owns the whole of it, down to the last tent. Tai-ge and I go to the edge of the rice paddy and set our feet on the steep trail that meanders down the hillside.

Before we can even get to the third tier down, the soldier prowling back and forth runs at us, hand on his gun. "Stop! Where are you coming from?" He gives our mussed City uniforms a once-over, though he doesn't look at my hand or my collar for stars.

"We were scouting some suspicious activity a few miles upriver." Tai-ge steps forward, deliberately flashing his two marks, though the guard's stony stare almost seems to harden as a result. "Some of the boys saw a heli in the air, though we didn't find anything. Is there a problem?"

The muscles in my jaw clench tight as the man steps closer, the details of his uniform muddy under the padded coat and fur-lined hood. Unmarked, so far as I can tell. He looks down his nose at us, with none of the friendly camaraderie I've always seen among Outside patrollers, as if surviving beyond City walls puts you in some kind of club. Only, I imagine the turnover rate is high and the snacks are subpar.

The patroller swears under his breath, speaking into a radio. "Scouts coming in from the north end of the rice paddies?" He narrows his eyes as silence draws out long from the radio, but then a confirmation crackles out from the speakers. When the person on the other end finishes speaking, the Red once again rolls his eyes over our disheveled uniforms. "They called everyone in for a meeting over an hour ago. Why are you so late?" He shoots a glare up at June's outline, barely there as the last bits of light fade. "Did she even stop you?"

"Of course she stopped us." I try to inject a measure of disbelief and offended pride into my voice.

"I can't believe any of you are still alive." The man still hasn't let go of his gun, hand tense on the handle. "Go."

Any of *you*. As if he isn't one of us . . . one of the Reds, anyway. I keep my nod brief and start toward the camp, Tai-ge close beside me. "What do you think he meant by that?" I whisper once we're a safe distance away.

"Maybe the Outside Patrollers are sick of dealing with people who aren't used to being Outside. There's a different set of rules out here. I had to learn them too, right?" Tai-ge peers out at the soft glow of lanterns pockmarking the camp, then back the way we came, though the whole mountainside is dark now. June's upright form is lost in the shadows above us, the cluster of patrollers only a few steps down from her nothing but glints of metal and teeth, and I can't help but think of the owl's nest perched above our things.

"At least we know they saw us land." I pitch my voice low, nodding to another Red as we pass, this one with the City seal stitched into her coat. "Or they wouldn't have bought the story about us coming back from searching for it."

Tai-ge nods, pulling his hood up as we descend the last set of stairs into the Chairman's domain.

The camp is set up in a series of circles arranged into ranks. The more important you are, the closer your tent is to the Chairman's. Lanterns dot the perfectly spaced tents. I look up to where the black flag should mark the center of the camp, but it's lost in night's grasp.

"If we're trusting Howl, he said there are only two encryption keys. One with the new Red General, the other possibly with the Chairman. Except Howl seemed to think he doesn't carry it around." Tai-ge slows a step, keeping his voice down.

"The Chairman's tent space will be guarded more heavily than the General. Shall we try her first?"

"Her? Did you hear who it is on the radio?"

Tai-ge shakes his head, the movement slow as he watches the stream of Reds walking among tents, all seeming to head toward the north side of the camp. "Not names."

"Well, whoever she is, the new General will probably be towing around Reds behind her on a sled. I don't think I ever saw your father alone." A thought nibbles at the back of my mind, my stomach sinking a bit. Tai-ge's father died during the invasion. His mother, though . . . What if she's here in this camp?

Tai-ge blinks as if he's wondering the same thing. But whatever it is, memories of his father, questions about his mother, he lets the thoughts slide down like water off his newly granite-made skin.

Our backs unbend as we enter the next row of tents, walking casually as if we belong. Tai-ge waves to a patrolling Red, giving him a good gander at the two stars pinned to his collar, but the man stops, an angry breath scratching out through the filters of his gas mask as he raises a hand for us to stop. "Hey! What do you two think you are doing?"

"We just came back from a scouting mission and wanted to check our filters before going to the . . . meeting." Tai-ge stands straight, just like his father. A general down to the very cadence of his voice, making the approaching soldier check himself, wondering who it is he's talking to. These masks muddle everything.

Thankfully.

The Red lets his hand fall, Ta-ge's confidence killing his abrasive manner. "Orders are everyone goes over there now, except for key guard positions." The soldier adjusts the gun holstered at his side, more out of discomfort than a warning. "The Chairman has been so . . . well, it's not my place to say. I just wouldn't be surprised if they take your mask and chuck you into the forest for being late."

The Chairman? Howl mentioned the First leader was based here, but he made it sound like the Chairman was touring the camps, making sure everyone had food, masks. Boosting morale. He wasn't supposed to be *here*. A hollow sort of anxiety scours my chest, the shadowy figure I've hardly ever seen off a telescreen suddenly looming overhead. He'll know we're here, somehow. He'll stop us.

I jump when Tai-ge laughs. Attempting to set the Red at ease, though the warmth of Tai-ge's laugh is sucked out as it crackles from the nose of his mask. "He's speaking to us in person?" Which is when I realize it might not be acting. That it might be panic fueling Tai-ge, too.

I put a hand on his arm, attempting to add a jocular dose to my tone. "Should have let those Outsiders invade years ago, just so we could see his face."

The Red rolls his eyes. "I'm supposed to be clearing the tents to make sure everyone is in the mess area. I'll have to escort you there."

He gestures for us to follow him. Tai-ge's muscles are so tense it's pulling his walk off-kilter, as if all his joints have frozen. "It's okay," I whisper, low enough the Red won't hear. "No one will be looking for us under these masks."

"What if someone sees your scar?" Tai-ge asks. "Or your birthmark? What if the meeting takes all two hours and June sets off—"

"We'll just have to make sure none of that happens. You're

pretty recognizable yourself, you know. Don't preemptively blame *me* for getting caught."

Tai-ge gives a humorless sort of laugh.

The mess area is open dirt, the remains of snow making the ground feel sloshy and unstable under my feet. It's mostly sets of two stars I see muddy and rusted on uniform collars. I'd have expected ranks and lines, Reds organizing as they love to do, but the soldiers are in a messy clot, coagulating in wary-looking groups. Every person here is masked, their combined breaths droning in and out as if I'm one in a swarm of flies. Divided from where the Reds stand, there are lines of benches set up, the occupants a little too round-shouldered to be soldiers, with gray-clad men and women walking through their ranks with platters of food. Firsts being served by Thirds. There's an unnatural hush over the hundreds of people, as if their vocal cords have all been cut.

A figure strides from the tent at the far end of the crowded area, ringed by a group of Reds, their guns at the ready as if they expect an attack here in the center of their own domain. I can see the single star on the man's collar from here.

The Chairman. A slick of dread coats everything inside of me. The man Howl lived with for two years, hoping he wouldn't notice his son had been replaced by a gore in disguise. He wears nonchalance like a coat, as if the City didn't just get slit down its sides by a Menghu knife. He won't look out at the crowd, as if the people here are nothing to him but a spate of fog, the tendrils curling around him, moisture beading on his coat, and only worth the attention it takes to wipe them away.

Tai-ge nudges me when one of the soldiers guarding the Chairman moves to admit a newcomer to come closer. "Isn't that . . ."

My eyes are caught on the soldier who moved, his gas mask

smudged over with mud and the evening's shadows. Not enough to hide the design painted over the filters. Teeth. Gore teeth.

I've only seen one person with teeth on her gas mask. Cale, from the Mountain. My eyes rake over the soldier, looking for hints of dirty-blond hair and cold blue eyes, panic racing in my veins. Could the Menghu have infiltrated this camp? Are we in the middle of what is about to be a massacre?

I left Cale Asleep in Yizhi, machines hardly able to detect her heartbeat. It's difficult to see much from this distance, but the soldier is obviously male. Masked, so he couldn't be infected the way Cale must be now. My panic dulls down a bit, and I take slow breaths, attempting to counter the flood of adrenaline in my veins. The soldier looks sort of familiar, though I didn't run with Reds often. High cheekbones. Hair slicked to the side . . .

"*Sevvy.*"

I refrain from swearing when Tai-ge's sharp elbow finds my ribs, but only just. *"What?"*

"Sorry. I didn't mean to . . ." Tai-ge clears his throat, lowering his voice when the soldier standing on his other side looks at us, his overgrown eyebrows knitted together in annoyance. "It's him. Isn't it?" Tai-ge nods toward the man who joined the Chairman inside his circle of guards, the former obscured by the tubes of his gas mask as he rasps something into the Chairman's ear. Salt-and-pepper hair, rumpled uniform . . .

Dr. Yang.

There's not enough oxygen making it through my mask's grille. My hand finds Tai-ge's, gripping so tight it feels as if our fingers might fuse together. Dr. Yang was at the Mountain. He was the one who argued to invade the City. He was the one who killed half the First Circle. He was the one who put my mother to sleep when she wouldn't give him the cure she'd invented.

My panic returns, rising up inside me like bile. Dr. Yang belongs to the Mountain. At least, I thought he'd cast his lot in that direction when he helped lead Menghu into the City, bringing his contagious strain of SS. How is he standing by the Chairman's side?

The Chairman raises a hand to get everyone's attention, though every eye is already glued to his broad-shouldered form.

"Many men and women have died since Kamar attacked our walls." The Chairman's voice rings out over our heads, melodic underneath the grasp of his gas mask. "But we are strong. We will not be conquered, not by sickness, not by bullets or famine!" Not the voice of a killer. I don't suppose he's ever killed with his own hands—why should he when he can kill with just his signature, stamped in red ink? "You, my friends, my family, are strong. Your lives have been dedicated to honing the City's strength to razor-sharp. When we return to our walls, we will take them back from Kamar!"

He pauses, as if hoping for applause, and there are a few cheers and claps, but most of the crowd waits. I feel sick, every word boiling my panic into a terrified sort of anger. How can the Chairman blame the invasion on Kamar, a fictional military devised to frighten the City into submission, when the real terror, the real enemy, is standing right beside him? The air around me feels electrified.

"The General has just radioed new information regarding Kamar that makes an attack imperative," the Chairman continues. "We've been forced to rely on Mantis for so many years that a cure seemed impossible—"

"Kamar? They're the ones who brought the contagious strain of SS," a voice hisses behind me. Other murmurs of dissent ripple out from the one protest. "What's the point of attacking them? Kamar must be completely Seph-eaten by now."

"What about my sisters? They're still back in the City. . . ."

"Before I was transferred here, a whole section of the camp went down to SS, and when they checked their mask filters, they'd been *disconnected*. . . ."

"SS could take all of us in one night! No one has enough Mantis to keep us all sane."

A voice breaks out from the murmurs simmering all around me. "What are Firsts doing to fix this?" No one hushes him.

The Chairman nods, welcoming the question. "This camp is working to find out what is different about this new strain of SS. We know that it speeds up the Sleep stage, and that there is a period of contagion that lasts about two weeks after initial infection. We also know that our gas masks are still effective in blocking it. As long as you are covered, you are safe." His words sound tinny and mechanical grinding out through the mask, insufficient to quell the questions that weigh heavy on this camp, these people who have been safe behind walls. Mantis in their mouths and children laughing on their knees. I can almost hear the questions no one is brave enough to ask. How can we survive outside the City? How can we kiss our partners or hug our children when we have masks permanently bonded to our faces?

How do we live like this?

The Chairman raises his hands. "There is hope, comrades. Both for us, and for your families still inside the City. We have reason to believe SS, contagious or otherwise, has a solution that will put our years of research to rest. We believe the reason Kamar was able to attack us at all is because they have found a cure to SS."

It should be a solid declaration, a First bombshell that causes spontaneous songs and adulation, but I can feel the Reds around me shift and squirm. Dr. Yang's face is inscrutable behind his mask. Kamar is just a fake name the City gave people from the Mountain. I can't believe Dr. Yang would want to lead an attack on the Menghu, his own soldiers. If Menghu have the cure, it's because Dr. Yang gave it to them. What is going on here?

I look to my right and left, wondering whether the men and woman around me can finally see the lies bubbling out from the Chairman's mouth like tar. Why would Kamar invade the City and continue going after our Mantis stockpiles if they've already cured SS? How could *Kamar* have a cure when *we've* spent a hundred years searching, a whole segment of our society dedicated to finding a cure while the rest of us give over our lives to feed and defend them?

The last thought seems so loud I can't drown it out. The soldiers standing around me shift, some toward the Chairman and some away into groups, their heads bowed together. Whispers spiderweb out from the little groups like cracks in glass.

The Chairman gestures for Dr. Yang to step forward, and my shoulders shrink down as if I can somehow hide inside myself to avoid his notice. The doctor stands military straight, his voice ringing out over our heads. "We must be strong. It was spies, weak men wishing for glory and riches, who allowed Kamar to infiltrate our walls, just the way invaders did during the Influenza War. We shall fight. We shall reclaim our City, our safety, and our *lives*." The soldier standing guard next to the Chairman stands a little straighter as the doctor speaks, lantern light glinting from the teeth painted across his mask. Where have I seen him before?

Dr. Yang's voice rises, the men and women around me focused on him, their breaths coming faster. I can feel the heat of their excitement surge with each word. "This camp is made up from the best. The brightest. The unconquered." The toothy-masked soldier looks to the side, exchanging a whisper with one of the other guards, a girl a few inches shorter than him. There's a flash of white, something at her wrist. . . . "You have not been tainted by SS. In seven days we move against Kamar's own city in the land below our mountains. The General will be here in a matter of hours, ready to coordinate the attack after analyzing their bases with the best scouts we have. We cannot fail. This is our only hope. I know my hope is safe because it rides on your backs. It will be realized by your strength!" He spreads his arms wide over the crowd as if he can embrace them all, hold them close, and I can feel them all standing a bit straighter. "We will not let these monsters poison our air and take our families any longer. We will take the cure and be done with them!"

Anger is like a blade inside me, cutting off my air. If only I could speak now. If only I could tell them what their precious Chairman has done to their wives, their daughters and sons, bombing them, infecting them, and torturing them in the Sanatorium. Tell them exactly where Dr. Yang's hope lies and how many have died to realize it. Firsts had the cure all along. None of this would have happened if the Chairman hadn't used the cure to secure his place on his throne.

Dr. Yang might be even worse. I only know some of what he has done, setting SS free, trapping Mother, letting her die. Murdering everyone in the City who knew how to make the cure because he thought he had it safe in his pocket.

I look over my shoulder into the mass of Reds behind me, some faces strangely bland, as if they aren't sure what to make of this news. Some are openly hopeful, determined. The Firsts on their benches don't cheer, their mouths bulging with food. The Thirds who were serving seem to be absent, not important enough to know this news.

I don't understand, though. What do Dr. Yang and the Chairman mean by Kamar? Kamar isn't real. Where are they really going, if not the Mountain? Is it possible that "Kamar" is actually Port North, the place Mother told me to go?

The Chairman continues speaking, his voice boiling the crowd into a frenzy. The Reds immediately around me begin to clap, one even going so far as to pump his fist against the air. How can they believe promises of change mean something? Nothing ever changed back in the City. Nothing ever got better, no matter how many times they broadcasted the Chairman's voice over the loudspeakers, promising bombs would stop, factory shifts would get shorter, life would improve if we could just hold on a little longer. It never did, and I know now the Chairman never meant it to.

I pull my bowed shoulders back, pulling on my hand linked with Tai-ge's. We'll find the key, the maps. If this place they're going to get the cure is Port North, then we'll just have to get there first.

"Seven days?" Tai-ge pulls back, leaning close to speak in my ear. "If they're headed the same place we are, then we have seven days to get in and out first."

I nod, mind whirling. Even with a map, we don't have the heli anymore. But, for June, for Lihua and everyone else in this entire camp who will end up branded and fit like cogs into Dr. Yang's new order, we will figure it out.

"How long until we have a real answer? Something concrete. An actual cured Seph?" a voice rings out from behind us, snaking out from between cheers and claps. "And when will we have contact with the other camps? I don't even know if my wife is still alive."

I look back to find the dissenting voice, my eyes flitting from face to face as the Reds' feet shuffle, their eyes focused and unblinking on the Chairman's form as if that would deflect any sort of blame.

Except one. He's far away from where the voice originated, but he's looking around the way I am. But not for the speaker. His eyes find mine. Dark brown. Familiar. Deadly.

Howl.

My stomach lurches and I face forward, his eyes a hot poker burning at the back of my neck. I squeeze Tai-ge's hand in mine, the ground suddenly feeling much weaker under my feet, only seconds from swallowing me. Howl didn't tell us Dr. Yang would be here. He told us the Chairman *wouldn't* be here. This is where we have to move our stones, to use the competing confusion to slip through . . . only it isn't confusion. Dr. Yang and the Chairman are standing before the crowd of Reds in a united front while Howl's at our backs, waiting to shepherd us toward them.

I try to fit the pieces together. Dr. Yang doesn't want me to leak the things he told me over Mother's dead body—easy to ensure if I'm dead. The odds against Howl were too high back in the heli, so he followed us here. I can't think of another explanation.

As the Chairman begins speaking again, addressing concerns with his rust-corroded voice, I clock the distance between me and the tents beyond the edge of the crowd. If we run now, Tai-ge and I would be too noticeable.

The Chairman finishes with a roar, "We will take the cure. I promise you, you and your families will be safe again!" This time the faithful cheer is deafening.

The soldier with the grinning gore mask yells along with

everyone else, the girl beside him raising her arms in excitement. A full flash of white catches my eye, the bracelet at her wrist catching the firelight.

Bones. She's wearing bones around her wrist. Like a Menghu.

The last bits of me reserved against panic disintegrate as I realize where I've seen the soldier in the Chairman's guard. Slicked hair, Cale's toothy mask. High cheekbones that cut like knives. My heart's off-kilter gallop leaves me gasping for breath. The soldier in the painted mask is Helix.

CHAPTER 18

"WE HAVE TO GO," I YELL OVER THE TUMULT, PULLING on Tai-ge's hand. There are *Menghu* here surrounding the Chairman. Only ones with dark hair and City features, or the Reds would know. They haven't yet caught us, but it's only a matter of time.

The crowd begins to jostle us, as people move toward the long table set on the far end of the cleared space where Thirds are setting out tubs of rice and vegetables. The Chairman goes to the head of the tables, ladle in hand. Serving the Reds as he has always claimed to. The crowd seems fastened to him by the eyes, by the hearts, even as the invaders who took their City, infected their families, stand to either side of him. *It will be all right,* they say to each other. *Look, there's the Chairman, serving me rice with his own hands.*

Tai-ge follows my lead as I slip through the crowds. I don't see Howl in the sea of bobbing heads, but I know he must be following us. Herding us toward the other gores so they can come at us from all sides.

I pull Tai-ge into the first ring of tents, only pausing for a moment before slithering across the pathway dividing the first

ring from the second. A Red walks along the pathway behind us, a
bowl of rice in hand. Another, darker form—a Menghu slithering
after us into the flickers of lamplight? No, it's just a Third taking
a breath from the food line's grabby hands.

"Do you think the Chairman meant what he said about—
Sevvy?" Tai-ge puts a hand on my shoulder. "You're shaking.
What's the matter?"

Yes. I'm shaking. Menghu in the camp, and Howl watching
from between tents . . . "Howl was in the crowd. And those were
Menghu around the Chairman."

"That's impossible." Tai-ge scoffs. "How would Menghu get
into the camp? And there's no way Howl—"

"There are Menghu here, Howl is here, and we can't afford to
hope they aren't working together." I grab his arm and drag him to
the next ring of tents, look toward the paddies cut into the hillsides
above us. "None of the stones are on the board where we expected.
Some of them aren't even the right *colors*. We have to run."

That patroller on the paddies—no stars, and disgust in his
eyes as he looked at us. Was that whole group Menghu too? My
skin crawls at the thought of June standing just above a pack of
gores hiding in plain sight.

"We can't, Sevvy." Tai-ge's voice pulls my attention away from
the mountainside. He rubs his eyes, looking back toward where we
left the crowds eating their rice. Tai-ge starts walking again, his
shoulders hunched, waiting a second until I follow. "We have to
get the maps or Dr. Yang wins." He swallows. "Do you think the
Chairman and the General know about him?"

"I have no idea."

We quiet as a group of soldiers pass us, one of the men sending another stumbling toward us with a laugh. The stumbling man

manages to stop before bumping into Tai-ge, but only just, giving us an apologetic wave before hurrying after his friends.

I let out the breath trapped in my lungs, my eyes crawling over the shadows like spiders, waiting for Howl to appear. "You're right. We can't just run." I swallow. "Howl told us to go after the Chairman's tent for maps and the key. I thought it was just so we'd have to let him come with us. We would have needed his stars to get in."

"So we should go after the General's instead?" Tai-ge sounds hopeful. "Maybe there's some way we could warn the Reds about Dr. Yang—"

"How? Leave a note?" I look up at him in the dark, then shrug. "I mean, maybe we could. Almost everyone is tied up in the mess area, and we know the General isn't due back for a few hours. So let's go."

I start walking, Tai-ge close behind. "The Red strategy tents are probably near the First section of the camp. They might even be inside the Firsts' area so the Chairman doesn't have to leave in order to join meetings." He falls into step next to me, nodding up to the flagpole in the center, tall enough we can see the City's falcon-and-beaker seal flapping overhead.

Lanterns grow more and more numerous as we draw near to the flagpole, as if Chairman Sun is determined to keep all the light for himself. When we get to the sixth ring of tents, there's a fence barring entrance to any who would go farther, something Howl failed to mention but which Tai-ge and I anticipated. Firsts don't like to mix with everyone else, not even in the close quarters of camp.

I look back into the lamp-strewn lines of tents, eyes darting from shadow to shadow, person to person. No one seems to be following us. But would I be able to see Howl or any of the other Menghu if they didn't want me to? I try not to think too hard about the people about to march into an attack without even knowing who they are really fighting for. It's not just Outsiders who need help, and it isn't just SS that needs a cure.

I hope we *can* leave some kind of warning for the new General.

We follow the fence until we come to a gate illuminated by bright lamps. Men and women are beginning to walk the pathways between tents, released with food and an assurance that the Chairman has a plan to fix all the wrongs in the world. Those who come near the gate, though, are rewarded with a severe frown from the guard standing in front of it, his hand tight on the gun at his side.

Tai-ge veers off the walkway into the lines of tents, and I follow, keeping an eye on the hastily erected fence, looking for gaps. It's not an impossible barrier—only chain link, a healthy space between it and the tents on either side. No guards. No spotlights. We walk until we come to a dim area between lanterns. Opening his bag, Tai-ge extracts a pair of pliers with a sharp wire-cutting edge, a tool we found in the heli. Hopefully strong enough for the fence. Tai-ge shoves the tool into his outside pocket, then slips over to the fence, checking both directions before he kneels down, much more visible than I would like.

"Interesting plan." The voice comes from right behind me. My stomach contracts down to a pinhole, and I grab for the inhibitor spray, but before I've even turned around, Howl grabs my arm and pries the spray from my fingers.

"No, thank you, Sev." He rasps from inside a gas mask, his expression hidden by the dark. "I don't feel like being knocked out at the moment. If you and Tai-ge actually want that encryption key, maybe you should let me take you to it." He cocks his head, eyes falling to the double stars at my collar. "Those are cute."

"Tai-ge!" I jerk my arm away from Howl, backing into the

no-man's-land around the fence, wanting to run but not wanting
to leave Tai-ge behind. The spray probably wouldn't have worked
anyway. Not with him wearing a mask.

Tai-ge looks up from the chain link, standing when he sees
Howl's shadowed outline standing just beyond the tents.

Howl sticks his hands in his pockets. I tense, waiting for a
knife, a gun . . . but he just nods to Tai-ge. "There's a Red patrolling the fence, about to come around the corner. I'd move away
from the fence if I were you."

And so would Howl. Sweat slides down my temple as Tai-ge
slides back into the cover of the tents, and Howl sidesteps so
we're sandwiched between him and the fence with nowhere to
run. A woman in a City uniform comes strolling down around
the curve of the fence as Howl predicted, pausing to look us over.
"Stay back from the fence, please," she says, then keeps walking.

Howl's hand circles my wrist, and I have to force myself to
hold still until she's out of sight. His fingers clamp down when I
try to pull away.

"If you run, people are going to notice you, Sev," he says quietly. "And you can't get in there without me."

"You'd let me run?" I whisper, anger grating against my
vocal cords. If I scream or try to fight him off, the Reds walking through might come to investigate, and looking closer would
reveal Howl, the Chairman's fake son, grappling with two traitors.
It's not hard to imagine what would happen next. "If you're going
to hurt us or turn us in, just do it."

Howl shrugs. "I'd rather get the encryption key, if it's all the
same to you. I still think the Chairman's tent is our best chance.
The General could arrive any minute, so her tents are probably
being prepared for her return."

"You want to help us after we left you locked in the heli?" Tai-ge asks, his eyes narrowing at Howl's hand around my wrist. My heart hammers against my rib cage, desperate to escape.

"Reds like shooting people." He shrugs. "So I decided not to sit and wait for them to find the heli. Following you seemed as good a plan as any."

"What do you *want*, Howl?" I try to jerk my hand away from him, but he doesn't let go. "Didn't you hear the speech? Like I've already said, Dr. Yang doesn't need you. There really is a cure. You can go home." The words fall in an ugly rush. "Just leave us alone!"

Howl's face is an inscrutable mask. "You still think I'm trying to hurt you?"

"You're hurting me right now." I look down at his hand around my wrist.

He lets go, putting a hand up when Tai-ge twitches forward, though I don't know what a scuffle will help at the moment. "Dr. Yang wasn't in the camp when I was here before," Howl says. "And did you see the Menghu?"

I give a hesitant nod.

"Then you know we don't have enough time to hash this out at the moment. I don't know what's going on in this camp, but I don't like it. We need to get the key and get out of here."

"There has never been a *we*, Howl." I hate the way my voice stumbles over the words, the way Tai-ge's brow furrows, looking from me to Howl. Turning away, I start along the fence again, looking for another spot to cut through. If Howl isn't going to knife us or shout for his Menghu friends, then I'm going to do what we came to do.

"Remember all those times you told Tai-ge you were worried

I'd get free and kill all of you, Sev?" Howl calls after me. I turn to look at him. "Guess what! I got free, and you're still alive. And there are plenty of people here who'd be interested to know you're in the camp—"

"Are there?" I cut in. "Yet another thing you forgot to mention while we were asking you about Dazhai?"

"No. You're not worth anything to the Reds, so far as I know." I hate the coldness in Howl's voice. "Traitors set on thieving, however, would get some attention. I didn't know the Menghu were here, but until they see an actual working cure, you're an asset worth holding on to."

"If they still believe that, then so are you."

"It wouldn't be that hard to focus their attention on you and not me, Sev." He takes a step back, giving an exaggerated shrug. "But you're still standing there. Breathing and everything."

Tai-ge draws up next to me, the two of us shoulder to shoulder, not sure which direction to step.

Howl turns away from us, walking back toward the fence. "I came for the encryption key. Come or don't, it's up to you."

CHAPTER 19

THE WORLD SEEMS TO BE TIPPING SIDEWAYS AS I follow Howl's familiar outline, his hands stuffed into his pockets as he walks. There isn't enough room in my head to burn through all the conflicting thoughts and emotions carving bloody trails in my brain.

"What do we do?" Tai-ge whispers, so low I hardly hear.

"I'm thinking," I whisper back, but my feet keep following Howl, leading us to the bright lights at the gate.

The guard eyes Howl warily, eyes flicking over his weathered City coat and the single star at its collar. He must not recognize Howl under the gas mask. "Where are you headed, sir?"

"Command tent. These two just came in with reports of contagion just south of here, but the symptoms are a little different from what we saw during the outbreak back in the City." Howl doesn't ever really stop walking, pulling back his sleeve to bare the single white line on his hand that marks him a First with an offhanded flick before pushing through the gate, as if argument from the guard is something he hasn't even considered. He turns back to meet the guard's gaze. "Keep your eyes open. Even with masks to keep cases down, we don't know what to expect. Hopefully the containment panel will know what to make of the new information." Howl's attention slides off the guard to Tai-ge and me, giving us an impatient gesture to follow. "Don't waste my time. Come on."

I quicken my steps, nodding to the guard as I follow Howl through the gate. The Red holds it open for me, waiting until Tai-ge catches up to let it swing closed. We follow Howl toward the lights, the brighter they shine, the longer his shadow creeps out behind him. I lag back a step, not wanting to be caught inside it.

"How long before June sneaks off?" Howl rasps over his shoulder.

Tai-ge glances at me, and I can almost feel him echo the shivers fingering down my spine. Howl must have been watching us all day. "We have at least an hour."

"This way." Howl swings to the left, ducking behind a group of tents, a strange sort of smell issuing from inside that burns my nostrils through the gas mask. I cough, putting a gloved hand to my mask's snout. Labs? What are they brewing in there that gets through masks?

"The Chairman's main tent is over here." Howl crouches next to the lab tent, a snowy breath misting from the filters of his mask when he looks back at us. "Shall we?"

"Wait, we're just walking in?" Tai-ge starts, just as I say, "If we're caught, we can't pretend to be anything but thieves."

Howl shrugs. "Or assassins. It's true. But he's not likely to come back here once he's done feeding Reds."

"How do you know?" I ask.

Pulling me down to kneel next to him in the snow, Howl

points toward the aisle of tents. "Because the place he sleeps is outside the fence. It's supposed to keep him safer, I guess. Hard to kill someone in their sleep if you can't find the right bed." Howl looks out over the aisle between tents, pointing toward the largest one in the cluster near the flagpole. "He has a guard posted on his official tent where most of his things are, but when he's actually planning to be there, they aren't lounging around the back door. Look."

The entrance Howl is pointing to is manned by a single Red, who shuffles her feet every few minutes, then looks down to pick at a spot on her sleeve.

"You know where to look in there?" Tai-ge asks.

"I think so. If he hasn't moved it." Howl stands, walking out into the brightly lit circle at the center of the tents where the flag waves above us. He walks straight across, head held high, only looking back once to make sure we're following.

When we slip around the back side of the Chairman's tent, Howl stops us. "There's one outside, and one just inside. Can you help me?" He waits for Tai-ge's answering nod.

"And you?" Howl looks at me. When I don't answer, he pulls his mask down around his throat, pulling the tinny rasp of the filters away from his voice. "You always did pretty well when we were running around Outside before. I didn't bring any grenades this time around, though. Or a tree branch."

"You don't have any guns up your sleeve this time?" I ask, my voice burning.

"A sleeve wouldn't be a very good place to hide a gun." He pulls at the cuff of his sleeve, fingering the material. "How would you get it out?"

"It's a figure of speech." When the gun came out back in the

forest, it had been a surprise. One that he'd put into my hand, saying he couldn't shoot it.

"Right. One that doesn't apply to guns." Howl loops the mask
back over his nose and mouth. "You going to help or not?"

When I stumble toward the Chairman's tent, the woman standing
guard pulls out her gun sleek and slow, the nose following my every
move. I can almost feel its attention burning holes through my
jacket, straight through to my skin, nothing but metal and a little
black hole that mean my death. The Red squares her shoulders, all
boredom evaporated into the night sky. "Back away, Comrade."

"I need to speak to the Chairman." The title sucks the last of
the air out of me, and I fall to my knees, tearing the mask from my
face. "Please. When the scouts came back, they—"

Tai-ge flies into the guard from around the tent's corner,
catching her in the side as she swings the gun around to point
at him. She's falling before I can even register the wrench cracking into her head, leaving the woman still in the snow. There's a
spot of blood on her temple, the wound looking black and sickly
against her skin. Drips of red trail along behind her as Tai-ge
drags her into the mouth of the tent. I dust the snow from my
knees, feeling the bite of wet and ice through my canvas pants as I
follow. Howl stands just inside, another still form at his feet. He
and Tai-ge pull the masks off the two immobilized guards, and
I come in with the inhibitor spray, pressing the trigger until it's
gone to ensure they won't wake up. Not for a while, anyway.

I try not to notice how frail they look, lying on the ground,
their images sticking with me even after Howl and Tai-ge drag
them into one of the tent's rooms out of sight.

Once the guards are hidden and tied up, Howl leads us down the tent's length, long and thin like a hallway. Rooms open up on both sides, partitioned off with lengths of canvas. A space with what looks like a bathtub, one with a cot and a pile of books, one with a chest of drawers and a dressing table. Howl stops short of where the tent opens into a main area, with seats and a large table, taking us into a small side room with a desk instead.

Tai-ge goes to a bookshelf up against the far wall, paned glass doors over the front. "What does the key look like?" He squints through the bubbled glass. "What I wouldn't do for a quicklight right now."

"It's a metal disc. With a ridge around the outside." Howl yanks at one of the locked drawers until wood begins to creak.

I pick through the items on the desk, accidentally sending a glass paperweight rolling and knocking over the Chairman's seal, his name and title stained red with ink.

"There's something that might be . . ." Tai-ge points beyond the glass. He touches the door, trying to fit his fingers between the wooden trim and the frame. "Anyone good at breaking glass quietly?"

Howl looks up, hand slipping into his pants pocket. It takes a second to register that the thing he pulls out is a knife until he flicks the blade free from its leather sheath.

"Tai-ge . . . !" I jump up as Howl steps toward Tai-ge's exposed back.

But Howl's holding the knife out handle-first.

"Try breaking the lock." Howl says, waiting until Tai-ge takes the knife before looking back at me, a challenge in his eyes.

Tai-ge wiggles the knife between the frame and the trim around the glass, using it as a lever to bend the locking mechanism. Wood splinters, the door groaning as he puts his weight on it until finally a chunk of wood flies out from under the knife. The door swings open.

Knife still in hand, Tai-ge pulls something from inside, the darkness of the tent making it difficult to see what the object is. Howl takes it from Tai-ge, running his hand across the top.

"Well? Is that what we're looking for?" Tai-ge asks. "Because if it isn't, then we need to . . ." He trails off, looking down at the knife as he rubs his thumb across the handgrip.

Howl pockets the disc. "I think it's the beginning of a lucky evening." He holds out his hand for the knife, but Tai-ge—staring down at it as if it's begun to glow—doesn't move to give it to him.

"Where did you get this knife?" Tai-ge asks.

"Magic." Howl steps closer as if he means to take it back whether or not Tai-ge's willing, and suddenly the air turns sharp. "Same way I undid the tape and got out of the storage closet."

I step up, whisking the knife from Tai-ge's hands. "Come on. Let's get out of here." I hold my hand out for the weapon's leather sheath, and Howl reluctantly hands it over. The notched blade catches on the leather covering as I slip it on, but the lightning-strike quality to the air seems to dissipate once the weapon is properly sheathed and in my pocket. Howl watches me put it away but doesn't say anything before heading out of the room.

"Did you see . . . ? On the handle, Sev," Tai-ge whispers.

"It doesn't matter how he got his hands on a knife right now." Taking hold of Tai-ge's arm, I pull him into the hallway after Howl. "We have to get to the edge of camp before June starts—"

Something harsh and metallic echoes over the camp. Howl skids to a stop in front of me, and I narrowly miss barreling straight into him. We're are too close, my shoulder against Howl's side and Tai-ge's ribs squished against mine as we all listen hard.

Gunfire.

CHAPTER 20

"THAT CAN'T BE BECAUSE OF JUNE, CAN IT?" TAI-GE whispers. "I didn't hear an explosion."

"Unless someone saw the guard we left in the trough . . ." I try to push past Howl, attempting to calm my rising panic.

"Or maybe it isn't June. Running out there without thinking isn't going to do anything but send bullets toward your head." Howl seems to unfold in front of me, filling the little hallway to block the door. "With Menghu and Reds together in the camp, I don't think it would take much for guns to come out. Stay close to me." He grabs my arm and pulls me toward the door. The darkness seems to thicken around him as I try to pull my arm free, worming a hand into my pocket for the inhibitor spray, only to remember it's empty.

"Let *go!*" My whisper is sharp enough to cut.

Tai-ge's arm snakes between me and Howl, but before he can do whatever it is he has planned, I kick Howl in the side of the knee. Howl lets go of me with a curse and limps back a step, his hands up. "Sorry. You can't just run out there. The guard around the other side of the tent—"

Voices filter back from the front of the tent, the three of us turning to see light blossoming in the tent's receiving room.

"Hide!" Howl hisses, ducking into the side room immediately next to us, the one with the tub. He beckons to me, but I skip away, slipping back into the room with the desk, only one sheet of canvas away from the receiving room. Tai-ge slides in next to me, still bristling at Howl taking charge.

Shadows dance across the canvas wall between us and the receiving room, quicklights burning yellow across the canvas, the thin fabric billowing back and forth as the tent's main doors open and shut, letting in a gust of wind.

Panic fizzes across my skin as three more shots ring out over the camp. It makes it difficult to even want to listen to the voices rising in the receiving room.

That is, until I recognize them.

"We did not discuss bringing Outsiders into this camp, Dr. Yang." It's Chairman Sun. "The invasion was price enough. It was part of our agreement to ensure the safety of—"

"It was also part of our agreement that you wouldn't send Reds poking around into Menghu-controlled ground."

Silence. Another shot blasts the night air, shattering the strain on the other side of the wall into something that sounds like a scuffle.

"Whatever is happening out there, you can't just send me to a bunker. We have to stop it."

"*I* will stop it. The *Menghu* will stop it. They're much better disciplined than anything turned out of your City."

"Just leave us alone! I did what you asked to facilitate the invasion. You have all the equipment you need now. We bombed all the places you told us to. Got rid of all the Mountain leaders who were sitting between you and . . . whatever your end goal is here."

The Chairman's voice is soft. "You've chased us away from the City, away from any chance of fleeing contagion. You've taken our factories, our farms. You got want you wanted, now leave us be."

The Chairman bombed the places Dr. Yang wanted? Got rid of Mountain leaders? He *facilitated* the invasion of the City? I cover my mouth, trying to dampen the sound of my breaths, Tai-ge alert beside me.

"Nothing belongs to you anymore, Chairman," Dr. Yang says. "Who will follow you once they know you provided targets for the invasion in order to ease this transition for you? Your order to purge General Hong leaders won't go over well with Reds."

I glance at Tai-ge, his jaw set in stone. His father had been called a First in all but markings. The Aihu Bridge bomb—the one that sent me scurrying out of the City in Howl's shadow for fear of repercussions against me—may well have been targeting Tai-ge as warning to the General to take a step back.

But even if the Chairman felt as if he didn't have enough control over the City, why let the Menghu in? What could the Chairman have possibly wanted so much that he traded his home and everyone who lived there for a rust-and-tentpole empire filled to the brim with people who can't close their eyes for fear of what sort of Sleep will find them? Getting rid of General Hong or any other leaders encroaching on the Chairman's power couldn't possibly have been worth giving away . . . everything.

"We both know the political reshuffling was your idea. You can't pin that on me." The Chairman's voice is dismissive.

"I can do whatever I want." The smile in Dr. Yang's voice is bloody. "You knew that the moment you saw the photograph."

The photograph? I lean toward the wall, as if I can somehow hear what the two men are thinking if I listen hard enough.

"You are incapable of leading. All the Firsts are." The doctor's voice rattles through his mask. "And I'm not the only one who sees it now."

"*You* are a First, Dr. Yang."

"I'm everything Firsts were supposed to be. Open to new ideas, to genius and learning instead of preserving what is already comfortable. You had the whole City at your disposal, but you were too stupid to know what to do with it. The City died because it couldn't listen to those of us who were smart enough to see that we wouldn't last hidden away up there. People are dying every day because of you, and I'm going to stop it."

I bite my lip. Dr. Yang murdered six people just to keep the cure away from Firsts back when my mother rediscovered it. He was willing to let her rot away, frozen alive in her glass coffin. Willing to allow hate-filled Menghu to run unchecked through City streets, their guns drawn, just so he could gain control.

Forgive me if I'm not quite convinced he cares about people dying.

"I found the cure you kept back from the suffering people in your city. Infecting them on *purpose* so you could let your Firsts play around with their bones and organs. And still you pretend you are somehow better than I am." Dr. Yang's voice is heated. "Get him underground."

My skin goes cold, the scuffling noises we heard when they first started talking finally making sense. I know who Dr. Yang would have in his entourage, who could be so close without making their presences known. Menghu.

"Do not touch me." The Chairman's voice rises as they move into the hall, elbows brushing into the canvas, almost hitting me. I pull away from the wall, curling up beside the desk, trying to make myself as small as possible, Tai-ge pressed in next to me. "You grew up with food on your table." The Chairman hardly deigns to raise his voice. "With anything you could ever want. You chose your studies, your friends, your research without ever having to worry about whether rain would make your bed wet. Why do any of this? I gave you—"

"You and the other Circle members passed over me and my work, my warnings about the Mountain becoming more stable, about the farms becoming more autonomous." The doctor's voice grows sharper, almost wounded, as if he can't believe the Chairman doesn't understand. "You didn't listen when I said work on the cure had stopped. You could have told me we already had a cure. You could have been honest and said you thought I was *less*. You thought you could treat me like one of *them* because my parents worked Outside for so long."

Another volley of shots shatter the night air. Dr. Yang pauses for a moment. "They're coming closer. We'll go to the helis, then."

"Please let me find out what is going on so we can—"

"As far as you are concerned, nothing is going on. Helix, would you . . . ?"

My blood freezes in my veins. Not just any Menghu. Helix. Here. Only a few feet away from me. It seems as if he's never been far, his face most often the one that reappears in dreams where everyone I love dies, his eye the one behind the gun site.

I press my hands to my forehead, this new take on the Chairman and the Reds leaving holes in my brain. Dr. Yang set contagious SS loose on the Mountain and the City, planning to use the cure to bring the poor afflicted people begging for alms at his feet. He has Menghu support. He has some sort of hold over the Chairman, who is forcing the Reds to kowtow. And now he's pointed all of them toward Kamar—Port North, if I'm not mistaken—like an arrow, with Dr. Yang bending the bow.

"Just think," Dr. Yang continues, "if you had a single compassionate cell inside you, you'd care how many lives you are saving by standing next to me. The dead rotting in the forest, the bombs, the walls . . . all of that will be over." His voice grows louder, and I clamp my hands down over my own wrists, as if it will somehow keep him from finding us in here. "Continue saying the things I've told you to say," he instructs. "Maybe something inside you will change. Maybe you'll learn to see people out there, not census records, factory rosters, and rifle counts, all of it weighing against whether the sun was hot enough on the south farms to make a decent grape for your wine."

They move farther down the hall, past where Howl must be. I hold my breath, my eyes clenched shut. Will they notice the guards are gone, Howl hovering over their inert bodies? The doctor's voice a harsh rasp. "Even if it doesn't, I won't let another generation break because your thumb is pressing down on them."

Who is it Dr. Yang thinks he's saved so far? By my count, contagious SS has done more to destroy lives than the City could have even dreamed.

The tent flap opens and I hold myself still as death. I must imagine the flash of tiger-head insignia snarling at me from the unmarked collars, the Chairman a lone spot of black and red in the midst of muddy brown. And then they're all gone.

Before the flap over my door even has time to settle, Howl gusts through, pulling both of us to our feet. We stop just inside the door the Chairman and Dr. Yang just exited.

"What do we do? Follow them out?"

"They're going to lock this part of the camp down." Howl

growls. "There's still gunfire. If we want to get out of here alive, we'll have to move fast."

Tai-ge and I look at each other, and I can hardly feel myself breathe, as if my lungs have given out. But if there's one thing I do know, it's that Howl doesn't want to die.

The gunfire is coming faster now, peppering the air with frantic bursts. Howl doesn't look back to see if we obey as he picks his way over the downed guards and peeks out the back of the tent. Wherever the shots are coming from now, it's not from where June was waiting. Not unless she's running straight down the middle of the camp.

Adjusting his mask, Howl points outside, his whisper rough. "You see weapons on fallen soldiers as we go, take them. Check for extra ammunition if we have time."

Cold washes over me at his flat tone. As if finding dead men and women isn't something to think too hard about. Tai-ge stands so close behind me I can feel his recycled breath blowing at the hairs on the back of my neck. Howl pushes the tent flap aside and slinks through, boots silent outside.

"You still want to get away from him?" Tai-ge asks.

I nod, even as I take a step forward, "How, though? We can't get past the fence without his stars. And he has the encryption key."

"I'll think of something."

"Me too. I'll think of three or four."

Outside, there's no sign of the Chairman, Dr. Yang, or their Menghu guard. Howl creeps behind the rows of tents just ahead, and I wait for Tai-ge to go first before following closely behind. Once we're past the Chairman's flag, about halfway to the fence, Howl straightens from his Menghu slither to put on the rigid, royal demeanor I remember from the Mountain when he was facing down someone who didn't agree with him. Shoulders square as if he expects the whole world to bow and bring him a hot drink.

There are three Reds at the gate now, and when they see Howl's single red star, his white smile, his Chairman-like disdain, they don't wave him through. The first Red grabs him. The second pushes him away from us. The third levels a gun at Tai-ge and me, his hands shaking.

"No one is allowed in or out." The man with the gun seems unhinged, ready to shoot rather than ask for an explanation. He nods to the one standing between us and Howl. "Take him down to the helis."

"These two have vital information I have to get to my father." Howl picks himself up, standing a few inches taller than the Red with the gun, who seems to shrink back as he recognizes Howl. "He was supposed to meet us in his tent. What is going on out there?"

"We don't know. It started over by the paddies."

My stomach drops. June.

The Red who was holding Howl lets go, his hands held contritely at his sides. "I'm sorry, sir, but we need to get you to safety right now."

"This is too important. Put your weapons down and open that gate. Now."

The three seem to wish the ground would open them up and swallow them, the angry sounds of fighting rumbling closer. There are shots so close I can almost feel the aftershock, the *zing* of bullets through the frozen air. The cries of men and women gasping their last breaths.

"Please, sir. It's not worth your life. Or mine." The Red who grabbed Howl steps forward. "We have orders, and we can't break them. It's not safe out there. Not for you or us. I'll escort you to—"

"These two are my escorts." Howl waves a hand at me and Tai-ge without really looking, steps back from the gate, and walks into the tents without checking to see if we follow.

The moment we're out of reach of the gate's glaring lights, I grab Tai-ge's arm and pull him through gaps between tents toward the fence's length. "This way. We'll have to go over. Or through."

"You don't think they'll shoot anyone they see on the fence?" Howl is just behind us.

"Even your First mark can't get us through the gate. Have a better idea, Sun Yi-lai?" Tai-ge asks. I almost want to laugh at the irony in the question, the barb behind Howl's assumed name. Firsts are supposed to be smart.

Howl actually smiles. "Nope. Let's go. Grab your wire cutters and your bulletproof skin. I'll be standing next to you, so I suppose I'll be the one they take down first."

Tai-ge slides to a stop in a shadowed place along the chain link, glancing up nervously as a group of Reds run down the aisles between tents parallel to the fence, lantern light catching here and there on City uniforms. Howl and I hover over Tai-ge as he brings out the pliers and cuts through links until there's a hole big enough to squeeze through. He tugs the jagged edges up to allow me to go belly-flat underneath, the sharp ends of the metal ripping into my coat's padding. He comes next, then grabs my arm and takes off into the tents before Howl can follow.

CHAPTER 21

I LOOK OVER MY SHOULDER TO SEE HOWL SCRUNCHING and twisting to fit through the hole, losing sight when Tai-ge wrenches me into a tent. Our breath streams from our masks in a fog, clouding the close air inside. Tai-ge edges up to the door, lamplight streaming in through the narrow gap between the flap and the tent wall to mark his face with a line of gray.

"Is he following?" I whisper, feeling in my coat pocket for the empty canister of inhibitor spray, only to have my hand close around the knife's handle instead.

"I don't think he saw us come in here." Tai-ge flinches back from the door as footsteps tromp closer, shadows flashing across the tent's canvas. A black sea of arms and heads, soldiers looking for whoever is responsible for the barrage of shots still echoing through the camp. Or perhaps the ones who are doing the shooting.

"What about the encryption key?" I whisper.

Tai-ge reaches into his pocket and pulls out a metal disk, holding it out in my direction. He doesn't look back to watch me take it, too busy squinting out at the shadow soldiers as they flit past.

The disk fits in my palm, a glass window in the top and a series of lines cut into the outer rim of the metal leaving prints in my skin. "How did you get this?" I ask. Tai-ge isn't the type to pick pockets. At least, I didn't *think* he was.

Tai-ge doesn't answer, pointing up toward the mountain, where the rice paddies are sketched against the sky in stripes of darkness and moonlight. "I knew we needed it, so I took it—"

Orange light blooms in the trees, the sound of the explosion taking a moment before it blasts over us. June's distraction. Tai-ge hardly blinks. "Great. We can go out toward the fields and circle back into the mountains."

The calluses on my fingertips snag against the key's rough exterior as I trace the lines around its edge. "What about June?"

"If she managed to get that explosion off, then she'll meet us under the owl's nest like we planned."

A chill runs through me. Under the owl's nest. Whose grave will it be calling for us to dig when we get back?

I shove the key into my pants pocket next to the knife, thinking I should probably zip it into one of my outer pockets, but worried I'll somehow lose it if I can't feel it pressing into my skin.

Tai-ge tenses. "They're coming this way. Let's—"

A shot cracks through the air, splintering my ears and sending the shadows dancing across the tent wall into chaos. Tai-ge pushes me back from the tent's mouth. My feet catch on something, and I fall into the back canvas wall, the divider between the tent's outer room and an inner one pulling free. Wood clatters, and there's a plasticky crackle of tarp as I go down, catching myself on one hand. It comes down on something soft.

Hair.

A scream curdles the air inside the tent, and the hair yanks out from under my hand. Canvas is twined around my arms and over my head, but I still try to grab the woman screaming, as if I can stop the footsteps now headed in our direction. How was she sleeping here, after the gunshots, the explosion?

But then I pull the canvas free and find her staring at me, her mask pulled askew to leave her mouth naked and exposed. The broken tubing spills down the side of her face like a gushing wound, her mouth suddenly empty of screams as she stares at me. Her eyes close, squinching shut tight, then opening again to bore into me.

Was she *Asleep*? Only now waking up? Sleeping with a mask on couldn't be easy. . . . I don't know how the new strain works, only that it's fast. The woman seems to be frozen, as if she still can't quite move.

The shadows lined up outside are a snaky mess of limbs and shots, shouts and curses. Tai-ge grunts from the tent's mouth, tearing my horror-filled gaze away from the woman to find him scuffling with a soldier. Before I can do anything, the man he's fighting pulls free and runs, shouting about unfriendlies. Boots crash into the icy ground toward us. Tai-ge turns, searching for some sort of escape, but his eyes shudder to a stop on me. No, just behind me.

Fingers touch my arm. The woman is standing too close, her open mouth a black gash in her face, her breath hot against my cheek. I jerk away, fumbling for something to use as a weapon, my fingers shaking as they close around the empty inhibitor spray. She grabs at me, hardly flinching as the empty cannister hits the side of her head with a tinny ping.

The woman lunges at me, her fingers twining into my hair and jerking my head back, completely oblivious to my elbow as it jabs into her stomach or my boot when it smashes down on her bare foot. She pulls me in closer, her teeth bared.

The knife comes out, heavy in my hand.

Tai-ge crashes into my side, attempting to knock the woman away, but her fingers grasp tighter, her nails against my scalp sending sharp stabs of pain through my skull. I pull the knife free of its sheath, but with Tai-ge in the way, I only manage to land the flat of the blade across her arm with a fleshy slap.

She recoils, letting go of my hair, giving me a split second to slash through the tent wall. I stumble through the opening, Tai-ge only a breath behind. I can hear the woman behind us as we run, but she's not going fast enough to keep up, her run lopsided and painful-looking. When we duck between two tents, then zig and zag between the silent canvas structures, she doesn't follow.

I pull Tai-ge to a walk, trying to catch my breath. There are flashes of flame in the darkness, guns being fired into the night, shouts from all directions. I cover my face with my hands, wishing I could wipe away everything I think and feel. "The fields, right?"

Two bright flashes and an eardrum-bending *crack* echoes just a few rows of tents away, between us and the rice paddies.

"We're almost to the edge of camp. I can see the silos just over—" My words cut in two as Tai-ge wrenches away from my side, a shadowy form slamming him into the ground. I can only stare for a second before my body responds, slingshotting me back toward my friend, knife out.

I land on top of the attacker, grab the ties holding the mask to her face and slash them apart. The woman rolls off Tai-ge into a crouch, grasping the mask against her nose. Our eyes meet, the knife blade between us shining silver in the moon's glow. Just as my muscles tense to throw me toward the woman, my hood wrenches back from my head, and the snap holding my collar closed twists up tight against my windpipe. My knees hit the ground, and I drop the knife, fingers scrambling to find the zipper key, the two-star pin at my collar stabbing into my throat. My brain seems blank, nothing left but the zipper stuck against my windpipe and the hand pulling it tight at the back of my neck, choking me.

"The City won't touch another Menghu ever again," a woman's voice snarls into my ear. "We'll leave you all to die. Burn your precious Chairman and leave one big Seph-dead camp."

A hand tears my mask sideways, the air cold and metallic against my nose. I try to suck air down into my panicking lungs, but it only seems to be leaking out, squirming free of my mouth in reluctant gasps. My eyes start to blur. My brain feels like it's exploding from the pressure. There's a hand on the ground next to me, knuckles white as it grasps at the frostbitten ground. Tai-ge?

Just as my vision turns blind, my groping hand brushes against something metal. The knife. My knuckles barely move as I grasp at it, my fingers like swollen fish flapping against one another instead of grabbing hold.

I internally cry for my hands to work, fumbling to seize the knife and feeling the blade cut at the fleshy insides of my fingers. The person strangling me laughs. Until I stab the knife point-first into her boot.

My attacker swears, the metal teeth digging into my throat loosening. I still can't breathe, can't *move*, but I force myself to flail over and somehow catch the knife into something meaty.

A boot connects with the side of my head, leaving nothing inside me but a tumult of pain and crackling light. I lie there on the frozen ground, my entire body stinging, waiting for the blow that will finish me.

A gunshot cracks over me—more swearing, running boots.

Nothing touches me. Just frozen earth and pain.

Silence. So much *nothing* around me where only moments ago it was murder and rage. I feel as if I'm submerged underwater, sucked down so deep the world doesn't matter anymore because I'll never be able to find it again. The silence screams at me to move, to do *something* or it will be permanent.

It takes so *long*—days, lifetimes—before I can even bring myself to touch my throat, to command my trembling hands to unzip my jacket, welcoming the blast of cold air that washes over me when it's open. I force myself up from the ground, the world around me ashy white with snow.

I'm alone.

With one trembling hand, I unpin the two red stars from my collar, my blood muddying their tips, and let them fall to the ground.

The knife is still in my hand, my fingers shaking so badly I can barely hold on to it as I get to my feet. There are bloody bodies on the ground, eyes open and staring blankly at the sky, the shells of people who lived and breathed and laughed and cried before this night left them as nothing but an echo. I force myself to look down at them as I walk, searching for Tai-ge's closely cropped hair, his torn City jerkin, but I recognize no one. A gun lies abandoned in the snow, a streak of red coloring the ice underneath it.

Howl said to take their weapons and ammunition.

I stumble away instead, every breath whistling down my throat. My mask hangs lopsided, the coils of tubes broken and hissing. I tie it back over the lower half of my face, hoping it looks right, unable to keep myself from shuddering as the severed tubes brush against my half-crushed windpipe.

Gunshots pepper the night, and my body involuntarily flinches away from the assault. They sound muted and distant, though I know they can't be too far away, my ears dimmed by too much sound. I stagger away from the cacophony of fighting, across one aisle between tents. Two aisles. I stop when the tent canvases before me begin to ripple, shouts battering against my tortured eardrums like the harshest of whispers. People, City jerkins, weapons, just across the next aisle between tents. I shrink down, hoping somehow they won't notice the broken Fourth. But then I see him.

Tai-ge.

Two Reds are dragging him down the aisle in front of me. He sees me right as I see him, his eyes immediately glancing off me and going down into the dirt. As the group passes, he turns his head to the side and we lock eyes. He jerks his chin toward the fields and mouths one word: *Go!*

I take a step. In his direction.

A hand snakes around my wrist. "Wait." The gas mask's unhealthy wheeze fills my ears with a voice I don't want to hear. Howl.

Tai-ge's eyes widen, taking in Howl behind me. Waiting until they're well past, he suddenly gives the Red escorting him a violent shove, and the two men jerk to attention, restraining him instead of looking for Menghu hiding between tents. He twists around to look at me as they yank his arms behind his back. *Go!* he mouths again. *Move!*

One of his guards peers toward us. Howl pulls me out of sight behind the tent. Down an aisle, gunshots still burning in my ears.

"We're going to get out, okay?" He stops, bringing me around to meet his eyes, face so close to mine I can't look away. Can't see past him to where Tai-ge is being swallowed by Dazhai . . .

Howl's fingers dig into my shoulders. "We need to pretend we belong here. We're looking for Menghu. Finding any that haven't been rounded up yet. Got it?" Howl's voice rasps with each word. "Someone shot one of the Menghu up in the paddies right as some of the Red scouts came in. The Menghu started shooting the scouts, and now everyone's crying spy and Menghu are shooting at anything with stars."

"You . . . How did you . . . We can't leave Tai-ge!" I pull out of Howl's grip, stumbling to the side. My head swims. "I *won't* . . ."

"I promise you, we won't leave Tai-ge here." Howl moves ahead of me again, his voice so calm it makes me want to slap him. "We can't help him if we're dead, Sev. We need to get out and find June—"

A dark form crashes into Howl, knocking him to the ground.

My legs fold under me into a crouch, a cocktail of adrenaline and fear freezing all my limbs as I watch a woman slam Howl's head against the frozen mud, her uniform unmarked. The Menghu's fingers snake up through the tubes of Howl's gas mask, tearing it crooked and obscuring his vision. Howl's double identity is going to be the thing that brings him down, a Menghu attacking him because he's wearing a City uniform. Something hard presses through my shirt into my ribs as I hug my sides.

The knife. Stuck in my hand as if it's been burned into the skin.

It's heavy, heavier than the Menghu's hands, which are now creeping toward Howl's throat, heavier than the night sky pressing down on me so I cannot breathe. The two of them blur together, a swirl of violent energy as Howl tries to squirm out from under the Menghu's grip.

I could just run. Back to Tai-ge. Up to where June is supposed to be, to our packs under that blasted tree.

The thought tastes like acid, bitter on my tongue. *I have the encryption key. I don't need Howl anymore.*

Another shout goes up from a few aisles over, boots headed in our direction. Tossing all my thoughts aside, I shove the knife into my pocket and sprint toward Howl, crashing straight into the Menghu's back. My fingers snag in her braid, and I wrench her head back with one hand, tearing at her stranglehold around Howl's throat with the other. His gas mask lies on the ground next to us, limp and tangled like a dead animal.

Howl's eyes connect with mine over the woman's shoulder, and I throw my weight to the side, surprise bringing her down on top of me, so Howl can get an arm around her neck.

We leave her unconscious in the middle of the muddy path between tents, Howl's sweaty fingers slipping against mine as we run, the beehive of shouts and activity shrinking down to nothing as the dark reaches out to embrace us.

CHAPTER 22

THE SNOW IS COMING DOWN HEAVY AGAIN. HOWL
and I don't speak until the dark has curved around us, nothing left
but the calm swish of the river washing down the mountain.

"Why didn't anyone at the gates stop you?" I croak, finally
breaking the silence. "No one thought you were a traitor, or
kidnapped or . . . anything." I wish I could pretend this was all
Howl's fault, but this is one blame I can't put on him. "You've
been gone for days. Don't they notice when you disappear?"

"I was with the Chairman." Howl doesn't look at me, though I
wouldn't have been able to see his expression in the dark anyway.
"We stopped at a camp near your trading post and he told me I
couldn't go wherever it was he was headed. That he'd come back
for me when . . . *something* was settled. It's only been a few days,
and things are so disorganized, I thought I could bet on lower
ranks not knowing where I was supposed to be."

I nod, keeping my eyes on the snow at my feet. Every swallow
hurts, and my head still feels hot, as if touching it will ignite my

hair into a blazing torch. Tai-ge is back there, a gun to his head. June is . . . Where is June?

"You weren't meeting back up at the heli?" Howl pauses, his outline looking back at me. "Or were you? There's absolutely no chance they didn't see us land. It's not safe to go back there. June should have known better. . . ."

"Yes, *all* of us knew better." My throat constricts, as if the jagged zipper endings cut straight through it when the Menghu woman was choking me. I leave my jacket flapping open, unwilling to have the zipper anywhere near my throat, even if it means snow wetting my front. "We're meeting at a spot on the river."

I almost miss the outcropping of rocks with the tree grasping for purchase above them, but Howl stops to listen at a turn in the river just beneath it. When he nods for us to go on, I point up to the tree. But when we climb up over the rocks, there's no one there.

"Hu! Hu, huuuu!" The owl is close by, his ghostly call falling heavy on my shoulders. Dig. Death. Graves.

Howl doesn't seem to notice, pulling Tai-ge's pack out from under the rock, then mine and June's. Inspecting them like everything that happened was part of some plan, down to the zipper teeth marks on my neck. As if all his emotions have been extracted and replaced with gears and flashing lights. He extricates June's waterskin from her pack, takes a drink, then sits cross-legged on the ground.

When I don't follow suit, he looks up at me, my knees locked, my whole body tense. "I'm sure she'll be here soon," Howl says. "Then we can go back for Tai-ge."

I walk over to the tree's trunk, as far from Howl in this little bit of shelter as I can, and sink to the ground with my legs curled up to my chest. I rest my cheek on my knees, and tears start even as I order them away, hot as they drip down my face to freeze against my pant leg.

Howl doesn't say anything, the two of us alone in the claustrophobic dark, muted cracks of gunfire still echoing through the night.

When light leaks in through my eyelids, I'm surprised to find them closed. Even more surprised that I'm warm, and the light is coming from a concentrated area, as though I'm somehow in a cave. Sitting up sets bells ringing in my head, pain and bone-heavy fatigue settling like a fog that winds tight around me. My scalp brushes the ceiling overhead, and I flinch down, putting a hand up to feel it. Where am I?

The ceiling gives when I touch it, but not easily, as if it's been weighted down. A rough, weather-treated fabric. One of the tarps, now covered with snow. I'm right where I was before, in the outcropping of rocks with the packs, only Howl has rigged us a ceiling. Found me a sleeping bag.

Daylight slinks through a narrow opening to my left, painting the gnarled roots of the owl's tree. Something moves to block the opening, and I scuttle back as far from it as I can, my legs tangled in the soft bunches of a sleeping bag. The person blocking the light crouches down, and I catch a glimpse of black hair, the City seal. A single red star pin. Howl.

Only a few months ago I was in the same place. Outside. Running. With Howl. But now it's backward, a puzzle with all the pieces jammed together wrong. Instead of running from the people who tried to kill me, I'm running *with* one. Instead of escaping to keep Tai-ge's head from the chopping block next to mine, I left him there to save my own neck. I put a hand to my forehead, the images from last night blocking out Howl's outline, a hunched blot of darkness choking the light. Tai-ge with his arms bound, telling me to go. Howl with a Menghu's hands around his throat like a necklace. Me running from Tai-ge. Me *helping* Howl.

You had to help Howl. You couldn't have saved Tai-ge right then. If Howl's survival clause is aligning his goals with yours for the moment, isn't it good that he's here with you? Who better to break Tai-ge out of Dazhai?

But then I have to stop thinking, Dazhai a chasm in my brain. Gunshots, blood. Bodies. My whole body starts to shake again.

Howl finishes whatever he was doing and comes the rest of the way into the shelter, sitting across from me. "Awake?" he asks.

I shiver as the shadows twist around his face. *He followed you into the camp*, I think. *Brought you to the key. If all he wanted was the cure, he'd have taken the key and the maps and left.* But then I can't keep myself from continuing down that road: *If all he wanted back at the Mountain was for you to die, you'd be an ash-choked gust of wind by now.* Admitting that Howl might have done something good makes the dead coals of hope inside me want to reignite. To believe that somehow there's an explanation for all the lies Howl has told me.

But there's no place for wishes like that. There never has been.

My voice croaks painfully as I try to find words. "Has June come back?"

"Not yet. We were able to go straight to the river. If something happened and she had to circle around . . ." His outline gives away no hints as to what he's thinking or feeling, his voice calm. "There's no reason to worry yet. It's only been a few hours."

"No need to worry after a gunfight that might have started right in front of her?" I refrain from groaning as I lean back against the tree trunk. Everything is sore, as if I were trampled by a horde of Sephs. I reach up to touch my neck, but then stop, unable to make myself face whatever damage has been done. I'm alive. Breathing. That's all that matters. "You said the shots started up on the rice terraces."

Howl's outline nods. "I didn't want to leave you here alone. If you're feeling okay, I'll go see what I can find. Dodging Reds shouldn't be too difficult."

"Find . . . what?"

"I know where June was supposed to be when the fighting started, that she made it to your bomb. . . ." He gives an appreciative nod, as if a bomb is something to be proud of. "Maybe I'll be able to figure out where she went. And I can look into where they're most likely to be holding Tai-ge so we can start planning. He has the key, I'm guessing?"

I try to swallow down the hitch in my throat, but it won't go. I'm acutely aware of the key pressing into my leg where it sits in my pocket. Maybe Howl *would* have left with the maps and everything else if he knew the key was right here within reach. Putting my hands casually at my sides so I don't give it away, my fingers curl around something hard and felted on the ground. Something sharp pricks my skin as I pick it up only to fling it away. An owl pellet.

"June knows how to handle herself," Howl says. "So does Tai-ge. If anyone recognizes him, they'll keep their hands off until the Chairman or whoever is in charge of the Reds has had a say. We have time." He sits forward, light zigzagging across his face before I can catch his expression. "There's no reason to think the worst until it's happened."

I nod slowly. "How is it possible there are Menghu down there? You know the Chairman. What does Dr. Yang have on him to make him obey?" Something about a photograph.

Howl doesn't answer for a second, memories from last night crowding in to fill the silence. The way the Menghu bent under me as I pulled her hands away from Howl's throat, the feel of her hair tearing under my fingers. It's not like I've never had to hurt someone. I did more than once last night. And I would again for Tai-ge, for June. For Lihua and Peishan.

But for Howl?

It's okay not to want anyone *to get hurt, Sev. Including Howl.* The thought seems almost whiny in my head, like I have to justify the fact that I saved Howl even though he's put me in harm's way. But even I know it isn't a matter of stopping an act of violence because it was right in front of me. I helped him hurt that Menghu, whoever she was, to make sure he was the one who survived the fight. I don't need him anymore, but I couldn't leave him there either.

What is wrong with me?

"I know the Chairman likes shaved ice with mango." Howl's voice surprises me from my thoughts. "And honey in his tea. But that's about where it ends, Sev." He leans against the cave wall, his head tipping back. "I wouldn't have walked into Dazhai so confidently if I'd known Dr. Yang would be there. I wonder if that's why the Chairman left me . . ." His voice stalls, and he moves deeper into the cave, out of the glare of light, his gaze suddenly focused on his hand. There's a purplish glow teasing his features, leaving his eyes and high cheekbones shadowed and skull-like.

"What are you doing?" I ask. But I know. I can see the characters painted in light on the back of his hand. It's a link like the one he gave me in the Mountain, a tiny mechanism that let us send messages to each other when I was trapped in Yizhi. Only I don't know who's on the other end of this one. He's reporting.

I pick up one of the felted owl pellets, pulling it apart to find the poor creature's leftovers inside. Before Howl can look up, I lunge forward, stabbing his hand with the sharp end of a bone.

Howl flinches away, probably more in surprise than because of any damage the digested bone could do, but it's enough to loosen his grip on the link a fraction, allowing me to grab it.

"Who is left for you to report to, Howl?" I ask.

The darkness has retaken his face, and the air seems to hum around us, as if all the violence I've expected to find inside him is about to come pouring out. I squeeze the link, expecting him to come at me, but he doesn't move when the purple letters spill across the back of my hand.

Small contingent still holding East wing in Y. I look up from the message. Howl still hasn't moved. "What does this mean?" I ask.

"You can look at the other messages. The ones I've sent out." I recoil when he crawls toward me on his knees, but it's only to point to the arrow pulsing at the corner of the display, just underneath my pinkie knuckle.

I touch the arrow and a column of messages appears, scrolling slowly up until it comes to the oldest, dated near after when I left the Mountain. It's from Howl, his messages orange.

ETA three weeks. No tail. End count?

The response is purple like the one that first came up. *Quarantine came too late. Mei contained, but others still at large. Emergency protocols aren't going to be enough.*

Mei? She contracted the new strain of SS at the Mountain. The contagious strain. I'm still not sure how she managed to start compulsing without any typical SS warning signs. She never fell Asleep.

Howl's answer: *Get out. I'll double back.*

Not leaving while I can still help. You bring back Jiang Gui-hua. It's our only chance.

The next set of messages are just checking in to make sure

whoever he is talking to is still breathing, and then there's a gap. I glance up at Howl, still watching me impassively. It's probably hard to send messages on a link when your hands are taped together. The messages resume early this morning.

The messages start with a demand from Howl: *Tell me you're alive.*

Alive. Jiang Gui-hua?

Dead. It's a message all by itself. Bleak and hopeless. The next one doesn't come until hours later, as if Howl had to steel himself to ask for the report hiding behind that one word in the answer. *Alive. I'm with Sev. Potential cure formula in the north. Mountain status?*

The answer is the one that popped up when I first took it. *Small contingent holding East Wing in Y.* More of the message I hadn't seen scrolls up. *City invasion forces took most of the Mantis stockpile. No way to ID infected. Holed in emergency caches.*

This is what's happening back in the Mountain? A memory pierces my brain, Mei compulsing in the hospital room. The doctors back at the City seemed to think the contagious strain moved more quickly, more violently through its victims, but not without any symptoms at all. She slept so soundly the night we came back from the patrol that landed Kasim and Cale in the hospital. I couldn't sleep at all.

Was it possible that she contracted SS not from Cale in her hospital room but before that? From the bomb we accidentally set off? Spreading it with every step she took?

My question is more difficult than it should be. "The Mountain is overrun?"

Howl's head bobs up and down. "I guess we're even. Our homes are both destroyed." Pain bites through the sentence, breaking his voice. "One more thing we have in common. Family all killed off. Cured. Used. Exiled. And now, homeless."

It's the confession I wanted from before, from the moment I

saw him tied up in the storage closet. Admitting who he is, that he lied. But the bald admission doesn't make me feel better. His head and shoulders bow, and he looks ready to sink through the floor, to become a part of the scenery. To give up.

Human.

"How sure are you the cure is going to be at the end of this hunt?" he asks, voice so quiet it might as well be dead. "How much of a chance do we have?"

Anguish rushes through me like a sickness as I watch him bowed under the sad remains of what used to be his, tears welling up behind my hardened resolve. We are the same in ways that are hard to think about. Everything that mattered to us was stolen. Cursed by SS and then by the cure. I reach out and touch his ankle, the only bit of him close enough to reach.

Howl looks up, surprised.

"Sorry." I pull away and twist my hands behind my back, not sure if it's because I'm embarrassed that I touched him or because my attempt to help is so pathetic. Sorrys don't do much, but I don't have anything else to offer. "I don't know about the cure. I'm only going on what my mother told me."

He looks down again. "I'm sorry about what happened to her. I didn't know she would die."

The link buzzes in my palm, a new message appearing. *Glad you found Sev. I'm not sorry for giving her a choice. Think before you do anything else stupid. Or irreversible.*

The only person who gave me a choice was . . . "You're writing to Sole?" How is that possible? She was the one who *warned* me about Howl. "Is she safe? Will she be able to get out?"

He sits up, craning his neck to see the new writing scrolling across my hand, purple light catching in his eyes. "I don't know.

She won't leave while there's a chance she can help people. Her birthday happened sometime while I was gone. It feels wrong that she should be in there instead of . . ." He clears his throat. "Twenty-eight years of living under that rock. What if she never comes out?"

An image of Sole's shaking hands, the unsteady warble in her voice, whispers through my brain, the box of things she'd taken from the people she killed on her patrols with Howl. *If it comes down to a choice between you and him, Howl will be the one that lives. No matter what he told you, this is who he is.* Her testimony is what sent me running out of the Mountain as if there were a ruthless killer after me. Because I was half convinced there was.

And here she is, writing to him. As if he's a person. Someone she cares about. She's *glad* he found me? After telling me to run? If Howl's done enough evil in the world that Sole thought I was better off alone Outside than with him, then . . . how does this fit in?

Is there a place in a human heart to love someone, to want good things for them, even if you know every terrible thing they've done? When you worry there are *more* terrible things in their future?

I look at Howl, the monster mask I'd so firmly fixed over his face already morphed into something I don't understand, no matter how much easier it is to give him fangs and a gore's flat eyes. My whole world, painted in bold blacks and whites, has now somehow been swabbed over with a discomforting and many-hued gray.

CHAPTER 23

I HOLD UP THE LINK, SOLE'S MESSAGE SCROLLING in purple across my hand. "This is why you followed us. Why you're here. To get a cure back to Sole before it's too late for her. To help the people at the Mountain."

"No." Howl meets my eyes. "I didn't know about what your mother said until after I found you." He holds his hand out for the link. I give it to him, watching as he reads Sole's new message. He doesn't look at me again.

"Why, then?" I hate the ugly hope uncurling inside of me. That it even exists when the answer is so plain. Howl wanted to live and thought my brain held the cure, so Howl needed me. However human he may be, that's the answer that will never change.

I want it to. I'm ashamed of how much I want there to be a different reason, but Howl doesn't speak, the sun's slow rise outside now diffusing light through the cave instead of pouring through like a spotlight. We can finally see each other.

"I didn't expect your help last night," Howl says quietly, a question lurking in the depths. "All fights are a risk, and I think you tipped the scales for me last night. Thank you."

I clench my hands together, my fingers tingling where they touched him.

"Is your neck okay?" He comes closer, craning his head to look at the bite marks the zipper made in my skin. "What happened?"

"I'm fine," I rasp. "You aren't a medic, so gawking isn't going to help anyone."

He moves until he's right next to me. "I can apply anmicro and tie a bandage *just* well enough to make you look ridiculous—"

"No. Thank you."

"Okay." Howl slides back to his place by the entrance, his feet extended in front of him. "I think . . ." He shakes his head as if he can't quite grasp the right words for what he's thinking. "I'm getting the vibe that we're still stuck in that alternate reality where I was trying to kill you."

The half accusation jolts through me, like falling facedown and naked in the snow. "You . . . don't you *dare* try to pretend . . ."

"Pretend?" Something in his voice ignites over the word, as if Howl's thin veneer of calm has cracked, leaving something raw and angry exposed. "You haven't even *asked* what I wanted when I helped you escape the City or what my plan was. If you've got questions now, say them out loud, okay, Sev? Don't just make the answers up and expect me to kneel for the punishment."

"When I tried to ask questions before, you got sort of handsy." There. Now we're back to reality.

"Handsy?" Howl coughs, a hand sneaking up over his mouth. It's not strictly true, I suppose, but close enough. "I wouldn't say—"

"As a distraction tactic, it worked all right. You were so concerned, too, asking about my family, my sister. Telling me about your brother and sighing all over the two of us being alone. I

guess I should be glad you didn't try to take any more while I still
believed you."

"Wow. You've got me pegged, Sev. I always seduce my human
sacrifices before I tie them down for the hospital gods." Howl
leans forward, and the smile I thought was hiding behind his
hand isn't there, the light harsh on an expression much, much less
amused than his voice led me to believe. "If only I'd known you
were up for it."

"And now you sound like Helix."

"Just how far are you going to take this, Sev? You know I
wouldn't act like that. At least you *should*. I'm . . ." Howl takes a
deep breath, and it catches on its way out. "I'm sorry for the way
things happened." The words' steely edges seem to cut as they
leave his mouth, spat down between us in a pool of blood.

"You're *sorry*?" I pull the sleeping bag tight around me as if
it can hold me together. Everything inside me has been boiled
down to bones and raw terror at the blank spaces in the cave where
Tai-ge and June should be sitting. I can't take this conversation,
can't do anything other than fend him off. "Were you sorry for
any of the others?"

"Others?"

"Your other sacrifices. The other people you've killed." I pull
the knife out of my pocket—the one Howl handed to Tai-ge back
in the Chairman's tent, then tried to take back—and hold it up as
though it's some kind of proof. "How much blood does this have
on it?"

Howl's mouth thins into a tight line, hands clenched at his
sides. "Did you really just ask me that?"

My fingers catch on the rough ridges carved into the handle. I
lower it, squinting down at the marred wood, the marks resolving

into three characters: *Hong Tai-ge*. It's *my* knife. The one I brought with me as a sort of good-luck charm the day I left the orphanage, wondering how I was going to escape Traitor's Arch with the entire Watch after me. Howl took it away from me before we'd been together more than an hour.

The dull silver blade has been swapped out for an ugly notched version that curves up from the handle, as if the moment Howl took it, it turned into something violent, a twisted version of the original.

"Was this meant to be a trophy, like Sole's dolls and Cale's finger bones?" I hold it up again, the words spilling out before I can think them through. "Because you haven't quite earned it yet."

Howl's glare breaths are too slow, too measured. "I don't have to defend myself to you, Sev."

"No? I guess you don't if you stand by everything you did." Prodding the rabid dog. It feels good. Reckless, as if taking control here will bring June back faster. Will somehow pull Tai-ge out of whatever cell he's sitting in, wondering if today is the day he ends. I slide the leather sheath back over the knife, my anger a shield. "You lied. You would have gotten me killed if Sole hadn't—"

"Yes," Howl cuts in. "I lied to you. If I hadn't lied to you, you'd be a pile of ashes under Traitor's Arch, but somehow I'm still the cold-hearted killer who left my muddy handprints all over you? They probably would have had Tai-ge shoot you himself." Howl talks over me when I try to cut in, raising his voice. "He would have done anything they told him to. The future General Hong's first symbolic murder."

"Tai-ge never would have . . . I wouldn't have . . ." My fingers clench around the knife, Tai-ge's name poking into my skin.

"You don't think so? At least I saw you as a person. Not as a walking traitor brand or an inconvenient footnote on my childhood I couldn't quite get rid of." Howl snatches the knife from my hand, holding it up to show me Tai-ge's name carved into the handle. "There was too much proof you really meant something to him."

"I wasn't a person to you, Howl. I was the price you tried to pay in order to go back to your real life."

Howl sits back against the wall, one hand raking through his hair. "How can you think that?"

"What am I supposed to think? The next time I saw you after Sole told me the truth, you didn't wave and come in the front door. You tackled me and *put a knife to my throat.*"

"How else was I supposed to make you and Tai-ge listen? Seems like you're forgetting about that time Tai-ge *shot me.*" He looks down when I just stare at him, incredulous. "You know what? Fine. I am a terrible person. I thought through the situation the way I was trained to. Like a *Menghu.* I didn't know if you or Tai-ge still had a gun. I didn't want General Hong's Red-to-the-core son to shoot me *again* before he saw my First mark and could fall down on his knees."

"If you say one more thing about Tai-ge, I swear, I'll—"

"This isn't *about* Tai-ge." Howl twitches forward, his voice raised now. "I protected you every second we were in the Mountain. When did I ever do *anything* to make you think I was okay with letting Dr. Yang and his little Yizhi minions take you?"

"They were going to kill me and you knew it, Howl. Every step on the way to the Mountain you knew it, and you said nothing. You said less than nothing. You lied so I wouldn't run away."

Howl is quiet for a second, and when he finally speaks, his voice is barely a whisper. "Dr. Yang said there was a chance—"

"A chance they might not need to cut me open? That makes me feel *much* better. And you didn't just lie about why you wanted me to go with you. You lied about who you *are* to get me to trust you. They were *terrified* of you in the Mountain." The accusation makes me feel strong. I don't know why I didn't see it until Sole pointed it out. Helix—who plays a starring role in my nightmares—flinched away from Howl but was able to kill June's father without blinking. Cale practically dragged me to the cutting tables herself, but then folded the moment Howl stood up. "I saw the Menghu do some pretty awful things. What kind of monster could you possibly be to make someone like *Helix* scared?"

Howl stands up, hunching in the low space like a creature winding its muscles to spring an attack. The light behind him is blinding, but shadows crawl across his face, turning him into a featureless blur, darkness in human form.

"Don't . . ." I try to swallow my fear, but it sticks in my throat, raising my hands to brace for whatever violence is brewing in that shadow.

"Don't what?" He sort of laughs, the sound black and ugly. "You really *are* scared of me." He backs out of the opening and stands just outside, staring up into the owl's tree, the light harsh across his features. When he finally looks at me, his face is dead. "I thought you were just making it easier for yourself. Refusing to talk to me. Blaming me because it was the cleanest explanation. The one that made it so you didn't have to think or feel anything for yourself. Why don't you just stab me now, stop the evil from spreading? I'll hold still." He pulls the knife from his pocket and drops it on the ground in front of him like a challenge.

"I'll show you how, if you don't know." Howl points to the

spot just under his sternum. "Right here. Go ahead, Sev."

My whole body curls away from him. Away from the knife, and the sandpaper roughness to every word. I look down at my hands, dirt and pine needles pricking at my knuckles, ashamed to find tears freezing on my cheeks.

"What gives you the right to tell me I'm the twisted one, Sev? You have no idea what it's like to know that if you don't pull the trigger first, it'll be *your* blood melting the snow. You're worried about what I didn't tell you? You want to hear it now?" I feel him shift in front of me as if he's willing me to meet his gaze, but I won't. I can't. "Like how it feels to go hungry, because if anyone in my family went foraging, the chance of getting back home was almost nothing? How it feels to be the one who has to make decisions between lives? Is it the kids I know from the Mountain who get to live, or the men dragging truckloads of rice to whoever has to eat behind City walls?" His voice breaks, every word a knife between my ribs. "You want to know how it feels to stand guard over bodies that used to be your friends so they aren't dragged off into the forest piece by piece by gores or Sephs or whatever monsters are closest?"

The sleeping bag feels too tight now, smothering me.

"How would you feel sitting warm and safe, eating food so fancy it makes your stomach turn, having to laugh at jokes about the way Menghu smell after they die? Forced to smile across the table at the people who killed your family and friends? I couldn't stay there any longer. I didn't trust Dr. Yang. I just . . . couldn't do it anymore."

"It was worth it to you, then." My voice is a ghost, transparent wisps that are already long gone. "The only daughter of Jiang Gui-hua, the person who screwed up your life by curing you. You thought it was worth chancing my life so long as it got you out of there."

"Yeah. I did. If one life was all it was going to take to stop Reds from killing my friends, to stop Firsts from killing everyone else . . . ?" He shrugs. "And if it didn't even have to be *my* life? Yes. You're absolutely right. That was exactly what I was thinking when we left the City." Howl takes a step back from the opening, the white blaze of light reflecting up from the snow blurring his features. The raw honesty in his voice cuts. "But it only took a few days out there with you to realize that I couldn't . . . I got to know you, and . . ." He trails off, as if the confession that he was okay with me dying is easier to articulate than him changing his mind about it.

"Is that excuse—that I'm harder to truss up for the scalpel once you know my favorite color—supposed to make all this okay, Howl?"

"That's not where we're standing right now, and it hasn't been for a long time, Sev." He shakes his head. "What's your excuse? You left without me. If you were so sure Yizhi was going to kill you, then what did you think was going to happen when I was the only one left?"

Silence. Only the hiss of the wind, the hush of snow as it blows down from the trees. Every inch of me is frozen, paralyzed, not able to expel the high-pitched scream ringing in my head.

"I don't even know why I came after you. I hoped . . . but hope is useless." Howl takes another step back, and then another. "Life isn't a weiqi match, Sev. There isn't a grid or stones or rules that end the game with a polite bow. Not everything can be reduced to what colors you're wearing." He doesn't speak for a moment, then shakes his head. "And I don't know why I'm trying to convince you."

My hands claw through the dirt, my brain unable to process the raw awfulness singeing his voice.

"Whatever Sole said to you, I would never have let Dr. Yang hurt you. Hell, I was willing to leave the Mountain for *you*. I'm done with hurting people. With lying. With all of this."

When I finally look up, he's gone.

CHAPTER 24

IT'S COLD IN THE LITTLE SHELTER HOWL MADE FOR us, wind whistling over the tarp and through the branches above. The owl pellets under me make me feel dirty and diseased, as if I'm lying in a bed of bones and skin, but I can't move, exhaustion weighing me down.

I left him. I knew what I was doing too. I just assumed Howl would leave, the same way he left before. It isn't much of an excuse either, now that it's been lobbed at my head. I chose my life instead of his because he chose his life instead of mine.

The last glaring bits of daylight burn into my eyes when I force myself to sit up to the sounds of rustling in the tree above me. I should have listened the first time I heard the owl's call. Tai-ge in a cell. June . . . I can't think about June.

And Howl. Whatever goodwill he had for me might as well be dead too. All the anger and hurt and awfulness I've been refusing to acknowledge since I left the Mountain threatens to overwhelm me, to squelch out any last bits of the person I was before.

I pull myself up from the ground with a growl and storm out

from under the tarp. The nest is just above me in the tree, the clumps of dry grass and pine needles like a dead thing lodged in the branches. Ice burns at my palm as I pry a rock from the frozen ground.

When I lob the rock at the nest, it glances off, landing in the snow with an inept *plop*. My throat burns, an inarticulate scream clawing its way out of me, but even the satisfaction of an unrestrained cry is dampened by snow, the sound muffled and close. Swearing at the rocks and the dirt, the ice, I kneel down to pry another stone free.

But then something moves in the nest, the coppery rust of twilight blinding me as a shape bursts from the nest and up into the sky. The bird circles around, shadow falling directly on me as it dives down, landing on the branch just above me with a hiss.

My fingers wrap around a loose rock on the ground, the touch of ice like needles and acid against my skin. The owl stands with its shoulders hunched, as if all the ghosts of the dead are gathered in its shadow, the bird's yellow eyes glaring and reflective in the failing light. It hisses again, bobbing back and forth.

I throw the rock at the creature even as its talons come out, diving toward my face. The rock misses, but I don't move, arms spread wide as I scream a war cry at the demon bird. At the last moment, it veers to the side, then circles back around to perch on the edge of the nest. It cocks its head, looking down at me. A terrible chill needles down my spine. Parhat looked at me the same way, as if wondering how best to take me apart. Like Mei, right before she looped a wire around my throat.

The creature flaps its wings once, then takes off into the bruised evening light. I stand there staring long after it's gone, death flying on silent wings away from me into the forest.

Death. Insanity. SS. The real enemy. Dr. Yang already wields it like the long swords from a history book: too grand for us of the lower caste to hold, but not grand enough to stop the blades killing us. Howl is out there, either looking for June or scouting the camp or maybe gone forever, on his way to help Sole.

What am I doing?

I crawl inside the shelter and pull out my pack. The camp isn't too far away. Maybe I can go back to the paddies, find the spot June was, and somehow follow her footprints . . . I jerk to a stop halfway out of the shelter as the heavy crunch of footsteps shatters the silence.

Groping in my pocket for the knife, I find only fabric. Howl dropped the knife somewhere near the cave's entrance.

Anger boils in my throat. At myself for yelling at a stupid bird and attracting attention. At Howl for *everything*, at Tai-ge for getting caught and refusing to let me get caught with him, at June for her magical forest powers failing. At *all* of them for leaving me here alone under the owl's tree.

I scuttle back into the shelter and comb through the snow to find the knife. Once its frigid metal is in my hand, I crouch with my back to the rock wall by the hideout opening and wait.

The footsteps don't pause to explore this way or that, don't trip or slide. They come straight up the rocks. Scuffle over the top of the boulders and land outside with a thump that shakes a clump of snow down from the tarp just outside the opening.

I launch forward with a shriek, crashing into the person just as they bend to pull the tarp back and expose me. Boots and snaggy shoelace hooks, knobbly knees that give way to ice and dirt when the wiry form easily sidesteps my attack, shoving my face to the ground.

"Be quiet!" A girl's voice. "How can you ever hear anything when you are so *loud*?"

I let my cheek rest against the ice, something inside of me disengaging. And I can let myself cry because it's June, and she isn't dead at all.

CHAPTER 25

"ARE YOU ALL RIGHT?" I ASK ONCE WE'RE INSIDE, my cheek red and smarting from being shoved down into the ice. June might not be a trained fighter, but she's quick on her feet. I suppose a half-brained attack from me might not measure up to the full-to-the-brim insanity she must have dealt with when she was still with her father.

June nods, her eyes narrowing as they skid across my neck. She points at the marks there, eyebrows furrowed.

"It hurt." I press a tentative finger against the raw skin and shrug. "But I'm not dead."

June stares a second longer, her hand raised as if she wants to touch the scabby, bruised skin, but then sits down. It only takes a moment for her to extract her pack and the waterskin inside, though instead of drinking, she pokes it experimentally. It isn't all the way full.

"Howl drank from it. Not me." I can't keep from looking at her, as if she'll dissolve into a shimmer of golden hair and cold-night hallucinations if I look away. "He's out. . . ."

June nods to the doorway, not a single thread of surprise pulling the weave of her calm asunder.

"You've seen him?" I ask.

"Drew off the Menghu." June glares out at the coating of snow as if it's to blame for everything that went wrong. "They were following me."

So he didn't leave. Where is he now? I wonder. Is he coming back, or was that argument the end of Howl and me sharing the same space?

My thoughts all sludge together, my chest seeming to constrict as the last words he said repeat over and over in my head. That he's done. I suck in a deep breath, telling myself that it will be okay. Howl being gone is what I wanted anyway. He can go back to being dead.

I reach out to touch June's shoulder, mentally shoving the table holding my thoughts over, the bits and pieces skittering away in a violent burst. June's alive, and right now that's all that matters. "What happened last night?" I ask. "There were gunshots and then the explosion went off, and the Menghu started killing people. . . ."

She gulps down some water, then closes the waterskin. "Scouts came in. Maybe the ones after our heli. They saw my hair. Saw the patroller in the trench." June's mouth creases up to the side in a sort of grimace. She reaches into her coat and pulls out a gun, the dying embers of the sun glinting off the metal. It's the weapon she took from the guard at the top of the paddies.

"Oh, June." It's easy to forget how young she is, after all the planning she's done, all the sneaking and scouting. She seems as if she should be as small as Lihua back at the Post, the weight of the gun in her hand so staggering I feel as if I'll break just looking at her. When eyes don't leave the weapon, I reach out and gather her to me, hugging her close. "I'm so sorry."

It's like hugging a bundle of twigs, all long, bendy lines that don't give in the least.

"The ones below heard. Thought the scouts were attacking them. That I was too." Her voice is barely a whisper. She pulls the outer layer of her Outside patrol uniform off, the coat singed and damp.

"The Menghu below you all started shooting?" I ask.

June stows the waterskin and shoves her pack back under the rock. "Some of them followed me. Couldn't get back here without bringing them, too." She looks up at the ceiling, and I can see tears glimmering in her eyes, as if keeping them from streaming down will somehow negate their existence.

We sit in the dark for a while, June chewing on some dried meat and pears. I try to eat, but it all tastes like dirt, so I stop, listening to the frosted wind as it whistles over the snow-heavy tarp above us instead. Something shifts outside, and fear stabs through me. I grope for the knife again.

June turns to look, but it's a settled sort of movement, as if she isn't afraid. She did say Howl was out there, but I'm almost surprised at the relief warm inside my chest when his face appears in the opening. "Everything okay here?"

So he's not leaving. At least, not yet. I'm not sure how to look at him. I don't know if I was wrong or if he was, or if we both were together, or how we're supposed to exist in the same hemisphere anymore. It's an awful snarl of confusion that twists deep inside me, tight around my lungs. I don't know where we stand. I don't even know where I *want* to stand anymore.

Howl doesn't seem to notice my discomfort, waiting for me to nod that we're okay before pointing at June. "Get her warmed up, would you? Maybe even break a quicklight if you've got one?" He runs a hand along the edge of the shelter's opening. "If we cover the door, then no one will accidentally see it and things could potentially cheer up a little in here." He tries to smile, but it doesn't quite work. "What's a little death and destruction when you've got friends?"

"How long before they find us here?" I ask. "It's not snowing anymore, and unless you know something I don't, it's hard to hide when people can follow your footprints in the snow."

"The whole camp is locked down. I think they're flying all the Menghu out, and no one's come up this way since this morning, so I think we're okay for the night." Howl doesn't look at me as he speaks. "And June has proven herself a master of stealth and general woodscraftiness."

June's slow grin takes me by surprise, making my heart want to melt. "Even you couldn't have lasted out there so long, Howl."

"We'll have a contest later to see." This time his smile looks almost genuine. "I'm going to go check something. We can figure what to do about Tai-ge in the morning?" He says it like a question, but then goes outside without waiting for an answer. Unless he killed something out there, Howl hasn't eaten since before I woke up. Or been warm or anything else but a living shadow out in the woods. I concentrate on my sleeping bag, draping it over June's shoulders, my fingers tracing the City seal embroidered into the side in tiny measured stitches before pulling out a quicklight. Maybe he's happier as a shadow than trapped in here with me.

Maybe that's the way it needs to be.

In the morning, our little safe haven is tucked in tight, like the forts we used to make from blankets and bedsheets back at the orphanage, waiting for Sister Shang to storm our walls.

Only, Sister Shang is dead.

Six days until Dr. Yang and the Chairman move north. Six days to get Tai-ge out and to beat them to Port North. Maybe with the fighting last night they won't be able to leave so soon. Maybe we have more time now.

June snuggles in next to me, both of us under my sleeping bag and lying on top of hers. It feels safe, because I don't have to open my eyes to know June is here when I wake up from nightmares. Breathing. Safe.

On the other hand, Howl came back sometime during the night and is lying with his back brushing mine, barely enough room in the little space for all of us to lie down. Even if it is a little creepy that he managed to come in without waking me, I don't shrink from looking at him when I sit up. He's not asleep, just tracing the lines of the rock wall with his eyes. He looks sort of cold even bundled up in his coat, but he didn't pull Tai-ge's sleeping bag out or try to share a corner of mine.

"Did you find . . . ?" I can't ask the question. The owl said enough last night. Tai-ge's absence might as well have turned my heart to lead for how heavy it feels in my chest. But if Howl had found Tai-ge . . . even if he'd found him bloody and facedown in the snow, wouldn't he have told me already? "What chance do we have of getting Tai-ge out?"

"I'm not sure." Howl rolls onto his back to look at me, putting his arms behind his head, his elbow just missing June. "How much do you trust him?"

"He's alive? For sure?" *How did Howl get into the camp? Is that where he's been this whole time?* I push that thought away, hungry for his answer.

Howl nods. "No room for doubt."

The weight inside me lifts, and I have to dull the urge to go outside and push the owl's nest from the tree. Whatever the old stories say, it's just an owl. No one died last night. No one is going to die. I breathe again, my lungs finally working again, feeling the silly smile on my face. Howl's eyes narrow, waiting for my answer to his question. "What do you mean, how much do I trust Tai-ge? I trust him as much as . . . I can, I guess."

"He knew where the packs were, right? You didn't stash them without him?" Howl pulls a hand out from under his head to point at Tai-ge's pack, still stuffed beneath the rocky overhang. "He's sort of . . . militant, isn't he? How is it you convinced him to steal a heli and fly you out of the City?"

"I think gunshots and SS spreading like fire in a bomb factory did the arguing for me."

Howl closes his eyes without answering, as if he's playing through something in his head. June stirs next to me, then rolls out from under the sleeping bag. She gropes around until she finds her now-empty waterskin, pulls mine and Tai-ge's out from our packs, then crawls through the shelter's door. When I transfer my attention back to Howl, his eyes are open again, watching me, expression suspiciously blank. "I found something that I'm having a difficult time explaining to myself. Perhaps you and June can provide context?"

"What do you mean?"

"I'll explain as we walk. If Tai-ge . . . well, we shouldn't risk staying here." Howl sits up, the skin under his eyes smudged and dark with lack of sleep. He pulls Tai-ge's pack out with a jerk, flinching when the fabric of the outer pocket tears. "I'll carry this. Help me pull down the tarp."

June stands just outside in an unblemished patch of snow,

gathering bits of ice into the tops of all three waterskins. When she sees us pulling the packs out behind us, she drops the snow and runs to put the waterskins in each. Together we gather up the tarp covering the ground inside, then unmoor the corners of the top tarp, dumping bits of tree and the snow massed on top of it that masked our hiding spot. She doesn't ask any questions, whistling to herself in a way that's more air than notes as I fold up the tarp, then roll it into a tight cylinder to strap onto my pack.

We walk toward the river, Howl going slow, listening, and telling me to stop more than once before we even reach the banks, while June slithers on ahead.

"So, what did you find?" I ask, stopping yet again as we get to the half-melted coating of snow frozen over the river. The water peeks out in gaps and cracks through the snow, hurrying under the drifts where ice held it up from the water. If it weren't so loud, I'd be frightened of mistaking the icy floes as solid ground. "Are they holding Tai-ge inside the camp? Is he okay?"

"They're not holding Tai-ge." Howl nods to June as she sneaks back, and the three of us set off along the river's patchy edges. "He and another Red trekked out to the heli last night."

"Is that where we're going?" Another jolt of relief runs through me. Tai-ge's alive. Not a pile of ashes in the bottom of some prison, or sitting in line, waiting for the headsman. Damn the stupid owl.

But then the information starts to marinate in my head. "Someone must have recognized him and known he'd be able to lead them straight to the heli's landing site," I venture.

Howl leads as we start up the side of a hill, our path climbing high above the river and its rushing torrent. "He's not a prisoner so far as I can tell. Just him and one other Red. In the heli."

A sick sort of fear overlays the prickles rushing up and down my arms. June turns to look at me, calculation in her eye. She knows Tai-ge wanted to go back as well as I do. Did walking under the Chairman's flag take Tai-ge too close to the edge of the hole where I threw the Reds, his family, and the whole City with them?

The owl's ghostly call seems to echo in my ears. There's more than one way to die. But I don't want to believe the bits of Tai-ge that left him itching for rules and schedules and the correct uniform-pressing techniques could have suffocated the parts of him that are mine.

I shake my head as we walk. Tai-ge said he'd be right beside me. He wanted to find the cure. He couldn't have turned sides. And what's more, Tai-ge has never lied to me, has never done anything to make me believe I shouldn't trust him. Whatever is going on, it isn't because Tai-ge is turning us in. Not voluntarily.

At least, I hope not.

"If you're worried something is off with Tai-ge," I say, choosing each word carefully, "then why are we headed straight for him, Howl?"

Howl doesn't answer for a second, concentrating on his footing as the mountainside becomes steeper, the ground threatening to slide us into the frozen water below. But when he finally looks back, I can tell the delay was more for thought than slippery ground. "I assumed leaving Tai-ge behind wasn't a palatable option for certain members of our party. And I promised we would help him."

Howl stops on a relatively flat stretch of ground and scuffs his foot in the snow, trying to dislodge the crust of ice built up on his boot, and accidentally teeters sideways. "Am I wrong? Everyone's okay with dumping Tai-ge? If they're really moving out in six days—"

"We're not dumping *anyone*. If Tai-ge switched sides, he would have led soldiers to the packs, not the heli." I shoulder past him to walk with June. The side of her mouth quirks up in a shadow of a smile, but she keeps up the pace, picking her way through the rocks. "What are our chances of extracting him? Or of even taking the heli back?"

"Very good chance we could do both. That's what I'm worried about. Why would they send just one Red to find the heli with Tai-ge? We know the Reds have been looking for you."

"You think it's a trap? But not one that actually led to where Tai-ge knew we were going to be."

"You're right." Howl shrugs. "But he isn't restrained. He walked out of there with no weapons, and last I heard he was laughing at his new Red friend's jokes. What's your theory? That he miraculously escaped, but didn't come back to us? That the Reds somehow missed the heli in the snowstorm, and he went back to make sure it was safe before coming to get us?" He swears, almost losing his footing, sending a miniature avalanche of snow down the hillside before finding it again. "Or how about this: Dr. Yang heard Tai-ge got captured. He knows you're after the cure. If he's smart, then he knows he gave you a deadline and a very good reason to find quick transport. Seems like a good way to bet on where your competition is and eliminate them."

I feel my brow begin to furrow, not liking the cheery accusation. "The Reds definitely saw the heli," I reply carefully.

"Oh, you're sure about that? Sorry, I didn't realize you were telepathic." Howl grins at me when I look back at him, and I don't like how many teeth are showing. "Why didn't you say so before? You can just intuit the cure out of Port North, so we don't even need to look at the maps or get the key back from Tai-ge."

The key. Howl thinks Tai-ge has the encryption key. That's why we're headed toward the heli, why Howl's even still here. I brush my pant leg, feeling to make sure the metal disk is still snug in my pocket, hating the aftertaste of disappointment rank in my mouth.

"My telepathy was supposed to be a secret." I pitch my voice down a few degrees and raise my hands for effect. "But now my senses are telling me how much you wish a Wood Rat and a Fourth would sew your mouth shut, then leave you hog-tied in the snow."

"You want to try it?" Howl steps closer, between me and the steep rocks jutting out over the river, Tai-ge's pack unbuckled and hanging lopsided on his shoulders. He's uncomfortably near, still towering over me even though he's down the slope. The last time he offered to fight me was over an apple, and for some reason I'm just as unsure this time if he's serious. "You think your telepathy is working well enough to save your life if Tai-ge's two stars cut deeper than years of being too scared of his mother to touch you—?"

I jam my elbow into his side, then slam my shoulder into his chest, meaning to push him over. But, even with gravity on my side, Howl doesn't go more than a step down, quickly finding his footing, his hands twitching as if it's only self-control keeping them at his sides.

"How about you pretend my friend's life matters for a second." I square my shoulders, looking down at him from my higher spot on the trail. "He's the only reason we didn't just leave you back at the Post with your head tied to an anthill."

"Ants aren't very active during winter last I checked." Howl adjusts the pack on his shoulders, his dark brown eyes unapologetic. He puts his hands out, practically begging for me to come at him. "What's it going to be, Sev? Are you going to push me off this rock? Or are we going to talk this through like adults?"

"If you're too scared to help Tai-ge, there's no need to put yourself at risk. Is this what you're after?" I pull the encryption key out of my pocket and hold it up, Howl tipping his chin back so it doesn't jab him in the nose. "You have the maps in that pack. You have whatever it is you gleaned from eavesdropping in the heli. If you're going to take it, just take it."

We stare at each other, the rumble of the river loud below us.

"I'm not—why would I try to take that away from you?" Howl finally says.

"You want the cure. For Sole to fix things at the Mountain."

Howl scrubs a hand along his scalp, pulling at his hair. "That does seem like the best plan at the moment, yes. But I wasn't there for whatever happened with your mother. She sent *you* specifically to go looking for . . . however it was she documented the experiments she did on me and you, right? I have a feeling that will carry some weight once we find them."

"We?" I pocket the encryption key and fold my arms. "Why *shouldn't* I push you into the river right now, Howl? I'd sleep better if a member of the group wasn't a proven liar."

Howl presses his lips together, the skin around his mouth lightening from the pressure. "I'm not a Jiang, so I might not be able to get her papers. But you have the disadvantage of having spent almost zero time Outside." He shrugs. "June's helpful, but she's a lot better at running and hiding than she is at elbowing people in the face. I have connections. Training. Motivation to get the cure. I can help you."

June coughs from up the trail as if to remind us that she's there.

I take a deep breath, trying very, very hard not to throw up. It's true. Not about elbowing people in the face, but there's no way we would have found the encryption key so easily last night without him. I wouldn't have gotten out of the camp at all. June would probably still be playing duck, weave, and shoot with Menghu.

And I wouldn't have known about Tai-ge and this Red at the heli.

"I'm not saying that we should pretend everything is okay. It isn't." Howl lowers his voice, glancing at June and fiddling with the straps of the backpack. "But finding the cure sort of takes precedence at the moment, wouldn't you say? We probably have a better chance on the same team."

The same team. I swallow down the bile rising in my throat, trying to forget the last time he said that to me seriously. Right after we first got to the Mountain and I wasn't sure I wanted to stay. He's right about our group needing help, but some kinds of help are too dangerous.

Dangerous enough you already left him to die. The thought unwinds in my mind, leaving me feeling hollow, my insides about to collapse. I left him at the Mountain. I left him on the ground in the hangar, Tai-ge's and June's guns still smoking.

I've spent so much of my life hating that people kill each other. Couldn't shoot Seconds, even the one who broke June's nose, or the ones who I saw break a Menghu's leg and drag him back to their campfire. I could hardly pull the trigger to kill a gore when it was running at me, and yet Howl has brought out something much darker inside me. As if all those years I worried SS would take control, that the monster inside me would be all I was . . . it wasn't SS I should have been worried about.

It was me. Me making a decision about who gets to live and who gets to die. Then walking away, as if it somehow isn't my fault.

Is that better or worse than what the Menghu do, cutting trigger fingers from the enemies they've killed to remember each one? At least they own what they've done.

I take a deep breath and meet Howl's eyes. "If we find the cure, how can I trust you to not run off with it?"

"I'm planning on it, actually. All shady motivations out in the open. When we find the cure, I'm taking it straight back to Sole." He stares straight back at me, unblinking. "But I'll take you and June with me. Even Tai-ge, if my interpretation of what's going on with the heli is wrong. I'm with you in thinking everyone who needs the cure should have it, City, Outsider, and Menghu."

The part of me that has been wondering what under the Chairman's weeping sky we will be able to *do* with the cure once we find it perks up at the thought. Sole's a medic. She's used to working with scavenged materials, doing things in the field when the stakes are high. Keeping secrets. And she doesn't hold loyalty to the Mountain or the City. If she did, she'd never have helped me leave the Mountain in the first place. If Sole survives whatever mess is going on where she is now, she might be our best hope at giving the cure to anyone who needs it without becoming political.

I nod slowly. "Okay. But I have two provisions." I mimic his placid tone. "If we take it to Sole, I want to nail down specifics about who knows we're there, who works on it, how to get materials . . ."

"We'll come up with something that works for all of us. We can't afford to be on any side here. No one deserves to spend their lives wondering if compulsions are better than bowing to whoever has the cure."

I start to roll my eyes, but he holds my gaze. Both of us know what it's like to have our lives in someone else's hands because of who we are. Not being in control of where we live, who our friends are, whether or not we die.

The thought actually helps, my reservations fading a degree or two. "Okay. The other thing is, I need the first working dose. I have to take it to Lihua."

"Who?" Howl glances at June when she gives an approving nod.

"She's a little girl, she's infected, and she's going to get thrown out of her tree house if we can't help her. Soon."

"I like tree houses." Howl nods and sticks out his hand. "I'll take it to her myself if you need me to."

I hesitate for one more second, staring at his open palm. But then I take his hand and we shake. His hand is warmer than mine. Rough with calluses, and much less slimy than I was expecting.

"Done?" June rolls her eyes and starts off.

"Wait." Howl stops me when I turn to follow her. "If I'm in this group, then I'm in. My opinions matter. I get to ask questions about whether or not Tai-ge might be a risk. No one gets to threaten to abandon me in the middle of nowhere or lock me in a stuffy closet again. Or try to shoot me." He glances meaningfully at June.

"*Try* to shoot you?" June looks back at him, a hand on her hip.

Howl rubs a hand across his chest where the bullets hit his protective gear back in the City, the moment of seriousness sliding off his face. "Are you going to be the comic relief now? I thought that was Sev's self-appointed job." He starts walking, the three of us moving along the ledge that juts out over the river. "In fact, could that be another provision? If we're all going to do this together, then I demand entertainment."

"If you promise to use all of your magic Menghu powers to get Tai-ge and the heli back in one piece, I promise to make you laugh until your head explodes." I start walking, my mind already skating forward, wondering what we'll find ahead. If Tai-ge *could* be a threat. I don't want to think it. But the thought was in my head before Howl spoke, like a seed already planted, just waiting for a little nurturing to sprout.

"That's my girl. Entertaining *and* threatening." Howl isn't done, apparently. "Though that sounds kind of messy. Maybe just until my nose bleeds?"

"You call me your girl again and I'll show you blood. I'll go find a gore and shove your head in its mouth."

Howl laughs. Not a real, from-the-gut, wholehearted sort of laugh. But not a courtesy laugh either.

It's funny. Howl deciding that I'm joking sort of makes me want to laugh too.

CHAPTER 26

MY FEET ARE SOAKED THROUGH BY THE TIME THE
craft is visible through the snow-laden trees, light reflecting in a
white-hot flare from the uncovered propellers to each side of the
cockpit. There are two sets of footprints pointing straight toward
it, and none leading away.

"Still looks like it's Tai-ge and one other Red," Howl whispers, nodding to the snow turned up around the heli. "And . . . get
down!"

Howl, June, and I fall back, finding trees to put between us and
whoever it is walking under the heli's belly. The man's bare head is
shaggy with hair pointing in all directions. Definitely not Tai-ge.
June keeps her eyes on the coat-thick form for a few seconds
before she looks at us. *Not a soldier*, she mouths.

Howl nods and gestures for us to move forward. I stand there
for a second, not wanting to obey. If Howl is part of our group,
then who is in charge now? Before, when it was the three of us
headed toward the Mountain, it was easy to fall in line. There was
no reason to question one another or argue exactly what we were

going to do down to finer points. Howl knew where we going and understood what needed to happen, so I followed.

That is no longer the case.

But I don't know how to assault people who have taken up residence in my heli, so I go in the direction Howl indicated. June pulls out the gun she took from the Red on the rice terraces and offers it to Howl, but he shakes his head and pulls a knife from his pocket. *My* knife. When did he take that back?

Now's probably not the time to be annoyed about it.

When Howl looks at me, I hold up the can of inhibitor spray I had in my pack. The last one we have. He nods, then creeps off into the trees, circling around to the back of the heli. June does the same, dodging from snow-covered rock to rough tree trunk until she's on the far side of the craft. I start in from my side, attempting to keep out of sight.

Whoever this man is, June's point about him not being a soldier has been made. If he has a gun, it's hidden under one of the many layers zipped to his chin, and he doesn't even look up when June scampers by.

I tense as he begins grappling with his outer coat, pulling and cursing until . . . something. Squinting, I try to make out what he's so upset about, only to look down in embarrassment.

He's peeing in the snow. Right by the heli. Ew.

Because I'm looking at my feet, I miss it when Howl darts forward. The Red shouts as he falls, but by the time I get there, he's facedown in the snow, with however many pounds of Menghu Howl can claim on his back and a knife blade against his neck. June comes in from the side, her gun leveled at his head, and I fall into my place, inhibitor spray warm in my hand. Not that we need it.

"Okay!" The word comes out choked, the man gasping for air

through his gas mask and coming up with snow instead. "You've managed to push me over. Now what?"

"Where are the rest of the Reds?" Howl asks calmly.

The Red squirms to the side, his gas mask pulling sideways as he tries to find air, though he goes still when the knife blade shoves harder against his neck. "Couldn't you get off and we can talk this all out? I'm just a medic. There are rules about medics, aren't there?"

"Kill them first?" Howl asks. "So they don't undo all your good work?"

June nods solemnly, though I think Howl was joking.

"I was thinking more along the lines of letting me zip my pants before anything freezes off." The Red gives a compressed sort of laugh, the squashed sound coming out as more of a cough. "It's only me and Hong Tai-ge here. You're his friends, right?"

I frown as he gasps down another breath, trying to pull his face out of the compacted snow under him. Tai-ge might outrank whoever this is, but he's older than Tai-ge, and formality usually belongs to age. He continues, "I think he'll be mad if you shoot me, and I'd rather not upset a Hong."

"Where's Tai-ge?" I walk to stand directly in front of the man. "In the heli?"

"I'm here!" The voice turns us all toward the heli's hatch. Tai-ge jumps down, not bothering with the ladder. He runs at me, and I can almost feel Howl tense, ready to throw me the knife, or rocket between me and Tai-ge before he can crash into me. But Tai-ge is laughing, the toes of his boots catching on the ice-crusted snow. He stumbles as he gets to me, throwing his arms around me, a smile almost cracking his face in two. "Yuan's spinster sister, I was so worried! I didn't know if they'd found you or if it was even possible you were still alive . . . !"

I drop the spray and hug Tai-ge back, my arms slipping against his voluminous coat. Holding as tight as I can, as if somehow it won't be real, that my friend, whole and well before me, will turn to smoke if I let go. The dusting of ice on his coat freezes against my cheek and his gas mask filter presses an awful mesh pattern in my temple. But I don't care. Tai-ge's alive, he's not in trouble, and we're back together.

The owl was wrong. No, the owl didn't do anything but sit in its nest, unhappy to have teenagers take residence under her nest. Fear has colored my thoughts a little too brightly, until I couldn't see anything but spirits and ghosts. It was just an owl.

Pushing back from Tai-ge's hug, I look up at him, his cheeks ruddy with the cold. "Why are you here? I thought we agreed to meet at the packs."

"It's a long story, I—"

Both of us look up as Howl swears. "Put it down, June."

Howl has pulled the medic up from the snow, the man's gas mask hanging askew to reveal an awful, patchy-looking beard that clings to his chin in a rather unconvincing sort of way. Flecks of snow stick to the medic's cheeks and eyebrows, making it look as though he just came from a rather involved banquet that prominently featured powdered sugar. It's hard to tell under the snow, but I'd guess he's somewhere in his late twenties, at least ten years older than I am.

And then I see June. She's standing just where she was before, her face icy white as her eyes rake the medic's features over. The gun is shaking in her hands, its nose still pointed directly at the Red's head. Her finger squeezes against the trigger, only a fraction of a movement away from blowing a hole in him and Howl both.

CHAPTER 27

PANIC TRILLS THROUGH ME AS I RUN TOWARD HER,
the thought that SS might have snuck through little June's mask
and taken hold of her twisting my stomach into knots. When I
get her, she jumps, skittering back like a rat caught amid the millet bags. It isn't SS peering out through her eyes, taking hold of
her arms and legs to do its bidding. She's afraid, the gun wavering
back and forth between me, the sky, the medic, and Tai-ge, as if the
quiet, happier girl I've been watching the last few weeks just came
out of a coma and is now someone else.

"June, why don't you give that to me?" I take one step closer
and her gaze climbs up to my face. Her shoulders slump and the
gun falls down to her side. When I close the distance between us,
she doesn't flinch away, though it isn't easy to untangle her fingers from the gun's trigger.

"What's the matter?" I ask.

June doesn't move for a moment, her hands shaking at her
sides as if she means to grab the gun back, attack the medic where
he's kneeling in the snow, or perhaps just explode. Instead, she

turns and walks toward the heli, gaining speed with each lurching step. Dodging the ladder, June runs underneath the heli's torn belly and out into the trees beyond.

"Hey!" The medic's voice steams up, and I turn to find Howl pushing him over, brandishing the knife. The man rolls onto his knees, his pants thankfully zipped as far as I can see, his hands raised over his head. "I already said I give up, man. Really not good at knives until *after* they poke holes in people."

"How does June know you?" Howl asks. I hate the coldness in his voice—and that I feel an echo of it in myself as I wait for the answer.

"I've never seen that girl before in my life."

Tai-ge steps toward them. "It's okay. This man is my friend. His name is Chen Xuan. He came to help us."

"Help us do what, exactly?" Howl's voice is a shade too quiet.

"I . . . I know about the city north of here. The one they're going to invade." Xuan stutters as he gets a clear look at Howl's face for the first time. He keeps his hands in the air. "Say, you aren't contagious, are you? Running around out here without masks?"

"SS isn't going to be a problem for you if you don't give me a good reason for you being here." Howl doesn't raise his knife any higher, but it feels as if he's standing on an edge, waiting for an invitation to jump.

"We don't have time for vetting at the moment." Tai-ge walks to Xuan's side and pulls him up from the ground. "We have to get in the air before—"

"Tai-ge," I interrupt. "Explanation. Right now."

Tai-ge's eyes widen at my tone. "If the scouts found the heli, they didn't make it through the shooting last night to tell anyone. It's safe to take it. Unless Reds followed us out of the camp, in which case we need to—"

"No, Tai-ge, explain *that*." I point the butt of the gun toward the medic.

Tai-ge gives a harried shrug. "You need to know *now*? Okay, okay." He almost looks as if he's about to put his hands up in the air as well. I lower the gun, though the business end isn't pointed at anyone, wondering what exactly my face looks like to make Tai-ge back down so quickly. "I told the Seconds everything. That I needed to get to Port North." His hands go even higher when I narrow my eyes at all of our secrets being laid out for the Reds to see. "They know about the cure already, Sev. The whole camp heard about it during the meeting. Xuan heard from the soldiers who captured me what I'd been saying, and he came to me. He knows about Port North, Sevvy. He knows where we need to go."

"Things aren't going well in the camps," Xuan breaks in, keeping his eyes on the knife blade still pointed at him. "It doesn't take a First mathematician to see how many masks there are and how much Mantis is left, and divide by how many people were there were at Dazhai. Not to mention the . . . odd behavior we've seen from the Chairman. The way he's been buzzing in and out of the camp . . . something's not right. I figured my chances were better with Hong Tai-ge than with the rest of the Seconds."

I blink, trying to weigh the deluge of information against June running away at the sight of him. Howl looks from Xuan to Tai-ge, and for a moment I think the knife might switch targets. "Why did you come *here*, then? Why not back to the packs? How are we supposed to trust that the new General and the Chairman both aren't listening to this entire conversation?"

"I won't tell him if you don't. At least not if you let me get back on the heli." Xuan swallows, his eyes wide on the single red star still pinned to Howl's coat. He attempts a smile, voice taking on a jaunty sort of tone. "Last I checked, the Chairman's family wasn't supposed to be so interested in razor blades. I'd bow, but . . ." He shrugs, his hands still half-raised.

Tai-ge gives Xuan a push toward the ladder, facing off against Howl. "This is ridiculous. Just because the camp is on lockdown doesn't mean they aren't going to send someone out looking for the heli again. Resources are spread thin, if I'm not mistaken. We have to move fast. I didn't want to scare Sev by showing up with a Second at the packs. I wasn't even sure if she was *alive*." He looks at me, crinkles between his brow barely lifting when he catches my eye. "I was going to go back for the maps, just me, and hope that Sev was hiding there. But now I don't need to, and none of this is going to matter if we get patrollers out here before we lift off."

I take a deep breath, looking at his face. Tai-ge never could lie. But even if every word out of Xuan's mouth is the truth, it doesn't change that June seems to want to stake him through the eyes. "Okay." I avoid looking at the medic, not sure how to untangle things. The explanation makes enough sense that I'd rather not continue discussing it with Reds ranging out from the camp. "Okay. Let's go. We can figure out the rest in the air."

Howl's face is too blank to be a real reaction, doubt rising off him like a smoke screen.

"Good." Tai-ge lets out a deep breath, clapping Xuan on the shoulder and leading him toward the ladder. "We've got the key; we've got someone who knows what's on the ground." He does a double take when Howl starts after them, pointing at the knife in Howl's hand. "Is that mine?"

Howl glances at me, waiting until I nod at him to lower the knife before he does so, though he doesn't surrender it into Tai-ge's outstretched hand. He gives an exaggerated smile and gestures for Xuan to go up the ladder, waiting until Tai-ge follows him up before sheathing the knife and pocketing it.

When he looks at me, the smile is gone. He points down at June's footprints, stark and raw in the snow. "You're easier to talk to."

I nod in agreement. "I'll go after her. What are the odds Xuan is telling the truth?"

Howl starts up the ladder. "I'm going to say miniscule."

"You believe Tai-ge, though?"

Stopping, Howl looks down at me, his lips pressed tight together. Then crawls in the hatch.

Nerves flutter deep in my belly at leaving Howl alone with Tai-ge, but then I let go of the thought. We're working together now. Howl put the knife away when I asked. Keeping the heli is too much of an advantage to let go of, and it was Howl who said Tai-ge would be left out of any murder sprees so he'd have a reliable pilot.

That's going to have to be enough for now.

June isn't far, her tracks undisguised and leading straight to the tree she's sitting beneath, only a few back from the clearing around the heli. She fiddles with her coat as I approach and stares down into the snow.

"June?" I ask. "What's the matter?"

She glances up, just a flash of green before planting them straight back into the snow. Bone quiet. Like an empty skull, a doll dressed up in old clothes, but with no tongue to speak.

I kneel in the snow next to her and touch her arm. "How do you know that man?"

She flinches away from me. Like when I first met her. Her hair covered, her bones sticking out like twigs of a malnourished tree. When I put my arms around her, she doesn't respond. She does follow when I pull her up from the snow and guide her toward the heli, though. As we're passing under, a terrible roar of machinery envelops us, the propellers starting to turn.

June and I clutch at each other in surprise, her heart beating so hard I can feel it through her coat. For a moment she seems to be a bird ready to jump into flight. But she lets me take her the rest of the way to the ladder, and climbs up after me. Once we're inside, she only stops to throw off her pack before shouldering her way through the cargo bay doors and out of sight.

"I told you, we'll get off the ground and set final coordinates in the air." Tai-ge has to yell over the sound of the propellers with the hatch open, giving Howl, a step behind him, an annoyed look to accompany what he says. Xuan sits next to him at the control panel, gesturing at the map suspended on the screen above them. A frown pulls Howl's mouth crooked as his eyes follow June's flight into the cargo bay before latching on to me. He gestures for me to come over.

"What about fuel? We don't know how far we're going!" Howl yells, his hand resting on his pocket where I saw him stow the knife. "I understand just as well as you do how dangerous it is to be near the camp, but without an idea of what we're going to be landing in. . . ."

"You don't know anything about flying, Howl. Step back from the controls. I'll get us where we need to go." Tai-ge spins to the side in his control chair, glancing back at me before hitting a button that makes the heli jerk up from the ground. The hatch is still hanging open behind me and I dart to pull it closed, dulling the propellers' demanding scream to a slightly dimmer roar that vibrates up through the floor.

"We can't just take off," I call. Tai-ge looks up from the dials at my voice. "Especially since we don't know . . ." I glance at Xuan, June's hollow presence screaming at me from beyond the bay doors. "We have to look at the maps and put together a strategy."

"We have enough for three . . . maybe three and a half liftoffs." Tai-ge peers down at the gauges littering the console, my stomach dropping as the craft begins moving faster in a vertical ascent.

"What exactly is half a liftoff?" Howl deadpans. I can almost feel the weight of his stare on Xuan, mine no less barbed.

"It involves a lot of falling." Tai-ge clears his throat, yelling to be heard over the propellers, making his voice crack. "Solar should keep us in the air, though. We can go through the maps and set coordinates once we're up. Can we have this conversation once we're gliding so we don't have to shout?"

"But what about—" I start.

"I know you have questions," Tai-ge cuts me off, looking away from the controls, his voice cracking over the noise from outside. "You don't know Xuan, but I do. I promise, this is the right thing. Trust me, Sevvy."

My gaze skates past my friend back to Xuan, the medic's shoulders hunched all the way to his ears, what with Howl clouding the space directly behind him. I don't like the way he won't look up at me, won't make eye contact.

I can trust Tai-ge. But I know Tai-ge well enough to worry that Red stars weigh a lot more than they should in his estimation. I put a hand on Howl's shoulder. When he looks, I point to the storage closet behind his back where Tai-ge won't see. He gives a small nod.

Howl steps around Tai-ge's chair and puts a hand on Xuan's arm. "Let's get the maps out. Come over here—that's where the best light is. You can show us where to go."

I stay with Tai-ge as Howl shepherds Xuan away from the captain seats. He doesn't even look up, pulling at levers and blinking buttons surrounding the captain's chair as the heli makes a jerky parting with the ground, my knees bending as my feet press too hard against the floor. The propellers tilt, hitching to the side and then up again, clearing the lower hills we were sitting under and buzzing up to head over the mountains.

I walk over to join Howl and Xuan once I'm sure Tai-ge is absorbed, leaning toward the Red with a smile that makes me feel as though spiders are crawling straight from my mouth. I have to speak loud to be heard over the propellers, but not loud enough for Tai-ge to hear. "I think we'll all fit, don't you?" I gesture to Howl's storage closet, the jagged bits of tape left from him escaping still littered across the floor. "It can be your work space, Chen Xuan."

"You can just call me Xuan. And I think I'd prefer to stay out here." Xuan shrugs. "Community over self and all that. I'd *never* presume to . . ." He stops when Howl takes a step closer. "What I meant to say was *Yes, ma'am.* I didn't realize it was the Fourth who was in charge."

"Things get a little muddled once you step outside City walls." Howl gives Xuan a little push that puts him past the closet's open door.

Tai-ge glances over his shoulder, his brow crinkled. But then the heli gives a shudder and he goes back to the controls. Bending at the waist, Xuan gives me a mockingly grandiose bow from inside the closet, but he doesn't raise his voice or try to signal Tai-ge's attention. "I'm honored to be given such preferential treatment, my lady. My queen. Which do you prefer?"

"'Ma'am' will be fine, thank you. Unless you're feeling

particularly worshipful, and then I think I'd prefer Ms. Queen. We like to keep things informal around here."

I slap a hand against the wall as the floor lurches under us. Howl braces himself with one arm, and I'm oddly gratified that I'm not the only one. I lean closer so he'll hear me over the drone of the propellers without broadcasting everything I'm saying.

"What are you thinking? Spy? Saboteur?"

"That camp is locked down, Sev. The only way they could have gotten out honestly would have been on a burn pile, riddled full of holes."

"Ew." I wrinkle my nose. "Images not needed, thanks."

"Not to mention the heli was sitting there untouched, especially if they matched its description with Tai-ge. Tai-ge's right about resources being spread thin, and an air advantage isn't something you just leave out in the forest for anyone to take." He looks me up and down. "You've got that full can of inhibitor spray, right?"

"I think I left it on the ground when I went after June." My stomach sinks, the floor feeling a bit more unstable under my feet even than when we were taking off, and none of it has much to do with being in the air. I can't make myself look past Howl into the storage closet, afraid of what I'll see in Xuan's eyes. "You don't think he'd attack us, would he? There's three of us."

Howl glances at Tai-ge behind me. "Just keep your eyes open."

I nod. "You search the medic. I'll take care of June."

"Yes, *ma'am*." But there isn't any irony to the glint in Howl's eyes. It's all steel and bones.

CHAPTER 28

WHATEVER TAI-GE BELIEVES, HOWL IS RIGHT. WE CAN'T hope that our luck extends to magically being able to keep the heli with no consequences. Or to have found a Red with intimate knowledge of exactly where we need to go, who also happens to want to jump in a heli with the Chairman's absent-without-leave son, a traitor Second, a Fourth, and a Wood Rat when all the masks and food are in the camp he just vacated. Fate, instant karma, and destiny combined wouldn't be that generous, not even if I'd taken off my stars back in the City and become a nun.

The propellers clip on and off, as if Tai-ge's trying to find the right height, the right wind before defaulting on the quieter correctional propellers that allow us to glide in comparative quiet. Before I get to the cargo bay door, June peeks through into the cockpit all by herself. Her eyes search the cabin over before stilling on me. Instead of hopping up next to Tai-ge at the controls to watch Tai-ge fly as she usually does, June goes to her rucksack where she threw it down in the center of the floor. She drags it to a corner and sits, clutching it to her chest.

I pull open my pack where it's propped up by the storage closet and snag a handful of dried pears. The silence emanating from behind the storage closet door makes my spine tingle, as if any moment I'll hear shouts or screams or . . . something. I'm not sure what it is I'm afraid of happening. Xuan attacking Howl? Or perhaps Howl falling in line with all the nightmares I've had about Menghu. I didn't tell him to hurt Xuan, but now I'm second-guessing, wondering what Cale would have assumed I meant if I asked her to search a potentially dangerous Red.

When I sit down by June, her face is empty as the cockpit windows, pressed over with gray clouds. The drone from the propellers goes silent again. Hopefully Tai-ge has found the right altitude. "You going to tell me about it?" I whisper. "How do you know him?"

June doesn't blink. It seems as though she hasn't in a while, as if the split second of darkness will bring monsters. She points to the storage room, a question on her face.

I nod. "He's in there with Howl. And I need to know if we should let him get sucked out of the cargo bay while we're up high or if there should be torture involved first."

June doesn't smile. I don't blame her. It wasn't that funny. When she finally reaches out for a slice of pear, I feel the breath stream out of me in relief as if June breaking down would turn me catatonic and mute as well.

"I don't know." She flinches as the propellers burst into motion, assaulting our ears, then stuffs the pear into her mouth.

"You don't know whether we should torture him?"

"His face is wrong," she says around the slice of pear.

"Wrong?" I fight the manic laughter drumming to be released at just how many ways that could be taken. At least she's talking again and not pulling back into her girl-size turtle shell. "Okay. But you do know him, right? It isn't just that you don't like patchy beards?"

She nods slowly.

"How?"

June's stare might as well be boring holes in the floor. But she shakes her head.

"June, no matter what he is or what happens next, I will protect you. I think Howl would too." It jars to hear those words coming out of my mouth, but whatever it is Howl has done, I believe June's on the list of people he'd like to keep alive, if possible. "Please, June. Anything you tell me will help. You don't have to keep secrets. You don't have to be alone. I'm here."

She looks at me, her vacant stare slowly coming into focus. But then she sits up a bit straighter and pins me with that greenstone gaze. "It's from before."

A warmth blossoms in my chest, as if it can somehow leap from me to her and soothe the worry out of her. "From before you met us?" I ask.

"He was there when they took her."

"They? Took who?"

"My mother. We ran."

A chill creeps down my neck, making its way slowly to my heart. "What do you mean you ran?"

June blinks, but it's too slow, as if she's been hypnotized, one step before falling asleep. "My family had to. From them." She doesn't look at the storage closet again, but I know Xuan must be one of "them."

"Dad never explained," she continues. "Just said we had to find her. And then he said nothing. And then it was better if I said nothing too."

The storage door cracks open, and Howl comes out on silent feet, going to the cluster of maps stuck in Tai-ge's pack. Tucking them under his arm, he looks at me. "Can I borrow the key?"

Tai-ge tears his eyes away from the controls. "Can we wait a minute to plan? I can set us on autopilot once we're far enough from City camps that we should be safe. That way we'll all be able to talk."

"I thought . . ." I bite my lip, trying to find the right words. Howl raises his eyebrow at me. "I want to talk to him first, Tai-ge."

"Why? If I'm in there, then—"

"No." The air feels close in the heli, the wet smell of dirty slush from outside mixed with moldering clothes that haven't been washed filling my nose.

Tai-ge doesn't turn around to look at me, his shoulders unnaturally straight in his chair. I pull the key from my pocket and hold it out to Howl. He takes it, running his fingers along the rough edge, but doesn't turn to go in the room. "Is June okay?" he asks quietly.

June looks up at him, but it's only a quick flick of her eyelashes before she's back to melting holes in the floor with her gaze.

"I'm not trying to pretend you aren't here, June. I just . . ." Howl scratches at the scruff coating his jaw. "If you've already said it once, I didn't want to make you say it again."

"Whatever is wrong, you must be mistaking Xuan for someone else, June," Tai-ge says from his chair. He couldn't have heard my whispered conversation with June, but a burst of irritation hits me at hearing him so easily dismiss her all the same.

June almost seems to shrink, whatever makes her June pulling back from her skin to a safer place. I crouch down by her, putting a hand on one of her knees. "I believe you, June. You are safe. At least from Xuan."

Howl joins us on the floor. "I'm not above pushing him out. Really." It's hard to know if he means Xuan or Tai-ge, but I don't look away from June to clarify.

June holds his gaze, then looks back at me. Her shoulders relax a fraction, and she nods.

Howl touches my arm, and I forget to flinch away for a second. "Would you rather have Sev out here, or would it be okay for me to take her in with me?"

June holds her hands out for the dried pears I grabbed, then gestures at me to go. I stand, worried that if I leave, June would fall to pieces on the heli floor, but she gives another annoyed sort of wave with her hand, curling around the pears as if it's just her and them in the universe. A promise of food and a place to lay her head. I have to swallow down a sudden feeling of helplessness.

"Come on, Sev." Howl's still there, waiting. "There's still a lot we can do."

Where does Howl get the right to guess what I'm thinking? I nod once, unconvinced. Then again, determination flooding through me. If June can't face down this demon, I can. That's a start.

CHAPTER 29

THE STORAGE ROOM DOOR SHAKES WITH THE VIBRATION of the secondary propellers, and my chest tightens in anticipation when Howl opens it.

Inside, Xuan is propped up against the wall, much the way Howl was less than two days ago, though his hands aren't taped together. There isn't much room, and I have to choose between being a bit too close to Howl and straddling the medic's outstretched feet. Howl makes the decision for me, pulling me away from Xuan's overly friendly smile to have me stand between him and the door, our shoulders touching.

"You don't remember me, do you, Miss Jiang?" Xuan flicks his head sideways, attempting to relocate his shaggy hair out of his eyes. When it doesn't work, he puckers his lips and blows at the stray hairs.

"Should I know you?" I ask. "I didn't realize we had a celebrity medic in our midst."

Xuan points to my bulky coat, the snaps and zipper still hanging open. "Your ribs. And all the other souvenirs you got from the

Aihu Bridge bomb. I treated you, so a thank-you for making sure you didn't get any scars on that pretty face of yours wouldn't go amiss." He crosses one foot over the other, folding his arms across his stomach. "Thought I was going to have to testify at your denunciation. Glad it didn't go that far." He smiles again. "Nasty things, executions."

I bite my cheek, refusing to drop his gaze. "I'm so glad you weren't inconvenienced by my death."

"Me too." He looks around the room with a cheerful grimace. "Don't much like this, though. If this is going to turn painful, I suggest starting with chemistry equations." He nods at Howl's First mark, the smile turning cheeky. "You can talk me to death."

Howl sets the bundle of maps down, reaches into his pocket, and pulls out my knife, running a fingertip along the keen edge. "I don't care for chemistry, to be honest."

A worm of unease burrows through my stomach. We are not hurting anyone. Either Xuan tells us what's going on or he doesn't, but there isn't going to be any blood involved. Attempting to joke about torture with June is one thing, but this . . . My thoughts freeze when Howl catches my eye. He quirks his eyebrows with a *don't worry so much* sort of look before kneeling down and setting the knife and the sheath next to him on the floor.

I refrain from scowling. What else am I supposed to think if Howl brandishes knives at people?

"There's no need for any of that." Xuan sits forward, hands out in supplication, flashing his Second mark in our direction. A practiced move that might have served him well in the City, but flaunting status isn't going to get him anything here. "The entire point of me being here is to give you information. I'm good to talk."

Howl smiles, but there's nothing friendly in it. "I think I'd first rather hear the real story behind your escape. If you don't mind."

"Of course you do. Quite daring, if I say so myself." Xuan's smirk must be hurting his cheeks, and when he catches me staring, he actually winks at me. "There were rumors floating all over the place about Hong Tai-ge. That he threw his favorite little escaped spy over his shoulder, stole the Chairman's own heli, and made a speech about how the ranking system is broken before stabbing his own father in the back . . ."

I bite my lip, willing myself to stay calm. Howl doesn't move, his face a practiced blank.

Xuan looks back and forth between us as if he was expecting a bigger reaction and settles on a shrug. "Okay, I made most of that up. But I wasn't lying before. Things aren't going well in the camps. The Chairman announces one set of orders only to contradict himself a few hours later. Masks are disappearing, breaking, with no factories to make new ones. *Food* is disappearing, Mantis, too. Not to mention those . . . *people* who showed up with Dr. Yang."

I wait a beat, thinking he means to elaborate, but he doesn't. "You mean the Menghu? You knew they were in the camp, even with City uniforms?"

Xuan blinks at me, a fluffy layer of confusion not quite shrouding the calculation beneath. "I don't know what a Menghu is. I *have* spent enough time running between the City and Kamar to know Outside patrollers weren't defending City walls against anyone from those settlements. Those Outsiders at Dazhai . . . You can smell one of them a mile away, see it in their faces, as if they gnawed the fingers off every dead soldier from here to the ocean with their own teeth. I don't know what deals the Chairman made because of the invasion, but if those soldiers who appeared in the camp aren't Outsiders, you can shoot me now. Whatever lines the Chairman decided to cross, they were the wrong ones."

"Kamar settlements?" The question seems so calm and collected, as if Howl doesn't know that Kamar is a completely fictional place, with guns and heli-planes, and soldiers created solely to make Third children and parents alike wet their beds.

Xuan nods. "Kamar's far enough away they've mostly been protected from SS, and it seemed like the best direction to head." He fiddles with the mask looped around his neck, the tubes a spray of tentacles slithering down his chest. "Neither of *you* are on the wrong side of the Seph line, are you?"

Howl leans closer to me, jostling my shoulder before I can respond in an unmistakable signal to wait before speaking. It's hard to keep my mouth shut, but I comply, the questions about "Kamar" foaming up to coat my tongue. *They're not sick? And somehow this medic has been there? If it really is the same place Mother called Port North, then why does it have two names?* "Kamar" sounds foreign and cold; I'd always assumed it was a phonetic translation that wasn't supposed to mean anything but "Outside." Different from us. Fear.

Howl keeps his eyes on Xuan, his hand sliding down to touch the knife on the floor between us. "So they just let you walk out of Dazhai. With Hong Tai-ge, who hadn't been seen since the invasion. How did you even know Tai-ge was there? Seems like that, along with anything he spilled about plans to go north, would have been privileged information."

I nod, remembering what Howl told me before about the reports asking for Tai-ge to be brought in from the Post. Tai-ge showing up as a traitor would deplete what little morale there is for those who were loyal to General Hong before he was killed. That is to say, the entire Second Quarter. Maybe Thirds, too, since Reds were the only thing between them and "Kamar."

Considering the lengths to which the City goes to keep information sealed tight, the soldiers who captured Tai-ge during an Outsider attack wouldn't have been sharing *anything*. Not if they wanted to keep their positions.

"No problems getting the keys to his cell?" Howl continues. "Or sneaking past the perimeter guards? No one tried to stop you on your way out of Dazhai?" Howls eyes run the medic up and down, as if looking for bruises.

"What can I say? I'm an excellent sneaker." Xuan twiddles his fingers, staring down at them with his eyes a fraction too wide, annoyed at the question.

"No communication devices I've missed?" Howl prods. "I'd rather you told me about them now, so I don't have to cut them out of you later."

"You've already patted me down once. You want more than that, you'll have to give me some kind of compensation." Xuan starts to laugh. "I'm not the one here who knows something about escaping, though, am I? I didn't know this excursion was going to be staffed by the great and perpetually absent Sun Yi-lai."

"We need you to give us *something*, Xuan." I kneel down next to Howl, picking up the knife and shoving it in my pocket, still holding on to the hope that it's Xuan's annoying personality giving these shallow answers and not a ham-handed attempt at deflecting our questions. My empty stomach twists over having such a large question mark here with us in the heli, listening, maybe even transmitting everything he hears. I don't suppose trust was ever on the table in the first place, not with June hyperventilating in the next room, but he's not even giving us room to make a shaky alliance. "One more chance. How did you know about Tai-ge? How did you two get out of the camp? Use short sentences. Preferably the kind that start with 'I.' For example: *I threw up hot chili sauce all over Tai-ge's guard, and he was so upset he didn't notice when we walked out.*"

Xuan transfers his gaze to me. "*I honestly can't figure this out. That Tai-ge would go off with you makes sense. Everyone knew he wanted you.*" He looks at Howl again. "But with you here too . . . You must have expensive taste in pets, Jiang Sev."

Anger threads through me, not missing his clear evasion of my question. *This* is the man Tai-ge trusts? I shake my head, scooting back a few inches as Howl jerks Xuan's feet aside to make room for the maps.

I glance toward the door, the propellers' vibration buzzing up through the floor. Tai-ge will tell us what really happened once he's not concentrating on flying. He'll clear all this up, and even if we have to leave Xuan in a closet, we'll have a solid path forward.

But then, a small voice inside me: *What if Tai-ge lies too?*

Pushing the worry aside, I help Howl smooth down the last of the papers, the seals forming bumps and splotches on the paper where the wax stuck. The lines and marks look almost like a maze.

Howl pulls out the key. "All right. Show us the information you promised Tai-ge. Tell me everything you know about the settlements you mentioned. *Kamar.* Things that might be helpful, things that won't, and everything in between."

"That I can do." Xuan leans over the papers, checking some notation I don't understand at the corners of each sheet until he finds the one he wants, then settles it on top of the others. "Get the encryption key going, and we'll start with where to land."

Howl looks up from the encryption key's controls. "I think we'll need a bit more than a landing spot."

Xuan nods. "That's for sure. When we land, I'll tell you where to walk. And after we walk, I'll tell you what to say and when to duck."

"That doesn't work for me." Howl lowers the encryption key, his hand dropping down to brush my pocket where I stowed the knife, as if having this conversation unarmed is too much to ask of him.

"Yeah, well, getting shoved out of a heli doesn't suit me." Xuan shifts back from the maps, letting his legs stretch forward again, his boots leaving a streak of dirt across the stiff paper. "And you can't really afford to push me, Mr. Chairman's son. They'll kill you the minute they hear City words on your lips. Doesn't matter how pretty you talk. Unless Blondie out there speaks Kamari, you need me. And I'm guessing that if she did, you wouldn't need directions to Kamar." He presses two fingers to his lips, giving us an ugly smile.

Howl seems concentrated on smoothing the edges of the paper for a moment before he looks up again. When he does, a shiver runs down my spine at the blackness in his eyes, as if his pupils have dilated to take over his entire iris. "If you say another word about June, you'll find out exactly how it feels to get pushed out of a heli. And if you miraculously pull a set of wings out of that dirty uniform, I'll jump out after you and cut them off."

I try to find someplace inside me to set myself apart from the dead promise in those words. But I can't.

CHAPTER 30

LATER, HOWL AND I EXIT THE STORAGE CLOSET. I
spread the maps across the floor next to the cargo bay doors while
Howl pads the outside of the door with sleeping bags to keep Xuan
from listening. June keeps her seat at the cockpit wall farthest from
the makeshift cell door, ignoring me when I call her over to look at
the information Xuan gave us.

I whittle my voice down to a whisper when Howl finishes and
sits down at the map across from me. "Xuan isn't going to lead us
into anything immediately dangerous. He'd get killed too. And if
he wanted to turn us in, he could have done it while we were still
on the ground at Dazhai."

"That's the problem." Howl shrugs. "Maybe he really does
want to defect. But maybe someone at Dazhai saw this as an
opportunity to keep tabs on us. What if I'm right and your
mother only told *you* about the cure because you're the only one
who can get it? That has probably occurred to Dr. Yang as well."

"You think Dr. Yang would have sent a Red medic to keep an
eye on me?"

"Maybe. Xuan knows the area. Tai-ge told the Reds his plan, though, so Xuan could have been sent by someone in the Second ranks as well." Howl sighs. "And then there's June."

June. I glance over at her again. She looks *emptied*. Xuan did that.

I coil the anger in my chest down tight, gritting my teeth as I turn back to the map.

"I need whatever Xuan's got. Coordinates," Tai-ge calls from the halo of lights dancing around him on the console. "And an idea of what sorts of fortifications we can expect."

"We . . ." The words die in my mouth. What does Tai-ge really know about Xuan? And underneath that question, the one Howl asked me back by the tree. *How much do you trust Tai-ge?*

With everything. But that doesn't mean I don't see his weaknesses. "Before we do that, could you tell me how the two of you got out of the camp so easily?" I ask. "The whole place was locked down."

He doesn't look up from the controls. "I told you. Xuan let me out. I've known him for years—he used to work with my father. Don't you remember him from after the bombing, Sevvy? He's the one who fixed you up."

"Tai-ge, I want to know *how*. Did you sneak out through the fields? Steal uniforms? Hide in a pile of dead soldiers? How did you get out?"

Tai-ge's just an outline against the cockpit window, the sun's light painfully sharp where it touches him. "It isn't that complicated, Sev. He snuck into the prison, told me he could help me, and we ducked past the patrols."

Howl's eyebrows are cocked, his lips pressed so tight together his mouth has disappeared. When he looks at me, I raise my eyebrows in question, and he shakes his head, long and slow, dismissing the bullet-point list of an explanation.

"Did you get coordinates?" Tai-ge's shoulders relax as he lets go of the controls, then twists around in the captain's chair to look at me. "You were in there long enough to have charted us a course the whole way there and back again."

Howl looks back down at the map, his shoulders tense. I don't want to give in to doubt just yet. Tai-ge is flying. Distracted. Maybe there's still an explanation for everything. Maybe.

"We're . . . discussing what Xuan told us," I finally call back. "Give us a minute."

Not exactly a lie, but I hate the way it tastes, speaking less than the truth to my best friend. I don't much like Howl's approving nod at my closed mouth either.

Tai-ge looks toward the closet, getting up from his chair. "Are you still worried that Xuan is going to hurt us . . . ?"

"Is there a reason we should trust him, Tai-ge?" I slide between him and the closet door.

He cocks his eyebrows. "Because I do?"

I nod, trying to swallow but nothing will go down. "We need some room, Tai-ge. Just to . . . make sure." Howl looks up, his lips pressed together tight. His mind is already made up about who needs what information. "Anything you can add about how you two met and how you got out would be very helpful."

Tai-ge gives Howl's bowed head a long look before answering. "I don't think there's much to add." There's a ruddy sort of undertone creeping up in Tai-ge's cheeks, the last semblance of good humor slipping from his face. "Are we really keeping him in there?"

"For now." Maybe if I approach him later, he'll share more. We've spent so much time *not* talking in front of Howl, perhaps Tai-ge isn't comfortable saying anything now.

Tai-ge gives the closet another long look, disapproval unfolding across his features. I pull him around to where Howl has already spread the maps down over the ground, not exactly sure how to proceed. Howl sets the encryption key down in the center of the map, a frown puckering the skin between his eyebrows, as if *he* isn't comfortable with Tai-ge here listening.

It makes me want to knock their heads together, to create a safe space where we can all just talk through what needs to happen without worrying what the other will do. I can't, though, because I know why both of them have sealed their mouths shut. I'm watching every word I say too. It used to be easy to trust what people said. I spent my whole life doing what I was told, believing what I was told. Living the way I was told.

It was built from lies.

Then I met Howl, believed Howl. About a new life, a place where even City traitors could be safe, if only they knew the way. He was at the center of it, the one leading me into this new beginning, which turned out to be an end in disguise. Now believing anything is like some past life, a whole other girl who didn't think very hard about anything because it was easier to tell jokes and play pranks than deal with the world squashing her down into the ground.

A soft purple light blooms under Howl's fingers as he turns on the encryption key, still not looking up.

I hate this. I hate that there's a shadow of doubt in my mind about Tai-ge intentions. That I almost feel more comfortable talking through things with Howl because I'm pretty sure I know what he is and what he wants. I hate not trusting people, looking sideways at everyone and everything they say. I hate that I should have been doing it all along. That there isn't a place in this world the girl I was before could survive.

When Howl sets the key down on the map, the purple light washes over the unintelligible lines, seeming to lift them an inch or so, forming a rippling landscape of mountains and valleys suspended above the paper. I can't help the lurch of excitement as I look over the rise and fall of the terrain. This is where Mother told me to go.

Where she told me I'd find family. They're down there somewhere, hidden in the swirls of light.

Toward the edge of the map, the land ends in a crescent, like the moon peeking around the corner of the Earth's shadow. Beyond that, the topographical representation slumps into flatness that continues to the edge of the map. Hovering inside the crescent of land, there's a craggy circle poking up through the flat expanse, as if the map forgot what was all around it.

Tai-ge's eyes flick over the map, and he blinks at the flat portion. "Is it still encrypted? That area needs an extra level of clearance?"

"Xuan says it's water." An ocean, like all the rivers, rain, and snow I've ever seen poured into the same container. I go up on my knees, all of me sore and hurting after Dazhai, looking down at the map. I know *about* oceans, but the flatness on the map just seems wrong. The smell of the encryption key fills my nose, a sort of chemical tang that smells like heat, though the device itself is cold.

"He's right." June's voice jerks my attention up. She's crept closer while we were talking, stopping just outside our triangle around the map.

"Can you tell us more about the area?" I ask. "Anything about their military? Walls? Populated places?"

June kneels in response, her fingers marching across the land's curved edge, disrupting the key's beams of light wherever she touches. But then she shakes her head.

Tai-ge sits next to me, his arm brushing mine. I slide to the other side of the map so I'm between him and Howl, June across from me so we can all see. "So?" Tai-ge asks. "What did he say? What are we looking at?"

"This is supposed to be some kind of settlement. Towns and cities." I draw my finger along the crescent of land, the light rippling wherever I touch until I come to rest on the craggy circle out in the water. "And this is the island where the main city is."

Howl points to notations made in a Red's spiky hand well south of the crescent of land, a knobby outcropping along the coast with hills between it and the settlements. "That's a City helifield for sure. And that"—he points to an X scratched into the space between the helifield and the hills blocking the populated area—"looks like some kind of staging area. But why would they need it?" He looks over at me, the purple light from the key catching under his cheekbones. "I don't like this. We have no idea what we're flying into."

"Kamar wasn't supposed to be real." My eyes feel dry as I explore the blazing lines, as if with so much to look at, I've forgotten to blink. "It was just a story to distract everyone in the City from who it was they were actually fighting so defection wouldn't be a problem. Wasn't it?"

"No one knows about this place." Howl looks at Tai-ge. "And between the two of us, it seems like it should have come up. Who are they, do you think? How have they managed to stay stable out here by themselves for so long?"

"Maybe they aren't as stable as the City or Mountain?" I sit back and cross my legs, leaning forward against my knees, unable to keep still. "Less of a threat. Or maybe they're too far away."

"Cities mean stability. You all have to live together." Tai-ge points at the island. "Get enough food. Have people who can fix your roof when it starts to leak."

"And," Howl adds, scratching at his stubbly chin, "if Xuan is right and SS isn't a problem there, that sounds significantly more stable than where we're coming from." He looks at me. "A good place to run if defecting is your plan. But the rest of what he said sounds like it came straight from the propaganda pamphlets the First Circle used to feed the Third Quarter. 'The invaders who destroyed our country speak a different language. They'll kill us as soon as they realize where we're from.'" He sits forward. "But why would they? The City hasn't been fighting them so far as I know."

Tai-ge clears his throat in the silence that follows. June's lips seem to be sewn shut, her knees drawn up close to her chin. She looks up at me, her eyes narrowed.

"Do you know if he's telling the truth, June?" I ask. "Reds took your mother. From where?" I gesture helplessly toward the pile of maps, spread across the floor.

"They do speak different." She raises one finger, pointing at the land that cups around the island. "I would never have known how to find my way back. Left too little."

A bubble of surprise swells up inside me, bursting with a sharp *pop*. June speaks the way I do. When she speaks, that is.

It was better if I said nothing. How dangerous would it be for a Wood Rat trying to hide in our mountains with all the wrong words stuck in her mouth? Is that why June doesn't speak unless she has to?

"Can you talk for us? Can you speak their language?" I ask, hope rising inside me. If June can interpret, if she knows more about this place than we realized, we won't need to dance around Xuan. And, realistically, if what Xuan has hinted about Kamar not caring much for City-born coming down from the mountains is true, June would be a better advocate than he could hope to be.

June looks down at her hands, brow twisted over the question as though there isn't a right answer. She closes her eyes a few seconds too long to be a blink, then flicks them back open, her green-stone eyes hard. "Maybe," she finally whispers.

"We need to settle on a landing spot." Howl clears his throat, looking over the notations to where Xuan told us to land. South of the settlements, to the west of the staging area. Right within the reach of everyone we'd like to stay away from. "Xuan said we need to get to the island. But he also said if we land too close to the settlements or the island itself, we'll be shot down."

I catch Tai-ge nodding along with what he says. "Do you know something about that?" I ask.

Tai-ge shakes his head. "No, I'm just listening."

I feel as if I've swallowed a hunk of lead. I keep trying to trust but only get more reasons to doubt. "We need to find a spot that looks neutral," I say. "Only, Xuan won't tell us more than what he has already."

Howl nods, picking up almost before I can finish. "If we find a spot with enough cover to hide the heli, we can scout our own information so we don't have to rely on *him*." He glances back toward the storage closet before nudging me. "Unless your telepathy kicked in and is telling you to do what the creepy medic says."

"No, my telepathy doesn't work unless both of my feet are on the ground and I'm not worried about people shooting me while I'm asleep."

"He isn't creepy," Tai-ge interjects. "And what's the point of having him here if we don't follow his advice . . . ?"

Howl's mouth quirks in a smile, ignoring Tai-ge. "Well, that's useless. Wouldn't you need telepathy most when you're worried about dying?"

"I use my powers for the soft and gentle things of the world," I retort. "Where cook stashed the good cookies. That sort of thing." My hand hovers over a hilly space above the settlement, blank of any notation. "What about here? It doesn't look so different from the south. No huge mountains or big signs that say, *death to all who come this way.*"

"The City doesn't put up signs, usually. But maybe they're more polite in Port North." Howl leans over to look at the spot I'm pointing to, and suddenly he's too close. I inch away to keep from touching him, my stomach clenching.

"Did you hear what I said?" Tai-ge pulls back from the map, going up on knees so he's a head taller than the rest of us. June shrinks back an inch at the annoyance in his tone. "Xuan knows the area. He knows where people are, he knows where neutral territory is, and he'll be able to get us down safely. Where did he say to land?"

"He . . . didn't give us specifics." I hate the way the lie slides so easily from my lips as I tilt forward to touch the map. My hands slide over the area southwest of the settlements where Xuan told us to go, then creep up to the north side of the populated area, the spot Howl and I were talking about. It's blank of anything but a cluster of three hills we could hide behind. Howl gives a miniscule nod. June sits back as if the decision has been made. I look up at Tai-ge. "Xuan just told us to stay north of the settlement." I point to the three hills. "What about here? Looks like it's within hiking distance of the settlements and far enough from the Reds that they wouldn't be able to swarm us."

"If that's what Xuan said, then that sounds fine." Tai-ge eyes the northern area. "We're not supposed to fly over the settled areas or the island, right?" He waits for me to nod. "So we'll come at it from the other side. What else do we know about fortifications? Walls? Guards? Do they have an army, whoever they are?" Tai-ge transfers his gaze to Howl. "Helis or guns? Mantis?"

"He won't tell us," Howl replies. "Not yet." He sits back from the map, returning Tai-ge's stare with a smile. "Torture doesn't provide reliable intelligence, for the most part, or I'd press him a little harder."

The three of us around Howl go still. I can only imagine my face is woven into a horrified sort of surprise, though June looks vaguely interested. The angry set to Tai-ge's jaw could cut metal. "Xuan is not a prisoner. He came to help of his own free will, and—"

"Whoa." Howl puts his hands up. "Calm down. I was just kidding."

"Just *kidding*?" Tai-ge's thick eyebrows both go high on his forehead, and suddenly I'm glad I left the gun June took from the camp in the snow before we took off. "You already locked him in the same place we kept *you*—"

"No one is torturing anyone." I put a hand up when Howl starts to argue. "I know you were joking, Howl, just . . . keep your sense of humor to yourself. Tai-ge, let's choose some coordinates. June . . ." She's curled up again, her face hidden underneath her arms. My heart misses a beat. "Are you okay?"

She nods without moving her arms. At least I think that's what she's doing based on the way her arms jog up and down. Howl puts a hand on her shoulder and she peeks through her fingers. "What's up, June?"

She breathes deep, then she pushes herself up from the floor, her face pink at the cheeks. Her eyes flick up to rest on Tai-ge, a movement so small I almost don't catch it. "I'm fine."

I slide over to put an arm around her. For a second I think she'll pull away, but then she lets her head hang back down. She's so small. So hard on the outside. But that doesn't mean she's hard on the inside. Coming back here . . . coming back with the very person who chased her away . . . I swallow hard, holding her close with one arm, and with the other, I point to a clear spot on the map. "There."

June leans forward, her fingers weaving in between the lines to keep from disrupting the trails of light. She points to a spot just behind the triangle of hills I picked, near the ocean. "No, here," she whispers.

"Should we go that close to the water? We don't know if they have boats, or how so much water will behave . . ." Howl trails off as June shakes her head, pointing again to the spot, a curve between two hills just before the knife's-edge drop into the water.

"It's safe there. Everyone's gone." June pushes away from me to stand up, then goes back to her spot on the other side of the cabin.

My eyes hurt, staring at the stiff lines of her shoulders, as if she's buckling under whatever it is she remembers about this place.

Tai-ge touches the spot, his mouth knit tight as if he's going to argue, but then he just looks up at me. "We have the maps that show where we are now? And the space between?"

"Yes. I'll help you." Howl bundles up the maps and the key

and takes them over to the controls. After dropping them next to the captain's chair, he goes to June and whispers something in her ear. She rolls over to push him away, but there's a trace of a smile at her mouth before he goes back to the maps and Tai-ge.

June watches me cross the cabin, sitting up when I settle in next to her. She leans toward me to rest her head lightly on my shoulder. All of the tension swimming through the cabin seems to have drained. If things could be okay with June, then at least one corner of the world isn't smashed to bits.

"We're so close, June," I whisper, worried saying it too loud will somehow curse us. The moment I begin to hope, the heli propellers will jam or Dr. Yang will materialize in the cargo bay with a bullet for each of us. "If we find my mother's papers, it could be the end of Mantis. The end of . . . at least some of the fighting."

"No." June picks up her mask from the ground, holding it up next to her face. "It would be the end of this. The end of fear."

CHAPTER 31

IT'S HOURS BEFORE THE MAIN PROPELLERS REENGAGE, jostling me from my uncomfortable sleep curled up next to June on the heli floor. Tai-ge is sitting up straight in the captain's chair, eyes darting from the heli's representation of our position and the map's glitter. Howl perches on the copilot's chair, looking into the bland coating of cloud outside the windows, uniform and gray.

Tai-ge's talking, and I catch a hint of a smile on his face. ". . . but my dad couldn't tell anyone the entire supply of sorghum was confiscated from the Third barracks out in Nanchang, because he was afraid they'd refuse to distill it in the factories."

Howl laughs, the sound choking off as we descend a degree or two, and his hand slips down to press his stomach. "Are we going down?"

"Yes. We might want to wake up the girls. We'll be going down the rest of the way in a minute, I think. Got to see what things look like on the other side of these clouds."

"I'll go over once I'm sure. Neither of them got enough sleep last night. You're probably ready to get some real sleep too, yeah? After being in prison?"

Tai-ge nods. "That was not the most enjoyable experience I've ever had. It all feels kind of surreal. Being there, and now being out here. I'm so tired."

Howl spins in his chair, letting his feet trail along the floor. "Once we're down, you'll have to tell me if it's true that General Hong convinced the Chairman to eat that red pepper jelly . . ."

". . . and ended up having to make a formal apology?" Tai-ge actually snorts, a laugh wringing out of him. "He was mortified. At least until our front door closed, and then he couldn't stop laughing." The smile slips a little, and he looks back at the controls. "I keep thinking that he's still down there somewhere. That when this is all done, I'll be able to find him and my mother and . . . everything will be all right. But he's . . . not."

I inch closer to June's warmth, my ears perked. This is more than Tai-ge's said to me about it. He's so quiet, as if displaying some sort of emotional vulnerability will just show the best place to stab. Not difficult to imagine why, unfortunately. His mother alone would have taken any advantage he gave her and used it weigh down the chains that bound him to her. It's odd to see him confiding in Howl after the tense interchange earlier, the two of them swapping stories as if they're drinking tea and throwing insults from the General's table as they oversee the City Watch roll call.

"That's why we're up here, right?" Howl says, his voice so soft I almost miss it. "To try to keep anyone else's dad from dying?"

I clench my eyes shut, dismay wrinkling my brow. Tai-ge's smile is precious, and Howl—confession extractor extraordinaire—is the one who brought it out, however briefly. I wonder if it's hard for Howl to stop, or if he's actively trying to twist Tai-ge into a new shape. It bears watching.

I untangle myself from June and stand, though she hardly seems to notice, rolling over and pulling my sleeping bag over her head. Howl swivels in his chair at our movement, and his eyes follow me absently as I cross over to the storage closet to check on Xuan. I swallow down my annoyance at his attention and open the closet to find the medic curled against the wall asleep. Shutting the door instead of waking him up for our descent feels a little too delicious, as if all the nastiness he's caused will somehow be compensated for if he throws up during our steep descent.

Outside the cockpit windows, the heli seems suspended in a fluff of cotton, nothing but fog above and below us. The floor seems to pull at me, jostling my stomach as the craft begins to slow. June sits up, her frazzled hair making her look about three times more surprised at the sensation than she probably is in reality. Howl stays in his seat, but his white-knuckled grip on the chair reveals his discomfort. Tai-ge is the only one of us who doesn't seem to mind the drop.

"There's something odd . . ." Tai-ge jams a finger into the sea of buttons, cutting off the electronic voice suggesting he turn on the heli's main propellers. "I was hoping we could glide down, like our other landings. But the wind . . . I've never seen wind like this."

I grab hold of the console as the craft gives a gut-wrenching lurch to one side. Tai-ge swears, negating the heli's repeated entreaties that he turn the propellers on another two times until the air begins to toss us from side to side. The sigh of relief that streams out of me when he finally makes the command that allows the propellers to roar to life might have been a little embarrassing if I didn't hear a similar one coming from Howl's direction.

Going back to June, the two of us brace ourselves against the wall. My stomach gives a sickening slosh. The heli staggers as we fall, slows, then falls again with an awful lurch over and over. Just as it feels as though we're diving headfirst into the ground, the craft crashes into something hard, the force of it slamming my head into the metal wall.

Tai-ge hisses a string of particularly creative expletives, presses another button, and the propellers slow to silence. Hands covering her ears, June only waits about three seconds after the propellers have given their last sputtering complaint before she's up from the floor. She goes to the hatch, wrenches at the controls to open it, hopping impatiently from one foot to the other while it unlocks. When it's still only half-open, she crouches down to peer through the hole, gives a deep sniff that turns into a cough, and jumps out.

The propellers probably notified every person living within miles that we've arrived, but there's not much we can do about that now.

I stand with my toes peeking out over the open hatch, gusts of wind blowing up through the hole in quick stabs and flurries that seem to be reaching for me, attempting to drag me out as I peer out after June. Every breath sits heavy in my lungs, as if I'm gulping water rather than air.

"I'll help June scout things out." Howl unbuckles his seat restraint, then stands up and stretches. He looks in on Xuan, a trickle of swear words leaking out before he can shut the door again. "You didn't wake him up?" Howl raises an eyebrow.

I shrug. "He looked so comfortable."

"Remind me never to get on your bad side." He bends to recover his discarded jacket, pausing for a moment to look back at me, a smile crinkling the corners of his eyes, as if he didn't mean to say it and only now realizes how ridiculous it sounds. As if what's passed between us is some kind of inside joke rather than a few cuts short of death.

For some reason, I find myself wanting to laugh along with him, a reaction that makes my stomach clench . . . but then settle in confusion. Howl has always been able to make me laugh, and it isn't as if laughing will fundamentally change our positions here. He knows that, and so do I. Maybe making Tai-ge smile wasn't part of a grand plan either. It's just . . . Howl. And the fact that his personality hasn't been swapped out for a scarier one isn't so jarring as it was at first.

What did I ever do to make you think I was okay with Yizhi taking you?

My shoulders tense. I haven't let myself think about what he said yesterday under the owl's tree. And just that one unfinished thought is hard to push aside. If it really had all been manipulation and lies, he would have marched me straight to Dr. Yang's laboratory and strapped me to the operating table himself. But he tried to get us out, tried to find another way. I'll never know what he would have done if I'd stayed. I do think he meant for us both to survive, if he could finagle it. We both probably would have, since Dr. Yang didn't want to kill me after all.

That doesn't absolve Howl of anything, though. He knew what was going to happen to me, no matter what he decided to do about it later. And nothing can change the fact that Helix—who I saw kill four people in less than a minute—shivered whenever Howl looked at him for too long.

Howl walks over, pulling his coat on one arm at time. "You coming out?" He glances from Tai-ge—still fiddling with his instruments and staring at the map—to the storage closet, considering. He lowers his voice. "One of us should stay until we've figured out what exactly is going on. If they try something . . ."

"I'll stay. I want to try talking to Tai-ge again, anyway. See if he can clear some things up." I look at Tai-ge, the traces of my friend's dimples lined into his cheeks as he fixes something on the control panel. Maybe he really believes he and Xuan are skilled enough to have walked out of the camp without being challenged. If I can help him see why everything looks so suspicious, maybe he'll be able to help us deal with Xuan.

I take a step back from the opening, keeping my eyes on the open hatch so I don't have to acknowledge Howl waiting for me to answer. Perhaps in another world, another lifetime where SS hadn't turned the land between City and Mountain to killing fields, things between us could have been different. There wouldn't have been any blood, any guns, any brands or bad dreams.

But even as the thought materializes, I shoot it down. Whatever that world would be like, we don't live there and there's no point in wishing we did. Howl's made his choices, I've made mine, and I'm not sure how far this easiness will last past getting the cure. The stones have already been placed, and Howl likes his heart beating, just the way I do. If we're at cross-purposes after this, I know what to expect.

"Well." Howl zips his coat, and I can still feel his eyes on me, waiting for something. "If June and I don't come back before dark, maybe consider sending someone out to look for the pieces? Oh, hang on a second." My thoughts clatter to a stop as Howl reaches inside the coat and pulls out a gun. And then a second. I can't help but recall the last time this happened, out in the forest. Howl bristling with weapons when I thought all we had was a dull knife.

I touch my pocket, feeling for the knife. Once again, it isn't there.

"It'd probably be good to leave at least one with you, just in case. I picked this one up when we were in the camp." Howl holds out one of the guns toward me handle-first. "Xuan had this other one."

Tai-ge walks over and reaches for the second weapon, Howl hesitating a beat before letting him take it. Tai-ge weighs it in his hand, then checks the chamber with quick, practiced movements. "Ammunition?"

"In your pack."

I hesitated in accepting the gun Howl held out toward me, so Tai-ge reaches for it as well, raising his eyebrows when Howl doesn't let go.

"I'll take that one." I hold my hand out, attempting to cut through the tension suddenly thick around us again. I'm not particularly worried about Tai-ge shooting any of us, no matter what's going on with him. I don't want him to give one of the weapons back to Xuan, though. "Unless you need it while you're scouting, Howl?" If Howl's passing out guns, I have a hard time believing he didn't keep one for himself.

"I don't do guns." Howl gives me a bleak smile at the incredulous expression I can feel materializing on my face. "Or I suppose I should say that I don't do guns *anymore*."

He doesn't do guns anymore. Sole said she couldn't pick one back up after she saw Howl shoot a little girl who was trying to escape the City with her parents. They were Reds, and that was all they saw until after the bullets had done their work.

"I've got this, so I'm good to go." Howl pulls something out of his pocket and holds it up. The knife, Tai-ge's name dark in the wooden handle. Why does he keep taking it? *How* does he keep getting it from my pocket without me noticing? "You don't mind, do you, Tai-ge?"

Tai-ge stiffens beside me at the sight of it. "How is it you ended up with that? It's Sevvy's."

"Is it?" Howl looks down at the handle, fingers tracing Tai-ge's name. "My mistake. I'll bring it back, I promise." He climbs down the ladder before waiting for an answer.

I stare after him until he's out of sight. Is Howl with a knife any better than Howl with a gun? There must be more than just the girl Sole told me about. More bodies staring up into the night sky with sightless eyes, so many that even Howl can't shoulder the burden of pulling the trigger again.

When he can help it, anyway.

Tai-ge reaches for the gun in my hand, startling me. "You really want that, Sev?" he asks when I don't let go.

"Yes. I do."

Tai-ge lets his hand fall to his side. Howl's on my team right now as much as he can be; Tai-ge's the one I need to make sure of. How to word this? *You aren't thinking of betraying all of us, are you?* seems just a bit too aggressive.

"How . . . are you doing?" I try, an awful smile twisting my mouth at just how bad I am at this.

"I'm going to make sure Xuan's okay," he responds, turning toward the storage closet. "Tell him we've landed and see if he can add to the picture we've got already."

I grab his arm, stopping him. "Tai-ge, wait. I don't think you should be the one to talk to him until we've cleared some things up."

"Cleared some things . . . ?" Tai-ge's voice stretches tight, his brow furrowing when I don't let go of his coat. "What's bothering you, Sevvy?"

"It doesn't add up." I gesture helplessly toward the storage closet. "None of his story does. He just showed up outside your prison cell, happens to know the single bit of information we need, and also wants to defect? He won't even tell us how he found out you were in the camp. We can't trust someone who is going to lie about how he dropped into our laps. I'm worried . . ." I fumble for words that don't sound accusatory. "I'm worried the Seconds *let* the two of you go. And if they let you go, let us take the heli . . . that's not good. We still don't know how they found us before, what they wanted . . . but the City or Mountain, either one, would kill us for the cure if we get it first." I lower my voice. "We couldn't even land where he told us to because it's too dangerous."

Tai-ge takes a step back, pulling free from my grip. "This isn't where Xuan told us to go? And you are only telling me this *now*?" He smooths his coat down from where I grabbed him. "You talked it through with June and Howl and then lied to me. *Me*." He stares at me, his face stony. "It's not just Xuan you don't trust."

He takes another step back, but his foot catches on the raised floor behind him, sending him to the ground. He shakes his head, mouth open as if there are a million things that need to be said and he can't think of a single one.

"Xuan risked his life to get me out of that camp." Tai-ge doesn't get up, just sits hunched over and small. It makes me feel hollow, as if I've betrayed him by second-guessing Xuan. "His girlfriend went berserk and ran off into the forest after the contagious strain ran through the City. All the camps outside of Dazhai are dealing with broken equipment and Menghu waiting in the trees. Everyone is wondering when they're going to attack or if SS will strike first. . . ." He finally looks up, his face pained. "I—I'm not sure what you want from me, Sevvy. We escaped. I was so scared that I didn't pay attention to the details. After the Menghu went on their rampage—I'm still not sure how that stopped—things were a little disorganized. Xuan and I were lucky." He shrugs. "It seems callous to say it that way. Twenty-two soldiers died, and burning their bodies was enough of a distraction that we managed to sneak out." He opens his hands in a plea. "I thought you'd be . . . relieved, at least. Should I have stayed?"

"Of course not, Tai-ge." My frustration returns, bring out the edges in my words. "When they took you, I was about one step from trying to disarm the man holding you with my teeth. The only reason I don't have a bullet sprouting from my forehead is because Howl dragged me away." I sit next to him on the floor, folding my arms tight around my stomach. "I couldn't sleep, couldn't *function* knowing you were in a cell. Wondering if you even *were* in a cell, or if they'd shot you."

Tai-ge lets out a long breath, looking down at my knees instead of my face. "I promised you . . . I'm here with you. I'm trying to find the cure in the way that seems right. Do you trust me?"

"I . . ." I swallow, licking my lips. "I trust you, Tai-ge."

He scrubs a hand through his hair and finally meets my gaze, the irises of his eyes so dark it's hard to see where they end and his pupils start. "You're so different from before, I can't tell how *you're* doing. Something changed while you were out there with Howl and June. I'm worried . . ." He wrinkles his nose. "You couldn't even sleep in the heli with Howl trapped in the storage closet before, but now you're siding with him instead of me."

There's weight here, as if me not replying will cement the cold space between us—that trust goes both ways, and if I don't give, I can't expect to get his trust in return.

Choosing words feels like choosing a match for my own cremation, unwilling and wrong. But I try, even as they ignite one by one. "Howl and I made a deal after what happened at Dazhai. He promised to help get you out, and then I realized our objectives align at the moment. He's good at reading things. At sneaking and spying and saying all the right things to get what he wants. He used it *against* me before. It's sort of a miracle I'm still alive." I look down at my hands, not really wanting to go further into it. "He's after the cure, the way we are. But he's also the one who helped June get away from the camp, the one who led us to you." I shrug. "We found space that allowed us to not kill each other. That's all that has changed."

"It's a miracle you're still alive?" Tai-ge echoes. His face clouds. "In the camp he was the Chairman's son, and then when we were navigating it was the same. A First, down to the way he struts around this place. But he had those guns the whole time. And the way he took Xuan down . . . that doesn't line up with anything I would have thought he was capable of back in the City."

A truth Tai-ge couldn't quite accept from me, at least not until the proof was before his eyes in black and white.

I wait for the next inevitable questions about whether Howl having different goals than me really should have been enough to send me out of the heli to sleep in the snow.

I don't want to say it out loud. I don't want Tai-ge to think about me and Howl. Not together. Not . . . any of the things I thought we were.

"And the camp . . . what we overheard in the Chairman's tent," Tai-ge continues, and my chest relaxes. Tai-ge is either blind or doesn't want to pry any more than he already has. "We've been fighting Kamar—or what we thought was Kamar. Menghu—since Jiang Gui-hua . . . since your mother . . ." He looks helplessly down at the gun still clenched in his fist. "And the Chairman is working *with* them. He was bowing down to Dr. Yang while they were actively shooting up the camp. There were probably people I knew there, people who could be hurt . . ."

People he knew in the camp. I can see what Tai-ge really means in the lines of discomfort clenching at his jaw. Tai-ge's mother could have been there. So close, shots ricocheting back and forth through the canvas tents, nowhere to hide.

"The Chairman knew the invasion was coming. He asked them to target specific people." Tai-ge stands up and goes to the console, laying the gun down, the weapon's metal dark like a bead of blood squeezing out from a wound.

His father.

I follow Tai-ge to the console, words clogged in my throat as I poke at the captain's chair, making it circle back and forth. A few days ago, I would have hugged Tai-ge. Let him talk into my shoulder until all the words were spent, or just let him be silent. Now, though, there's a fire in his eyes that doesn't look safe, as if touching him might result in an explosion.

"I'm so sorry, Tai-ge. Everything is so . . . wrong." What else is there that I can say?

Looking out into the gray mist so I don't have to look at my friend's unfamiliar expression, I'm completely unprepared for when he pulls me away from the high-backed seat to fold his arms around me, gathering me close. I hug him back, closing my eyes, trying not to feel the prickle of scabs across my neck as they stretch with the movement.

He buries his face into my shoulder, just where I was thinking it wouldn't fit so well anymore. "I just . . . I can't even think about it," he whispers against my coat. "It's still happening, whatever it is the Chairman is doing. We were there in the middle of it. The shots, and the dead. When I saw you standing behind that tent as if you'd turned into a ghost . . . blood dripping down your neck, and Howl just behind you." A shudder ripples up through his chest. "The whole time I was sitting with my hands cuffed to my cell door, I was worried they'd seen you. That *I'd* never see you again."

Surprise wars with memories of the horror lodged in my gut from the moment I crossed out of Dazhai, as if the world had suddenly started to deflate because I'd left Tai-ge there with a gun to his head. Tai-ge's my best friend. The world needs him in it. It's a poor sort of silver lining to our situation, Xuan locked in the closet, hundreds of dead in the City and the Mountain, Lihua waiting for us back at the Post. Howl ranging outside like a gore. But I'm glad to know Tai-ge feels the same way I do about him.

"I'm here," I say. "You're here. We're okay, even if everything else is broken."

His arms are soft around me, asking for something. Support. Peace. Until he pulls me tight against him, arms dropping down to circle my waist, then curl up my back under my coat. His cheek slides next to mine, his lips on my ear. "We are going to fix this. You and me. Just like you've been telling me all along."

I can't move, goose bumps prickling out all over my body as I try to figure out what is happening. All of my muscles scrunch up, hollowing out where his hands are touching me, as if I could somehow extricate myself without him noticing.

There are no marks anymore. I'm not a Fourth, and he's not a Second. This won't destroy his future. There aren't any rules now. This is okay. The words sound so nice in my head, so perfect and plausible.

But then his fingers find the curve of my back, pulling me tight. He inches his head back, his cheek against mine.

Everything seems to go fuzzy, a white blur of panic pushing

everything out of my head, even as Tai-ge's lips trail along my jaw, searching until he finds my mouth.

I always wanted this. Before. Back in the City. I knew, deep down, that he did too. But my branded star and his bright City future had always shouted louder than anything I wanted. Tai-ge was the one who made sure I knew it wasn't a wall I could climb. But now, all I know is . . .

This isn't how it felt to kiss Howl.

I jerk away, anger at myself a tinny taste in my mouth. Howl has done enough damage. I'm not going to let him take Tai-ge, too. If I skip kissing Tai-ge, it is *not* going to be because of . . .

A barrage of memories pounds at my brain: Howl lying next to me after a nightmare, the two of us whispering back and forth until it faded. The way he laughed over games of weiqi with June, and then stood between me and the Yizhi doors. His smile less than ten minutes ago.

I force the images away. It doesn't matter how easy things were when we were running toward the Mountain, that Howl never once made me wonder what he would have to give up to be with me. It wasn't real.

Maybe. I don't know anymore.

Tai-ge looks at me, but he doesn't seem to notice the discomfort trilling through my every vein. He brings one hand up to my cheek, then extracts the necklace from my coat: stars, ring, and jade piece. My past. The bits of me I didn't want to forget, even if they were painful to look at. My mother, the City, and him.

"No matter what else happens, or maybe just *before* anything else happens . . ." He holds the ring up, rust flaking onto his fingers. "You don't need this to remember me anymore because I'm not going anywhere. I love you, Sevvy."

I love you? It feels wrong. Not the exciting wrong of forbidden romance, of doing what I want despite what the rules have dictated up until now. Just . . . *wrong.* I snatch the ring from him, tucking it back into my shirt. Trying to breathe, but he's stealing all the air, leaning toward me to close the distance between us as if kissing me is the only logical conclusion to his statement.

I step back, brushing his hands away, forcing space between us. "Tai-ge, I'm not . . . I don't . . ."

He stops. "You don't what?"

Silence. Too much silence. Xuan sitting in the room just behind us. Howl and June outside. Port North. The cure. My head spins, everything a whirlwind of an unsettled future too dangerous to turn away from. I bite my lip and make myself meet his eyes. "I don't think this is a good idea."

He lets me pull the rest of the way back, his hands slipping from inside my coat so we're not touching, watching me try to find something other than him to look at now that my words are hanging in the air between us. As if there is supposed to be a longer explanation, a reason. All I can do is shrug, mortification a heavy weight on my chest.

"What do you feel, Sevvy?" he asks. "What do you want?"

"I can't want *anything.*" I take a deep breath, trying to control my expression as tears prick in my eyes. "Not right now. You're my best friend, Tai-ge, and I love you too. When you were stuck in Dazhai, I thought if we couldn't get you back, I would *die.* But, please, just . . . don't."

Tai-ge nods slowly, folding his arms across his chest. "Just . . . right now?"

"I don't know if it's just right now. When all of this . . . people killing each other . . . people trying to kill *us* . . ." Until we figure

out how long it will be before Xuan sticks a knife in someone.
Until I find the family my mother sent me after . . . I can't quite
get a sentence out of my mouth, can't make any promises about
how I'll feel later. I don't know if the gap between us will somehow close in a month. Two months. A year. Ever.

Even back in the City, the thought of Tai-ge and me together
wasn't real. It was this dream I had, one I knew was impossible
and stupid and all the more alluring as a result. But now, with
him standing in front of me, all those years of him not dreaming the same thing—at least, not enough to do anything about
it—between us, it doesn't even make sense. Tai-ge shrugs, folding
his arms all the more tightly around himself. "Okay. I'm sorry. I
didn't mean to make things worse."

"No, not worse." Maybe worse. Why is this worse?

Images rush together of all the times we've been alone on this
heli, suddenly painfully clear. Tai-ge sitting close, Tai-ge touching
me, Tai-ge *waiting*. I didn't see it until right now. I didn't *care*.

It's not supposed to be this way.

"I'm . . . here, then. I love you. I'm sorry about the misunderstanding with Xuan, but I'm on your side. I'm here for you. I
don't need anything else for now."

For now? I nod slowly, wishing there were something else I
could say. But there isn't.

CHAPTER 32

JUNE'S HEAD APPEARS THROUGH THE HATCH, HER cheeks so pale, it's almost as if she's turning to ice herself. It's a relief to see her, the awkward silence between me and Tai-ge suffocating. All the questions I should have asked while we were alone dried up in trying to figure out why I didn't want to kiss him.

"Do you think we're clear to start toward the island?" I ask, squatting down by the hatch. There isn't much to see outside the cockpit windows, smudged over by a thick fog, and the uncertainty itches between my shoulders, as if someone is already out there watching us. Hopefully not the people Xuan warned us about, the ones who hate anything carved from City stone.

June shakes her head, gestures for me to follow her, then disappears down the ladder.

"I'm going out," I say, not looking at Tai-ge. "Please don't go in Xuan's cell. And make sure he doesn't try to run or anything."

"You're still worried about Xuan?" Tai-ge looks up from the console. "After what I told you? Or is it just that you need to talk to the others first?"

A flash of guilt singes my chest. "Please, Tai-ge. He's a risk. And hasn't been exactly helpful so far."

"Well, you did lock him in a storage closet." Tai-ge goes back to the buttons and lights flashing over the maps. The space between us feels empty, like a cramped and starving belly, but with no clear way to put something into it to take away the pain. He doesn't look up again, staring at his instruments. "You aren't . . . doing what we did before with Howl, are you? Going outside to plan?"

"No . . . June just wants me to come . . ." I breath deep, the air whisking in from outside pricking oddly in my nostrils. "What do you want me to say, Tai-ge? You know everything I do."

He frowns. "Then you'll explain to the others. About how we got out? Smooth things over so Howl and June won't push you into keeping that door locked?"

I can't quite articulate the anger that jabs inside me. I never had to argue with Tai-ge before we left the City. Just by principle of our ranking marks, it was obvious who had the answers. But now, since escaping the City, I wonder if Tai-ge would have even let me argue with him back then if I'd wanted to. In every discussion we have—even the subjects he has no experience with, like the existence of gores—he needs the evidence to pistol-whip him across the jaw before he grudgingly accepts that my thoughts could possibly have merit. About Firsts and Seconds, about SS having a cure, or even about Howl being the person I knew him to be rather than the one Tai-ge recognized. He's let me lead up until now, let me make decisions without expecting me to fall in line with what he thought, but I know, deep down, he expects I'll eventually come around.

"Xuan is going to have to do some more talking before we let him out of there, Tai-ge," I say. "It isn't Howl or June twisting my arm. It was my decision to lock him away."

"And I'll have to do the same before you let me hear what we're going to do next?"

"Tai-ge . . ." I can almost hear my teeth grinding together, and have to force myself to stop before they break. "We're just scouting, okay? Trust goes both ways. Please let me go look at what they've found, and stay away from Xuan so we don't . . . I don't know, find you with your head bashed in."

"Right." He rubs his neck, then stretches his arms out until his shoulders crack. Then he finally looks up from the console, meeting my eyes. "Okay. I can do that."

Something inside me relaxes a fraction. "I'll be back in a few minutes."

Howl and June are both on the ground outside, waiting until my feet hit the damp earth before leading me out into the wisps of gray and wet. Rain mists down from overhead, a salty aftertaste in the air that leaves my tongue curling my mouth. Wind whips my hair so the ends stab at my eyes and cheeks. The glare of sun penetrating the storm clouds seems to be coming from a few hours above the horizon, making it late afternoon. Buildings sulk just beyond the curve of the hill where we landed, looming like skeletons in the mist. Their outsides are bleached and spindly versions of what a home should be, their insides dark.

June stops under a tree just outside the clutches of the ghostly buildings and points to the ground, a pile of what looks unmistakably like excrement at her feet.

"Are we . . . skipping latrines this trip?" I ask.

"Gores," Howl supplies. He looks around, pointing to another spot just farther into the abandoned settlement where a tree hunches over the old buildings like an old crone. "A whole hutch of them, I'd guess."

The hairs rise on my arms, memories of black eyes eclipsing my vision. We haven't seen so much as a hair from a gore's tail since we flew out of the burning City. "Is that why there aren't any people here?"

June shakes her head, a violent jerk that dispels my visions of a gore feast.

"This place was evacuated, by the looks of it." Howl rubs the back of his neck with his hand, then pulls the collar of his coat up to his chin, shoulders hunched against the wind.

I try to look through the mist, wind agitating the gray air into what looks like a torrent that masks the empty buildings beyond. "How did you know to land here, June? Is this where they took your mother from?"

She touches the trunk of the tree, fingers tracing the rough lines of its bark as if she knows it better than the lines of her hands.

Howl leans forward. "Did they take lots of people all at once or sneak in and pick people off . . . ?"

June shakes her head, pointing to the village. "They took all of them."

Goose pimples on my arms prick like needles as she takes a step toward the houses, staring blank-eyed at the ghosts of what she used to know hovering out there in the mist.

Something moves in the long grass behind me. I spin to look, almost expecting a gore's throaty song to cut through the heavy pall, but there's nothing there. I rub my arms. "Should we go extract a direction out of Xuan and head out? With the language problem, though . . ."

"We probably have a little bit of breathing room before anyone notices we're here. In this kind of cover, even if someone saw us come down, it would be hard to pinpoint where exactly." Howl takes a deep breath, eyes scrunched against the wind. "We should probably not leave the heli until we're sure where we're headed, though. Not unless you want to come out looking like that." Howl gestures helplessly at the wind-battered buildings. "Especially with gores hunting in the area. And not knowing about where we'll find people, or where the water starts."

The ocean. Is that what is in this salty air? So much water it weighs down the wind and drinks up the sun? Every gust feels like a whip against my cheeks, tearing at my hair and pushing against me, as if this storm wants to herd us into the empty-eyed settlement.

"We don't have great visibility, but we should be able to see if anyone tries to come at us," Howl continues. "Safer than trying to hike closer and hope the gores eat Xuan first. We can take a look around to see what we're walking into, get a good night's rest, and make an early start tomorrow."

"We have how many days before the helis come? Five?"

Howl nods. "Five days until they leave from Dazhai. What they plan to do when they get here . . . I don't know. Xuan seems to think the island is impermeable." He looks back toward the skeleton houses. "Not sure why. You know anything about it, June?"

June shakes her head, taking another step toward the ghost village, nothing inside it but mist and memories, and suddenly I can see scorch marks on the walls, the last remembrances of a fight years dead. Will someone come for us in the night? Whoever it is the City wouldn't tell the Red General's son, the *Chairman's* son, about?

Here we are in a place where City words and scars are enough for a bullet in the head. I touch my traitor brand, the star lopsided as if it means to melt off my hand. "Let's go back inside before the gores come out."

"Gores don't hunt till after dark." June peers up into the sky, her hair a tempest of gold. She reaches out to touch my sleeve. "Come?"

An extra thread of uneasiness laces through the discomfort already belted around me. June, who has never once had something nice to say about my ability to stay quiet, would rather have me along to scout than be alone in this place?

I take a deep breath, the briny air stinging in my throat as I nod. I can appreciate not wanting to walk through the blasted remains of something that used to be mine alone. Grateful that she chose me. She needs a sister, not a scout.

June points to Howl and jabs her chin toward the heli. He waits for me to nod before heading back toward the ladder, flickers of light seeping out through the hatch into the blustery air. The worry I once had about Howl hurting Tai-ge vanished. Howl doesn't have a reason to. I've realized he's not so much a monstrous gore. Maybe a surgeon instead, planning which bits need to be cut in order to get him to his end goal.

Still, I don't feel the need to look back as we walk away. And that by itself is enough for me to blow out the candle lighting my thoughts.

CHAPTER 33

JUNE LEADS US INTO A BANK OF TREES THAT HUDDLE
together against the wind beyond the abandoned dwellings, blocking its harsh bursts. As we walk, something crunches under my
boot. I pause, expecting to find a bone half submerged in the mud
under my boot. It would fit this murky place.

But when I stoop to look at the pieces, I find the shattered bits
of a rice bowl. June turns to see what's stopped me, her nose wrinkling as I pick up one of the shards. A faded pattern of flowers is
stenciled along the rim, fragmented characters in measured strokes
just below.

Long life. Prosperity.

I set the shard back next to its fellows in the mud.

June watches, her eyes narrowed on the orphaned fragments
of pottery in their bed of muck, but then she turns back to the
trees, gesturing for me to follow. The trees seem almost purposely
planted, a windbreak for the village that used to be here, but left
long enough that the trees had children and grandchildren of their
own. We follow along the line, staying on the village side of the

trees until the wind begins to calm, mollified when the sun begins
to burn through the veil of mist overhead.

The vegetation grows thicker before I see signs of habitation
again—only they're not the sorts of signs that inspire hope. We
step over the rusted remains of an I-beam, our feet finding scat-
terings of brick and tile mired deep in the ground as if they'd
grown up from the earth itself. A shape in the trees ahead turns
into the starved outline of what looks like it was a building long
ago, nothing left but metal ribs and spine exposed to the elements.

A flutter of movement in the foliage to our left sends a cascade
of nervousness down my spine, but June only gives the waving
branches a casual glance. It's not until we've walked on that I see a
creature there I've never seen or heard of before, thick pelt heavy
and brown and an ungainly, heavy head. It watches us pass, then
goes back to grazing.

June points toward a line forming a belt across the tree trunks
ahead. A fence, sharpened posts pointed toward us. It's not new-
looking exactly, but the posts are scored wood. Much more recent
than the ruins, or the wood would have rotted and gone long ago.

We slip under the fence, sunlight hardly a flicker of warmth
against my back as light begins to filter through from ahead, space
between the trees giving hints at something beyond. June stops as
we get to the end of the trees, reaching one hand out to a nearby
trunk, as if to steady herself. I steel myself to look as I step up
next to her, only to have my breath stolen.

We're standing at the top of a hill. And beyond that hill
there's . . . nothing. A vast rolling mass of gray nothing. Water.
An *ocean*. The weight of it pins me to the ground, every inch
of me feeling the rush of waves below us as they churn up the

rocky beach, foaming fingers reaching up the stretch of pebbles toward us.

If eternity has a face, this is it.

I crouch to the ground, breathing the salted air, fear and wonder a complicated snarl in my chest. June ducks behind a large rock sprouting from the unstable sea of pebbles underfoot. She points down the beach.

There are boats bobbing along with the waves, ribbed cloth structures sticking up from each one, like a bat's wings. Beyond them, a shadowy hulk leers at us from out in the water, like a fortress suspended out on the waves. Three craggy points mark its top, and when the wind blows a column of mist past, I get a fleeting view of carved stone and sun on glass windows.

"Is that . . ." I try to catch my breath, but I'm full of salty air, full to exploding.

June edges back from the rock and up the beach into the trees, walking much more softly now. Following, I angle back the way we came, but she doesn't follow, staring at the wind-stripped trees, the trunks bald where they face the ocean. Her eyes are full of something I can't understand. Seawater instead of the hard, scratched jade I'm used to. And then she starts walking. Parallel to the tree-formed windbreak, toward the shadowy mass of rock and the bat-winged boats worshipping it below.

"June!" I whisper it as loud as I can, picking up the pace behind her, but she dodges and weaves through the trees, and it's all I can do to keep her snarled hair in sight, her curls a golden smudge against the blasted gray-green of this forest. The colors of this place are all wrong.

She hops over plants and around rocks until we come to a path. Slows to a jog when fences crop up, and the path turns into something that almost looks like a dirt road. And then to a walk when the first dwelling comes into view.

"June, we can't . . ." She waves me to silence, letting me catch up.

I touch her shoulder, knowing it won't be enough to stop her if she doesn't want to. "But we don't know . . ."

She shakes back her curls and walks forward, every step measured and confident. "*I* know."

Emotions collide in me. Worry and fear. Excitement and anticipation. And a shadow of surprise tinged with uncertainty. June knew where to set down the heli. She seems to know this road. And she isn't going to stop.

What will it mean if this road spills into a village where the children know June's name? Where she has real family, not the adopted Seph clan she was a part of when we found her? What if in all these weeks of looking for where we belonged, she finds a place already hollowed out for her, but there's no space for me? June is as good as my sister now. Neither of us had a place, so we made a new one together.

I keep pace, willing my steps not to slow. It isn't just June who might find something that fits here. Saying out loud what I hope for is too frightening, as if by voicing it, the universe will realize I want something and take it away. Will I find people here who read with my mother's same cadence? People wearing her eyes and mouth, who can look into my face and see something other than the secrets mother hid in my brain, or the scar on my hand?

June must have those same hopes, wondering about the people who might be waiting for her. Who might see her and welcome her in because they are the same. She looks over her shoulder to see what is slowing me down, giving an annoyed sort of jerk with her chin to keep up, as if nothing between us has changed by coming here. As if nothing could.

I smile. And keep up.

When we get to the house, it's almost shocking how normal it looks. Not the materials or the shape of it—the roof is heavily sloped against the wind, and the walls and chimney are made from some kind of rock I've never seen before, one laid right on top of the other. Not like anything from the City or the Mountain, Cai Ayi's Post, but it looks like a place people live. Permanent. A home.

Smoke issues from the chimney and there are boxes set into the ground to either side of the steps that lead to a red-painted front door. They look so similar to the Third Quarter garden boxes that I almost feel as if I should don gloves and rifle through the empty dirt looking for peppers.

A chimney, garden boxes, and a boy on the front steps. He looks up as we pass, ruddy round cheeks, a shock of hair splintered down his forehead, a chunk of wood in one hand and a thin knife in the other. The boy raises the knife-heavy hand, and I flinch before he speaks, expecting an alarm, a call to arms. Instead he waves, yelling one long, drawn-out syllable that reveals two missing front teeth but absolutely no meaning I can discern.

June raises a hand in return and keeps walking. Something inside me threatens to burst, salt wet in my eyes as we pass him.

He's not afraid.

June notices my tears and rolls her eyes, but then she slips her arm through mine as we continue down the dirt path. There are more houses, each low to the ground, leaving a whole world's worth of sky overhead. One has a cluster of silvered old men chatting together over tiny cups of tea just outside the front door. A woman walks by with a young child tethered to her back. They raise a hand to us as we walk, and June raises her hand back. Another woman, perched on a droopy fence, calls out to us. June gives her a sharp nod, and the woman's slack lips twist into a smile.

"What did she . . . ," I whisper once we're past, pulled along by a cacophony of voices ahead. "Did you understand her?"

June's mouth is buttoned shut, the edges turned down. But she puts one of her hands up and measures with her thumb and forefinger, a knuckle's worth of understanding. We pass a pen housing scruffy-furred animals, their heads down in the scrappy grass. Three old women sit in front of the gate, their wrinkly fingers sliding tiles in some kind of game back and forth. It's like the Mountain all over again, a riot of color where I'm used to a monochromatic selection of people. Olive skin and sunburned pink and warm brown. Snowy hair and ebony, sunlight and polished oak.

The farther we walk, the closer the buildings are together until the road turns to a street cobbled over in stones. A murmur sinks through the gaps in buildings, the washed-over sound of hundreds of voices smashed to make one soft roar. It makes me think there must be some sort of gathering nearby, the noise breaking through the weeks of solitude and silence I've endured. Memories of infected claw their way across my brain, the last time I was with lots of people. Being dragged across the Mountain Core, my boots squeaking against the stone floor, Yizhi doctor fingers digging into my arms and Cale's pale stare stabbing even deeper. Large group meetings in the City market square back before I left it all behind for Howl's stories, the speakers crying out over the crowd for us to look hard at our neighbors, as traitors could be anywhere.

What if the reason I didn't belong before was because *this* place was supposed to be my home?

June pulls me toward the noise, her steps hurried until we spill out into a street packed with people. A smile finds my lips as the people press in around me, booths lining the road with sellers yelling about how fresh their fish is, how dry their rice, how thin their china.

At least that's what I assume. I can't understand a single word. A man thrusts a whole fish in my direction, the dead creature's eyes fixing me in a ghastly stare, the salt-and-tepid-water smell humid in my nose. The stream of words splashing out from the man's mouth as he tries to offer me a trade feels so familiar, as if all the words belong to the same page torn from my dictionary.

June elbows her way in next to me, and for a moment, I think her mouth will open, that these foreign words will appear on her tongue, but instead, she waves him away and pulls me on through the crowd. A display of cups and plates catches my eye, beautiful calligraphy sweeping across the rims in blue that turns my stomach.

Long life. Prosperity.

Not broken. Not yet left forgotten in the mud.

A grandmother toting twin baby boys squeezes past me, one of the boys attempting to grab for my unevenly shorn hair. She smiles an apology before walking to a table loaded with treats I never could have imagined. The people clustered around the table argue with the man behind it as if there is something contrary about his bread. But it's a good-natured sort of argument. As if these people grew up bantering and know what the other is going to say before the words come out.

The idea of family . . . of fitting into a place like this . . . feels warm inside my chest.

That is, until a high-pitched siren suddenly takes the air, shattering the hubbub like glass shards to an eye.

The people around us look up to the sky, not the panicked floundering of a crowd about to stampede, but with quiet questions, anxious hands reaching out to touch their brothers and sisters, children, as if to make sure they're still there. The grandmother hauling her twin boys holds them close, not bothering to pull the boys' hands away from the bread forgotten on the table, the seller equally lost in the clouds above us. June links her arm through mine and pulls me close to her side, the two of us clutching each other as we search the sky. Perhaps there is no home without bombs, without danger lurking just out of sight.

The man with the fish points toward the sea with his curved fish-gutting knife, the hulking form of the island crouching just off the sandy shore. There's some kind of movement up at the tops of the three peaks stabbing up from its stony mass, like winking jewels in a crown.

And then the scream of heli propellers.

June ducks even before the sound finishes poisoning the air, dragging me toward one of the buildings. But the people don't seem to be worried so much as confused, following the heli's progress toward them.

"Friendly!" I shout to June, grabbing hold of her shoulders. "It's friendly, I think."

She puts a finger to her mouth with a hiss, looking from left to right to see if my City-tinged words will bring trouble faster than a heli ever could. The crowds seem to be on the move, a mother hoisting up her daughter to sit on her shoulders, patting her feet fondly even as her eyebrows pinch at the heli's steady progress toward us.

I point back the way we came, the safest way to ask that we go back. We know where the island is. That's what we came for.

June shakes her head, eyes glued to the heli. Now that it's closer, I can see its scored metal skin, the gutter of laboring gears making me wonder at its vintage. June cranes her neck to watch until the buildings block its final resting place on the other side of the town. Grabbing my arm, she moves with the crowd, toward the ancient mechanical beast.

The heli landed in a field, a scattering of animals prancing away from the air-churning propellers even as they power down. A woman and two men climb down from the heli's cockpit, the machine a much smaller creature than the one waiting with Tai-ge, Xuan, and Howl locked away inside. Beyond the heli, I see my first clear view of the bridge, probably half a mile farther down the beach, a stone statue of a woman standing with her hands raised on the other side.

The woman in front of us raises her hands too, but it's to quiet the crowd. Her hair is cut to a blunt line just below her chin, her hooded eyes and olive skin looking as if she could belong to the City.

Not just the City. She looks like *me*. Even with the unsettled shifting and the cry of a frightened child echoing out over our heads, excitement fills me, threatening to burst out. We're here. I can feel it in my bones. We're going to find my family here. My mother's cure.

These people aren't afraid. Are they strong enough to fight off whatever it is Dr. Yang and the Chairman bring to their doors?

The island's sharp peaks grin down at me, its secrets locked behind bars of stone. Xuan says it doesn't matter how many helis the Chairman sends; none will get in.

When the woman speaks, her voice is lower, huskier than I imagined it would be, sewn through with urgency. She points to the clouds above us, and then to the south. There's a reaction from the people around us, looking to one another and then to the island across the thin stretch of sea.

June tenses next to me.

The woman speaks again, and the people nod along, the current of unease rippling to form waves and then a storm. She raises her hands, entreating and calm, finally turning to point to the island herself. When the speech comes to an end, I'm unprepared. She's talking, and then all of a sudden she's not anymore, heading off the back of the platform, the clusters of people around me beginning to shuffle toward the edge of the open space.

June grabs my arm and pulls us back the way we came, pushing us to go faster and faster until we're past the market street, past the house where we saw the little boy, sprinting back toward the skeleton village and its broken china. The light has begun to fade to roses and gold, the air turning colder.

"You understood what she said!" The words come out in a gasp as we duck under the spiked fence, branches reaching out to slap at my face and arms. "What did she say? Was it about Dr. Yang and the invasion? She pointed south, toward the staging area we saw on the map."

"Speakers," she calls over her shoulder.

"Speakers?" I swear as a branch catches me across the collarbone, its sharp whip stinging. "What does that mean?"

"Speakers will protect them from the soldiers coming. On the island." June hops over a fallen log and trundles to the side to avoid a hole into the ground.

"Protect them how?" Are speakers like Reds? With generals and guns and bombs? "Can you speak back? You'll be able to tell them who we are and . . ."

A wind flushes past us, stealing the words from my mouth and setting the wide leaves on their hunched branches into an agitated fluster. June freezes, putting a hand out for me to stop as she swallows down a breath of thick air, her nose twitching. She puts a hand over her mouth, fingers clamping down.

"June?" I can hardly bring myself to whisper as every inch of her goes still, as if standing quietly enough will convince the grass and vines to slither up her legs and hide her.

"Run." It's a whisper that bites. She takes off into the trees, not quite the way we came. *"Run!"*

My heart batters at my rib cage in the split second it takes for me to launch after her, my insteps screaming as they pound against the uneven ground. Hands up to protect my face, vines and long grass tear at my feet, each trying to fell me as some kind of prey. Suddenly, June's bright head disappears in front of me, going down hard. I slide to a stop, finding her on the ground, a long skid in the mud where her foot caught on a rock.

Her chest heaves up and down, her eyes wide as she scrambles up, hardly able to stand upright, as if she can't decide whether to run or to hide. She grabs my arm, fingers painting bloodless white stripes across my skin.

One breath. Two. My lungs are too full of salt to inflate. I clench my eyes tight, waiting for teeth or claws, gunshots or knives to break the awful silence.

June raises her head, her vertebrae straightening one at a time as she listens to the forest. "They're awake," she whispers.

"Who?" I ask, my chest squeezing down until there's no room left for bones or flesh or air or *anything* but fear.

As if in answer, a long howl cuts through the air.

CHAPTER 34

RUNNING THE REST OF THE WAY BACK TO THE HELI
is like dashing along a cliff's edge in the dark—not so much wondering if you'll fall, but when. When my feet find the metal ladder,
the heli's bulbous frame reaching out to welcome me and June back
into safety, my insides still won't let go. Twisted down to nothing.

Tai-ge looks up from the controls, his fingers fiddling with
the buttons and knobs as if he's done nothing but wait until we
returned. Howl stands in one quick movement from where he's
stationed by the storage closet door, one moment sitting, the next
upright as if there wasn't anything that had to come in between.
"What's wrong? Are you okay?" His eyes rake June over, then turn
to me, looking for blood.

"We're okay," I gasp, pulling the hatch shut against the twilight leaking up into the heli as June crouches near her pack. "We
found a settlement. A big one."

"A settlement?" Tai-ge stands, and his voice is a degree or
two colder than it was before. Red creeps into my cheeks as I
remember him standing so close I couldn't breathe, his hands on

me until I moved out of reach. I'm not sure now if he's angry at all of us or just annoyed at me. "There are people within walking distance? Did they see you? Xuan said—"

"I think Dr. Yang's helis are landing early." I cut him off and immediately regret it. Xuan said what? And when? Did Tai-ge go into Xuan's room after promising not to?

"They're landing now? *Yuan's eyes.*" Howl smooths a hand over his mouth, fingers rough against his scruffy chin. "If they lock the island down because they expect an attack, we'll be stuck on the shore with no one to talk to but Reds as they march in." Howl pulls Tai-ge's pack down and checks inside before grabbing mine. "Is that why you ran back? Because we have to try to get to the island now?"

"We can't go anywhere. The gores are out." I swallow the words down when Tai-ge looks up to the ceiling, his mouth quirked to the side.

Howl looks up from my pack, his nose wrinkled and his hands full of one of my undershirts. "When is the last time you washed these?"

"Get your hands out of my stuff." I try not to think about the dried-sweat crinkle of the clothes I'm wearing now. It's difficult to find the willpower to peel out of so many layers when they're the only thing between you and the wintry sun.

"No judgment. I was just asking." He zips my pack closed and gives it a pat. "Just wanted to make sure we were ready to run. And I remember you being addicted to soap, so I'm just a little *surprised*—"

"I don't *like* them that way! And you've got no room to judge. I've met your friends with their muddy hair and dirty bedsheets. . . ." I break off when he starts to smile, a response ready on his tongue. This is not the time.

I clear my throat. "You're right about needing to move as soon as we can, though. Yes, we could get stuck out here with no way in if they close all the doors against Dr. Yang, but if they're moving everyone from the settlements in at once, then maybe we can sneak in with them."

"That does sound promising." Tai-ge stands, walks over to the boxes of supplies, and pulls out a stack of clean bowls. "Shall we bring Xuan out, see what kind of pitfalls we'll be up against?"

Bring him out. Like a beaten dog from its cage. Tai-ge won't meet my eyes, won't look at Howl, either. June is still beside me, focusing on Howl at the suggestion that Xuan should mingle out here. Howl gives her a small nod, sliding between Tai-ge and Xuan's door as if he's an extra level of separation.

"Let's eat. I'll talk to Xuan once we're done. Give June some space." I watch as Tai-ge pulls out a container of leftover rice from his pack, then starts digging through the picked-over supplies, coming up with a package of dried meat and ration crackers. His jaw is set as he walks back toward me, balancing the bowls in the cradle of his arms. "Are the waterskins still packed? I drank the one up on the console."

"We filled the ones in the packs with snowmelt," Howl volunteers, hands going to my pack again as if he means to pull mine out, but he puts them up when I glare in his direction. "Still needs decontaminating, though."

"Because mine was next to my dirty shirts?" I raise an eyebrow.

"Because we didn't purify it before, and I don't feel like dying," he assures me.

June extracts a bundle of water purifiers from her rucksack, flipping the packets across her fingers.

"I understand that something makes June uncomfortable about

Xuan, but do we really have time to make everyone comfortable?" Tai-ge sets the bowls down next to me. "If there's a window where we will be able to get in—"

"Tai-ge, it isn't up to you." I go up on my knees as he walks back toward the door, June shrinking down in her spot, hands balling into fists around the water purifiers.

"If we have to leave as soon as the *gores* stop hunting, we're going to need everything planned and put together, and we need *him*. . . ." Tai-ge blinks when Howl doesn't move away from the door. "At the very least, he has to eat. *I* need to talk to him. He has to help me . . ." Tai-ge trails off, every word he chooses seeming to displease him further.

"*You* specifically need to talk to him?" I suck in my cheeks, Howl's ears wide open from his spot by the door. "Tai-ge, do you know more about Port North than we do?"

Tai-ge licks his lips. "If he has to be our interpreter—"

"We might not need him," I break in. "June can—"

Tai-ge raises his voice, talking over me. "If we need him to interpret for us, treating him this way isn't going to make things go well for us." He turns away from the door to look at me. "I told you, Sev. He just wants to escape, the same as we do."

"Maybe," I ask quietly, sliding closer to June so our shoulders touch. She's a corpse beside me, waiting. "But are you really willing to risk all of our lives on bullheadedly assuming you understand the situation better than the rest of us?"

Tai-ge's face goes from hard to granite.

"No one followed you out of Dazhai and you knew it, Tai-ge," Howl's voice is quiet. "I've seen you Outside enough to know what kind of training you've had, and you didn't use it on your way to the heli. Neither of you stopped, circled back, never even looked over your shoulders, which makes me think you *knew* no one was going to follow you. And, if you were worried about Xuan scaring Sev—which"—he glances at me—"is sort of ridiculous, because Sev isn't the type to go off screaming into the woods at the first hint of a threat—you could have left Xuan behind a tree somewhere and explained things without taking him all the way to the heli. Most of a day's hike. You took him straight to the heli, then stayed there instead of coming for us."

"Us? You weren't supposed to make it *out* of the heli," Tai-ge retorts. I've only seen Tai-ge lose his temper once, back when I first found him before the invasion. He was cold and quiet, a firecracker only seconds from bursting. This seems as if the fuse has already run out, the deafening *pop* just hasn't hit our ears yet. He turns to me. "Weren't we supposed to get rid of *him?*" He almost yells it. "The traitor . . . Outsider . . . *whatever* he is who almost killed you? *He's* the reason you have Xuan all locked up—"

"If I hadn't come, both of you would still be in that camp." Howl glances at me. "At least Sev would be."

"Okay, stop." I stand up, moving between the two of them. "Arguing isn't going to help anything. Tai-ge didn't have the map key, Howl, so it's not like he and Xuan could have left without us—"

"How can I stop?" Tai-ge keeps talking over me. He clasps his hands and sits when I stare at him, his expression sparking as if he didn't just shout me down when I was defending him. "If you believe *any* of Howl's accusations against me, then what does that make me, Sevvy?"

"Stupid?" Howl says it under his breath, but it's not a real attempt to hide what he's saying. "At best."

Inside the storage compartment, Xuan starts to laugh.

Tai-ge looks down. "This isn't right, Sevvy. And don't tell me Xuan could be communicating with Dazhai or Dr. Yang or the Seph-cursed Chairman, because I know you searched him." When he finally meets my gaze, his are eyes hard. "You said you trust me. Is that the truth?"

"Tai-ge . . ." His name feels like a rock lodged in my throat.

"I don't see why basic decency—feeding Xuan, not locking him up—is wrong when he's the reason we've gotten this far. . . ." He pushes himself up from the floor, grabbing two of the bowls. "But whatever being Outside for so long did to you, Sevvy, I'm not going to be a part of it." He walks over to the door, towering over Howl. "I'm going to go in and eat with him, if that's all right. Maybe you all should get this over with and just shut the door after me."

Howl holds his spot in front of the door, not even bothering to sit up straight, his face written over with a cocky sort of disbelief as he looks up at Tai-ge. The air is so charged it's a wonder it hasn't yet ignited.

"Open the door." June whispers it, the electricity dancing between Howl and Tai-ge dimming to nothing when they turn toward her dead voice. "We need them. I—I don't speak."

I close my eyes, hating the ghosts in her tone. "You don't have to speak, June."

"I don't speak like *Port North*. Not anymore. When we were in the village . . ." June shrinks down, her shoulders folded clear up to her cheeks. "Xuan . . ." Her mouth forms his name like a nail, the point digging into the roof of her mouth. "We need him. And Tai-ge to fly us back."

Every word sounds like loss, cutting into my chest. My arm finds her shoulders and she doesn't move for a moment, her spine supporting all her own weight. But then she gives, just a fraction, letting me hold her.

Tai-ge gestures for Howl to move. He does, though it takes longer than it probably should, and he doesn't move far, forcing Tai-ge to brush past him. When Tai-ge opens the door, Xuan's waiting just on the other side, his chin propped up on his bound hands, his eyes a fraction too wide. He grins at us, flipping his awful hair out of his eyes. "What did I do in my last life to deserve such wonderful entertainment?"

CHAPTER 35

THE HELI IS A TOOTHFUL SORT OF QUIET. STARING down into my metal bowl, grains of rice like maggots over the bits of cold potato, I wait for the first of us to bite.

Tai-ge chose a seat next to me, with June on my other side. She's the only one of us eating. I suppose June has too recently been without to turn her nose up at stale rice. Howl has moved to lean against the elevated section of floor where he can see both the storage closet and Tai-ge. He props one booted foot on top of the other, his arms casually crossed inside his coat. Xuan knows enough to stay inside the closet, though the door remains open between us.

If he threw up during our descent, I don't see any signs of it now.

"May I borrow your knife, Sevvy?" Tai-ge looks at me in a way that isn't looking at all, his eyes focused on my shoulder. "I was going to cut up some of the dried meat."

My hand goes to my pocket. Empty. "Howl still has it."

"Right." His voice is a touch too even, and my memory sparks over the way he froze in the Chairman's tent, fingers running across the slash marks forming his name on the handle. "Can I use it, please?"

Howl pulls the weapon from his coat, looking at it for a second before tossing it toward Tai-ge, the sheathed blade landing next to his knee. "What is it with you two and this knife?" he asks, his tone a little too jovial.

I'm glad for a split second, grateful he's willing to try to make this okay—and grateful that Howl could probably take the knife back from Tai-ge before he could properly stick it into anything he wasn't supposed to.

Not that Tai-ge would do that.

I blink, hating my thoughts. *Have* I changed into something from Outside, like Tai-ge said? The stories they used to tell us about Outsiders are painful to think about now, and not all wrong.

Maybe I have changed to fit into the places I've been standing. I stare down into my rice, stirring it around until it's a globbed-together mess, attempting to mix it into something more appetizing and failing miserably. If I've changed, it's only to stand up taller, to ask more questions. To be in charge of whether I live or die, because I don't trust anyone else to make those decisions for me anymore. I never should have in the first place.

"No one's going to tell me about the knife? Is it a secret?" Howl asks. "Because I kind of get the feeling we could do with a story. Maybe one with a punchline?"

"It's just a knife." I shrug off the question before Tai-ge can answer. Tai-ge picks up the knife and uncovers the blade, eyes running down its notched edge with distaste. He puts it to the dried meat, cutting it into strips.

June, still fiddling with her pile of water purifiers, pulls one free, tossing it into Howl's lap. "Your favorite."

She freezes when we all look at her, as if she's caught in a gun sight. But then she shrugs it off, turning away from us. "Lychee."

I have a bite of rice halfway in my mouth and drop it all across my lap when she says the flavor, trying to choke down something between a groan and a laugh. Howl hates lychee. I used to give him lychee-flavored water purifier as retribution for . . . what was it for? Some prank. I glance at him and immediately tamp down what was left of the laugh because he's smiling too.

"If the knife's not a big deal, then can I have it back when you're done, Tai-ge?" Howl asks. "It's been good luck."

"I'm still kind of lost on how it ended up in your pocket in the first place." Tai-ge picks up the blade, looking at his own name carved into the handle before heading toward Xuan's with a bowl full of food.

"Finally! I'm so hungry my stomach started eating itself." The sharp edge of sarcasm hasn't left the medic's voice. "If I'd known you didn't like medics so much"—Xuan puts a hand up to accept the bowl of rice—"I would have brought a gun or a gold necklace or something. I didn't know you traitors have to trade with one another just to get a bite of plain rice."

"You did bring a gun. Lucky for you, we give out food for free. Making it edible, however, is extra." Howl cocks his head at Xuan, smiling when the medic looks down into the bowl of stale rice, a few strips of meat piled at one side. He turns his attention back to Tai-ge, pointing to the knife. "And I came by that knife honestly. She let me use it back when we first left the City. And it was up my sleeve when she taped my hands together, so I figure it's your fault I still had it. You were the one who was supposed to search me." He smiles at Tai-ge.

"I thought you didn't keep things up your sleeves," I say innocently.

"Not guns." Howl cradles his rice bowl against his chest, carefully taking a bite. "We've already established they don't fit. My arms are too big."

"Or your sleeves are too small."

"Bad habit, keeping knives up your sleeves," Xuan chimes in, his mouth half-full. "Slip up and your wrists are slit. Can't tell you how many times I've had to treat soldiers without enough brains to keep their knives in nonstupid places." He waves his chopsticks at us, swallowing. "Boots is another one. You can't just stick them in there. You have to have a special . . . holder? Or maybe I mean holster."

"Lashing?" Howl supplies, giving an infinitesimal shrug when I raise an eyebrow. "You need the proper sheath, too. Boots are stupid places to keep knives anyway. Unless you're not planning to use them."

"You mean unless you're not planning to use them *on* someone. Not a quick draw, like a sleeve?" Tai-ge looks at him, face a little too calm.

Howl nods. "Right."

Tai-ge picks up a bowl for himself, fingering the knife thoughtfully as he sits down next to me. "I'm guessing you did this?" He points to the ugly curve of the blade. The sort a Menghu would carry, nothing like the dull blade it had when I left the City. "How did that end up happening? I didn't think Sevvy would give it away. Especially not to someone who seems to have rubbed her a bit wrong."

"There was absolutely no rubbing involved." Howl pauses midreach for the bag of dried fruit when I shoot him a dirty look. "And, at the time, that knife wouldn't have even cut a cake. Wait, *is* there a story? It seems like there must be or you wouldn't care."

"I'm not—" I say at the same time Tai-ge starts, "It's kind of funny, actually—"

Tai-ge looks at me, his lips drawing tight.

"You know"—I smile, as if I'm returning the expression instead of trying to stave off his grimace—"I think a story *is* a good idea. What about the rabbit in the moon, or maybe about the time we fell out of the tree in the People's Garden?" I sniff, looking around the room before going back to my bowl of stale rice. "I broke my arm."

"Great story, Sev." Howl looks back at Tai-ge companionably, shoveling a load of rice into his mouth and talking around it. "I figured the knife was yours originally, because Sev doesn't seem to be the type to carve her secret crush's name into something."

"How long have you two known each other now? A few months at most?" Tai-ge's tone sets Howl very carefully outside our group. As if it's his decision who I know and how well.

Howl glances at me, swallowing his mouthful. "Hiking Outside for weeks has a way of forcing you to get to know people, even if you don't want to." He points back to the knife. "That, though . . . seems like giving a knife to a Fourth would be sort of . . . treasonous."

I pull my bowl close to my chest, the dehydrated smell of the dried meat decorating my rice making my tongue feel parched and sandy. "June, would you pass me another potato? How about one of your star legends, Howl?" I take the potato when June passes it to me, breaking it in half in my bowl. It smells old and dank, as if it's more dirt than potato. "Less depressing."

"Enough with the sidestepping," Xuan calls from inside his room, making us all look up. "You're blushing enough for all of us put together, Fourth. I've got news for you, Tai-ge: If that knife was supposed to be some kind of romantic gift, then you are the worst boyfriend ever. She probably thinks so too, since she gave it to Howl. And I think he might use it to torture people."

"Okay, fine." Howl shrugs and gives me a knowing sort of smile. "I'll leave it alone. I do know a good story about—"

"I'll tell it," Tai-ge cuts back in, his expression when he looks at me a little too vague to be anything but a mask. As if he's reaching out to shake me, to remind me who I'm supposed to trust the most. "It's from when we were, what, thirteen? Fourteen?"

I open my mouth and close it, my throat constricting. "Tai-ge, I don't *want* you to tell this story."

"Come on, Sevvy. He wants to know. And it is a good story." Tai-ge's words come in long, straight lines like a math equation, every variable spelled out. He turns to Howl, tapping the knife against his palm. "Sevvy had a new roommate at the orphanage. A Third whose parents were killed in an air raid. She was infected during the raid and angry about it."

"Her parents being dead didn't have anything to do with it?" Xuan calls.

June looks at the floor. Even if being with us helps her feel safer, Xuan's presence here as part of the conversation itches. Every time he speaks, I can almost feel June shrink. I start to get up to shut the door, but Tai-ge holds on to my arm, keeping me next to him.

"This girl was *big*," he continues. "At least seventeen. I still don't know why they put them together. Usually at the orphanage, they kept newly infected isolated until their Mantis doses were fine-tuned. But not this girl."

Wei was her name. And it was *not* a mistake that she was put in my room. But Tai-ge never believed that the nuns would do that. That the City would do that. Not on purpose. I can feel Howl's eyes on me as if my thoughts are shouting louder than Tai-ge's voice, but I don't feel like looking up.

"I had to run down to the orphanage one night after curfew. Sevvy left some of her schoolwork at my house." Leaving something was a tradition. It was always interesting to see what his mother deemed important enough to take to me. Homework, yes. Coat, no. "But when I got there, the nuns had all disappeared. I almost left. I didn't want to get banned for running around the girls' floor unescorted."

I finally look up to catch Howl's eye, and he goes back to staring at a package of dried fruit sitting in his lap with a tolerant sort of smile. I don't smile back. Following rules isn't something to be ashamed of.

"Sevvy really did need her homework, though, and it wasn't her fault the nuns all deserted their posts. So I went up to her room"—he pauses, laughing a little—"and opened the door to Sevvy with her roommate in a headlock."

June looks up with interest.

"Now, Sevvy isn't that big, and this girl was a monster. Completely out of control. But Sevvy just took her down. Didn't need my help." Tai-ge laughs again. "So after the nuns came and carted her away, I took Sev to the medics. . . ."

"Wait, I think you missed something." Howl chews slowly and methodically, speaking around the lump of fruit in his cheek. "I thought Sev won the fight."

"She finished it, but she didn't escape completely unscathed."

Wei bit my arm all the way to the bone and broke my wrist. She wasn't compulsing, either. She had a younger sister who got a full dose of SS during the attack, but she never woke up. Not everyone does.

A new factory was going up a few streets over, building materials strewn haphazardly throughout the site. I can only imagine that some Third missed the heavy wrench in the morning, but it's probably difficult to tell in that kind of chaos. Wei hid behind the door and waited for me to come home. It was only five years of living in an orphanage with Sephs—of being accustomed to paying attention to things that seemed a bit off—that saved me from a broken skull.

Wei spat on the floor as they dragged her out, screaming back at me, "Someday you'll get what you deserve, traitor!"

It was right after Aya died. Right as I was fully realizing what it meant to be the traitor's daughter. All of the facts and figures the City had been drilling into my head for years, the kids trapped inside their own skins in the Sanatorium and the fact that just about every person I knew set the blame at my mother's feet . . . it meant I was worthless. Worse than that. I was a stain, an aberration that anyone living up the Steppe would be glad to see scrubbed away. No matter what I thought, or what Tai-ge thought, no one in that orphanage was going to lift a finger to help me, not even when my life was at risk. Every time they looked at me and saw my mother's birthmark, it was reaffirmed. I was the problem. The symbol of everything we were fighting against.

It was a new beginning. I wasn't unhappy knowing what I was to those around me. But I knew I needed to watch myself, and to watch out for Tai-ge after that. That I should have known to watch out for Aya better than I did.

Maybe that's why the idea of the Mountain felt so hopeful, why I let Howl walk me there without asking the questions that seem so obvious now. Why Port North feels like the sun behind a cloud, waiting to come out. It's a promise of something I couldn't even admit that I wanted when the City filled up my whole world, horizon to horizon, nothing but madness and violence waiting outside of it.

I can feel Howl's eyes on me again, quickly darting back and forth over my arms and legs as though he'll be able to discern what happened, but when I catch him looking, he returns his attention to Tai-ge.

"And you're right, Howl. Fourths aren't allowed to have weapons." Tai-ge sucks his cheeks in, "I don't think infected are in general. But it was such a close call . . . I was afraid the next time something happened, Sevvy wouldn't be ready. That she wouldn't be able to protect herself. I snuck the knife to her the next day. Just in case. I've always been right behind Sev, making sure she's okay." His arm, which was brushing mine, settles behind me, as if he wishes he could put it around my shoulders.

A spark of anger ignites inside me. How could Tai-ge have ever thought handing me a dull knife would be enough?

Why did *I* ever think it was enough?

June's eyes are in her bowl, uninterested in a story that doesn't end with a good fight. Xuan is against the far wall in his room, bent knees and boots all I can see through the door. Only Howl's eyes are on Tai-ge, the heli's soft lights sinking into the spaces between his knuckles and fingers as he eats one slow bite at a time.

CHAPTER 36

HOWL AND I CLEAN UP THE DISHES AS JUNE SETS herself up at the base of the ladder to take the first watch. Xuan makes a show of stretching his legs, then sits back against the wall with his head propped up against his two hands. "Do you eat anything other than dried-out rice around here? Let prisoners use the facilities?"

Tai-ge moves toward the door. "You're not a prisoner. I'll take you out."

"No, Tai-ge . . ."

He stops, crossing his arms as he looks at me. "Are you going to do it?"

"I'd rather she didn't." Xuan coughs again, crawling to the closet's doorway. "And I wouldn't mind keeping the Chairman's gorish son away while I have anything valuable out."

"I don't want you to . . ." There isn't anything to finish that sentence that won't make Tai-ge more angry. Not to mention the gores we heard calling outside. But I don't care for the idea of cleaning out the storage closet if bathroom breaks are off.

So, I stop talking. Go to the pile of supplies and dig until I find the heavy tape we used to restrain Howl. I dart to intercept Tai-ge as he extends a hand to help Xuan up and hold out the tape. Tai-ge takes a deep breath, patience and annoyance a grieved swirl across his face, but then he shakes his head, brushing the tape away. The air inside the little room tastes toxic. Not the smell itself, just the lack of space between me and someone who did . . . whatever it was that happened to June's family, with Tai-ge so firmly on the wrong side.

"We can't just let him out without taking precautions, Tai-ge," I whisper, discomforted by Xuan's chipper expression as he listens. "We . . . need him. He said he wanted to escape. This could be a good time."

"Fine." Tai-ge thinks for a second, then walks over to his pack and unzips it to reveal a set of handcuffs. "Will this be good enough? More comfortable than tape. And easier to remove once we're back inside."

"Where did those come from?" I ask. The metal swings from his hand in a smooth arc, the keys dangling from the locking mechanism. They look scratched and worn, as if they've had more than their share of use.

"They were mine, back in the camp. Complimentary jewelry for lodging in the prison. Kept me nice and close to the bars of my cell. Xuan charmed the keys out of the guard." He walks over to Xuan's door, opening one of the bracelets. "Seemed smart to keep them."

That would have been useful earlier, when we first found Xuan urinating next to the heli ladder, but saying that out loud isn't going to help anything. "Stay close enough for June to see you, okay? The sun is already down and I'd rather not have another close look at gores."

Tai-ge rolls his eyes. "Are you serious? Didn't we used to joke that gores . . . ?" He raises his hands at my serious expression. "Fine. I'll watch out for the *gores*." He holds a hand out again to help Xuan up from the ground. "Shall we?"

Xuan pulls himself up, then smooths his shaggily cut hair down across his forehead before letting Tai-ge pull his hands together in front of him, then lock the handcuffs over his wrists. "Don't worry, Jiang Sev. If I get too feisty, Tai-ge can just push me into the ocean. I never was much for swimming."

I hold my hand out for the key, tucking it into my pocket when Tai-ge hands it over. No point in sending Xuan out shackled if the key is within reach. "If you try anything, I'm just going to yell for help as loud as I can and hope that whoever comes shoots you first."

Xuan wrinkles his nose. "You aren't very good at threatening people, Jiang Sev. It'll do you good to trust someone. Maybe we'll even part as friends, with you running headfirst into whatever trouble you have cooked up and me headed toward a hot beverage."

"If only the people here hadn't abandoned this place. I could do with some tea. Do you think gore scat would make a good flavor?"

"Abandoned . . ." Xuan narrows his eyes at me, then looks at Tai-ge. "You didn't land where I told you to."

Neither of us answers. He'll see well enough when he goes outside. Tai-ge leads Xuan toward the hatch, waiting for him to go first before climbing down after him.

"I'm sorry about earlier." Howl's voice snaps my attention back to him.

"You're sorry?" I blink.

He comes closer, glancing at June and lowering his voice as if she somehow won't hear. "I shouldn't have brought that up. About the knife, I mean. I didn't realize it would be like . . . prying, I guess." His eyes run up and down my bare arms as if he'll be able to decide which of my scars belongs to Wei, the seventeen-year-old Seph who didn't deserve to be in that orphanage any more than I did. "I'm going to go keep an eye on them. Just to be safe."

I nod, not quite sure how to respond, a sorry for something that seems sort of ridiculous when measured against the hole blasted through the memories we share. An apology is an apology, though. No matter what Howl is trying to say about Tai-ge for telling it when I didn't want him to.

Things I'm trying not to think myself. So I settle for another nod. "Thanks for saying that."

"Thanks?" A smile starts in the crinkles around his eyes as he starts down the ladder after Tai-ge and Xuan. He moves over to let June slip down the ladder next to him. I guess we're all risking the gores at the same time.

Howl continues, "I wish I'd thought before handing it to Tai-ge in the tent. It was all . . ." The smile reaches his mouth, but it's sort of awkward now, as if he wished he'd stopped talking.

"It was all what?" I sit forward. Ready for a punch line after the bad memories tonight.

"It was all I had left. Of you." His eyes are a fraction too wide. An entire kaleidoscope of butterflies erupts into flight inside my stomach and up into my throat. I can almost feel my mouth drop open, as if there are words that should be in it, but it's just butterflies, butterflies, butterflies.

Until he speaks again. "I guess it's better that he has it. You don't like the tree house idea anymore, so I think we're done stabbing that particular dead gore."

My stomach sinks, and I look down, trying to arrange all the things I wanted to say into something new, something to turn it into a joke or even into a clumsy sort of laugh. Anything to negate what I was just allowing to happen inside of me. I know what he wants, and it isn't me. It might have been before. I think . . . I'm pretty sure it *was* before, at least to some degree.

The thought feels like . . . something. Like it should mean something, but I'm too afraid to look. It's clear that I've said and done enough to make Howl's end goal change. Which is good. I don't think there's room inside me to go back to where we were before. Because where we were before wasn't real.

I know what he is now. And it probably isn't something anyone should want in their life permanently.

Before I can force any words into some sort of acceptable reply, June gives a shout from below. "He's running!"

Howl's down the ladder before I can surge to my feet, but I'm only a breath behind once I hit the ground. Xuan and Tai-ge are already hidden by the heavy fog swirling up to lick my ankles. Howl takes off into the mist, and I can only follow, hoping he can read the ground and the trees, and find Xuan's trail.

It's not until we've passed the first row of emaciated dwellings that I spot a dark form lying in the grass. Howl skids to a stop, already on his knees by Tai-ge's side with a hand around his wrist checking for a pulse. I crash down next to him, my hands finding Tai-ge's hair, his forehead, and there's blood in scattered droplets on my fingertips. Scarlet against the pale cast to his face.

A haunting cry sneaks up through the curling mist. Goose pimples on my arms prick into knives as the cry ends in a chilling cackle.

A gore's hunting call.

"Tai-ge's alive. But Xuan may not be for much longer. Stay here." Howl's off before I can respond, ghosting into the maze of houses, their wasted remains closing around him like skeletal claws.

It couldn't have been a gore that hurt Tai-ge. Of course not. There would be more blood and less of my friend. My hands shake as I tear a length of fabric from Tai-ge's tattered shirt and press it to the gash in his head. I look out into the mist. Where's Xuan? We can't lose him. Not if he's our only chance to talk our way into Port North. June materializes out of the mist, her feet hardly touching the ground as she runs to my side.

Tai-ge's eyelashes flutter, his brown eyes glazed and unfocused when they open. "Sevvy?"

"Take him back, June. I'm going to help Howl." Another howl slashes like a razor against my eardrums, freezing my hands on Tai-ge's bloody forehead. June shoves something heavy and metal at me before pulling Tai-ge up into a sitting position. It's a gun.

"Go!" she yells.

I stumble to my feet, momentum almost throwing me back to the ground until I find my stride and run in the direction Howl went. But there are gunshots going off in my head and Parhat's on the ground in front of me, blood dripping down his nose. And gores are charging into a Red-filled clearing in the forest, bullets burning smoking trails in the beasts' thick pelts. Kasim, Howl's best friend, lying helpless on the ground, blood littering his unconscious form as they tear a man apart right over him. The real world is a blur, the scratch of dry grass against my ankles, rocks catching at my boots. I can hardly see anything in front of me, tears streaming down my face as I run. But I do run until Howl's shape rears up in front of me in the dark.

He waits a moment for me to catch up, then sets off again. My lungs burn and I duck under branches and through scrub that's too wet, too green even in the feathered gray of twilight. The air feels soggy and wet in my lungs, molding my insides as I choke down each breath. Howl darts between two of the weathered houses, and a shout rings out before I get around the corner. My side catches on splintered wood because I turn too sharply, almost tripping over Howl. He's on top of Xuan, knees digging into his back. The handcuffs glint silver, shoved into the dirt over Xuan's head.

Another of the awful baying howls shudders through the houses ahead of us. And then another off to my right. "It's too late. I thought it would be the Kamari who killed us, landing here. But I chose the wrong moment to escape." Xuan's voice sends chills down my spine, dry and raspy, like dead leaves rustling. "I guess none of us win."

"Get back to the heli!" Howl yells at me.

"You get off me. I'm going to run. I'm better off with the gores than you." Xuan gulps. "I think. But if I have to get eaten, I won't complain if you stay out here and get eaten too."

My gaze drops down to Xuan's hands, and I grope through my jacket pocket to find the key I just zipped inside it. My fingers are slippery with sweat, glancing off the other odds and ends shoved into my pockets. When the key finally comes out, another beastly wail jerks my head out toward the line of houses to the left of us. Gores hunt in packs. Come at their prey from more than one side. How long before they get here?

"What are you doing, Sev?" Howl yells. "Get out of here! I can bring him back!"

"Get off him!" I growl back. Howl doesn't move off Xuan's back until the key clicks into the lock, opening one side of the cuffs. Xuan shakes his hand free, swearing at me when I clap the empty bracelet over my own wrist.

"What did you do that for?"

"We need him. We need him to translate for us, or we'll never get the cure," I say.

Howl grabs my wrist and drags me up from the ground, barely giving Xuan time to find his feet before beginning to run. Xuan stumbles as we take off, wrenching me back, though he follows rather than waiting to be torn apart the way he threatened.

The gores' teeth-chattering wails are bearing down on us from two directions now, immediately behind and now off to my right, though the silence seems to crackle along my left side as we sprint. Howl pushes me and Xuan to go first, keeping up just behind us, the howls seeming only to be a few steps behind him.

The heli looms like a great beast up ahead, shadowy and vague except for where cockpit lights pierce the mist. Xuan keeps pace beside me, our arms tangling us with every stride. He groans just as I'm about to give a shout of relief. We're only twenty feet from the ladder when I turn to look over my shoulder for Howl.

He's there. Only twenty or so feet behind him there's a streaking blur of shadow, the last bits of sunlight seeming to burn in its black eyes. A gore.

The ladder is only a few yards away. Only a few steps. But the sound of paws brushing over the loamy earth lopes up behind us, the loud huff of a charging predator eating away at my ears. A huge weight slams into me from behind, a dead pulse of fear blocking everything out but the press of dirt against my face when I hit the ground. Stripes of burning pain cut into my back, everything silent in the panic of finding myself pressed down into the grass with one arm trapped under me. When sound catches up to me, snarling yips pierce my eardrums, each violent bark puncturing the air. Xuan is next to me on the ground, his eyes full of something too terrible to articulate.

A clear window appears in the terrified frenzy controlling my brain. *You aren't dead. Do something.* My trapped arm has a lump pressing into it.

The gun.

A whining yelp rips through the air, raising goose bumps all over my body, but the weight lessens for a moment. I take the opening, throwing myself over, bringing the gun up, my finger groping for the trigger.

It isn't a gore on top of me. It's Howl, his back to me, wide frame dwarfed underneath the monster towering over us. Long yellow teeth frame the mouth gaping open above us, black tongue arching as the creature screams, a reek of long-rotted meat enveloping me. Blood drips down its muzzle and lower jaw.

Before it can bite, I bring my arm around Howl and pull the trigger, the explosion of sound seeming to crack my skull, the gun kicking my hand back with a violent jolt. The bullet catches the gore in its high, hyena-like cheekbone, but glances off. Lurching back, the gore swipes at its eye and muzzle with a gargantuan paw. Howl lunges forward as it recoils, one of his hands jamming up under the beast's jaw. The gore squeals, then pounces on Howl.

The sound of more gunfire hardly penetrates through the blood rushing through my ears. I have to get to Howl, my whole body crying out as the world starts to turn over, flashes of movement blurring everything in front of me to slashing strokes of color. Xuan's dead weight pulls me down to the ground in a pathetic crawl, tugging at my tethered arm as I fight to reach Howl, trapped in the gore's embrace.

Another shot splinters from the heli's direction. The gore goes eerily still, turning its black gaze on me, one of its eyes a red, chunky mess oozing down its cheek. I freeze, hypnotized by the intense one-eyed stare. When the gore's snarl-wrinkled snout relaxes, it falls, the whole of its powerful shoulders and destroyed head slamming down directly onto Howl's limp form.

CHAPTER 37

HANDS GRASP MY SHOULDERS, FORCING ME TO LOOK up. It's June, her eyes hidden under a worried scowl. Half a second of inspection later, she gives a jerky nod and rushes over to Howl and the dead gore on top of him. Another baying cry rips through the air over us. More gores are coming.

The pull from Xuan's handcuff suddenly changes direction as he charges after June. My hands ball into fists, ready to pull our shackled hands behind him, jump on his back, or raise my gun and shoot until he stops trying to attack. But instead of lashing out at June, he tugs at the gore's hulking shoulders, attempting to pull the creature's dead weight off Howl. Tai-ge appears next to me, moving with an almost drunken slowness, our hands twisting deep into the mottled brown-and-black fur to help move the monster.

I can hardly look when the gore finally rolls off Howl. It seems impossible that he could still be alive under the dark wash of red thick across his skin. He doesn't move, staring blankly at us.

June kneels, tugging at one of his shoulders, but Xuan pulls her back. "We can't pick him up." His voice is eerily calm. "If his back or neck is injured—"

"Then he's dead anyway." June doesn't let him finish, another gore's awful cry echoing out from the trees as if to punctuate the sentence.

Together we lift him, June at his feet, Tai-ge and Xuan at his shoulders and torso, with me bracing Howl's neck, walking backward to get him to the heli. One of his shoulders is a bloody mess, a jagged hint of his collarbone stabbing up through his skin. Howl stares up at me as we rush him toward the heli ladder, eyes seeming almost black against his ashen skin.

When we get to the ladder, it looks impossibly tall, a climb I hardly even thought about five minutes ago suddenly an insurmountable barrier. Movement in the mist flickers out from the odd scrubby trees, twisting fear through my chest. We don't have time to figure out how to get Howl up into the heli.

A shudder runs through Howl and he blinks, finally tearing his eyes away from my face. He jerks one foot away from June, and she sets the other on the ground, Tai-ge and Xuan lowering the rest of him to the grass. The handcuffs pull as I try to help him sit upright.

"We have to get you inside," I say. We're so close, I can't see anything but Howl's blanched skin, feeling his whole frame shake as if it's *my* muscles shuddering out of control. But he nods.

Slowly, painfully, he rolls onto his knees, his bloody, broken shoulder slumping to one side. I pull his good arm over my shoulder, groaning at his weight as we walk to the ladder. Xuan helps from the other side, carefully pulling here and there without touching the broken clavicle, or Howl's arm dangling painfully down. June snakes up the ladder past us, stationing herself at the top, where she can pull at Howl from above. The gallop of Howl's heart raps out through his side, the beat too fast, too hard. He attempts to link one arm through the first rung and use it to leverage himself up, and Tai-ge lodges himself beneath Howl, half climbing, half carrying him up from the ladder as June pulls from above.

Feeling useless, I try to stay out of the way to allow the two of them to get him the rest of the way into the heli. The world feels too close, Tai-ge's boots in my face when he climbs above me, Xuan and the handcuff pulling at my wrist as we bend and crawl all over each other trying to get inside. When my head clears the hatch, all I can see are Howl's boots lying on the stained carpet.

"Shut the hatch," Xuan orders once we're in, crouching next to Howl's side. "And someone get me towels. Something clean to stop him bleeding. And water. And where's your medikit?"

The length of chain between the cuffs pulls as he leans over the jagged edges of the wound. Howl thrashes away, his breaths coming in a hyperventilated frenzy as he tries to put space between himself and Xuan. June hovers protectively over his bloody shoulder, her fists clenched.

"You stay away from him!" I shove myself between Xuan and Howl. Tai-ge stands next to me, medikit in one hand, gun in his other, the barrel pointed at Xuan's chest.

"Move." Xuan's voice is cold, shattering my panic into a thousand fizzing pieces. But when he tugs on the handcuff to encourage me to obey him, it's gentle. "You want him to live, then get out of my way. I'm a medic, remember?"

"That just means you know what will kill us fastest. It wasn't a gore that knocked out Tai-ge."

Tai-ge holds the medikit out to me, keeping the gun trained

on Xuan's chest. "He attacked me and ran. I didn't even hear the gores until after June came."

I grab the medikit, but I can hardly look at the gash in Howl's shoulder, the gouges cutting through his shirt and across his chest. Blood soaks into the carpet from his arms and hands, like a sponge being squeezed out. One of Howl's hands twitches toward mine, fingers curling around my wrist, his knuckles banging against the medikit's metal case. I could help people at the orphanage. Clean up cuts and bruises. I've set broken bones. But this . . .

Xuan's finger jabs toward the long gash in Howl's shoulder, the bone peeking up through the open flesh. "If we don't get him taped shut, he's going to bleed to death."

Howl moans, the first sound he's made. His grip around my wrist is getting tighter by the moment. "If you hurt him . . ." I close my eyes and move to the side, letting Xuan pull the medikit away from me. He barks at June to get him a waterskin and something clean to stanch the bleeding, ignoring June's features twisted over in fear and anger as she goes. His hands pick through the different bandages and packages in the medikit, my stomach squirming when he comes up with a short blade. After everything Howl's fought in his life, is he going to die with a Red's hands inside of him?

Xuan rejects a blanket, a dirty towel, and June's mussed sleeping bag, finally accepting two clean shirts June stole from Tai-ge's pack as suitable. He presses one against the gash that tears through Howl's shoulder and back, then hands the other shirt to me to stanch the blood trickling from the cuts running the length of Howl's arm. Taking the rejected sleeping bag, June drapes it over Howl's legs, rearing back when he kicks it off, jostling himself onto his side. Xuan firmly pushes him back to the floor.

"Would you try to keep him still, Blondie?" Xuan nods to June. She freezes, a stone-faced expression flashing across her features, but it only lasts for a second before she's kneeling by Howl's head. Xuan twists all the air out of the waterskin, then keeps twisting until it bulges with pressure. He pulls back the now-bloodied shirt, jabs a hole in the bottom of the waterskin with the blade, then sprays the hard stream of water into Howl's blood-black wounds. Howl flinches away from the strong bursts of water, June trying to hold his head still. I sit down next to her, my free hand on his unmarked shoulder to try to keep the rest of him from moving, the other following Xuan around as he ransacks the medikit, spreading the white-packaged medical supplies all over the floor around him.

"Could you please unlock these?" Xuan growls, giving the handcuffs an annoyed shake. "I'm sure you're very nice and all, but I'd prefer to work without the extra limbs, thank you." He finds the package he was looking for, breaking the plastic and extracting a syringe and what I recognize as a vial of sedative.

I pull my free hand back from Howl's shoulder. Search my jacket pockets. Then my pants pockets. I come up with three pieces of old paper, a single white bean. No key. "I must have dropped it."

Xuan pauses, a funny sort of grin flashing across his mouth. "If karma were instant, I'd be the prime example." He pulls some kind of tape from the piles of supplies on the floor, lodging it in the wound in a way I don't understand. Bandages come next, more tape, until Howl looks as though he's more bandage than human.

It's easier to look at him now that the awful broken pieces of him are hidden, only the scratches on Howl's chest and arms still visible. The gouges in his arms run from shoulder to wrist, as if

Howl dragged his arms along the points of the monster's teeth without being bitten. His tight hold around my wrist slackens as the drugs take hold, but I don't want to let go, threading my fingers through his. Red, white, red.

Howl, who I've only ever seen taking charge, running, fighting, arguing, smiling and joking . . . he's limp, curled between me and June. Small. Broken. Unforgivably mortal.

CHAPTER 38

WHEN HOWL'S EYES CLOSE, XUAN MOVES TO THE slashes across his chest, moving slower now as he cleans them out. He smears ointment across the gore-torn skin, then tapes it closed. Xuan looks at me once it's done and lets out a breath that seems to have been trapped in his lungs. "So, is this going to be permanent?" He raises our cuffed hands.

I start checking my pockets again, but slower this time. I know the key isn't here. And the fact that there's no key means Xuan can't try to run away again. At least, not without me.

"I must have done something awful in my last life to deserve all of this." Xuan tiredly drags a hand down the side of his face, leaving a smear of blood across his forehead. "Though I suppose being handcuffed to a pretty girl is a fun result." He cocks his head, looking at me. "You are a bit dirty, though."

I look down at Howl's still form. "Is he going to be okay?"

"I can't do much more. Not without a full medikit." Xuan gestures for June to pull back from Howl's head. "I'm going to wash his arms and bandage them up. Maybe we can move him into the storage room after that? Wouldn't want anyone to trip over the Chairman's royal son."

The joking tone grates. He takes a hint from my silence and doesn't say anything else until Howl's blood-streaked arms are clean, bandages covering the ugly red gashes.

Tai-ge hesitates before slipping the gun back into his coat, then kneels to help us move Howl into the storage room, leaving a soggy reddish-brown blur on the floor. I hold his head steady as we lift him up, making sure to keep it from hitting when we set him down on the cold floor. Tai-ge steps back into the doorway, watching as we pull blankets over Howl. With June crowding in next to Howl's head, Xuan and me to either side of him, there isn't enough room for Tai-ge in the little room. He stares down at Howl for a second, his eyes jarring to a stop on my hand on Howl's, then turns to leave, blood a dried trickle of black down his temple.

Once Howl's bandage-drowned form is situated on a sleeping bag, I can't seem to move, staring down at his ashen cheeks. Xuan stands up, pulling my wrist along with him. "You got some love too, Miss Jiang." He points to my back. "Shall we fix you?"

I blink, my brain blank. But then the memory of pain in my back registers. Whatever the gore did to me, I can't feel anything now. My hand, still knit with Howls, doesn't seem to want to let go. What if the moment I stop watching, Howl forgets to inhale?

"Come on." Xuan gives my wrist bound to his a tug. "Sitting here isn't going to help anyone. But those claw marks in your back will probably turn nasty, and I don't do nasty, no matter what promises I made when I became a medic. I'd rather let you decompose than drain *anything*."

I shudder at an image of slash marks black and festering across

my spine. June sits on the other side of Howl, her eyes tracking
Xuan as if she's some kind of animal, ready to attack if he makes
the wrong move.

"I don't mean to pull rank or anything, but I'm a medic. A
Second to your Fourth." Xuan's voice is too calm. The one I used
to use with orphans crying off the last vestiges of a compulsion.
"Let me help you."

"You hurt Tai-ge. Are you going to bandage my back or make
the cuts wider?"

Xuan makes a face. "You and Sun Yi-lai didn't have to come
after me."

"I can truthfully tell you it wasn't with your benefit in mind."

"Then I guess you're going to have to trust I don't go for the
flesh-eating bacteria samples that come with every City medikit."
Xuan waits for a second as if he's expecting a laugh and looks
down at the floor when it doesn't come. "I wasn't trying to kill
Tai-ge. You landed in the wrong place, on Kamari-controlled land.
If you were trying to . . . I don't know, make it so I couldn't trap
you somehow by landing somewhere other than where I told you
to, it didn't work. I figured arguing would just bring that knife a
little closer to my throat, and that maybe there wasn't even *time* to
argue anymore by the time I realized where we were. If they find
us out here alone . . ." He sighs and scrubs a hand through his
hair. "Trusting one another doesn't have to be this hard. I'm still
alive, when I should probably have gore teeth sticking from my
abdomen. I'm out here away from all the megalomaniacs playing
Ping-Pong with SS bombs. The least I can do is smear anmicro on
your back."

Something inside me unbends, remembering Howl with his
wrists taped together. *I want to live through this, just like everyone else.* I

can't begrudge Xuan the same wish. It's difficult to untangle my fingers from Howl's, blood sticking our fingers together. When I reach out to touch June's shoulder, she shivers. "Stay with him?"

June pulls her gaze down from Xuan to look at me, weighing something. She nods, then reaches for Howl's empty hand, holding it between her two small ones.

"Thanks."

It's a bit of a dance for Xuan and me get out of the room linked together the way we are without stepping on Howl or June or just falling over, but we manage to get back to the cockpit without any wounds. Tai-ge stands up from the captain's chair as we come out, hand reaching for the gun on the console. Xuan puts his hands up, dragging one of mine up next to his in the air, the short chain linking our handcuffs together clinking.

"I'm not going to hit anyone else, I promise." Xuan smiles, but there's no humor in the expression. "Just want to make sure your traitor friend here hasn't been cut in two."

Tai-ge's eyes coldly weigh the length of metal binding my wrist to Xuan's. "How did you two end up like that?"

"She really, really likes me. That's what." Xuan flinches when Tai-ge pulls the gun from the console, letting it weigh his hand down. "I'm sorry. We had a deal. I broke it."

Discomfort boils up inside me. What deal? Tai-ge didn't mention a deal.

"You *attacked* me. You promised to lead us into the city and help us—" Tai-ge starts.

"Yes, but certain members of . . ." Xuan swallows whatever he was going to say at a black look from Tai-ge. "You're right. Your friends were right not to trust me." He flicks his head toward me. "I'm even more of a coward than you or anyone else thought. I'm going to patch your friend up, and I suggest you move the heli while I'm doing it. To the hills east of the Kamari city."

The expression shadowing Tai-ge's face makes my stomach wriggle uncomfortably, as if I just discovered my insides are home to a nest of cockroaches.

"If we take off again, we're stuck." Tai-ge rubs his forehead, flinching when his fingers get too close to the blood cutting across his temple. "Only enough fuel to get off the ground one more time. And I'm assuming Howl isn't up to walking all the way back to the City." He meets my eyes. "Unless this is the excuse you've been looking for."

The excuse I've been looking for? My hand goes to my stomach, everything crawling inside. We were going to leave Howl behind. Leave him in the exact spot he's lying right now, locked in the storage room for Reds to crack open like a nut.

"He just saved my life, Tai-ge." I barely have the voice to say it. "Probably yours, too, since he found you before the gores did. And you want to leave him out there for them?"

Tai-ge can't hold my gaze, biting his lip.

"Well, if we can't take off . . ." Xuan waits for a second, his head cocked toward Tai-ge. "Would you prefer to shoot me before or after I clean up Ms. Jiang's back? And, if it's after, would you mind putting that down?" He points to the gun. "I'm very easily distracted."

Tai-ge looks down at the weapon, then back at us. He sets it carefully on the console, keeping his back to the window. He's so careful about it, I wonder what it is outside that he doesn't want to look at. The dead gore? Hard proof that Tai-ge once again didn't listen, that the world is a bit larger than he realized.

"If you please, Ms. Jiang?" Xuan beckons to the floor.

The back of my shirt hangs in tatters, slashed open to leave the front ballooning around me in an uncomfortably breezy way. Xuan has me lie on my stomach, feet stretched toward Howl's door, my head cradled across one arm, the arm linked to the medic awkwardly pulled up behind me as he crouches next to me. Pain splashes down my back as Xuan sprays the cuts out with another of the waterskins.

"You're lucky. These aren't from the gore." Xuan's voice is muffled, as though he's chewing on the inside of his cheek as he works.

I grit my teeth through the sting, skin crawling as his fingers trace the arc of the cuts across my bare back. "What else would they be from?"

Tai-ge's voice makes me look up. "Howl. He knocked you down." He twists back and forth in the captain's chair, now studiously avoiding looking at me as well as the window. "The gore was going for you, Sevvy, and he . . ." Tai-ge shakes his head. "I've never seen anything like those things. Never. I don't even know how I held my hand steady to shoot it."

"It came after *me*?" Everything inside me is stone. Heavy, cold, impenetrable, as if I couldn't absorb information even if I drilled it in. My thoughts won't seem to focus, flitting from Tai-ge's paled expression to the slashes of pain on my back to Howl lying limp in the storage closet.

Sole said if it ever came to a decision between my life and Howl's, he'd choose himself.

So why is he lying half-dead in the storage closet right now when I'm out here with barely a scratch?

The ointment feels like ice, goose bumps prickling all the way up my neck and down my spine as Xuan slathers it across my skin, then sets cool lengths of bandage across the cuts and tapes them down.

"I don't know how Howl jumping on you would have slashed up your back," Xuan muses as he pats the last of the tape down onto my skin. "Unless he's wearing a studded bracelet or something. These cuts look like they came from a blade." He tugs at the edge of my destroyed shirt. "Not to mention this fantastic alteration to your shirt."

I could put on a dirty shirt from my pack, I suppose, but with my hand linked to Xuan's, I'm not sure how I would get it on. He pulls me up from the floor, a bandage crinkling the skin on my back, and I try to ignore the way my tattered shirt hangs around me. I turn toward the storage closet, the door open only a sliver. All I can see is one tiny wedge of June, curled around Howl's head and whispering in his ear, though his eyes are closed.

"It isn't going to be enough." Xuan's voice is too quiet, the cuffs clanking between us as he whispers. Information meant only for me. "Not with gore teeth."

"I thought you said it wasn't gore teeth." I crane my neck around trying to look at the bandage on my back and end up going in a circle with the handcuffs looped all around me.

Xuan shakes his head. "I mean your pal in there. Sun Yi-lai."

"His name is Howl."

"Sure. Howl. If only I had a throne to sit on, I'd think up a cute nickname too. Whoever he is, that shoulder wound is bad enough without the right supplies, but with gores . . . They'll eat anything. Humans, animals, even things that have died from sickness or poison. There's no telling what is in those wounds." Xuan pulls against the handcuff, twirling me around so I'm not caught between my own hands, but it's gentle. "When I was stationed in the camp south of here, they'd use poisoned lures to try to get gore numbers down, and it didn't work so well. They would just eat the bait, the chemicals would stay in their mouths and in their systems . . . I've seen more than one soldier walk away from a dead gore with not much more than a scratch, then die from exposure to whatever was caught in its teeth."

"What do we need to do, then?" I whisper. "Is Howl going to . . ." I don't want to say the word. Out loud, it might come true.

When the sentence doesn't end, Xuan shrugs. "It might have been a healthy gore. But if not, your medikit doesn't have the stuff to treat it. Flesh-eating bacteria and all."

Fear swirls in my chest, Howl's face swimming in my sea of consciousness, chalky white. My thoughts seem hot and cold at once, everything tasting of tears.

It's going to come down to one of you. That's what Dr. Yang said to Howl, the most damning thing of all that happened between us. He said that he knew it. That he knew what was waiting for me when we got to the Mountain. If I weren't there for Howl to hide behind, Dr. Yang would've killed *him*. I was a buffer. His way to get back home.

But it was only hours after the doctor reminded him one of us had to die that Howl asked if I was game to leave. If I was brave enough to find my own way Outside, away from the rules and the expectations and the danger. To go live in a tree house, high enough that gores and Sephs would never find us. If I'd walk away—escape—so we could be on our own team.

He wanted to survive. Wanted me to survive too, if he could swing it.

I'm not going to let him die. He doesn't deserve it. The thought surprises me, as if it's been hiding deep inside me behind all the bluster and anger. All I can see when I close my eyes is his outline between me and a jagged circle of fangs. The gore came after *me*, not him. He could have run. Could have stayed back, gotten to safety once the gore was occupied. But he didn't. He took my spot inside the gore's jaws.

All I can see is Howl, the survivor, who may have just killed himself saving me.

I walk into the little room and shoo June out, bending Xuan in half so we both fit next to Howl. Xuan grumbles a bit, but it isn't long until sleep drags his eyelids down, lengthening his breaths into an annoying snore. Howl doesn't wake when I sit up, his skin too hot under my fingers as I search his pockets. I find a gore tooth, the same one he gave me back in the Mountain. The one his brother hollowed out and put on a necklace, that Sole couldn't keep her eyes off. The communication link is inside.

Purple light stings my eyes as I write out the message to Sole explaining what happened. When I'm done, I lie down, squashed between Howl's bandages and Xuan's snores, the link clutched in my fist. Waiting for the slight vibration that will mean Sole can help me. That she'll know some way to fix this.

"Howl." My whisper is rough and worn. "You can't . . . you can't survive June and Tai-ge *shooting* you, only to be taken out by little scratches like these." I stare straight ahead, cringing every time Xuan exhales in my face. I can't force myself to turn over, can't look at Howl, his chalky pallor, his bandages already showing blotches of red. My eyes burn, tears salty and wet on my cheeks.

I take a ragged breath, his side scorching hot against my back "Just please don't die," I whisper. "I don't want you to die."

CHAPTER 39

NO DREAMS OF GORES' YELLOW TEETH TONIGHT. No Parhat, Liu, or Tian, their faces black with blood, or Helix and his long spidery fingers as he grasps at his gun. No Cale with her hair a halo of fire, no infected billowing from the Third Quarter like a cloud of smoke.

Instead I dream of Howl and me siting on a rock under the endless night sky. He tells me the story of Zhinu the star and her husband, Niulang, the two of them trapped in their separate parts of the sky. We walk up to the strawberry beds in the Mountain greenhouses . . . and then he has a knife at my throat. And he's tied up in the storage closet. And then looking down at me from under the owl tree, anger and despair a toxic cocktail that lines his face. *"I don't even know why I came after you."*

I stop him in the dream. We sit. I listen without trying to argue. He listens too. We write a truce together in the dirt, the whole truth in exchange for my traitor star and his Menghu coat. And a promise to get rid of all the lychee water purifiers and to eat green apples every day and live in his stupid tree house. But just as we reach out to shake hands, Howl crumbles into sand, and then I'm awake, Howl's broken body thrashing beside me.

Xuan sits up, grabbing hold of Howl to keep him still, calling for water. For bandages and medicine. For things I don't understand, the whole world foggy around me as if it will all just blank out in a moment because I'm so, so tired. June hands me the only waterskin left after Xuan used the others to spray out wounds yesterday. She keeps her eyes on Xuan as he checks the bandages, asks me to help prop Howl up so he doesn't choke as we pour liquid down his throat.

Tai-ge is as silent as yesterday, though his eyes follow me as I help Xuan check the bleeding on his arms and chest. Heat begins to burn in my cheeks as I hold the new swaths of gauze in place for Xuan to tape, the last bits we have, finishing as quickly as possible to get my hands away from his bare skin.

Xuan bites his lip as he peels the thick bandaging from Howl's shoulder, avoiding my eyes when he asks for help again in dressing it. Answer enough to the question I can't bear to ask. How long before chemicals eat away Howl's skin, tear into his bones and poison his blood? I can see nothing in Xuan's face, no future.

The last measure of sedative in the medikit goes into Howl's bloodstream, and I sit with my eyes locked to his, his hand grasping mine too tight as we wait for the medicine to take hold. His face is so pale, nothing but a ghost of the person I know must be fighting inside, strangled and suffocated underneath all the bandages. But once his eyes close and his fingers relax from their frantic grip, I can't sit still any longer. Can't stay. The world seems out of focus and sickly as I trip my way out of the storage closet. Down the ladder and out of the heli. Xuan's protests as I drag him along after me are nothing but a mindless buzz that I can't make myself pay attention to.

Outside, the sun has burned the mist from the air, leaving a clear view of the three hills we landed behind and the odd, grasping, and gangly trees clustered at their base. And past that . . . the ocean, a disorienting monochromatic horizon that seems to go on forever. The air still feels wet and smells of something I can't place, leaving a brackish taste across my tongue, the world all over in teals and grays, as if we're in the center of a storm cloud and the colors have all been stolen.

Bloodstains splash the grass all around the heli, the creature we left dead on the ground pulled into gruesome bits, the heaps of flesh that used to be the huge beast strung out all around the clearing and gathering flies. I pull Xuan a step closer to the spot I fell last night and have to bite back a retch as the wind blows the gamey scent of unwashed fur and death into my face.

"Is there a reason you want to stand out here? I'm getting blood on my boots." Xuan complains.

Tai-ge comes down the ladder after us, and I have to think for a minute to remember why he decided to bring the gun out with him. Xuan. He tried to hurt Tai-ge. Tried to run.

"It's not safe out here." Tai-ge's voice is terse. "There were more gores." He bends down near what is left of the gore's head, wrinkling his nose. "Somehow I don't think there was enough here to feed them all."

"Gores are nocturnal, Tai-ge." I wrinkle my nose, stepping over a blood-caked spot in the grass. "Not that you're listening." The last part is under my breath.

The creatures ate the one that almost killed us. Or some of it, anyway. Something catches sunlight under the monster's detached jaw. Xuan points to it just as I walk forward, reaching to pluck it out of the bloodied remains of the gore's maw.

The knife. It pulls out easily, stink of feral beast mixing with the tang of congealed blood in my nose. Underneath the blood I find Tai-ge's name. "Howl must have stabbed the roof of its mouth so it wouldn't bite him." Trying to remember what happened last night is like trying to walk back through a nightmare, the images jerky and incomplete. I do remember blood on the gore's muzzle and cheek, the bloody remains of the creature's eye. Howl must have stabbed it there, too.

"So, you two must be pretty close, right?" Xuan's voice makes me jump, reeling me back from the thoughts clouding my mind.

"Close?" I glance over at Tai-ge, who has gone back to the ladder, his eyes hard as he watches us. He cocks his head, waiting for me to answer. "What do you mean?"

"You and the Chairman's son? It's not every day you see someone jump between a gore and its prey." His teeth glint in the afternoon light in an all-too-knowing smile as he gives my shoulder a nudge. "Seems like the City has more reason to be hunting you than I thought, Fourth. Everyone always used to talk about Tai-ge, but I'd side with you on this one. Howl's definitely got something."

I wipe the curved blade off on my pants, the notched edge catching against the fabric. "Go write your romance novel somewhere else."

Xuan laughs, jingling the handcuffs between us. "If only I could. Does that mean Tai-ge is after Blondie instead?"

"Stop calling her that."

Xuan ignores me, his hand tugging against the handcuffs as he bends down to pick something out of the churned-up earth. "Here's another mystery solved."

In his hand are four metal stars joined at the points to make a line. Mine. My hand goes to my neck, the leather cord that usually holds them gone. I didn't notice it missing in the adrenaline-soaked hours since the gore charged us. Twisting around, my fingers barely touch the bandage pasted between my shoulder blades, about the right distance for my cuts to have been from the necklace. Xuan holds the stars out to me, careful of the sharpened points. City red barely shows through under the rusty brown wash.

I take them and drop to my knees, feeling the ground for the rose-colored jade piece my mother gave to me when I was young, but the blood-soaked dirt divulges no secrets.

The rusted ring is gone too, lost forever down a monster's gullet. Of the three pasts strung around my neck, it *would* be my traitor stars that stuck with me, too sharp even for a gore to swallow.

"How long do you think we have before the people from Port North—from Kamar, I guess—notice we're here?" I ask.

The hint of smile that always seems to be on Xuan's face drops. "I don't know. Maybe Kamar is too occupied evacuating to the island to pay attention to us."

Panic twinges in my stomach. "We're supposed to have another three days."

"They sent out the first forces the night of the Chairman's meeting. The main force hasn't gone over yet, but . . ."

"They're already at the staging area? I saw a heli yesterday from Port North—a woman came in it to evacuate the people in the village. Do you think Dr. Yang has already sent people to the island?" My heart sinks. What if it's already too late? I stand, scratching at the blood crusted on my hands. We couldn't move now even if we wanted to. Not with Howl lying broken in the storage closet like that poor bird from the orphanage, trapped in its cage.

"I don't think so." Xuan looks south, toward where Port North is supposed to be, absently rubbing the Second mark scarred into the skin between his thumb and forefinger. "I was supposed to ship out with the main group tomorrow and meet up with them at the permanent camp south of Kamar."

I follow his gaze, hopelessly looking for some clue as to where Port North starts or a hint of the Red staging area I saw on the map south of it. Where Dr. Yang and the Chairman probably are at this very moment, plotting how best to take the one thing my mother left for me: the cure.

CHAPTER 40

TAI-GE CALLS OUT WHEN I START TOWARD THE empty dwellings, Xuan trailing behind me. "I should come with you, shouldn't I?" He glances at Xuan, hand on the gun.

"No. I need to think." I probably shouldn't be angry at Tai-ge. Xuan was the one who ran and brought the gores down on us. But Tai-ge was the one who wouldn't listen to me or Howl in the first place.

"I can't drag her into the woods and expect Kamar not to figure out where we came from," Xuan breaks into my thoughts, directing the comment at Tai-ge. "Blending into a crowd is difficult when there are handcuffs and a less-than-compliant teenager attached to your wrist. A dead teenager would probably attract even *more* attention." He squints at me, sizing me up. "You're smallish, though. Maybe if I found an overcoat, I could stash you under it and pretend I spend too much time in the cafeteria."

Tai-ge doesn't laugh. "We need to get moving. If getting to the island during the evacuation is our only chance . . ." He glances toward the heli.

"I need some time to think about it, Tai-ge. We can't leave Howl."

"We *can't* leave Howl? Isn't that what you've wanted to do all along?" Tai-ge raises his eyebrows, waiting expectantly. As if now that he's finally done tolerating Howl, I'll be the one to open the hatch and throw him out.

"Things have changed." I clear my throat and take a step toward the hatch. "We're stuck in plain sight of a bunch of people who might want to poke holes in our vital organs. Give me a few minutes to figure it out."

"We had a plan. One that doesn't require a Menghu." Tai-ge waits for a second, then impatiently waves his hand, as if commanding me to explain myself. "You're going to risk losing the cure to Dr. Yang over this?"

I take a deep, steadying breath. "Just let me—"

"And you're going to wander off with *him*." Tai-ge looks at Xuan. "After he attacked me and ran?"

"What exactly did you have in mind?" The words explode out of me, patience gone. I hold up my wrist, handcuffed to Xuan's. "Should we saw his arm off? We're going to go look for the key, and I'm going to figure out a way to not abandon the person who just saved my life and still get to the island before Dr. Yang. I'd rather do it without you yelling at me."

"Sevvy, I . . ." Tai-ge looks down at his boots, but looks up immediately, the slosh of blood and hair underfoot too gruesome to meditate upon. "Sorry. I'll . . . get things ready to go here."

"We'll talk when I get back, okay?" I tug on the handcuffs and whistle at Xuan. "Come on, little puppy!"

Xuan groans theatrically. "I think I'm more upset about being tethered to you than being stuck in the middle of enemy territory."

"Wait. Take one of the guns." Tai-ge holds it out to me.

I grudgingly take the weapon, sticking it into my waistband. If Xuan does decide he has a better chance at survival running away, even if it means dragging my dead body along behind him, then he has access to a weapon now. Actually, if I were dead, he could probably figure out a way chop off my arm, then hide the cuffs. On the other hand, if Xuan wanted to kill me he probably could have done it with medical supplies and blamed the gore. I don't trust people as easily as I used to, but Xuan did help us with Howl.

Walking to the spot Howl had Xuan pinned isn't as difficult as I'd expected, our footprints from last night scarring the ground as if we dragged shovels through the plants. It's sort of eerie, the marks we made between the houses making me realize just how long this place has been abandoned. There are no signs of any other humans. What happened here?

The wet dirt sticks under my fingernails and in the lines of my knuckles as Xuan and I search the scrubby grass for the tiniest hint of silver. Maybe if we dig long enough, I'll wake up. This whole nightmare will be over and . . . I'll be back in my bed at the orphanage with absolutely no future, wishing Tai-ge's two stars didn't weigh down his shoulders quite so much, and patiently waiting for the headsman to call my name.

I stand, the abrupt movement startling an expletive out of Xuan. Is that what I am doing? Walking toward an early death, no matter which path I take? How is it I managed to drag so many people with me? How long until there are Reds or Port Northians or more gores peeking up through the heli's hatch? How many of us will even get close to Mother's cure, or will we all get shot, bitten, or killed one by one? My mind trips over the horrible image

of Howl burned into my brain, hovering a breath or two away
from the line between living and dead. Could I have done something different last night to change what happened?

Last night is over. What can I do now?

Xuan touches my shoulder, surprising me into pulling the gun
out of my waistband and shoving it into his face before I can think.

"Whoa." He puts his free hand over his head, the other tugging
at the chain that connects us. "I just thought you might like to
know that you are talking to yourself."

I groan, the sound chafing against my throat as I lower the gun.

"What is it you're so twisted up about?" he asks. "Getting into
Kamar now that you have a mostly dead guy to carry around? Or
is it the dead guy himself you're worried about? What to do about
Sun Yi-lai, who so dashingly just saved your life?"

"Please do not refer to him as 'the dead guy.' He's not dead."

Xuan rolls his eyes, but then he sighs and sits on the ground,
pulling me down next to him. "There's not much we can do for
him. The tape inside him is going to dissolve before it can do
any good. All you have here are medical supplies that are meant
to keep someone alive until they're flown back to a hospital. He
needs a scalder for the chemicals. And an anmicro wash and bond
to close it all up. We don't have that stuff."

"But . . ." I look out to the empty horizon, the lack of mountains and heavy tree cover making me feel exposed. "That staging
area south of here? Would they?"

Xuan gives a slow nod. "Probably. But they'd also have some
less comfortable sorts of things for us if we tried asking for medical supplies. I don't know who down there is . . ." He goes silent,
looking at the ground.

"Don't know who is what?"

He tips his chin back up. "Did I tell you how lovely those bandages make you look? They really set off your skin tone."

"The girl who is holding a gun is about to lose patience with you, Xuan."

"What is it you want me to do? Sneak into the camp? With you and your traitor brand attached to me? If they got your mask off, anyone would know who you were, and they'd take us both to the Arch." Xuan points to the mark under my ear, the one that links me to Mother, then shakes his head. "Or whatever they're using for ceremonial killings these days. I'm not quite that desperate yet."

I flick his hand away from me. "But if it means the difference between Howl living and dying . . ." My mind is still running faster than I can keep up. If we got medical supplies somehow, then what? Expending the time it would take to get them would eat up any chance we have of getting to the island before Dr. Yang.

"I'm not going to walk back into a City camp, Sev. I did what I was supposed to do in the City—and didn't ask questions—but now I have a chance to get away from all that. I'm not going to waste it because the Chairman's stupid son let a gore get its teeth into him. If you ask me, him fading away might help the situation a little bit here."

"He's not the Chairman's son." Gun loose in my hand, I curl up, my free arm around my legs and my cheek against my knee as if I can squish small enough that the world will forget I exist. As if I'm somehow the one who did all of this and if I wink out of existence, then everything will go back right. Tears burn behind my eyes.

"Sure he's not the Chairman's son. I was ready to cut off my marks to get away too."

I shake my head, not willing to argue. "If we just sit here, we'll lose the cure. We might all get killed. But I can't just watch him . . ."

"That's the problem, isn't it?" Xuan points at me when I trail off, his eyes narrowed. "You don't want him to die, but even admitting that is hard for you. Why?" I shake my head at him, unable to answer. "I'd ask if you want a hug . . ." He backs away an inch when I wrinkle my nose, his hands going up. "A very nice, platonic, comforting sort of hug from an older brotherly type who is not even a little bit interested in you, I promise . . . but I don't really want that thing any closer to me." He points to the gun, which is still absently pointed in his direction.

A week ago, Howl being eaten by gores was hardly punishment enough for what he'd done. But now, actually watching as his cheeks hollow and eyes go glassy is completely different. I can't block out the image of him facing down the gore. Or the memory of him carrying me away from the Reds after we pulled June from their tent and I ended up with the butt of a gun to the head. Of his face in the dark, starlight dotting his nose like freckles.

Xuan pats the ground next to him with a patronizing smile. "Talk to me, honey. I'm good at love problems."

Annoyance boils up dangerously inside of me, every word out of his mouth a dire chance that he won't make it back to the heli alive. *Why do I feel like this?* my head screams. *I must be going insane. Suddenly I'm ready to kill? For Howl?*

Xuan sort of laughs. "I gave E. coli to the last girl I liked." He states it matter-of-factly, a hopeless smile curling in his mouth. "So really, being the reason Yi-lai got bitten in half is nice in comparison."

"You . . . what?" I tuck the gun back into my waistband, Xuan's explanation putting wrinkles in my forehead.

"It was an accident. Sort of." He tears a stalk of the rough grass from the soil, spiky seeds blistering from the top.

I watch as he picks the seeds off one by one, rolling them between his fingers and throwing them into the grass. "How do you accidentally give someone E. coli?"

"I was working in one of the labs up on the Steppe. She taught a class a few doors down. We used to cross paths on the way to self-criticism. But she was a First."

"She didn't like you back? So you gave her E. coli . . . to put her out of her misery?" I think for a second, my mind fuzzy. "To put her out of *your* misery?"

Xuan smiles, a thin veneer of humor over a less-than-happy memory. "I took the slides her class was working with out of their protective unit—lots of different colors: red, pink, blue, green—and spelled *I love you* on her desk. She wouldn't have known it was me. I just wanted to see what she would do." He shifts over, running his fingers through the grass, bent from our search. "Turns out it was an infectious disease lab and all the different colors were different strains of E. coli. She didn't come back for a long time."

"You're a medic. You didn't look at the labels?"

"It was a First-only lab. None of their research that's out where people can read it is labeled in a way that's public-consumption friendly."

I give a halfhearted smile. "At least she recovered."

"She didn't even know who I was." He lifts his hand to show me the two lines carved into his hand, dragging my hand up with it. "Second. I don't think she even saw me until they checked the surveillance and she came herself to yell at me. It's hard to be the one who wants to start things. I couldn't, because she outranked me. She might as well have been a different species. Living on another planet."

"What happened?"

He shrugs. "I made her laugh. We got to talking. Things were . . . good. For a while." He looks down, and suddenly I remember Tai-ge's explanation of Xuan wanting to leave. That his girlfriend had gone mad and run off into the woods. "At least you don't have to toe the line with Howl. If he wants you, all *you* have to do is say yes or no."

A sigh bubbles up out of me, tangling with the wind rushing past us in cold currents. "Howl doesn't want me. He just wants the cure."

CHAPTER 41

I PINCH MY MOUTH SHUT OVER THE WORDS, FORCING them to sound like the truth. *Howl just wants the cure.* I can't face any other explanation right now. Anything else and everything will start to break.

"Is that right." Xuan widens his eyes, propping his chin up on his fist as if he's entranced. "Tell me everything."

"It's kind of a long story. . . ."

"Which I don't particularly want to hear." He puts up a hand to stop me. "Your story already doesn't make sense."

"This is how you solve my problems? Not letting me tell the story?"

"What do you have to do with the cure, Ms. Jiang? If it's *not* a ridiculous, made-up story to force the City to continue listening to the Chairman, it's hidden in Kamar somewhere, right? Why would Howl need you?"

"Because my mother—"

"Blah, blah, blah, be quiet. I hate to be the one to say this, but you are sort of annoying. And I'm not just saying that because of these." Xuan shakes the handcuff, making my hand jerk to the side. "Last I checked, Yi-lai—*Howl*—was suffering from acute gore attack, resulting from an overactive sense of protectiveness." Xuan's stiff, emotionless tone is one hundred percent medic, the ridiculous diagnosis hammered out from behind a straight face. "There are set procedures in dealing with annoying people, and *saving* an annoying person from a gore when a gore could just take care of the problem for you is not one of them."

I can hear the smile in his voice, and it makes me want to slap him. But instead, I go back to the ground, focusing on one thing I can do. My fingers look thick and clumsy threading through the clumps of dry grass. In the hours since Howl attempted to fight the gore off with Tai-ge's knife, I've thought of all the things Xuan is implying—minus being annoying; I'm not annoying—but it hurts too much to let any of those thoughts solidify. After tying Howl up and yelling at him and accusing him . . . after leaving him at the Mountain. After telling June and Tai-ge to shoot him. After he threw down the knife and told me to kill him myself . . . It's too much.

And if he does still want me . . . I bite my lip, not sure where my thoughts are supposed to go after that. Too scared to look.

The key. It has to be here somewhere.

"I told you. I *am* good at love problems." Xuan leans back, looking up into the sun. "I'll tell you how to fix it on one condition."

A gasp rips out of me as I accidentally wrap my fingers around a prickly plant, the barbs sinking deep into my fingers. "We don't have time for this. It's too late to fix things with Howl." If I say it enough times, maybe my brain will stop trying to convince me otherwise.

One thing I do know, though: Tai-ge's right that we can't let Howl be the reason we give up and let Dr. Yang get the cure. The thought is an awful wrinkle inside me, an answer that feels wrong.

Xuan continues, "And that condition is you have to call me 'doctor.' Or, if you really want to, you can call me 'doc.' Doc Xuan. Doc Chen." He clears his throat. "Love Doc. Any of those is acceptable."

My fingers brush something metal, and I jump, losing hold of it for a second. I take a deep breath, closing my hand tight over the tiny key, carefully sitting back to look at Xuan. "Are you finished?"

"Are you finished, *Doc*?" he corrects.

I will my temper to cool before I end up ramming the key up Xuan's nose. "So, back to where this conversation started. If I could unlock these handcuffs, is there a chance we could get medicine from the staging area?"

He sits up straight. "You found the key. Where is it?" He pulls my handcuffed arm toward him, suddenly flexing muscles I didn't know were there.

I pull the gun out and point it at the sky, waiting.

He lets me go, wrinkling his nose. "You can't go into that camp. And I can't help you, Jiang Sev. Even if walking in and taking what we wanted were easy, I wouldn't be able to make any promises. I don't know what kind of junk is in those wounds."

"Is it possible that having Howl—the Chairman's son, right?—in your debt might be a better bargaining chip than dancing for the dead General's son?"

"The dead General . . ." Xuan scrubs his shaggy hair back, looking up at the sky. "It's the new General I'm worried about. If

I'm not mistaken, the Chairman should be worried, too."

"What about the new General? What does she have to do with your deal with Tai-ge?"

"I was promised a wave good-bye in exchange for a low-profile entry into Kamar."

"But you tried to run."

"It's hard to hold up the terms of a deal when you're pretty sure all of it is about to get blown to pieces."

I narrow my eyes, waiting for him to look up at me, but he doesn't. "You haven't been yelling to Tai-ge about mistreatment."

"When the vipers know where you sleep, Ms. Jiang, you don't yell."

"Tai-ge's a viper? He's been on your side this whole time. You wanted to defect, and he flew you to the ocean."

Xuan presses his lips together. "That would be a marvelous story, wouldn't it? Unfortunately, he's not the only viper who knows the location of the heli. And my superiors have a history of not keeping promises."

If there are promises Reds are supposed to be keeping, then Tai-ge . . . My stomach knots. "So you *are* a plant. Getting us in to Port North . . . why?"

"Not all the vipers agree about who has the right of things and what will happen after we invade, Miss Jiang."

"You aren't just trying to run because of where we landed, then. You're worried your wave good-bye isn't going to happen. That *Tai-ge*"—the knots in my stomach come alive, hissing like snakes—"or *whoever* is in charge in the camps is going to hold on to you instead of letting you escape."

Xuan nods. "And, unless you can promise something better, I'm afraid I can't share much more than that. Technically, I'm probably already Arch fodder, so if you don't mind . . ." He makes a grab for the key.

I whisk it out of reach and hold up the gun, hating the way my finger looks so close to the trigger. "I'll make you a deal. We need to get Howl medicine. If you won't help me, I'll swallow the key. And maybe shoot you in the head. Or somewhere worse."

"I take it back about Howl being the gore-ish one. You are officially much creepier." Rubbing a hand through his uneven hair, Xuan rolls his eyes. "You might as well drop that thing, because if you were going to use it, you already would have. I'm willing to pretend for a second that I can't just take the key away from you. What do you have to offer me other than . . . not shooting me in the head?"

I let the gun sag down to the ground. "I'll make sure they forget you existed. You get us medicine, get us onto that island—"

"Sneaking into Kamar while they're evacuating was never a great idea." Xuan holds up his dirt-smudged hand and points at the two white lines marking him a Second. "If Tai-ge, Howl, and I all show up with mangled hands, they'll know exactly what we are. I honestly considered cutting off my hand." He looks down at his arm with a shiver, the chain linking us together bright in the sun. "But even with June swearing we were all trying to escape the City, they'll kill us."

"Why?"

Xuan sighs. "That staging area? It's a worker processing unit. We send troops in, take anyone who looks healthy, and then send them south to work on our farms. What do you think happened to the people in these houses?"

"The City just . . . takes people?" My stomach churns, sick bubbling up inside of me, the empty houses seeming to stare at my back. "Those people in the other town June and I walked through—"

"The island has some kind of weapon that shakes helis out of the sky. There are settlements across the areas where the weapons reach—one on each of the three highest points of the island, we think. Those places are safe. But places like this . . ." He gestures around us. "We're out of the weapon's reach."

The bleached wood and stone of the settlement are even more ominous now.

"And it's not just here. They didn't realize what was happening at first. I was in one of the first groups to come here when the Chairman started expanding City farms. The people came out to meet us when we landed. We put them in cages. All strictly secret. Hardly anyone knows where Kamar is or what it's like. Or that it isn't made up of light-haired, light-eyed people who want to kill all of us. It's just a place. A nicer place than the City, if I'm not mistaken. Fewer weapons, more places to hide, if you're lucky enough to get onto the island."

I go up on my knees, inching away from him. "You came here. You *stole* people. . . ."

"I didn't steal people. I did physicals. Designations for types of labor the people we took were best suited to. No point in kidnapping someone to do your hard labor if they're diseased. Or sending them to a mine if they're too tall, or to a field if they're too old."

"And June's mom? You were the one who took her?"

Xuan scrunches his eyes closed for a second. "Probably. I must have been, if June remembers me."

My arm linked to his seems to be tingling, as if I've been sitting here talking to him for too long and now whatever's wrong with him will seep into me. He's processed so many slaves, helped kidnap so many people he doesn't even remember? "I hate that I'm talking to you. That I have to ask for your help now."

"I didn't . . ." His eyes lower, mouth pinched shut. "I didn't *want* to do it. You know how things are in the City. You obey, or you end up with SS. Or an execution sentence. It's not just because of SS and the masks that I want to leave. . . ." Xuan puts a hand to his forehead, the tendons and muscles standing out. "I was *glad* when they started fighting back. It was so hard to just walk in and . . ." He takes a moment before continuing. "We started taking people right around the same time your mother went to sleep. It probably took another year after that before they got those heli-killers running, before their fighting force got organized enough to do anything but cry as we pulled people out from under them—most of the people the City processes now are fighters—they call themselves Baohujia. The family of protectors. They're the only ones out where the City can get to them without having to risk their own forces, patrolling the settlements and protecting them against soldiers who come on foot to get around the heli problem. Kamar's version of Seconds."

My whole body goes cold, all the little strings of hope I'd braided together crusting over with ice. *The family. Find the family.*

A family of people who protect the island, the settlements . . . would protect the cure, if they had it. My breath catches in my throat, a sob I have to choke down. Could it be that Mother didn't mean *my* family or hers? Not blood, not people who will see my face and know I belong to them.

Before I can even say anything, I know I'm right. This must have been what she meant. She wanted me to find the protectors of Port North. And those same protectors are going to find our heli and kill us before we can come up with a plan to get to the cure, if Xuan is to be believed. All because of the things Xuan and the other Reds have done.

Howl was wrong. It doesn't matter who I am, and there's no one here waiting for me.

I don't know if I should scream or point my gun at Xuan and pull the trigger. I can't do either because the world isn't made up of rights and wrongs anymore. Every right seems to have the wrong motivation, and every wrong a thousand justifications, and who's to say which is right or wrong anyway? It depends on who is talking. I know exactly how it feels to be told what to do, the Arch singing a death song behind me to combat every rebellious thought. And even without that, Howl is dying. The *world* could die if SS spreads far enough. I bite my lip, willing it not to quiver. Instruct my spine to straighten. Look Xuan straight in the eye. "How long will it take us to get to the staging area?"

"We?" Xuan's head gives an exaggerated shake. "I'm not getting caught with you anywhere, Ms. Jiang. And I'm not good at gauging distances. Probably two days on foot? How would we survive the gores?"

Two days. There are already helis on the ground, Reds forming up to push past the island's defenses. Past the *family*. The Baohujia. I ignore the ripples of regret. Mother was City through and through. It was silly of me to hope. And it's time to move past my silly assumptions about the world.

There have been too many. I don't think my heart can assume anything else or it will shatter completely.

I grit my teeth and sit forward. "June's not your best way in, Xuan. I am. I know people inside Kamar. You know my mother was a spy for them." Lies. I hate the way the words taste, but I have to say them anyway or Xuan won't listen to me. "The Baohujia knows I'm coming."

Maybe. Probably not. But it's possible, even if it isn't blood linking me to them, they'll know what Mother wanted to do with her notes. "Mother told me to find them. If you get medicine for Howl, I'll make sure you get in. With all your limbs attached and everything." I give his scarred hand a meaningful look.

Xuan's eyes narrow. "How am I supposed to believe that? You didn't even know where Kamar *was*."

"Mother died before she could tell me how to get here. But she's the one who formulated the cure. She's the one who left it here with them, and she's the one who used her last words to tell me to come get it. My mother wouldn't have sent me to Kamar just to be shot down. They know I'm coming for the cure." It sounds so perfect, but there isn't any hope left in me to think it could be true. "Maybe that's why whoever it is who sent you is watching us. Because they know I have a better chance than anyone else to get it." I smooth my hair back behind my ear, the shorn ends still feeling wrong. "And you don't have a choice here. It's believe me or get killed by the Kamaris when they come, because if you don't help me, I'm not going to do any advocating for you." I point south. "Or you could go back to that camp and find yourself a nice tent. Stay with the Reds and hope they have a mask for you."

I'm just as bad as Howl. Bending the truth to get what I want. Putting Xuan's life on the line, even as I promise to save him. But it comes down to this: I don't have it in me to leave Howl here to die. And if there's no real hope that we can sneak onto the island, then doing what I can to preserve Howl's life is the only thing I can do.

Two days to get to the staging area. That's two there, two

back. We'll think of another way while Xuan is gone. A way to get in with the soldiers, maybe even to go after Dr. Yang himself after he gets what he came for. It doesn't matter who I take the cure from, so long as it ends up in my pocket and not a Menghu's.

Xuan bites his lip, staring at me through the strings of hair trailing down his forehead. He leans forward, and all my muscles tense, my fist balling around the key. But it's a nod, not an attack. "Okay." He says it slowly, as if he isn't sure what he's saying is true, the idea too foreign to compute. "I'll help. If you agree to a few things first."

A trill of hope rises in my chest. "I'm not calling you Doc."

"I need supplies. A way to get past gores that doesn't involve huge weapons." He gives me a smile. "I'm not much of a shot. And I've seen too much to believe guns would be a sure bet against them even if I were."

"There are hammocks in the heli. I'll leave one out for you, and you can use it to sleep up in a tree where the gores can't get you." I open my hand, the key on my palm. Not sure if this is right, if I can really trust him, but he leans forward and takes it before I can think any more, unlocking his side of the handcuffs. When the scratched silver falls free from his wrist, it hits the dirt with a *thud*, weighing my hand to the ground.

"I can trust you to come back with medicine?" I ask. "In return for getting you into Port North?"

Xuan smiles, a dark, bleak sort of expression that twists my stomach. He rubs his wrist where the handcuff chafed against his skin. "Sure you can."

"Xuan." I look him in the eyes, pleading full in my voice. I don't have another choice. Not if I want Howl to live. "Please give me a reason to trust you."

He shrugs. "I'm done with SS. I'm ready to weather this out in a bunker, eating fresh food and playing weiqi. If you're lying, I'm dead anyway. It's just a matter of whose bullet finds me first. You just had better be here when I get back. I wouldn't worry about Reds getting to that island before we do either, not unless they walk in on foot, and then the Baohujia would pick them off one by one as they cross the bridge. There's no way to get in unless Kamar wants you there." He glances back in the direction of the heli. "Or at least it won't be on my head if they do."

"What do you mean?"

Xuan pulls himself up from the ground, offering me a hand up. "I said there were things—things, *plural*—I need you to agree to in order for me to help. And the second one is this: When I get back, Hong Tai-ge had better be somewhere else. He doesn't come into Kamar with us, and as of today, as far as he is concerned, I'm dead. It's the only way you're going to be able to keep up your side of the bargain." He stands up from the ground, brushing off his knees. "And, friendly, unsolicited advice: Unless you're planning to hand over the entire island and the cure along with it to the City, I'd suggest that once you get him out of the heli, you lock the doors and don't let him back in."

Fear is an ice shard inside me, a knife. "Why?"

Xuan flexes his newly freed hand. Then he looks at me. Smiles. And tells me.

CHAPTER 42

THE GROUND SEEMS TO SLIP AND SLIDE UNDER MY feet as I walk back, pushing me toward the heli against my will. This is what happened in the Mountain, everyone telling me Howl wasn't the person I thought he was. And he wasn't. I didn't want to believe it, so I chose to trust him. I didn't know him well enough to be able to absorb or discount the information, had to hope I guessed right.

Tai-ge, however, I do know. Where all the evidence stacked up against Howl didn't make sense to me, Xuan's story fits exactly into Hong Tai-ge's shape. I knew something was wrong. I just didn't realize how much.

The owl's image pulses through my brain, the one who cried all night at me to bury my dead as I sat under its tree, wondering which of my friends the Reds had killed. The bird that stared me down when I tried to push it out of my mind, hissed when I threw rocks, then flew at me just to make sure I was listening. I thought it was a superstition, a fear that bled out of my head to plague us while we tried to sleep. But it was right. Someone did die that night.

Dying isn't always about pulses and lungs and blood flow. Sometimes it's a memory, an incorrect perception that dies inside you, leaving the world less a person you love.

Tai-ge looks up when I whisper the hatch open and climb up through its craw. His eyes catch on the blank air next to me, wildly grasping at the space Xuan is supposed to occupy. He runs to the hatch, holding a hand out to help me in. "You got the cuffs open. Where's Xuan?"

"I let him go. He'll probably get eaten by a gore before he gets anywhere near Port North."

"You let him . . . !" Tai-ge swears, swatting the hatch out of my hand as I start to close it, the metal banging against the floor. "Get out of the way, Sevvy, we need him. What were you thinking?"

Keeping my face calm, I use both hands to close the hatch, forcing Tai-ge away from the opening. When I turn and stand up, I look him full in the eyes, searching for the part of him that's different. As if betrayal should show up like smoke behind his irises. But he just seems confused.

"Where is the other gun, Tai-ge?" I ask.

He pulls it from his coat, and I hold my hand out for it.

He doesn't give it to me, looking down at its silver barrel. "Move, Sevvy. You don't understand—"

I grab the gun from Tai-ge's loose grip. The weapon is heavy, the metal warm where it was against his skin inside the coat. Walking to the heli's flight control panel feels almost as if I'm floating on air, vertigo nibbling harder and harder at the sides of my vision when I get to the heli's flight control panel of blinking lights and point it toward the navigation screen. Raise the gun.

Fire.

It isn't as deafening as I'd like, something on the gun's muzzle muting the sound, and it makes me even more angry, wanting it to be as loud as I am angry.

"*Sevvy!* What in the name of Yuan's axe are you—" Tai-ge ducks as I shoot the control panel itself, the buttons and levers, anything that looks fragile, until one of the bullets ricochets into the ceiling with an infuriated *twang*. Tai-ge crashes into me, pinning my shoulders and arms to the cold metal wall while he wrestles the gun from my hands. It doesn't matter, though. It's empty.

The door to the storage closet flies open, and suddenly June is elbowing her way between me and Tai-ge, standing between us with her arms extended as if she's the wall that will protect me from him.

"Go back in with Howl, June." My voice is so steady, I can hardly tell it's coming from my own throat. "Give us a minute."

Tai-ge's mouth is still open, unspoken profanities practically dripping out as he looks from me to the ruined console, hardly acknowledging June when she doesn't move.

"I'm fine, June. Go make sure I didn't wake Howl up. Please?"

She turns to stare up at me, her cheeks red, nose uneven where it was broken a few months ago. But then she steps down from raised portion of the floor, only looking back once before she goes back into the storage closet.

My shoulder hurts, my hand numb. I slide to the ground, not moving as the console bleats a sharp metallic protest, every system I hit attempting to beg for mercy. Tai-ge's hands go to his hair as he turns toward the pleading cries. "Sevvy, why did you . . . What is *wrong with you*?"

I don't move from the floor. "What is it I don't understand, Tai-ge?"

"You don't understand how important Xuan was—"

"Because he was supposed to help you find a way to disable their towers." Tai-ge doesn't move, his face too surprised, too shocked to emit any sound. "Xuan's seen them working, seen Port North take helis out of the sky. You told her everything. About the cure. What Mother said about Port North." Every word comes out as a growl. "You and Xuan were the best plan she could come up with, the best chance General Hong had of getting helis to the island before Dr. Yang gets Menghu on the ground. If you disabled the towers, she could fly right in, take the cure before they get even close." I swallow, and it feels like gulping down a knife blade, every inch a searing pain. Why didn't I see that when the first General Hong fell, there were only so many candidates who could take his place? "I'm not going to let your mother take the cure."

Tai-ge shakes his head, holding a hand out to me as he steps closer. "Sevvy, I think you need to calm down. . . ."

"You've been talking to her this whole time. You told her about me being cured, that we were on to something, going after Port North."

He steps back and slumps into the chair. "Sevvy . . ."

"My whole life you've been nodding along when people called *me* a traitor. As if it's in my blood to go against everything I'd been taught. To *want* to hurt the people I loved. But what is a traitor, really?" I fold my arms tight against my chest, as if it might hold all the pieces inside me threatening to blast apart together. "Someone who goes against everything they are, against what they believe? Someone willing to abandon their friends so they'll win? Tai-ge, you got out of that camp because the new General—your *mother*—escorted you out."

Tai-ge's eyebrows furrow down, making one thick line. "It was Seconds who found me in that camp. Of course they took me to her when they realized who I was."

"She gave you new maps, a new key, and told you to leave me and June on the ground where we wouldn't bother you anymore." I look him over, trying to decide where he was hiding it. Whether he meant to come back for me at all. "Is it better than the Chairman's? Maybe it isn't such an offensive purple color?"

His hand twitches toward his jacket pocket, but he shakes his head. "I wasn't going to leave you there, Sevvy. She wanted me to, but I would never . . ." He swallows hard, gesturing up to the heli. "She gave us an opportunity, Sevvy. How else were we supposed to get to the cure before Dr. Yang? With the Chairman selling everything we had to those monsters? I had to tell her what he was doing—"

"You've been talking to her a lot longer than that. *Yuan's bloated head*, I am so stupid. How else would Howl have heard reports about where we were? How else would those Reds have been able to walk up to the Post and ask for us *by name?* You were so angry when June showed us where we were on the map that day because you gave the Reds bad coordinates."

His mouth opens, but nothing comes out for a moment before it closes again, the hard-set lines I've become accustomed to since his father died settling over his features. "We needed help, Sevvy. We knew the cure was a real thing, and people were dying. . . . The moment we had a plan I thought would work, I stopped talking to her."

"For the whole twenty-four hours until we went into Dazhai, Tai-ge? Now you're a full-blown traitor just like me. What makes it okay for you to say the Chairman needs to be taken down? Your dad dying? I never got that option when he killed *my* father."

"Stop. Talking." Tai-ge's face contorts, his accustomed calm unable to keep its grip. He sinks down into the pilot chair, his shoulders sagging. "My mother is not a traitor. She is trying to mitigate damage the Chairman is doing to our people, Sevvy. It isn't just those Menghu he let run through Dazhai with guns. He let the Menghu into the City. He had my father killed. Had Firsts airlift all the Mantis along with more than half the City's gas masks and turn them all over to Dr. Yang, according to Mother. She didn't know he'd arranged with Dr. Yang to open the walls in the first place. With all of us so used to bowing to First marks . . ." Tai-ge scrubs a hand through his hair, as if even now he can't bear to say anything negative out loud about Firsts. "Mother's doing her best to keep Dr. Yang away from our resources. Most of the helis are out on the farms; most of the *food* in these Mountains is out where Seconds are in control. She doesn't want to exchange the Chairman for someone new who favors Outsiders over City people . . . and isn't that why we're out here? To stop him?" He sighs, looking at me as if I must understand now that he's been speaking for a minute or so, like I'd accept any words, any explanation, so long as it came from his mouth. "This is how we keep the Menghu from exterminating us."

"You think the Reds are going to follow a general who goes against the Chairman?" I spit the words at him like acid, wishing they were.

"It's not easy to be at war, Sevvy," Tai-ge spits right back. "Would you rather she watched them all die? She's going to save the City. That means . . . *this.*" He gestures to the heli, to the two of us and the island beyond. "It means doing things you wouldn't—things you *shouldn't*—do, because it means it's the difference between annihilation of everything in this world that is good and not."

The Hong family, still twisting and manipulating. What was it they used to say in the City? That General Hong practically *was* a First, even if he had two stars weighing down his collar. Isn't that part of the reason Firsts tried to pin that bomb on me, back when Tai-ge and I were flailing in the Aihu River at the beginning of all this? Howl said Firsts might have been targeting Tai-ge. Trying to warn the General to take a step back. Some Reds follow the General first. But based on what we saw in that camp, I could almost see the divide between Reds who are still loyal and the ones who aren't sure the Chairman is a good face for the City anymore.

"She's negotiating with Menghu when they just shot up her camp?" I ask. "That's a compromise you're okay with?"

"Until we get the cure? Yes. But not after. Not even Dr. Yang meant for the Menghu to kill anyone at Dazhai. It was a mistake." Tai-ge looks down. "Menghu were up on the paddies to make sure no one was sneaking food out of Dazhai. And in the heli-field, loading up everything they could carry to send toward Menghu camps. They only started shooting because of *June.* That whole massacre shouldn't have happened." He looks over the radio, poking at the now-silent knobs and dials. "We'll get the cure, and then there won't be any mistakes. There won't be any Outsiders stealing our food or our masks, killing our soldiers just because they can." The rust in his voice makes me pull away, as if something in Tai-ge has changed.

Or maybe it hasn't. Maybe I just never saw this deep before.

"You're the one who started this, Sevvy," Tai-ge continues. "If Dr. Yang gets the cure, there won't be any hope of getting away from him. Not for the City, for any of the Seconds or Firsts or Thirds or anyone else." He points to me. "But with us on the ground, with Xuan helping us—"

"Did Xuan even *want* to help?" I cut in. "He's just as scared of you as he was of the Menghu."

"What does it matter what any of us want, Sevvy? This could be the end of the City, of us and everything we know. If Dr. Yang has the cure, he can decide all of us are farm slaves and we won't be able to argue. But if we can take out Kamar's towers—"

"Mother called it Port North, Tai-ge. Kamar is what the City calls the place where they've been kidnapping and killing the people for the last eight years." I put a hand over my mouth, so angry I can't even find words to put into understandable sentences. I lick my lips, the dry skin cracking under my tongue. "If we let your mother get the cure, then *nothing is going to change*. I'll still be a traitor. They will *shoot June*, and instead of saving Lihua, they'll just create a hundred more reasons to experiment on little kids. You're letting helis invade Port North without thinking about all the people who will die because of it."

"They're not our people, Sevvy! They've been holding the cure back—"

I stand up from my spot on the ground and walk over to the packs. "You're trying to save *yourself*, Tai-ge. What about the rest of us?"

Every word Tai-ge says blisters. "What were you planning to do with your mother's notes anyway? We have one medic—who *I* brought, by the way—one heli-pilot, one half-dead impostor, one Outsider, and one . . ." He gestures helplessly. "You. Whatever you are. Even if your mother made ten thousand doses of the cure with your name written across them, how would it help anything? Even if we had a way to give them out, it would only stop the people out there killing one another *accidentally* through compulsions—not those who *want* to kill, like the Menghu."

I shake my head, pulling his pack from the pile and tying a hammock to the top of it. "The only way to stop everyone from fighting over the cure is to have people outside the City and Mountain develop it. Everyone will *have* to stop fighting." It sounds naive, idiotic even, now that I've said it out loud, but I can't stop now. "They'll *have* to kill the ranking systems and the slave labor in order to deal with us. Either that or face living with a mask, hoping SS doesn't get in. People will come to us. Howl says—"

"Whatever Howl says is going to take you straight back to the Mountain and all the Menghu you're so scared of." Tai-ge's hand is on the pack, jerking it away from me, but when I turn to face him, his expression softens. "Menghu have done nothing but hurt us and the people we love. If we get the cure, I can protect you. We'll be safe."

"I haven't been a part of the City's 'we' since I was eight." I walk to the hatch, dropping the pack next to it on the metal floor. "For me, it won't matter if it's Dr. Yang or your mother who gets the cure. They won't give it to people like me, or June, or the families they dragged away from that skeleton village to work until their fingers froze." I jam the lever that controls the hatch, and it slides open, the wafts of brackish air tangling in my hair. "They'll give it to the people who keep them in power."

I kick his pack through the hatch, waiting until I hear it *thunk* on the ground below before turning back to Tai-ge. "Now get out."

Tai-ge's mouth hangs open, staring at the gaping open hatch. "Sevvy—"

"No. I'm not going to explain this to you anymore. I shouldn't have to, and it's too dangerous to try. Get out."

"I tried to do it your way." Tai-ge's voice is quiet. "I got the growth regulators to get us out of Dazhai. I *snuck into a Red camp* with you. Stole from them." Tai-ge rises slowly to his feet, his fists clenched. "I *wanted* it to work, but it just . . . hasn't. I love you, Sevvy—"

"No, Tai-ge, I really don't think you do. And I'm done with this conversation." I raise the gun, my hands shaking. It's empty of bullets, but pointing it at someone I've wasted so much time on shudders through me like a sickness. "*Get ou—*"

The sound of shattering glass slices through my sentence, and suddenly the cockpit window behind Tai-ge's head fills my vision, cracks spreading like grasping fingers across the paned windows. Shards of glass scatter across the floor in a glittering assault, a gaping hole just in front of the pilot's chair.

Tai-ge crashes into me just as something flies through the hole, bouncing across the metal floor until it clatters to a stop right at our feet.

"Let go of me!" I scream, but I'm caught in the snare of Tai-ge's arms, Tai-ge trying to stay between me and it, even as I try to kick the device out through the hatch. The grenade falls into two perfect halves, the pieces beginning to spin with a high-pitched scream.

White gas pours from the two spinning halves even as I worm my way out from the tentacled snarl of Tai-ge's arms. Eyes stinging, suddenly all I can feel is cold metal against my cheek, pressing against my shoulders and stomach, the smell of burning.

And then, nothing.

PART III

CHAPTER 43

SHOUTS CLUNK ABOUT INSIDE MY SKULL AS IF MY
brain has been replaced with a set of weiqi stones. Hands touch my
arms and hands, my neck, my hair. My eyelids feel as if they've been
fused together, petrified, leaving me only a stone version of the girl
I thought I was.

Pain pierces the inside of my arm. Then my neck, fiery trails
of pain burning merrily down the length of my body until the
screams trapped inside my stone mouth are worse than the agony.

The voices recede, pokes and prods replaced by the metal
groan of a hinge. I try to slow my breathing, to open my eyes,
but my body doesn't listen. Memories of Sleep slink in through
the cracks, oily and black, as I try again to move and none of my
muscles respond. Panic buzzes at the back of my mouth, foaming
down into my chest and stomach, and I strain to force something,
anything to obey. A finger. A toe, even. Anything that will let me be
alive, that will prove I'm not trapped inside my own body again.

When my eyelids finally crack, a scream of triumph tears up
through my throat but catches, hot and stinging, in my mouth.

Black. Black all around me, the room so close I can feel my breath rebounding back into my face from a ceiling only inches from my nose, the walls brushing my arms even as they hug my sides.

A coffin, like they used to bury people in.

My chest presses against the lid of the box when I breathe. Letting my eyes flutter shut, I try to convince my panicking lungs to slow. If I don't touch anything, I can pretend it's just dark. A moonless night. Safe, even if the air around me feels warm and sick, as though it has already been stripped of oxygen.

I shift uncomfortably, trying to concentrate on what I heard instead of the close air. The shouting was like those men I met at the Post. The man with his erhu and the two friends muttering to themselves in gibberish. But as much as I try to hold on to the image of the Post, the song, try to remember the words the men said, the walls seem to push in on me. Tears tickle down my cheeks, and I can't even wipe them away. Just as my body begins to shake, a small square directly over my face pulls back. My hands knock against the top of the box, as if I could somehow contort myself up through the hole and crawl out, but the space is so tight I can't bend my arms up toward it. A waft of cold air hits my nose and snakes down into my lungs as I greedily inhale, the brackish aftertaste hardly noticeable after the stale air inside the box. Something blocks the light streaming in, and then there's a pair of deep brown eyes peering curiously at me.

A man. He speaks, more of the garbled syllables that don't make sense. It sounds like a question. A stupid question my brain can't quite latch on to.

"Let me out," I interrupt.

The eyes narrow for a moment, and a jolt of familiarity buzzes through me, but it's gone, buried under my anxiety as quickly as it came. There's a moment of silence before his mouth opens again, this time full of words I understand. "Who are you? They said you have the mark, but you can't understand me? You can't be *both*."

Both of what? Gasps rip through me, tears blurring my vision.

"You really don't understand?" He cocks his head, the words formed with that same patched-together quality I remember from the erhu player at the Post. "

I don't know the right way to answer, my hands and arms ready to start scratching through the heavy roof to my prison, now that I know there's more than dirt on the other side. "Please." It comes out in a gasp. "Let me out."

"What can you tell me about the helis with soldiers flying to the camp south of here?" he asks. "What are they planning?"

"We're not part of the invasion."

"An invasion? They're going to brave the island? That seems uncharacteristically stupid for the Chairman."

"I'm here for . . . family. My mother said . . ." I can't even string the words together, my lungs forcing the little air inside me out as my ribs contract. There's no family for me here.

The man is silent for a moment, unblinking stare almost heavier than my lungs, which are almost out of air. "What is it you want, exactly?"

"I want you to let me out of this box." I try to hold back the hyperventilating gasps threatening to take hold of my lungs. "I can't remember anything else."

His smile is less than kind, but not malicious. Curious. "All right. You must understand that I personally don't care for the manner you've been kept here, but if I let you out and you try to hurt me, I will not feel bad when the others in this room kill you."

I blink, and he takes that as an answer.

A series of clicks vibrate through the box, and the top of my prison swings up like a lid. My eyes go dark as I sit up too fast, the blood pounding in my head making me feel faint. My body screams at me to get up, to get out of the box, away from even the possibility of being shut in again, but I stare down at my hands, filling my lungs long and slow until my arms stop shaking.

When I can see properly, I take stock of the room. It's small, the walls made up from blocks cut from stone with a tiny window near the top admitting dusted streams of sunlight. The floor shines as if polished from having been walked on by generations of feet. As promised, there are two people other than the man who was speaking to me in the room, dressed in the long tunics I remember on the erhu player and his friends at the Post. I don't see any guns.

I suppose he didn't say they would shoot me. Just kill me.

The man who opened the box steps out from behind the lid, and my breath catches. It *is* the man I met at the Post, though there's no erhu strapped to his back now. He walks to sit in front of the two guards, settling himself comfortably on a stool. One guard has her eyes fixed like gems in a setting, unblinking as she stares at me, curly hair pulled into a loose ponytail at the nape of her neck. The other—a man who looks as if he could be from the City—oddly enough, is watching the erhu player.

"Interesting." Erhu Player reaches out to touch the edge of my now-open casket, gaze following the deliberately slow rise and fall of my shoulders. "I didn't expect someone I'd met before. Did you follow me here, somehow? We don't use aircraft much, and I suppose I don't know how easily they can be tracked."

An aircraft. Does he have one of the ancient helis like the one I saw in the settlement? It doesn't matter, I suppose. I shake my head. "I didn't follow you here. Not on purpose. Though if I'd known you belonged to Port North, I would have."

"Port North?" He turns the words over in his mouth as if he's never heard them before. "Very interesting. How did you come by that mark?" He points to my chin, where Mother's birthmark curls up from under my ear. "I didn't see it when we met in the mountains or I would have asked you questions rather than play for you."

"It's a birthmark." I touch it self-consciously. "I need to talk to the family. To . . . I think they're called Baohujia. They have something for me."

"These two are Baohujia." Erhu Player's fingers flick toward the guards behind him, though he doesn't unscrew his gaze from my birthmark. "What is it you want from them?"

My hands hurt as I unclasp them, clenching and unclenching them in the hopes that the blood will return to my fingers. "Some papers. My mother came here and left some very important documents." He must know. Even Xuan believed SS had been eradicated from the island. That was one of his reasons for coming. The cure is here.

I try not to notice the speculative gleam in the erhu player's eyes as they sink from my birthmark to settle on my wrists. "You're a *Fourth*." His gaze climbs back up to meet mine, mouth quirked in an impassive smile. "What's your name? I must have heard it back at the Post, but I can't remember now."

My arms prickle with cold, and I fold them tight around me. I don't want to share my name when I don't know what or who will be burned as a result. Answering questions with questions isn't doing much, but I'm not sure how else to survive.

What would Howl do?

Howl.

An ache settles in behind my eyes, stabbing like icy shards of glass. His shoulder bitten through to the bone. Xuan, in the woods, waiting for the supplies I was supposed to give him. June's pale fear. Tai-ge, the *liar* . . . I push the thought of him away. "Where are my friends? There was a girl from here and two boys about my age. . . . One was hurt. The other had a Second mark." I hold up my hand and touch the star melted into my skin. Xuan wasn't in the heli when . . . whatever it was happened. Maybe he got away.

"A Second, too? They didn't tell me that." Erhu Player shakes his head. "We disabled your aircraft and recovered those of you who seemed most useful. I'm afraid we don't keep Seconds. Firsts—the one who was hurt?—are good collateral. Thirds and Fourths usually mean us no harm, or are interesting in any case. We're still not sure how the Outsider girl fits into this. Seconds, though . . . They aren't valuable enough to your City to recover, and they're usually too violent and indoctrinated to assimilate."

"You're saying they . . ." I was so angry at Tai-ge, but the thought of him lying still—wounded and left for the gores—shudders through me. "You brought the others here, but not him?"

The erhu player shifts to one side, readjusting his long tunic. The guard watching from behind hardly blinks as his eyes follow the erhu player's every move, but his shoulders pull taught. Tension seems to swell in the room, as though something deadly walked in, fangs bared, and somehow I'm the only one who can't see. But then he sits straight again, folding his arms into his sleeves. The two guards relax.

"Are you saying . . ." The words break apart as they come out of my mouth, and I swallow, trying to find the air to speak. "Are you saying Tai-ge isn't here because . . . they *killed him*? That you kept my other two friends, but Tai-ge's *dead*?" The shock of it strikes me through the chest, and I know it's true without anyone telling me. Of course they would kill any soldiers they could. Reds have been stealing their children for eight years.

My stomach heaves, but there's nothing inside to expel, the dry gag leaving nothing but bright spots for me to look at across my vision, tears streaming down my cheeks.

I was ready to send Tai-ge out with the gores, to never see him again. But Tai-ge was my best friend when no one else could stand the sight of me. He stood up for me when his father yelled. He believed me when I told him there was a cure, and that we could find it together.

Only, he didn't.

But it doesn't change the glaring hole in my heart where he used to sit.

The erhu player sighs, his calm, unblinking stare now holding a trace of pity. "If you are not a part of this proposed invasion, perhaps you'd like to tell me what you are doing here, little sister?" he asks quietly.

The word rankles, an empty substitute for what I'd hoped to find in this place. "I'm *not* your little sister."

"Apologies. It was meant as a kindness." He inclines his head. "I would like an answer to that question, though."

My face hot and my feet cold and curling up should crush all the despair inside me, but it isn't working. "My mother told me to come because of SS. She didn't know about the contagious strain, but . . ."

The man looks up at that, a reaction so exaggerated in

comparison to his slow nods that all of us in the room go still. "Please continue. Contagious SS?"

I shiver again, rubbing my arms up and down as if that will brush away the needle points pricking out all over my skin. "Yes. One of the Firsts manufactured a new strain that is communicable—"

"And these papers have something in them that will help." He pulls a hand from his wide sleeves to rub across his chin, eyes narrowed. "Why would they be here? How can you be marked the way you are, when you are so obviously from the City? Our people do not often meet."

"I don't know." Uncertainty flickers through me. The man's agitation over the idea of contagious SS sends drips of fear down my throat. If the cure is here, why would contagion matter? But Mother said to come here. Dr. Yang wouldn't be expending so many resources to invade if the cure weren't here. Of course, even if they do have the cure, this place may not be willing to just hand it over. I narrow my eyes, and sit forward, attempting to convince myself I'm the questioner instead of the one awaiting judgment. "Maybe you can tell me. My mother's name was Jiang Gui-hua. She came here almost nine years ago with research she wanted to hide from . . . a man. Dr. Yang. I'm her only living child, and I'm here to collect it."

The curly-haired guard watching me flinches, and her eyes flick to my questioner.

The erhu player leans back, the only indication he heard a miniscule line between his eyebrows. After a moment, he twists around to speak to the guards, my ears straining over the familiar-sounding words to catch something that makes sense.

The curly-haired guard shakes her head with an almost abrasive-sounding reply. As the light touches her cheek, my heart jumps. There's a brown curl of pigmentation creeping out from under her ear. The same side my birthmark is. The same shape. Stark against her pinkish skin, as if somehow we're connected and I don't know how.

I put a hand to my cheek, covering my own mark.

Erhu Player responds to her terse remark, his speech submersed in fluid vowels and sharp cuts. Finally, the curly-haired guard gives a slow nod, then leads the other toward a metal seam in the wall. She places a hand against the metal, and a door slides sideways into the wall. They step through, and the guard gives me one last hard look before pressing her hand to the outside wall, shutting the door.

"What . . ." I swallow down my question, switching it for another, my fingers pushing hard into my cheek. "What did you tell them?"

"That I'll call for help if I need it. Or that you will." The erhu player pauses a second as if waiting for confirmation I understand, and I hardly know whether to nod. When I don't say anything, he shrugs. "The First who we found with you—"

"Is he all right? He needs help. His shoulder—"

"He's being cared for, though I believe our medics' assessment wasn't extremely optimistic. With the amassing forces to the south, I wondered if it was him they were after. It isn't often you find a First traveling with a Fourth and a *Wood Rat*." The words come out with a hint of venom new to his speech that takes me aback, a challenge to the slang so strong I can't make sense of it. "Tell me his name. Fewer lives will be lost if we can make this an easy negotiation with the Chairman."

"He's not really a First." I shake my head, panic spiking in my belly. Is Howl a potential chip on the negotiating table for this place? "He only has a First mark because he was a spy in the City."

"A spy?" The man sits forward. "For who?"

"Another group. They were fighting the City too—"

"He's from the Mountain, then?" The man's jaw clenches. "Perhaps his death wouldn't be such a terrible loss after all."

My chest sinks at the idea that Howl's death is already a fore-gone conclusion, and that instead of taking him off the table, I've just taken away any reason the people here had to treat his gore bites. If they even can.

The man presses his lips together, and just like it did back at the Post, that feeling of familiarity thrums through me again as if I've seen him before. Seen him a million times. But can't quite connect his face to where and how. "You, however, might be use-ful." He stands, his back seeming almost unbearably straight as he nods to me. "I'll ask the Baohujia to bring you food. Water. I'll be back."

"Wait!" My insides seem to melt into one stringy mess at the idea of June boxed in. "What about my friends? The girl from here, June. She didn't do anything to hurt anyone. And Howl might not be a good negotiating tool, but he . . ." What can I say to argue for Howl?

How did it come to this? Once again it's me who is grasping for arguments to support Howl, when it was only a week ago that I was shouting the loudest against him.

A draft blows across me, and I realize the erhu player is still standing there, staring down at me, his hand frozen against the metal strip, the door hanging open. "What did you say?" he asks.

I bury my head in my hands, trying to wipe away the raw emo-tion I know is written across my face. This place is just as bad as the

City or the Mountain, and this man, no matter how beautifully he plays the erhu, is going to use the things I want against me.

I'm not a Menghu. I'm not a First or a Second, trained to keep a straight face. I'm just a person. And I can't help it. "I just want to know if my friends are all right." I say it into my hands, the words squished and muffled. "June scares so easy . . . and if Howl isn't . . . I want to see him."

"Howl." I look up at the strained quality to his voice, choking on my friend's name. "*Sun* Howl? A spy from the Mountain."

I never knew Howl's last name. I'd always assumed sharing a last name with the Chairman was part of his charade back in the City. For my benefit, when we went to the Mountain. I stare at him, not sure if nodding will make it worse or better.

The erhu player blinks, his expression a mask, and I can't begin to guess what lies underneath. After a moment, he turns away from me and walks out. He doesn't look back.

CHAPTER 44

WHEN THE ERHU PLAYER FINALLY RETURNS, I'M LYING with my back against the wall, my eyelids warring between exhaustion and horror, the one forcing them to close, the other jabbing them open every time a dream begins. There are too many shadows in my mind—of Sleep, of Menghu, of Tai-ge's body rotting next to the mutilated gores by our heli.

"Oh, good. You're awake." Erhu Player runs an appraising eye over me as I scramble to sit up, weighing on the tears in my shirt and the bandage peeking through. "Would you like something to eat?"

The two guards from before follow close behind him. The girl sets a wooden bowl next to me on the ground, the scent so thick with spices I can hardly tell it's food, only the grains of rice and what looks like some kind of meat telling me it's meant to be consumed. The other guard holds out a waterskin to me, then hovers over me after I take it. The waterskin feels leathery against my fingertips, not plastic like the ones I've used before, and it's stitched over with flowers that don't seem to have any practical purpose. Not to bind the seams, or to designate a unit or an owner. They're just *there*, as if it's supposed to be pretty.

I run my fingers over the bumpy stitches, the flowers' yellow middles bright and cheerful. I like it. But once I've opened it and wet my lips, the man grabs it from my hands and tucks it back under his arm.

Erhu Player gestures for the man to give it back, once again using the clipped syllables I can't quite divine. Even when I listen hard to the two answering him, staring at their mouths as they fold around the familiar sounds, I can't seem to pick out a single word that belongs to me. The guard shrugs an apology and hands it back gently, as if he's not sure how to treat me now.

The mark is still there on the woman's cheek. And now that I'm looking, I see the same mark on the man's jaw, though it's harder to see against his darker coloring. As the two of them talk with the erhu player, my eyes snag over and over on those tiny curls of brown skin. I touch my cheek again, one thing that linked me to Mother for all these years, as if birthmarks were somehow hereditary. I thought it set me apart. In a bad way, for most of my life. But now it seems I was marked as an Outsider long before they burned a traitor's mark into my hand.

You can't be both, the erhu player said. Both from the City and marked. But here I am. Caught between yet another two worlds, and not fitting in either one.

"You are not going to eat?" I look up to find the erhu player still contemplating me.

I push the bowl away, my stomach churning. "No thank you."

"Come with me, then." He extends a hand to help me stand, but I get up on my own, dusting off my knees and arms, trying to ignore the damp cling of my shirt against my skin. "I've a story to tell you, little sister."

"Don't call me that."

"I'm sorry. Habits are difficult to break, especially when I've little motivation."

I look over at the jab, surprised to find that ghost of a smile that seems to hover about this man's face, as if he thinks he's teasing me. Out in the hallway, cold soaks through my bare feet as we walk down a bleak hall. The two guards walk just behind us down the long corridor, the woman trailing a hand along the geometric lines that mark the pale, porous stone walls.

The erhu player walks between me and the inner wall, where open doorways lead to less than inviting dark tunnels. He almost seems to glide, his hands tucked into his sleeves as we walk. "If you like my story, will you be good enough to answer a question for me at the end? I hope we can help you."

"You want to help me? You've already killed my . . ." I trail off. Not "friend." Tai-ge wasn't my friend. I thought he was, and the realization that he very much wasn't still feels like vertigo.

The erhu player's mouth quirks. "I haven't killed anyone, Jiang Sev. The Baohujia do what they must to keep us safe from what lurks outside our territory. We Speakers work with them to keep those inside the territory happy."

"You're a Speaker?" Wasn't that what the woman back in the village said? What June understood, anyway. Go to the island to be safe with the Speakers. They'll protect you. "What does that mean?"

"I speak for the people here, advocate, mediate. Help make rules. And the Baohujia make sure we're all alive to follow those rules."

"They both have . . ." I look back at the two guards trailing us, brushing the spot on my chin where the mark lies. "They're marked the way I am. Did Mother give it to me hoping it would help me sneak in here, and—"

"My story will answer that question. Just listen. Gao Shun wants you to hear before she speaks to you."

"Who is Gao Shun?" We come to a set of stairs, beams of light suffusing the air with particles of dust that seem to sparkle, though the windows are too high on the wall for me to see anything but gray, cloudy skies outside. For a prison, this place isn't what I would have expected. Compared to the dark and dank hopelessness I remember from the Hole—the underground prison in the City—this place feels almost airy. Empty, though. Echoing and distant, as if the warm touch of friendly banter and good meals have never once graced this hallway.

"Gao Shun is the head of the Baohujia," Erhu Player responds. "She sends thanks for the warning about contagious SS."

"And you? What is your name?"

"My name is Luokai." He pauses on the stairs, eyebrows raised. "Is that enough? Can I continue?"

I swallow my frustration, the informal introduction rankling. No last name, but I have no idea what that means here. I grew up holding my name close, like a treasure to be shared only with those who deserved it. Before my surname became a target, anyway. At the Mountain, people seemed quite free with their names, sharing given names and surnames as if they could be interchanged. Is Luokai being rude? Familiar? Maybe Luokai is a title and he isn't telling me anything but how far below him I am. There were enough in the City who did much the same.

He's been so careful to use *my* full name, though, so it must mean something. What if it's like Comrade Hong—*General* Hong now—Forcing Tai-ge to use my full name as some sort of shield against me, a barrier to others deciding we might be friends if they heard only my given name on his lips. Worse. A *nickname*.

Sevvy. My stomach twists. No one will ever call me that again. But then I straighten my shoulders, thrusting my chin up. No one will *ever* call me that again.

It was an excuse. A cover. A *lie*.

"There haven't been many crossovers between our territory and yours until recent years." Luokai looks up at the tiny slits that make windows near the ceiling, as if he can see clear to the mountains through them. "There was a war. Between this country before it was broken by SS and a country from over the ocean, a man at their head named Cameron."

Cameron. The word feels foreign even on his tongue, his mouth twisting it almost to sound like the City's word for this place. Kamar. Ka-mah-re.

Luokai continues, "It was the worst kind of war where men and woman forgot themselves and became even less than the beasts. War does that to all who partake, but this was a special sort of loss. Your humanity could be *ripped* from you rather than given up one compromise or threat at a time. Many tried to hide from the scourge, the fear of catching such a terrible sickness driving them to the highest reaches of the mountains. To islands in the sea." He raises a hand as we get to the top of the stairs, gesturing to the stone hallway. The whole building.

We're on the island. On Port North. Made of stone and stairs and foreign words, with none of the warmth I dreamt of.

I bite my lip, ramming my disappointment down, willing myself not to interrupt, not to tell him to go jump in the ocean himself because everyone knows the history of SS and the Influenza War.

We come to a grate set into the wall, the bars set so close together, I couldn't fit my arm through. Two Baohujia sit on the other side. They jump up at the sight of Luokai, bowing their heads respectfully as they open a door in the grate to allow us through.

Once we're past, Luokai continues, "The people here were safe. Even those who swam to our island, parts of the army that brought the sickness from across the seas. The scourge across the water seemed to die out, only cropping up naturally here and there among our own people, as if the war had broken a barrier of some kind in our brains."

Naturally occurring SS? I shudder. Did they send their sick out into the forest to die, like they did in the Mountain? But then I check myself. Whatever happened on this island, it's better than what Yuan Zhiwei did, consistently reinfecting his own people to force them to rely on Mantis. On him.

"By the time you from the mountains and we from the island found one another again, generations had past. We did not want war, and it seemed you did not either. Your City could not forget the guns, the bombs, the sickness that had spread at the hands of those who had come from across the sea. General Cameron was not one of the refugees who came here, though his name was a powerful tool. Calling us by his name served as a declaration of separation, as if somehow the monks and others who lived on this island during the war were corrupted by those who came from Cameron's army seeking asylum. Those from the invading army and from the mainland who took refuge here left descendants, people who had harbored in our homes, then married into our families and worked in our fields. We were incurably different to you mountain folk. Frightening. To protect our peace and ensure no more killing would happen, the City took a hostage."

"The City? Took a hostage from here?" My head seems to be swimming with fatigue. We come to another stairway, the steps curved so I cannot see what's the top. Sunlight pours over us in a liquid stream from the windows above, forcing me to squint. There are chisel marks in the stone, forming a rough assortment of bending waves that coil up the stairs, marking each one.

"We demanded a hostage in return, so it became an exchange. A child of your ruler traded for the child of ours."

"A Speaker?" I ask.

"Speakers do not have children. That sacrifice was left to head of the Baohujia. What parent could plan an attack when it is your own blood that would be spilled in the streets? And not just your own child, but cousins from the sister who was given a generation before, grandchildren after your child is grown and a father or mother themselves. We knew sickness still raged in your city, that the hills and mountains were full to the brim with violence and cross-dealing. But we were at peace. Until Jiang Gui-hua."

Fear fingers its way through my lungs, pressing hard so they refuse to inflate. This is where we find out if they have the things I came for. But if Mother was the person who brought war, how likely is it these people will help me? "She came. She brought—"

The man looks up. "She came?" He shakes his head. "No, Jiang Sev. She was *from* here."

CHAPTER 45

"MOTHER WAS . . . FROM HERE?" THE AIR SEEMS
trapped in my lungs. Mother. A Baohujia. A daughter of one of the
head families here.

Luokai nods. "She was. And your people killed her." He points
to my mark. "She must have given you that tattoo herself."

Tattoo? My hand creeps up to touch the skin of my cheek,
as if I could feel the mark there. Ice and stone seem to bloom in
my chest, burning and freezing and falling and *heavy* all at once.
Mother was a First, married to a First. She looked like the City,
had a City name . . . but that thought stalls. I've met all sorts of
people since I've been outside. Including people who look and talk
the way I do. Who have much more City-sounding names than I
do, even though they've never set foot inside City walls.

My name. Mother gave it to me. A funny, Outside-sounding
name, because she *was* an Outsider.

But how could Mother have been some kind of political hostage? And if she was, how is it that no one in the City knew, given
that we were supposed to be at war with Kamar?

Then another thought hits me. When Mother told me to find the family, I thought she meant lost grandparents or aunts or uncles who had escaped the City. I never once imagined that I could have had family who were *born* here.

What was it that Luokai said about the families of the hostages? *That sacrifice was left to head of the Baohujia.*

The head of the Baohujia. Gao Shun.

What if . . . ? *No.* I bar the doors surrounding that question, not ready to ask yet. I want to hold the hope inside me before real answers can dash me to pieces.

My hand strays to the mark again, as if I should be able to feel it poking out from my skin. "What does this mean?"

"Everyone is supposed to serve with the Baohujia when they turn sixteen." Luokai touches his own chin, blank of a mark. "Most of us, anyway. Being marked is an honor. At eighteen, we can leave the Baohujia if we choose. It's a mark of truly belonging to . . . what did you call our island?"

Belonging? My cheek feels hot, my cool fingers brushing against it. "Port North?"

"Yes, that's it. People who have Baohujia's mark are true members of the community. They love this place enough to give up some of themselves to *Port North*." Luokai shakes his, head smiling over the words.

"Why is calling this place Port North funny?" I ask.

"I think it's a literal translation. What we call our island made to fit your mouth. It only could have come from someone who had lived both places."

Literal translation? I wonder if that's why June didn't recognize it when I first told her where Mother told us to go. June has been gone so long she only understands some of what is going on, much less a name my Mother made up.

I wonder how Dr. Yang knew?

The swirls of stone decorating the wall grow larger, and I realize they're waves of water, dotted with ships and little figures peering down at the churning eddies. "Are there others from the City here?" I ask. "What happened to them when Mother was put to sleep?"

"A new hostage was sent every ten years. And there *was* talk of retribution at first. But Speakers spoke for the hostages who had been brought here. They'd lived here most of their lives. They had married. Had children and grandchildren. They were more ours than the City they left behind. To punish them for the crimes of the place they were born would be to punish our own daughters and sons."

"And they're still here?" I ask.

"Yes. Though I don't know how you would tell them from the others of us here. They belong to us now."

"And people from here are still in the City?" I bite my lip. Among the Firsts, perhaps?

Luokai doesn't quite look at me when he answers, his lips pressing together tightly, an expression that once again brings a spark of recognition. "That I do not know."

"Why didn't Port North attack the City?" I ask. "The City killed their hostage."

"We are not a warlike people, Jiang Sev." Luokai sighs, his breathing perfectly even as we ascend, though mine is beginning to cut short, protesting each step. "Not in mind or in tools. Your City has planes and bombs and guns that would overtake us a thousand times. We can hide, but moving against the mountains was as impossible then as it is now."

A landing comes into view ahead, the sculpted whirls washing up the wall to twine around a figure carved into the rock. It's a woman, her lantern raised against a crashing storm of stone waves, the light from the windows catching in drips and pools in her robes and in the swirls of her hair. The carving has been worn smooth from hands touching the wheels of water at her feet, her long skirts and the wild streams of hair twirling around her, but her eyes are calm and piercing as she looks down at me.

"She protects us from the sea. Or she did, before." Luokai's voice jerks my attention back to him, his eyes pointed up at the stone woman. Down the hall are full-length windows cut into the outside wall, the source of the gusty winds whistling through this place. A stone bannister blocks any risk of falling over by accident.

And on the other side of the bannister . . . My heart stutters. All I can see is gray. Gray sky and gray water all around us, stabbed through with towering rocks, their bases gnawed away under the water's careless bite. The sea never seems to end, reaching long past the horizon as if I'm in some other world. My body tingles as if I'm already falling into the void so many stories below us, the white-tinged waves undulating toward us as if they can reach up and grab me.

"Are you all right?" Luokai pauses, cocking his head.

"There's just so much . . ." I shake my head, and I almost feel dizzy, as by looking down at those waves so far down below me, the stone has begun to roll under my feet. I point to the woman carved into the wall. "How does she protect you? Doesn't stone sink when you throw it in the water?"

"Stone does well enough when heli-planes crash into it." Luokai shrugs. "They're more worrisome than water these days."

Forcing myself to keep walking, I find shelter in looking at the woman on the wall, anything to pretend those gaping windows to the sea aren't pulling at me, waiting to swallow me down. The stone woman finds something solid inside me, something calm. Her halo of hair and her calm eyes remind me of Mother, who stood tall and proud even frozen in Sleep, a hostage in her own body.

Hostage. If the City and Port North each extracted a hostage from the other every ten years . . . There is one boy I can think of who was missing, and no one seemed to know why.

Sun Yi-lai.

I grab hold of Luokai's sleeve, pulling him to a stop. "The Chairman's son. He was the exchange. He was here."

Luokai nods. "Yes. He came to us when he was about two years old."

"That's why no one knew where he was. He's been here since before the treaty broke." I bite my lip, doing the math in my head. "But . . . my friend Howl. He was pretending to be the Chairman's son. That's how he got into the City to spy. If the real Sun Yi-lai was supposed to be here, then wouldn't the Chairman have known Howl didn't belong to him?"

Luokai's eyes narrow at Howl's name, and he continues down the hall with an extra kick in his step as if he's just realized he's late for a self-criticism session. "That is a question I'd also like the answer to. Sun Yi-lai hasn't been here for many many years. By the time we got word of Jiang Gui-hua's Sleep, he'd already left."

"Where did he go? Is he alive?"

Luokai stops in the hall, nothing around us but stone and strips of silver marking the wall. "No one knows. At first we thought he'd been kidnapped, taken back to the City. But then your Chairman demanded that he be produced. That if we wanted to keep helis and soldiers far from our cities, we would give him back his son. We had nothing to give him." Luokai's eyes close, old memories heavy on his shoulders. "Speakers still go up into the mountains looking for any sign of him. Something we've yet to find."

Could it be that each child stolen from the settlements is the Chairman's price, a price exacted a hundred times over for whatever happened to his son? That doesn't make sense either, though, because if it were some kind of revenge, the kidnappings would have stopped once Howl came to him. The Chairman got his son back.

But the Chairman didn't stop.

Maybe once you have a justification to start taking, it's hard to find a reason to pull your hand back out of the jar.

My feet drag to a stop when Luokai stops in front of another silver strip, much like the ones down in the cells. "Was that the end of your story?" I ask. "You said you wanted to ask me a question."

He's already halfway to touching the silver strip, but stops, looking back at me. "All of this started when Jiang Gui-hua hid her things here. What was so important it was worth a war to your mother? What was worth dying for?"

My forehead puckers. If Luokai really doesn't know what was in Mother's papers, what are the chances he'll hand them over if I tell him? With a contagious strain of SS headed this way, giving away the cure wouldn't be a good choice.

Meeting his eyes isn't difficult. Maybe it would have been a few months ago, but now I know the value of secrets. "You said the head of the Baohujia wanted to talk to me?" A tremor runs through me. The head of the Baohujia. Family.

Luokai nods.

"Well, then I'll tell her all about it. Is she in there?" I point to the door.

"No." Luokai presses his hand to the silver strip. "This is my room. It's only my brother inside."

The door swishes open, the room inside dark, a sleeping figure swaddled in blankets on a pallet on the left-hand wall all I can see. "Why are you bringing me to your . . ." My words dry up when a light set high on the wall begins to glow, illuminating a floppy head of hair and a shoulder swathed over in bandages.

Howl.

CHAPTER 46

HOWL'S CHEST RISES AND FALLS WITH A REGULARITY that seems almost miraculous. I hardly know how I cross the floor or feel it when my knees collapse at his side, both terrified to really look at him and hopeful he'll somehow be better. He lies flat on his back, a thick gray blanket tucked neatly up to his chin, his eyes closed. His skin is cool when I pull back the blanket to touch his wrist, his pulse slowed down from the suicide sprint it was attempting the last time I checked on the heli. My friend still looks shrunken and small, as if some part of Howl escaped into the night the moment the gore bit him.

Is that what Howl is now? My friend?

I try not to hold my breath as I check his bandages for the chemical reek that seemed to crawl out of the wounds before. Under the white cloths, Howl's skin is an angry red, crisscrossed with an awful black thread, as if they sewed the break in Howl's skin shut rather than using adhesive. But instead of the rank, hostile smell from before, something herbal and tangy wafts up from his skin that makes me want to sneeze. Not pleasant exactly, but healthy. Alive.

Luokai kneels beside me, reaching out to take Howl's other hand, still limp on the pallet. Not to check his pulse, but to examine the single white line carved into the skin between his forefinger and thumb.

Howl's eyelids twitch, then crinkle open to squint up at me, blinking as if he can't quite remember how it is he got here or why I'd be at his bedside watching him sleep. He glances over to Luokai, who is still contemplating the scar marring Howl's skin, then to mark the ceiling, the contours of the room, and the silver strip lining the open door.

He closes his eyes again, and I can almost feel the gears in his mind beginning to whir, calculations forming on how far he is from the door, to where I'm sitting, to the height and build of the man sitting next to me. Howl slowly twists the wrist I'm holding around so his hand is wrapped around my wrist as well, fingers squeezing gently.

"You're awake." Luokai carefully sets Howl's hand down on the mat and sits back on his heels. "I don't know much about medicine, but I think that's supposed to be a good sign."

"How are you feeling?" I ask.

Howl opens his eyes again and there's a hint of a smile at the corner of his mouth. His throat convulses as if he's summoning the courage to speak, but it comes out in a cough that curves him forward.

"Something to drink?" I ask. "Where's your medic?" I look toward Luokai, but he doesn't respond for a moment, eyes still heavy on Howl's First mark. Finally, he goes to the door, speaking in low tones to the guards we left outside.

"Where are we?" Howl croaks between coughs.

"On the island."

His eyes widen and he tries to take a deep breath, to stop the coughs racking his chest. "And?"

"And . . . I'm not sure. I was in a cell until they brought me here," I whisper.

"June?"

"I don't know."

"That stupid medic?"

"I let him go."

Howl's head ticks to the side, processing. "Tai-ge?"

I lick my lips, my fingers around his wrist compulsively tightening before I realize. Luokai returns with a small cup of water, steam wafting from its surface. Howl's chin comes forward as he attempts to sit up, but that's as far as he gets, his eyes clenching shut in pain. I shift so I'm by his head and help lift him into a sitting position.

He groans, but he can support himself once he's up. I try not to think about the fact that he's bare to the waist, wearing nothing but bandages.

I've never seen him without a shirt before—not like this, anyway. His skin ripples over the muscles that rope up his torso . . . and then I can't look anymore because he'll notice. Just the thought of him catching me staring at him causes enough heat in my cheeks to roast taro.

Howl tries to reach out for the cup with his scabby, bitten arm and swears. His shoulders curve forward around his broken collarbone as he gathers the arm under his wounded shoulder and cradles it against his chest.

This isn't the gray, mostly dead boy from the heli. Even with my limited orphan-style medic experience, I know just how close Howl was to stepping over the line into black after the gore bit him. Now he's not even contemplating it, just wishing he could, probably. He's much, much better.

"How long have we been here?" I ask Luokai. A recovery this miraculous didn't happen in a matter of hours. "Helis are supposed to attack in . . ." I don't know how many days.

"You *do* know their plans?" Luokai tears his attention away from Howl. "You'll help us, then?"

Howl's eyes meet mine, his years spent up to his necks in lies and manipulation mixing with my brushes with lies and promises unkept over the last few months. I don't know the sorts of things that would be helpful to know about the invasion, in any case. Only that Dr. Yang said seven days and what he means to take. Hope. The future. Everything that's important to me.

I turn a fraction, toward Luokai. "I want to see June first. And my mother's papers. And have a way out of here that doesn't involve weapons."

Luokai swivels toward the door, barking an order at the two Baohujia standing there. One gives a minute bow and slips out of the doorway, out of sight. Luokai nods to the other guard before looking back at me. "I can show you your friend. But as for the papers and safe passage off the island, you'll have to take that up with Gao Shun."

"I'd like to speak with her as soon as possible, then." I turn back to Howl, the warmth of hope crackling in my chest. He hasn't tried to reach for the cup again, so I take it from Luokai, the bulky pottery warm against my clammy skin. Before I can offer to help him drink, Howl takes it out of my hands, the cup wobbling as he tries to hold it to his lips.

Dr. Yang took Howl, too. Made him into whatever it was Howl became inside the Mountain. A person who believed only a gun could preserve his home. That no matter what, Reds would never stop, would never share their food, their medicine, or anything he needed to live. But that only lasted until the Mountain tried taking Howl's life too, and he was caught between a tiger and a falcon, both hungry for his flesh.

What was it Howl said when we were in the cave, under the owl's tree? That I *can't* understand. Not any more than he can step into my shoes and know what it was like to have my sister shot in the street, to live with Mother looking down at the City with her dead eyes, waiting for it to be my turn.

Well, this war can't have any more of us. Dr. Yang can't have Lihua or Peishan. He can't have June. He can't have the rest of me, or what's left of Howl. Not if I have anything to say about it.

Swearing again under his breath, Howl's throat constricts as he drinks, his whole frame shaking. Even if he isn't being poisoned from the inside anymore, Howl isn't going to be running anywhere. He finally seems to feel me watching him, but instead of raising an eyebrow and cracking a joke about being irresistible, Howl pulls the blanket up around him as if he's cold. Or embarrassed to be sitting here half-naked.

Vulnerable, perhaps. A state to which Howl is not accustomed.

"Can I have something to make a sling for his arm?" I ask Luokai. "I'm guessing he didn't need it while he was asleep, but now that he's awake, every time he moves it will hurt. Broken collarbones hurt everything else, too."

The man starts to bow his assent, but a typhoon made from a gas mask and golden curls pours into the room before he can finish. Blond hair catching the dim light, June slides to her knees away from the guard who seems to be her escort, pivots, and rams straight into him. A groan leaks out of him as she kicks him in the groin. I jump up, not sure if I should be helping June or restraining her, but before she can plant her elbow into the other guard's ribs or her teeth into someone's skin, a third guard grabs hold of her from behind, tackling her to the ground, wrapping his arms around her and squeezing until June stops fighting. Her gas mask obscures half of her face, making her sharp nose and chin into a long ugly snout.

"June?" I run to her, pulling at the guard's arms wrapped so tightly around her middle. The panicked rasp of air sucking in and out through the filters of her mask makes the hair on my arms prickle. "Let go of her! June, are you all right?"

One of the other Baohujia moves to grab me, but Luokai calls him off. "Tell her to stop, or we'll put her back in a box where she can't hurt anyone," he instructs.

I fall to my knees, one hand still pulling at the guard's arms, but he doesn't even look at me, doesn't give an inch. When I put a hand to June's cheek just above the curve of her mask, she rears back, hiding her covered nose and mouth against the guard's arm, as if I were going to pull the filters away from her.

"I wasn't going to take it off, June," I whisper as calmly as I can manage.

June won't look at me, every breath jerking, panic screaming out of every twitch she makes. I touch the guard's arm again and meet his eyes. "Let me take her. She won't hurt anyone if I'm holding her."

I hope June is listening, even if she won't look at me. Luokai translates, and the man loosens his grip. June tumbles forward into my arms, and I grab her around the middle, pinning her arms before she can attempt to inflict any more damage. She only twists against my hold once before wilting against me, her limp form frighteningly still. Each breath comes in a rusty wheeze, her eyes wide in terror, like a caged animal. I hold her firmly against me just in case she's waiting for the right moment to bolt.

"You've seen her," Luokai says from behind me. "I'd like to take you up to Gao Shun now. Time presses against us." He gestures for the guard to take June back, but I curve my arms around her and glare up at him.

"Let her stay." The steel in my voice grinds the words out in a heavy, unmovable shield.

"She won't hurt anyone if you let her stay with us," Howl croaks. "And Tai-ge, too. Where is he?"

June's weight feels heavy against my chest. It's comforting to have someone touching me, holding me down.

"Sev?" I look up, and Howl's eyes are on me. "Have they told you where he is yet?"

He holds my gaze, the mist of pain and grogginess seeming to slip when I don't answer. I look away to find Luokai's stare instead.

I feel my heart freeze for a moment, looking from one to the other. Their heavy brows, the shape of Luokai's nose, just a bit flatter and wider than Howl's. Their dark eyes narrowed to almost the exact same degree. Even the way Luokai stands, straight-backed and leaning toward me looks like something I've seen a thousand times. It's the mouth that clinches it, though.

What was it Luokai said before opening the door? In the mixed panic and relief of seeing Howl alive, I hadn't quite processed it. Howl and this man look as if they were broken from the same mold.

They look like brothers.

CHAPTER 47

"WHAT'S WRONG, SEV?" HOWL ASKS.

I point to Luokai, my mouth hanging open for a moment before words come. "You said Howl was related. . . . I think you'd better explain."

Luokai takes a long breath, then carefully lowers himself to the ground to sit across from us, focusing on Howl. "I probably should. I would never have had a First brought to my own room or allowed an entire heli's worth of invaders into the same room together if not for you, Howl."

"How do you know my name?" Howl's eyes sharpen, and for a moment I wonder if he's putting on the sickness, if he's stronger than he's acting.

Luokai tucks his hands into his sleeves as if steeling himself before continuing. "Sun Howl. From the Mountain, no? Your parents, Chen Hui and Sun Baoli, defected from the City during a purge of the Chairman's family. Sun Baoli was the Chairman's youngest brother."

An ugly flutter of ash stirs up inside me, not sure where to go.

Howl is related to Chairman Sun? If the Chairman was removing any challenges to his hand around the First Circle's neck, it wouldn't surprise me to find he'd sent members of his extended family to starve outside City walls.

It would also, after all of the pretending and lying and ridiculousness, be horrifyingly ironic.

Howl glances at me, brow furrowed. I wait for him to correct the erhu player, but he doesn't. "And you are . . . creepy Port North guy. Who has not tried to kill me yet, even though you know my name and my entire family history, so I shouldn't worry?"

"You worry that anyone who knows you will start with a weapon?" Luokai smiles. "I suppose that's in line with what I remember of you, though I hoped you would grow out of it. I'm your brother."

Howl jerks away and begins coughing again. "My *what*?" A tear tracks down his cheek as he flinches with each barrage of coughs, clutching his arm close to his chest.

"Your brother."

"Seth—my brother—is dead. He's been dead since I was little."

"I suppose I am. The man I was before most certainly is. I don't use that name anymore. It was a concession our parents shouldn't have made. I use the name they gave me when I was born: Sun Luokai." Luokai breathes in, holding the air in a second too long before letting it back out again. He looks down at his hands, tracing the skin between his forefinger and his thumb decorated with a single scarred line, faded almost to nothing as though he got it very young and never had it redrawn. "I was a child when our parents escaped the City. But old enough to be marked. You, however, were born in the Mountain."

I want to laugh and cry at the same time. But it's not the time to do either, because Howl is shaking his head. "Scars don't prove anything."

A ghost of a smile flits across Luokai's face, pain a sharp seasoning. "The Mountain was closed back then. They were afraid if we went out, we'd lead Reds right to our hiding place. Or worse, that SS would find its way in. It was hard to find enough food for everyone, so they organized raiding parties. Volunteers to risk contracting SS in exchange for food to put in their children's starving bellies—"

"Stop," Howl interrupts, sliding off the pallet as if he wants to stand and walk away. But for once, he can't. He slides toward me and June, as if having the two of us at his back somehow makes him stronger, but only makes it a few inches.

"Stop? Why?" Luokai looks down at his hands. "I wanted to believe you were still alive. I remember the way you looked the day I went out with them. You were only five or six, ribs sticking out like a sick gore, begging to come with us. I was barely old enough to go at sixteen. Those City supply lines from the farms had all the food we could ever need." He speaks in a straight line, unwavering and direct, inevitably drawing closer and closer to the chasm, the great hole I know is coming. "We didn't even get a chance to attack. A City scout circled around behind us and threw a grenade right in the middle of our group. I still remember how it bounced, coming apart right at my feet, each piece trailing little wisps of smoke. Mother jumped in front of me.

"We managed to carry her out, Father and me. But it didn't matter. She was probably gone before I picked up her feet. Father collapsed less than a mile later. I didn't even know he was hurt. We couldn't bring their bodies back. I didn't know what the grenade was, what *I* was, because I'd been standing so close to it. I fell Asleep only hours after getting back."

Howl's face crumples, jaw tight. Even more vulnerable than a ghostly shell of the boy from before, missing a shirt and bled dry. He looks like that little boy first realizing his parents aren't coming back in from the forest. June wheezes underneath the mask and a teardrop falls on my arm.

"Were you looking for Howl? When I saw you at the Post?" I want to let go of June, to put my arm around Howl and smooth out the painful line of his back, but I'm afraid that any leeway I give to June will be returned tenfold with violence.

Afraid that after everything, a touch from me wouldn't be comforting anyway.

I can't help but wonder if I looked . . . if I went far enough . . . Howl said it when we were sitting outside the Mountain, gazing up at the stars like we had some sort of control over our lives. Sole told me this story when I was still at the Mountain, hiding in her bathtub, waiting for the demons to come steal my brain. She said something else, too, about why he left. Fear crawls down my arms, the studied way the Baohujia watched Luokai suddenly taking on a new meaning.

"No," Luokai answers. "When you met me at the Post, I was looking for stories of Sun Yi-lai. We've been ranging out farther and farther, hoping to somehow stop . . ." Luokai takes a deep breath, his eyes closing for a moment, his hands perfectly still on his knees, as if he can banish whatever feelings are roiling in his chest. "I wish I could have looked for you, Howl."

"You *wish* . . ." Howl clears his throat, the words jagged and sharp. The space between them feels awkward and prickled, two brothers who always meant to find one another, only to end up in a cell together, one a prisoner. "What happened to you, then?"

Luokai fingers his ear where a gold ring pierces the skin. "I breathed in the wrong air, and I ceased to be a human being according to the people inside the Mountain. Chan was with us that day too. Both of us were asked to leave the moment we woke up."

The name Luokai picks at the edge of my brain. Chan. That was the other boy Sole mentioned the night she told me this story. Her brother. Banished for contracting SS, because back then allowing Sephs to mix with the uninfected was too dangerous.

It's *still* too dangerous. I find myself curling down over June, edging toward Howl as if I can somehow protect them from what could be coming next. Even if breathing the same air won't poison any of us, compulsions could do just as bad or worse.

"I don't know what they told you," Luokai looks at Howl, his eyes soft. "Just that they wouldn't let me see you to say goodbye. Maybe it was kinder that way. They didn't make you watch us leave, wondering when the compulsions would take us, if we'd die by Red fire or by our own hands. We had to leave everything, everyone." He takes a breath, flashes of emotion flooding his eyes in quick bursts, but disappearing as if he can control them. "Chan and I protected each other, helped when compulsions were bad. But it wasn't enough in the end. We came to a building standing alone in the forest. It seemed so tall, like nothing either of us had ever seen before. I still remember the rusty red braces sticking out from the old walls like bones from a rotting corpse." Luokai licks his lips. "I couldn't stop him that time. Running up the stairs as though the whole world were chasing him. Up on the roof, the whole building swayed under him until he jumped." Luokai shuts his eyes, shaking his head a fraction. "I still don't know if it was a compulsion, or just . . ."

Howl leans back, the hand less abused by the gore coming up

to cover his face. I slide June down to the floor, relaxing my grip on her arms. She remains still, eyes closed like she's asleep, her raspy breaths through the mask long and steady. Sliding a few inches closer to Howl, I put my hand on his back. I can't watch anymore. Can't let him sit through this alone. When my fingers press against his bare skin, he takes a long, shuddering breath that catches against his ribs and leans back against it. Against me.

Luokai flinches, eyes glued to my hand on Howl's back. The way he's focusing makes every inch of me buzz, waiting for something to happen. For him to lurch toward us, or to move away. Wondering if the compulsion will be violent or harmless. He doesn't move, though, his straightforward gaze sliding from my hand on Howl's back to thoughtfully meet mine. I feel as if he's looking under my skin, examining all the pieces that put me together.

"There must not be very many like you here. Infected, I mean." I clear my throat, inching closer to Howl. He turns away from Luokai and the dry, dead recount of his journey here, presented like a list of chores, easing toward me until he and June and I are all touching. "How else would you survive?"

"Speakers serve. We lead. Hand in hand with Baohujia. They protect, we advise."

"Speakers? You mean . . . all Speakers are infected? Everyone in charge here has SS?" A clan of infected are ruling those of sound mind? Remembering the grip of the medicine-induced compulsion I had, the hallucinations, the difficulty distinguishing between reality and the nightmares my brain superimposed on the world around me . . . these are the people Port North chooses to lead? How can you rely upon a leader who may not see the world in colors and shapes, but rather as a monster he is fighting?

"Is that what I am? An 'infected'?" Luokai raises his eyebrows, his voice a tinge too calm. "Am I some other species than you?"

"I didn't mean . . ." My stomach sinks as I realize what it was I just said. What I've said all along. What everyone says. When I thought I was infected, I didn't feel like a human being so much as a faulty gear in the City's machine, something inside of me twisted so far amiss that I didn't belong to them anymore. But that's not the truth. Luokai isn't "an infected" any more than *I* would claim to be the personification of the cure. Reduced to the lesions or lack thereof in my brain. I'm not a cure, a Fourth, a traitor, a Seph, or anything other than me. A person.

The fact that it never occurred to me to think of it that way hurts. "I'm sorry I said it that way."

He smiles, nodding to accept the apology. "There are not as many of us affected by the disease here, it's true."

"You were looking for the Chairman's son . . . so Port North will be able to stop the City kidnapping people out of range of your towers. Until the City finds a way to push them down, anyway."

The look Luokai gives me sends goose bumps rippling across my skin. "What do you know about the towers?"

"I'll tell you anything you want to know once Mother's papers are in my hand."

Luokai's placid glance has gone steely, and he gets up from the floor. "Let's go, then. I fear that I went to find your Chairman's son and came back with something much worse." He draws an aged breath that pricks the attention of the guard outside, her curly hair framing her face as the light streams through it.

Before she can step inside, the guard puts a hand out to lean against the doorjamb, her head lolling down against her chest. She tumbles to the ground, Luokai barely managing to catch her before her head cracks to pieces on the stone floor. He eases her down onto the floor just outside the doorway, his face solemn.

June tenses, suddenly solid as a statue. She very slowly puts a hand over the part of her mask covering her nose, as if every breathful of air is scribbled over in ink.

"What happened?" I untangle from June and Howl, scrambling to help. I heard no footsteps or helis, no gunfire. I wrap a hand around the girl's wrist, grasping for a pulse, but there's nothing there. Her chest lies still, one moment awake and alive, the next . . . gone.

I tip her chin back, meaning to breathe into her mouth, do chest compressions until the life flickers back into her eyes, but Luokai pulls me away. "It is too late, I'm afraid."

Too late. My brain wants to explode, grasping for an explanation to fit what is happening right in front of me. Howl and June stay behind me, tense as statues. "How can you be so calm? Is it usual for people to spontaneously die?" I lean down, determined to help, even if he thinks it's too late.

Luokai arranges the guard's arms across her chest. "She's Asleep, Jiang Sev."

"Asleep?" I look up at Luokai, dread a deadly blossom in my chest. "She went with you to the mountains? You were exposed?"

Luokai shakes his head. "She wasn't there. I couldn't understand it until you mentioned the contagious strain." He swallows, looking up and down the hall. "Baohujia protect me. And others, when I am not myself. The two who came with me to the mountains have already fallen ill. Into a coma of Sleep that lasted only hours instead of weeks. One woke showing the symptoms of compulsion. The other did not wake at all. Three other cases of SS have manifested since then. Baohujia who were assigned to be my companions."

"You're *contagious*?" Dread blossoms in a deadly flower inside my chest. "How can you be? You contracted SS a long time ago!"

Luokai gestures to the girl, every bit of her loose and relaxed as if it's only a matter of time before she falls apart. "Do you have another explanation?"

I look back at Howl. "But *we* haven't . . ." He gives a violent shake of the head, telling me to be quiet. If they know we've been cured, it will raise too many questions about what it is we want from Mother's papers. Who would trade the cure for information about an invasion that supposedly won't be able to get past their heli-killing towers?

I go back to June, hugging her close. Howl and I were both exposed to contagious SS. June is still well, though. Tai-ge never showed symptoms either, though they went without masks around us much of the time we were in the heli. Whatever cured SS in me and Howl must keep us from being carriers of the new strain, though Luokai is not so lucky.

Luokai focuses on me. "How long does contagion last? Have I been spreading it every moment since I got back here? The two who were with me are as well?"

I shake my head. "I'm not sure how long contagion lasts. We've been on the move, but I think I heard something like two weeks?" Dread creeps up and down my arms, the thick walls of the cell suddenly feeling like a shield as much as a prison. How long did it take for the Mountain to fall with Mei, the first contagious case of SS there, roaming free through its glass-and-stone intestines? And the City, turning from a few troubled blemishes of infection to a festering boil in the matter of a few days, sending our heli off with a snarl and complimentary bite marks. The new strain seems to be even more devastating, moving more quickly, finding the basest parts of the brain and exploiting them.

June's wheezing breaths begin to speed up, her eyes ricocheting between Luokai, the hidden door, the blankets and pallet, the barred window, as if trying to find some sort of escape.

"We need to get out of here," Howl whispers, his bandaged shoulder brushing mine. His voice is dead, sunken deep inside, as if his thoughts mirror mine, and after weighing every strategy, running is the only viable option.

I nod, trying not to think of what might be boiling up past our quiet hallway. Of the frenzy we left at the City. Howl knows better than I do, because I left him in the middle of it, two bullets lodged in his protective gear.

"You'd attempt to leave without getting what you came for?" Luokai cocks his head. "If your mother's things were not so important to this war, you wouldn't have risked coming here. Either of you." Luokai's eyes go back to Howl, a soft sort of longing hungry behind his expression. But he bows his head when Howl does not look back.

The image puts me in mind of another set of bowed shoulders. Sole, staring at the gore tooth, telling me it was Howl's older brother who had given it to him. That she and he were . . . something. Before he'd contracted SS. Before her parents and her brother disappeared, leaving her with nothing but revenge and a gun.

Does he remember her? His life before? When I told him Howl was from the Mountain—before I said his name—Luokai seemed only to be made of judgment. Perhaps remembering a family that was supposed to belong to him but that banished him to die instead.

"You must come with me, Jiang Sev," Luokai finally says, scrubbing a hand across his closely cut hair, pressing his lips together, and it's as if I can see Howl inside him, peering out, only he's all stress and no swagger. "I'm afraid contagion adds another level of complication to the conversation we must have with Gao Shun."

I draw June close to me again, her body still limp, Howl bent over the two of us in a way that's more frightening than the gore's teeth marks under his bandages. "Give us a moment. This adds a level of complication for us as well."

Luokai narrows his eyes at me as if he's waiting for something. For me to cover my mouth, throw my arms up in panic at being in the presence of an infected breathing his sickness into the air. At least Howl and I are safe. "There are quarantines being set as we speak," he says. "I'll give you the time it takes me to find new Baohujia willing to accompany me."

My stomach drops when he stops at the door, contemplating the metal strip in the wall, one hand creeping up to touch the side of his mouth. "You're going to spread SS wherever you go," I say. "Would a mask keep it in?"

"I don't believe masks work that way. And even if it were possible, you already have two fewer than you need." Luokai's smile is blank, though he does glance at June. She shrinks toward me, making herself small, hands still splayed over her mask. "We must move forward, trusting that our future will not be cut short so long as we do not allow it to be."

Allow it to be? A chill of memory needles through me. Of worrying whether or not SS had left me enough to even claim humanity anymore. Of watching the way people's eyes glossed uncomfortably past me to look toward the Sanatorium, of Tai-ge's wall between us and thinking it was justified. I take a deep breath, trying not to draw a line between me and Luokai. "You don't believe SS will cut it short for you?"

Luokai pauses on the other side of the open door, his loose robes wisping around him like a butterfly's wings. "SS may visit me during unguarded moments, but it does not choose who I am or what I become, Jiang Sev. I am not my sickness. Life is a series of choices and opportunities, not a line of blocks to stumble over."

"You say that as if SS isn't about to swallow Port North whole."

"Even the sickest of men can see the good in his life. It is a choice." Luokai smiles at me once, his eyes flicking to Howl and back again before he reaches for the panel to shut the door. "Everything is a choice."

CHAPTER 48

HOWL DOESN'T MOVE AFTER THE DOOR SHUTS BEHIND his brother, as if even the afterimage of Luokai's presence is too much for him. Arm cradled against his bare chest, he almost seems to teeter toward me, the weight of him leaning into my shoulder feeling like some sort of concession. June huddles close on my other side, the three of us connected, as if somehow that will force the universe to right, the prison doors to open, and Mother's cure to unroll itself at our feet.

It's like the family I wanted so much to find here. A circle of protection, each of us leaning on the other.

"Can I help you, Howl?" I whisper, the spot where he's touching me seeming too warm.

Howl pulls away from me, straightening his spine one vertebrae at a time, a sort of rabid energy replacing the dejected slump to his shoulders. He looks around the room, each movement a quick jerk that reminds me of June's caged panic, first eyeing the narrow window, and then the metal strip marking the door. "What's on the other side of that?"

"A hallway. A very long drop straight into the ocean." I nudge June over, settling her onto the floor with her back against Howl's leg, and go over to the pallet. "Food that smells as if it's meant to be consumed by nostril rather than mouth."

"Help me think. What did you see on your way here? Windows . . . any way out?" He watches as I pull the ragged blanket up and hold it up to the light, breath stuttering over the soft, tangy scent of whatever medicine is on Howl's wounds, clean linen, and a pleasant sort of undertone that I know belongs to Howl himself. It only takes a moment to find a rip in the threadbare fabric and tear a long strip free from the blanket. "Come on, anything could help."

"You just found your dead brother." I kneel in front of Howl, but he won't look at me, the tattered fabric light in my hands. "You don't need a moment to think it through?"

"Rather than plan how to survive this?" He rocks to the side and almost falls over, as if he meant to leap to his feet and over-balanced instead.

"We have to talk to Gao Shun before we go anywhere. She has Mother's papers." She might be the one Mother gave them to. Gao Shun might belong to me. I breathe deep, itching just to see her, to see if I can draw lines between us.

"Having them and giving them to us are two different things."

Howl is probably right to doubt, but he's not going to be able to do anything at all if he doesn't stop moving around. I go up onto my knees, holding the fabric I tore from the blanket out. "Hold still, would you? The more you move your arm, the more pain you're going to be in."

For a moment I think he won't obey, hectic energy streaming from him like sweat. But I don't move, meeting his eyes full-on,

refusing to budge. Finally, he nods, letting me loop the strip of
fabric around his wrist and knot it behind his neck, though his
momentary stillness is nothing like submission. The makeshift
sling barely reaches around his arm and up to his neck, my fingers
tracing the lines of his neck and shoulders as I tie the sling tight.

"Thank you." He adjusts his arm. The pained, lopsided set to
his shoulders doesn't exactly straighten, but I can almost feel him
relax a hair. He takes deep breath, still staring toward the door. "I
can't . . . process Luokai right now. What are our options? Do we
have any resources?"

"Just what is here."

"And Tai-ge? The heli is probably our best shot to get away
from here, and he's the only one who knows how to fly. Do you
know where they took him?"

"No."

Howl shifts to the side, frustration setting his jaw in an angry
line. "You don't know? Or you don't want to say it out loud?"

Tai-ge's face swims up in front of my eyes, the argument about
the cure and his mother and Reds and Menghu and *Howl* . . . and
then Howl's hand touches my arm, an anchor when I'm drowning
in air.

He tries to catch my eye, but I won't look. "Tell me."

I turn away so I don't have to see that awful mix of patience
and sympathy in Howl's eyes, as if somehow my heart should be
bleeding out through my chest.

If it is, I can't feel it. I can't feel anything but numb. Off-
balance, perhaps. Empty, even.

I should be sad. My best friend is dead.

Maybe I am sad. But the way it happened cauterized the
wound, sealing the rot and hurt inside. I knit my fingers together,

feeling the blank space where I wore that stupid ring. It wasn't even *his* ring. It was a ring I made for myself and assigned to him, the rusty metal staining my skin until I put it on my necklace of pasts. I've known my whole life what Tai-ge was. It's like Xuan said. If he'd wanted me, all he would have had to do was ask. But he didn't ask until there were no other options, until I'd already cut all the nerves that led back to him.

It was bad enough to have only thought of Howl when Tai-ge kissed me. But worse is the wrongness inside me that finally feels right. As if the last bits of wire and twine binding me to the City have now been ripped free.

"I know you two are . . . close. I'm sorry. . . ." His voice is soft, eyes searching my face. "Talk to me, Sev. Let it out."

I blink, waiting for tears or panic or anger or anything at all, but everything just feels empty and dead. "There's nothing to let out, Howl. He was . . . he was talking to the Reds." I try to swallow the words down, but they vomit out of me, my whole chest and throat straining to keep the burning bile down. But at his expression, I take a deep breath and look down. "Tai-ge was talking to the Reds the whole time."

Howl's eyes widen. "So I was . . ." He presses his lips together.

"You can say you were right. You were." I smooth my hair back behind my ears, nose wrinkling when the uneven strands fall right back into my eyes. "I think he wanted to believe that we could find the cure and stop the fighting somehow. But when it came down to it, he didn't have the faith in me. Or in himself. He couldn't see past the City walls." Saying it out loud feels as if I'm admitting something. Something I didn't even want to admit to myself. Tai-ge didn't trust me. He thought I wasn't smart enough or capable enough to listen to, even when I had more information than he did. That so long as he was safe, he assumed the rest of us would be too. "They don't take Reds prisoners here."

Howl blinks, looking away. "Sev, I'm sorry. I know I said . . ." He trails off, then meets my eye again. "I'm sorry."

It feels concrete. Real. A new world where I completely misjudged the one constant that's been in my life for eight years and nearly got all of us killed. And I don't need to waste any more time muddling through it right now. "I'm fine. I would love to have this conversation some other time. Right now, I'm going to go get the cure and get us out of here."

"You'd *love* to. Great." Howl raises an eyebrow, and June gives a sort of huff from my lap that almost sounds like a laugh.

I point to Howl's pallet. "I can't do this by myself, and you won't be much help if you can't move. Go lie down before whatever they've done to make you not-dead wears off."

Howl gives me a lopsided smile that doesn't hide the strain as he shifts toward the pallet. "You were a little sad about me being dead. Even if you do still hate me."

"A little."

"You hate me a little, or you were sad a little?"

"Be quiet, Howl." It almost feels like a bigger admission to brush off the question, as if by refusing to joke with him, I made it into something serious. I ease June off my lap, feeling as he turns toward me, watching me settle June with her head on the pallet. Every movement I make, even when I smooth a snarl of hair back from June's face, feels exaggerated because know his eyes are tracing every one. She grabs hold of my wrist when I start to get up, the green jade of her eyes cloudy. "It's okay," I whisper to her. "I'll be back soon. You take care of Howl."

June tightens her grip on my wrist as if she won't let go, but then relaxes it, letting her hand fall away. I can't make myself look back at Howl because he's still watching me, something stretched tight between us. Of course I don't hate him. I sat in that storage closet by him and cried when I should have been sneaking onto the island; let Xuan go, hoping he would come back with medicine, although I had no collateral or faith in him. I risked June's life, Tai-ge's, and mine, staying in the heli when we knew Port Northians would come after us. All over caring about whether or not Howl stayed alive. I don't know whether Howl was aware enough to hear those things happening, so it feels like a secret. A secret I'm not quite ready to share.

"Sev?" Howl's voice stops me as I stand, so quiet I'm suddenly sure it isn't a secret at all. "I . . . I'm not sure . . ."

I turn toward the door, trying to ignore the trails of fire burning through my stomach at the way Howl stutters over the words, willing Luokai to come back *now*. I take a deep breath, filling my lungs until they'll take no more, even though it feels like sucking air through a mask, every molecule getting caught on its way down. This is not the time or place to begin a conversation about us.

I don't even know what to think myself. I was angry at Howl for real reasons. My eyes crinkle shut, as if I can block out my thoughts, block out the part of me that wants to turn around and kneel at his side even though June is lying right here. To give in to the wanting inside me, curling up like tendrils of smoke in my lungs.

"Sev? I can't . . ."

I turn slowly, caught in amber and stone, willing myself to stop, but I can't. Howl is still sitting a good two feet away from the pallet, his shoulders stiff and his arm curled tight next to his chest. He isn't trying to catch my eye, rather contemplating the space just above my left collarbone. A trickle of surprise threads through me when I catch the glimmer of wet at the corners of his eyes. He blinks furiously when a tear spills down his cheek, but doesn't move to brush it away.

Which is when I realize what it is he's struggling to say. It isn't some declaration of war or peace or love. It isn't an apology or even another joke.

Howl can't pull himself back onto the pallet without help, and he can't make himself say it out loud.

June twists to look at Howl when I walk over to him, then gets up from the pallet to help. I slide my arm under his good shoulder, then ease him over the empty space between him and the pallet. June supports his neck as we lower him down onto the bedding, then slides around me to spread the blanket over him.

"Thank you," he says quietly, his eyes shut, as if by not looking at us he can somehow pretend it didn't happen. "I'm officially helpless. Someone give me a medal."

A flutter of amusement wings it way through me, a spot of brightness in this dark stone room. "You want a medal from me, it's going to have my face on it."

June leans against me. "Mine, too," she whispers. "I helped."

The spot of brightness widens into a warm glow inside my chest. The world has cracks and holes, but there's a light here, among the three of us, making it seem a little less cold.

CHAPTER 49

WHEN LUOKAI COMES BACK FOR ME, HE'S ALONE.

No Baohujia volunteered to share his air, I suppose, and I find myself feeling similarly, watching Luokai from the corner of my eye as we walk, waiting for the shadows I know are trapped inside him to come fluttering out. He doesn't seem to notice, though he does point out that we're walking up stairs once I've tripped over the first three, landing in a sort of alcove and grabbing a tiered stone marker set squarely in its middle to keep from falling. It's sort of like the old buildings from the First Quarter, with tight-lipped smiles for each roof, growing smaller and smaller toward the top.

"I'd be careful if I were you," Luokai says calmly, though I can almost see a hint of smile twitching at his cheek. "The Speakers wouldn't have cared for you trying to hug them. Disrespectful, you know."

I push off the pillar of stone, keeping my head down as I try to make up for the distance he walked while I was finding my feet. "What do you mean?"

"Only the most revered of them got a permanent remembrance, the way they used to do for the monks who lived here." He nods to the alcoves set into the wall every ten or so steps. "Though the most important ones are outside. One for Gao Lishun, who first thought to use tunnels as vents for air. Zhang Sheyi, who argued to give safe haven to anyone attempting to escape the mainland. Wartime gives great opportunity for great deeds, great arguments. Great mercy. That was before the towers, though, so most of their stones have long fallen."

"The towers did something to their statues?"

Luokai's brows furrow, but he doesn't elaborate.

We move up continually, though we seem to be moving away from the windows, all the stone corridors deserted except for the two of us. Luokai doesn't look the way I'd expect someone suffering from unmedicated SS would. Parhat, from June's Seph clan, had been marked all over with scars, his mind so full of SS he was looking out at the world through a diseased well of water, the light refracting in a way that made him jump and squirm. June's father wasn't so damaged, though he bore the marks of infection. His tongue had been cut out.

Luokai looks at peace, gliding along with his hands tucked into the wide yellow sleeves of his tunic. Upright. Unscarred. I can't even tell how old he is, his hair black, his skin smooth. He couldn't possibly be more than twelve or thirteen years older than I am.

"Watch your head, Jiang Sev," Luokai warns as we turn into another passage, hunching to fit into the low-ceilinged hallway. "I'm sorry I cannot show you more of Port North, but this is the best we can do to keep SS back."

"Where are we going?"

"We're going to follow one of the vents up to the top of the island where Gao Shun is."

A light flashes ahead, Luokai's outline stark as the first brush-stroke on rice paper. There are still tool marks in the stone, the rough texture grating across my fingertips as we pass. The silence feels too close, until I have to crack it open. "Those statues . . . were all Speakers infected with SS from the beginning?"

"No. This was a monastery's Before, and so it was they who began as leaders, welcoming those who were infected into their midst. Now it seems difficult to see it any other way. Can you think of a better group of people to dedicate themselves to serving others than those who are infected?" There's a tic in Luokai's jaw pushing through the layers of calm. "I cannot safely be alone, so I cannot have a family. I have close friends, I suppose, but it's difficult to face someone whom you have attempted to kill." The hallway widens as Luokai speaks, until it empties us out onto a wide concourse, the ceiling a dark wall of rock. The wide area itself is brightly lit with paper lamps that remind me of home. There's no fire in these lamps, though, their hearts glowing with a yellowish orange light that reminds me of quicklights, only much brighter. "It's much better than the way they handled things at the Mountain," Luokai continues, "as if I'd been transformed into something less than human. Here I work with the other Speakers to do what must be done. I'm a useful sort of burden instead of a monster."

Luokai leads me past a forest of columns toward what looks like the edge of a cliff, darkness seeming to wait on the other side, barely warmed over by the glow of lanterns below. The railing is framed by an arch cut straight from the stone, a lookout over a much wider cave below. When we get to the railing, I'm surprised to find some kind of glass shimmering between me and the rest of the cave.

Beyond the glass and the railing, there are steps that lead to what looks like a market nestled into the heart of the rock, lanterns hanging in patterns all across the top. People mill down what look like streets, and there's a low grumble that seems to vibrate up from the floor. Generators, perhaps. But why have the steps if you're going to block them off? They lead straight down into the market from where we're standing, but with the glass barrier, there's no way to descend to where people are chatting with one another. We're in a world apart, observing like scientists with screens and statistics, waiting for something to happen. My eyes catch on a young boy as he threads his way through the clumps of people below us with what looks like a mischievous spring to his step. Is this what Luokai does? Watch people?

I reach out to touch the glass, and it's rough, as if it was sprayed into place rather than cut to fit the doorway. At the edges, there are beads of glue, shining as though they're still wet. My eyes eat at the stream of people below as if I'll be able to catch sight of a familiar earlobe or jawline. My family could be here somewhere.

And if Gao Shun is family? Will it change how she looks at me? I pull back from the glass, looking around the wide platform for a way out. "Can we keep going? We've already used so much time, and the helis are—"

"Be calm, Jiang Sev." Luokai takes a deep breath and lets it out, his hand propped up against the glass, and suddenly I'm afraid. "I need a moment to be calm."

My throat constricts. I hold myself still as a corpse, as if a sudden movement will bring Luokai's infection out where I can see it. With no Baohujia and a barrier between me and the rest of these people, if Luokai has a violent compulsion, I'm the only one here to receive it. "You can't keep compulsions back, can you?"

"What are compulsions but products of your mind? Your stray thoughts and feelings." Luokai takes in another deep breath, the air filling him out like the fat belly of a full waterskin before he lets it out. "If I control my thoughts and feelings, then what thoughts will SS have to work with but good ones?"

"You can control it? Keeping control of your thoughts makes you safe all the time?"

Luokai finally stands straight, looking me in the eye. "No one has that much control, Jiang Sev." He turns to face the glass, his eyes catching on the little boy traipsing up the steps toward us. I feel my shoulders tense, waiting for an angry shout, or for the shadows hiding the boy's face to resolve into sharp hunger lines and a frown. He sprints up toward us and barely stops at the glass, pretending to slam into it.

It's the little boy I saw back in the village sitting in the safety of his doorway. Black hair hanging down his forehead and no fear in his eyes.

He mashes his face into the glass. I startle back, my hands coming up to somehow protect myself, but the boy doesn't try to get through. He pushes his nose up against the glass until all we can see is a squashed cheek and stretched nostrils, the boy's face comically askew as his soft giggles filter through the thin barrier. Luokai begins to laugh, the sound almost foreign in my ears, as if this place of darkness and compulsions should be full of nothing but frowns and anger.

But then I see the smile on the boy's face. He isn't compulsing. He's making faces at us. And when I look over at Luokai for some kind of explanation, he's making a face *back*.

I close my eyes and bite down on my lip. Who have I become? This scared little creature, assuming even one look in my direction means harm? *I* used to be the one who made faces back. Was Tai-ge right about me? That I'm something new now, something too used to being Outside? Fear of compulsions was something that lived in me long before I set foot outside the walls, but it isn't something I want to hang on to. Hand against my chest to calm the awful pounding of my heart, I open my eyes again and try a smile.

The little boy is already skipping back down the stairs. Happy and carefree, even though he's stuck in the dark. Like little Lihua playing games with us up in the trading post. My heart misses a beat when a woman peels away from her group to grab hold of the little boy's hand to tow him away down the street, her other hand ruffling through his hair.

Not like Lihua.

Free.

I turn away from the glass to find that Luokai has already begun to walk parallel to the wall with the railing, toward a flight of stairs. "Do you always live down here in the dark? To keep away from the bombs?" I ask, thinking of the Mountain with its recirculated air and artificial lights.

Luokai shakes his head. "Most of the time we live on the surface. But with helis coming, we want to take precautions."

"If they get to the island, you don't think they'll worm their way down here?"

"It's unlikely they'll get anywhere near the island." Luokai glances at me as he walks, "The towers can read the frequency of heli propellers, then feed it back. It shakes them to pieces. Unfortunately, there are other things on the island's surface that react to the same frequency. Stone. Walls. Glass. It's dangerous to be out there during an attack. This time we've had enough warning to bring anyone who would come in where they'll be safe. If helis come, we'll drop them from the sky. If soldiers come on foot, they won't make it past the doors once we shut them behind us."

Luokai continues up the stairs, all openings between us and the people below glassed in like with the balcony below, where the boy was standing. A thin flow of air wafts down from the stairwell, ruffling my hair as we climb, the stairs twisting until the balcony and the market below it are out of sight. "Do you remember the Mountain?" I ask. I want Luokai to fit in a mold I can recognize, which makes me think of someone else just as broken as he should be. The girl who still remembers him. "You knew Howl. What about Sole—"

"There's something you ought to know before we talk to Gao Shun." Luokai cuts me off, looking out through one of the glassed-in openings to below as we pass, the cheery light catching in the hollows of his cheeks. He shakes his hand free of his sleeve, reaching out to touch the rough stone wall. "You've probably already thought this through, but let me make it clear."

Luokai stops at a set of lanterns hanging on either side of a door that's empty of glass, rushes of air brushing at the red fabric that forms a door. "Gao Shun isn't going to go easy on you just because you're young. She'll want to know everything. About the invasion, about SS. How much they know about the towers and what's in the papers you came for. Anything you might know about the City, the soldiers who are waiting to descend on us and their leaders. She'll want to know why you came here and why she should help you."

"As long as she gives me Mother's papers, I'll tell her anything she wants." I shrug. "But if she won't, I don't know that I can help. Will that be enough?"

Luokai pauses, one hand extended to pull the fabric back. "I hope so."

"She's related to me, isn't she? We're family. We must be." I look at him, my heart beating hard.

Luokai presses his lips together, staring down at my shoes, as if I've deduced an answer he doesn't want to give. But when he looks at me, it's compassion in his eyes. "Yes. She's your mother's sister."

My lungs contract, the wafts of air blowing out from inside the room catching at my throat, drying me from the inside out. The walls I'd been taking down, the empty spaces I'd been preparing for this place compressing inside me. I reach for the wall, steadying myself as if I can feel where she is, feel the weight of blood joining us together. In this place where the children have no fear.

But Luokai's tight-lipped smile only hints at one emotion, and I don't like it. It looks like pity. "It will not help you, Jiang Sev. Your mother brought us war, and Gao Shun has never forgiven her."

CHAPTER 50

ON THE OTHER SIDE OF THE RED CURTAINS, SEA AIR congeals in my nose, the soft breeze turning into a gale that tears at my hair and streaks my cheeks with tears. Luokai leads me around a corner and natural light stabs straight through my eyes, leaving jagged cuts of purple and green across my vision. At the end of the long room, a fan fits perfectly into the tunnel's mouth, taller than I am and strong enough to be appropriate ventilation for the most toxic of factory floors. The blades whir into a gray haze.

And, on the other side of the fan, a backlit blur of a woman.

Shadows crawl down over her face, hiding her features and expression, leaving me with nothing to see but a black-and-white excuse of a person, an impossible blaze of light illuminating the true depth of darkness inside.

Luokai opens a box sitting at the base of the fan, his tunic and loose pants rippling like water under a storm as he pulls out an odd-looking pair of disks, plated with scratched-up brass. They're connected with a half-moon of flexible metal, and I try not to flinch back as Luokai fits the two disks over my ears, the bendy metal linking them together resting on the crown of my head.

The disks are padded with a leathery cushion, blocking out most of the fan's noise. But there's a steady sort of hum that comes from the disks themselves buzzing in my ears, almost like the whine of a speaker back in the City right before the Chairman spoke. Maybe that's what they are. Loudspeakers from Before, when there was a reason for only one person to listen to something without everyone having to partake.

Luokai slips a similar pair of disks over his ears, though his are not quite so crisscrossed with scratches as mine. "Can you hear me?" he asks, his voice loud as if he's speaking straight into my ear over the fan's noise.

I nod. Luokai turns to the willowed shadow on the other side of the fan, shot through with blazing sun, saying something in the close vowels and consonants of this place. A new voice slips into my ear through the disks, like the worst and best memories I have braided together, crackled over with age, though I can't understand the words. I'm lost in both trying to fit the syllables together and trying not to. Trying not to see my own mother's mouth moving, as if she somehow came back from the death I gave her at the top of Traitor's Arch.

But it's more familiar than anything I can fit into a memory, her voice. I've heard it before. Where could I have heard it?

Once Gao Shun is done speaking, Luokai looks at me, concentration wrinkling his brow, the fans blowing the bristled hair on his head. "Tell me what the invasion force is after. They've never brought so many helis, so many soldiers. They've never tried to move against the island. What is their plan?"

I stare at the fan, at the muddled shadow just beyond, tears pricking in my eyes. She's right there. My aunt. My blood. My skin prickles over in fear and wanting, the two warring with each other as if it matters somehow what I want. "Can I please see her?"

Luokai shakes his head slowly.

I nod, swallowing my emotions as best I can. "They know about your towers. Where they are. Tai-ge—my friend you killed—he meant to break them somehow, I think. I know the date they mean to invade."

The woman speaks again, her tongue lisping over the harsh syllables. He nods along with each word, then looks at me. "Invade? Why invade here? If they bring SS here, they spoil their own slave pens."

I shake my head. "I'd like to see my mother's things before I say anything else."

Gao Shun's outline goes still, as if she's taking stock of my posture, my raggedly clothes, the space between my eyes. When her voice continues, it holds an aftertaste of questions. Luokai translates, "If SS truly is contagious, how is it you walk so calmly next to Luokai . . . ?" He blinks. "Next to me, that is. Do they have a new method of filtering air? Internal, perhaps?"

My mind whirrs, wondering what it is I should say.

The shadow shifts to the side, sunlight flickering behind her to stab into my eyes. Her husky voice sounds in my ears, the words lining up in slow, intentional lines, a heavier accent than Luokai's weighing them down. "That's what the invasion force is after, isn't it? They're here for Gui-Hua's things."

I take too long to respond, the shock of her speaking in my own language either a good sign or a bad one. But then her shadow nods, as if my silence is answer enough by itself.

"You can't give anything to them." My step toward the fan almost feels compulsive, the wind from the fan tearing at my hair.

"Mother sent me to get her things before Dr. Yang could or he'll use them to control—"

Gao Shun launches into a tirade of clipped syllables cutting me off. Luokai waits until she's done before turning to me. "I'd suggest not telling her what to do," he says softly—not a strict translation, I'd guess. "She wants to know what is in those papers. We can't read them—not the words and letters. The notations and the purpose are foreign to us."

"It's hard to explain."

"Your Red friend didn't have anything special with him when we found him." My chest goes cold as Gao Shun's smooth syllables slip through the headphones. "Odd, considering the dire situation you say your people are in with SS. He had no internal filtering system, no external gas mask, at least not that he was wearing when we found him." Luokai's eyes glaze as he simultaneously listens to her and translates for me. It sounds almost like they dissected Tai-ge and left him in pieces out in that skeleton village. "They have to be coming here because of contagion. That's the only thing that has changed."

Gao Shun takes a deep breath and once again speaks in my language, the switch taking my breath away. "You can't catch SS, can you? You're impervious. My sister did it to you somehow. And that's why they killed her, because SS is their weapon of choice."

She has me again, caught with no words in my mouth because I don't know where any of her stones are. I don't know where or how to place mine because I'm not even sure we're playing on the same board.

I didn't even think I was walking into a game. As if somehow a force that has been fighting the City for so long would automatically fall on my side. My mother told me to come here. I thought that would be enough.

What was I thinking? I've spent so much time concentrating on getting here. Why didn't I think about what I would find?

My hands tremble against my legs, twisting words into my mouth to tell her about Outsiders, about her own people being kept on farms, about SS and how it will take them all, and that Dr. Yang did it on purpose . . . how Sole can help us . . . but Gao Shun isn't done talking.

". . . if that *dog-headed* Gui-hua had done her duty and left the balance in place the way she was supposed to, none of this would have happened. We wouldn't have Seconds cutting us down, lapping at our blood—"

"Don't talk about my mother that way!" The air screams across my face, my eyes so dry they ache, but I keep them open, standing up to the wind pounding across every inch of exposed skin. Only weeks ago, I would have agreed with this shadow from my past. But I can see my mother for who she was now, her frail voice loud in my ears, saying she loves me. "She was trying to help. She was trying to stop . . . They infected *me!*" I roar it into the fan, ignoring Luokai as he tries to pull me back. "They were hurting me, so she had to do it. She couldn't stop researching. She couldn't leave us all to the Firsts. What do you know about SS as a weapon when you're out here away from it all? Your life doesn't start or stop based on your Mantis supply."

The shadow is nodding now. "She came up with some kind of cure and then she left the cursed formulas here for them to come after. Never thinking once about the people who would die, the danger she was putting us all in. Gui-hua knew *that man* was a snake, and she still set bait for him here, not caring a moment if we survived once he'd bitten." Gao Shun swears. Takes a deep breath.

"She was trying to help people." My voice feels shredded and limp. "*I'm* trying to help—"

"Your City killed my parents. Every last one of my sisters and brothers, caught by your slavers or with bullets in their heads. Your mother left me here alone with no bargaining chips." Gao Shun takes a deep breath and lets it out in a staticky rattle that sends a high-pitched buzz ricocheting off my eardrum. "We finally have something they want. Who is in charge of the camp?"

"*No.* You can't give it to anyone in those camps. Dr. Yang won't give it to everyone who needs it. He'll use it against us, against *you*—"

"*Do not tell me what I can and cannot do.*" Her voice stings, even as it thins out through the headphones. "Who taught you that you are better than your elders, better than your own blood?"

"What's to stop them dropping SS bombs here, too, if they have the cure?" I scream toward her, Luokai forgotten at my feet. "You've been safe until now because the Chairman needed you to be well so your people could work on City farms. But if you hand over the cure, they won't even have to kidnap your people. You'll have to come groveling to Dr. Yang for even a hope of survival."

"Thank you for your help." The shadow turns and walks away, into the light, every step abrupt enough to be a stomp. All I can see of her is a loose robe to match the other Baohujia, the shifty darkness of her burning up as the daylight wraps its fingers around her as if Gao Shun is nothing but a ghost. The last glittering hope I have, vanishing on the wind.

I'm as close to the fan's deathly airstream as I can be without getting my nose caught in the blades. She has to be able to see me, daylight streaming down on my face even as it obscures her features. "Your only chance is to give it to me! Contagious SS is already here in Port North. You don't even have Mantis, and Dr. Yang isn't going to share with you. *I will.* I want to help."

Luokai's hand closes around my shoulder, startling me away from the fan's blades. "Go. She can't hear you." He removes the headset from my ears and drags me back through the shrouded doorway, back into the darkness, where two Baohujia have appeared. The fan's muted *whirr* scrambles my ears, everything lost in the rush of wind. "Take her back to my room!" he yells over the sound.

I pull away from him to look around the room for something to break the fan from its moorings. For anything that will give these people a reason to listen to me. "I have to convince her. I can't—"

Luokai grabs hold of my shoulders, forcing me to look him full in the face, to be still. "Answer me truthfully. Is that really what is in those papers? A cure?"

Luokai's rangy outline towers over me, but his hands are gentle. "Yes," I answer. "Will you help me? You're in charge here, not Gao Shun."

"Speakers don't act individually, Jiang Sev. We do what is best for everyone." He gestures to the Baohujia behind me, and their hands are like shackles around my wrists, wrenching me back the way I came before I can make any more arguments. Down the dark hall, wind slipping its salty fingers through my hair, anger shuddering through me as we push through the red curtains and down the stone stairway. Gao Shun's words twist around me like tentacles, squeezing at my throat, at my ribs and heart. Every word was an accusation, a challenge, as if somehow I were the one who sent the Chairman to haze her. But every step feels as if I'm tearing apart, leaving something of myself sitting there at the foot of the fan, wishing I could see Gao Shun's face.

Her voice is so familiar. But where I thought it was like mine, the similarity cuts, as if instead of sharing blood, she'd like to inspect mine drop by drop.

When we get back to Luokai's room, my guard palms the door open and jerks me inside, forcing it to shut before I can say anything to him. Perhaps now that they've gotten what they need from us, being polite and gentle isn't on the agenda anymore. I'm not important anymore. A meaningless stray from a people they hate.

I suppose I can understand. All I've seen of this place are remembrances and the stone walls that protect them from the City—from people like me.

But I know how it feels to be waiting for SS's hooks to show up at the corners of my vision. For the creature living inside my chest to rear its monstrous head. To be exposed, to be chosen, even when you didn't want to be. My Baohujia guard has been exposed to Luokai, so what could he be thinking now? That he's only got hours, minutes even, before his eyes could close. And, if he's been guarding Speakers his whole life, he knows exactly what it is he'll be giving up.

If he wakes up at all.

I try to shake off the heavy web of misery sticking to my shoulders, but it doesn't fall away. This place could be just as cursed as the Mountain, as the City, within hours. What are the chances they'll ever recover from the plague about to descend if they hand everything to Dr. Yang? What could I have said differently while I was facing down the shadow that was all I could see of my aunt through the fan? Could I have been more guarded? Pretended to be afraid when Luokai told us he was sick? It didn't even occur to me.

I put a hand to my stomach, wishing I could calm the wriggling dread deep inside me and sink to the floor, my hands clawing through my hair, clamping down tight as if that's the only way my head will stay attached.

Howl's blankets twitch, his eyes open and looking at me, June a lump under a blanket just next to him.

"Are you okay?" Howl whispers.

I blink, surprised when tears overflow down my cheeks.

He lifts one edge of the blanket, smoothing out the side of the pallet. "There's room for one more down here."

"How many people have to take the things I want before I'll stop trusting them?" The words rake their long claws down my throat. My eyes clench shut, shards of pain slivering out to my temples, the sharp edges delving deep into my brain. I crouch down, curling in on myself as if I could crush all the feelings out of me. "I didn't mean to tell her what is in those papers . . . and now she's going to use them . . ."

An arm closes around my shoulders—Howl, somehow up from the pallet, crouching next to me. He holds me close, and I sob until there's nothing left inside me but ache.

CHAPTER 51

I SLEEP. NOT THE COMFORTABLE SLEEP OF A BED AND four walls around you, but the dead sleep that digs its claws into your brain, leaving scores deep in your dreams. Dreams of the box. No. Worse. Dreams of Mother's voice crying over me. Dreams of being trapped in my own body once again, daring every muscle of mine to move, of pleading and then screaming in anger when not even a finger will obey. Screams that echo inside my skull, lie panting on my tongue, because I cannot force my own mouth to open or my throat to obey.

Pressure hums inside my head like a fire blazing to escape, building inside my nasal cavity until I finally force a word out between my teeth. The world seems to fall to pieces around me as my eyes find a blank ceiling, and I sit up, my lungs choking down a full breath of air.

Light-headed with the gasps raking my throat, I look around Luokai's room, empty of anything he could break or use to hurt himself. As much a prison as the box I lay in downstairs. I can move, but is this dark hole in Port North's rock much better than being Asleep? No one can hear me speak. No one would listen even if they could. My life and that of my friends are probably already forfeit. But it isn't only us who will die if Gao Shun hands the cure to Dr. Yang.

The warm weight beside me resolves into Howl, curled around his broken collarbone. His arm lies in its sling across his chest, his other arm lined up along my side, as if he fell asleep wanting me to know I wasn't alone. My throat clenches, and I move away, tears prickling across my eyes.

I should have known the moment I started hoping to find a place here in Port North that it was hopeless. Fairy tales and hope are for stories. We wouldn't love them so much if that were the way our lives really were. I should have expected my aunt to be holding a gun with one hand, using the other to protect an entire island's worth of people who she'd rather see survive over me.

Howl and June asleep next to me seems like the worst sort of story, because I can still feel hope when I look at them, and all I can do is curve around that shiny bit of nothing and wait for it to be taken away.

Family. What does sharing an ancestor even mean? I pull at strands of my hair, trying to distract myself from the fire burning everything inside me to ash. June and I are family, no matter what blood says. We chose each other, me in the first moment I saw her standing there in the dark next to her father.

She chose me when we burned his body.

Nothing, not even blood ties, will break that. We're sisters—not because either of us needs replacements for sisters or fathers or mothers who disappeared into the weeping air, but because we are better together than apart.

And Howl . . . No matter how backward and unraveled the two

of us are, he was willing to fight for my life. And I'm willing to fight for his. Of all the people I could have have at my back, I'm glad it's him.

But Howl isn't my brother the way June feels like a sister. I don't want him to be. And, at the same time, I can't find a place inside that isn't shaded over in doubt, wondering how either of us could move past the broken bits of bone and death tied between us so tight it suffocates.

There's a tray set just next to the silver strip marking where the door opens, a teapot, three small cups, three bowls of rice, and a whole fish, its eye glazed over, staring blankly at the ceiling.

Taking a deep breath, I reach over Howl and June to touch the wall, the stone cold against my fingers. It doesn't matter if we're stuck. Doesn't matter if my aunt would rather have never seen me, might try to use me as some kind of bargaining chip.

I'm not Asleep. I can move. I can breathe. I'm not laid out on a platter, staring into eternity, waiting to be eaten. Despair never helped anyone win.

"Sev?"

I jump at Howl's voice, looking over to find his eyes open.

"Are you all right?" he asks. "You were dreaming again."

Heat starts a slow burn in my cheeks as if somehow he could hear everything I was thinking as I looked over at him, so quiet next to me on the floor. "How'd you guess?"

"You were calling for your mother before you woke up." He slides over to his side, laboriously attempting to sit up, grimacing when I lean down to help him up into a sitting position. "You still dream about her? You did when we first left the City."

I feel my face flush, my cheeks warming. "I've been awake for a while. Have you been lying here . . ." Putting hands against my cheeks, I clear my throat. "How do you know I used to dream about her?"

"Because you'd wrap yourself up around that brand." He glances down at the star melted into my hand. "You'd say her name. I thought it was, you know, being out in the middle of nowhere, wondering when the Sephs would come at you. Taking medicine that messed with your head. Giving up everything you knew for everything you were afraid of . . . all in the company of a boy you'd never met but who was devastatingly attractive . . ."

A smile curls uncomfortably at my mouth, both because he's right and so very wrong. "I never said that, and you know it."

"You did. It took getting hit in the head first, but you said it." Howl grins, but he looks down, breaking eye contact. "Sorry. I probably shouldn't tease you, considering . . . everything."

The pit in my stomach deepens, swirling around like a vat of tar. I can't help but answer, though. "You know I like jokes better than moping. Moping doesn't help anyone." It's good to say it out loud. Then maybe everything will go away and I can go back to . . .

I close my eyes. Go back to what? Unless June and Howl came up with a brilliant escape plan while I was gone, there isn't much we can do.

"That's the real reason I came running after you with those maps, you know." Howl yawns, leaning back against the wall with an uncomfortable grunt. "Got addicted to perkiness and couldn't find it anywhere. Menghu are so serious all the time. Firsts, too." He points toward a clay-looking pot sitting in the corner opposite June. "There's a pot over there to use if you need it. You know, if that look of consternation is more than wishing I would be quiet." He looks at the pot, brow furrowed. "At least I think it's for peeing in. If not, whoever comes in here next is in for a surprise."

I give a theatrical sniff. "Well, wouldn't you know it? You fouled the only water left on this whole island."

"That'll show them." He nods to the tray of food by the door. "Seriously, though, is that something to drink over there?"

"If you can get up to pee in a pot, you can get your own water." But then I pull myself up from the ground and walk over to the tray. "Would you like weak tea or something stronger?" I gesture to the pot.

Howl laughs, then grimaces, putting his good hand to his shoulder. "No more urine jokes. My poor, gore-bitten side can't take it."

Dragging the tray over, I pour a cup of tea and hand it to him, watching as he drinks before pouring my own. It isn't until the liquid hits my tongue that I realize how dry my mouth is, like a wet sponge left to bake in the sun.

"You want to tell me what happened with Gao Shun?" he asks quietly.

I finish my sip and carefully set the cup down. "She figured out that I'm cured. And that she might be able to use Mother's papers to get the invasion to stop. So she isn't going to hand them over to us."

He nods slowly. "Good. We came up with an epic escape plan that would be a shame to waste. It involves stealing your mother's stuff and then miraculously teleporting back to Sole."

"You can teleport, too? Why didn't you tell me?" I smile a little. "Let's . . . eat. And then we can plan."

He nods again, waiting until I pick up one of the spoons and take a bite before extracting his own bite of rice with only one hand, grimacing at the movement. "So with Gao Shun. You must have seen—"

"Can we . . . not?" I cut him off. "Just for a minute?" I want to think of anything other than my statue for an aunt, of what might happen to us next. We need to plan, but I need a moment to regroup. "Tell me a story."

"A story?" Howl absently touches the bandage at his shoulder, rubbing the edges between his fingers. "About what?"

I pour us both some more tea. "Tell me something I don't know about you. Tell me what your life was like before my mother pushed everything out of balance."

Howl doesn't say anything for a moment, looking down into the cup I set next to him. When he finally does, the words are careful. "I think your mother was trying to push things back *into* some kind of balance for me."

"What do you mean?"

Howl picks up his bowl, attempting to carve out another bite of rice, but scattering about half of the little grains before they get to his mouth, and he sets the spoon down, pressing his lips together. I try to take his spoon to help, but he bats my hand away before continuing what he was saying. The awkwardness of his silence feels personal, as if there are a million things he could say, but none of them would be comfortable because I'm the one listening.

It rankles. But I don't want to pry any more than he accidentally did about the knife back on the heli, so I breathe deeply, preparing myself for a discussion of stone hallways and cliffs—to the island and how we might get off it—but he speaks before I can.

"I mean . . . Jiang Gui-hua cared whether or not I died. You heard Luokai earlier. My parents changed his *name* just so people at the Mountain would leave him alone. At least, so people couldn't peg him as a purged City-born just from an introduction."

We sit there, silence like a weight on us, a rock waiting to crush us both into the stone floor. There are five thousand things I want to say all at once. That I want to know about his life, even though my brain screams to stay on my side of the wall we've built to separate us. That I can see he hurts, and that I want to fix it. That somehow I'll be able to listen to all the things that came before and somehow rearrange them for him the way he did for me all those months back when Mother was a rotting corpse lodged in my brain and there was nothing I could do but gag over and over.

"Why you?" I don't like walls. None of the ones I've ever had in my life have been good. The other side was always radically different from what I thought, and I'd rather know the truth about Howl than make one up. "Why did my mother choose you to be the one who got cured?"

Howl contemplates another half-filled spoonful of rice and actually gets it into his mouth without too many losses. Chewing slowly, he waits until he's swallowed before answering, and even then, every word is made from molasses. "I've got all the wrong marks. For the City and the Mountain." A grimace of a smile creases one cheek and he looks up from his rice bowl to meet my eyes. "Do you remember the way Mei looked at me when she first saw my First mark?"

I nod, remembering how the Menghu-in-training had gone cold. It didn't matter that Howl had left the City, that he was fighting for her side so far as she knew. The mark itself was reason enough for Mei to hate him. Howl sets his spoon down and touches the single line scored into his limp hand, as if it means more somehow than a brand he had to take on in order to look the part of the Chairman's son. He shakes his head, picking the spoon back up. "The Mountain is full of defectors from the City, but unless you brought something with you, either a history of being repressed, or a lot of resources to make up for doing the oppressing . . . My parents escaped the City, but they were still marked. I was marked too, even though I didn't have the scars. Dr. Yang chose me because there wasn't anyone to say no. No one would have missed me much if it didn't work."

She's the only one like me. He said it when we first met, when he thought I couldn't hear him. I thought it was because we'd both been cured, but maybe that's not where it ends.

"What was it like to grow up in the Mountain?" I ask. "What were the good things? The things you wanted to go back to?"

Howl's brow furrows. "I remember playing Hawk Catches the Chicks with other kids in Jiaoyang. Playing jianzi with my teacher's featherball in the dark with Kasim until we broke something. We were always together, laughing through lessons about the City, pretending to take on the Chairman ourselves and bringing back food and Mantis for everyone like heroes. Teasing Helix. You saw the Mountain. It was my home. I loved it."

I wait for a second, wondering what more there could be, hiding behind Howl's eyes clouded with memories. The City was mine, too. Even though they didn't want me.

As if he's reading my mind, Howl shrugs again, something painful creasing his forehead. "I was . . . angry. And lonely. I didn't have anyone who was mine. Who wanted to take care of me no matter what happened. No matter who I was or where I'd come from." He looks up at me again. "Then *she* told me that even if I ended up with SS, I wouldn't be sent away like my brother was. That I could be a part of her family. I couldn't admit it at the time, but I wanted what she was offering. A lot."

"She said . . ." I close my eyes, my mind blank. "She wanted you to come live with us? Why didn't you?"

"The only person who wanted me was an enemy, even if she did claim to be helping us." He frowns. "And to this day I am still ashamed that I told her as much. That her scars made her a monster, and I didn't want anything to do with her or her family. She just told me to think about it. That she would be there for me when I wanted it." He finally meets my eyes, the dark brown clear as the day I met him. "They did infection trials. I remember her watching me from the other side of the glass, smiling at me. Making silly faces so I'd laugh."

I remember the faces she'd make when Father wasn't looking.

"But when it was all done, when I was still SS-free . . ." He looks down again. "She disappeared. She left without even saying good-bye. Presented me with this idea that I could be something other than the leftovers of old City trash . . . then slipped away during the night with it in her pocket."

The words seem to fall forever, lost somehow in the dim gray tinting everything around me. Tinting the whole world. "You think she left you on purpose? That she never meant . . . but you said—"

"I thought she lied about wanting to take me with her." Howl sets the cup down, staring at the wall instead of looking back at me. I want to touch him again, to somehow comfort him over things that have long been cried out. "It made me hate the City even more. They killed my parents. Labeled me. It made me think that maybe having a City scar really did turn you into something that wasn't human anymore. Willing to do *anything* so long as you got the outcome you wanted." He stares at the single mark on his hand, an angry red scab splitting the line in half. "Maybe that much is true."

Now it's my turn to look down.

"I didn't know she went back for you. That the Chairman took her before she could come back for me. That *Dr. Yang* took her," he corrects himself. "Not until I was playing the Chairman's son, and he took me to the City Center. She was propped up in her box, her eyes shut, all those tubes feeding into her. And all I could feel was . . ." His voice catches. "All those years of hating the City, of hating *her* . . . and she was there on the Arch the whole time. Worse than dead. She said something to me after I told her that I didn't want to live with a City monster. That when you look close-up, most enemies look like people too."

My heart seems to twinge with each beat, and I feel cold, hugging my knees to my chest.

"I wouldn't look. Not in all my years as a Menghu. I didn't care." He looks down at his hands, clenching the uninjured one into a fist. "But I saw her up there . . . saw *you* bowing for the Reds and laughing at yourself even as your knees bent . . . and suddenly I could see so much more than stars on collars. There were men and women in that City who were nothing but evil, murdering, lying gore bastards, but it wasn't their stars that made them that way. There were good people too. People who were kind, who just wanted to be safe, to be happy. To laugh. There was this little old Third who made me tea every morning. She wanted nothing more than for me to find a nice First to bring home for dinner. And a Second on one of my committees who could make me laugh for no reason at all. And the Chairman . . ." He scrubs a hand through his hair. "The Chairman was the worst part. He was kind to me. Distant, but he'd bring me honey in my tea when I had a cold, and asked about how I liked working on this committee or taking a class from some First he'd worked with before. He cared."

June shifts in the corner, rolling so I see a smidgen of one closed eye, her long eyelashes a smudge of golden brown against her cheek. She's so relaxed and calm, as if all her cares in the world disappeared the moment her eyes closed. "Why does everything have to be so complicated?" I whisper.

"No matter how right you think you are, no matter what you think is at stake, when you fight, there's someone who deserves to live who . . . won't. But if you don't fight, then you're the one who falls. At least, I used to believe that." Howl's voice whittles down to a whisper, as if he can't quite say it out loud. Silence spools between us, filling up all the space, the air. His hand snakes into my vision, touching my hand where it rests in my lap, his fingers soft.

My chest and lungs contract as I stare at his hand on mine, my mind flashing through things I don't want to see. Howl kneeling on the ground, a gun to his head. Helix smiling as he told me Howl wanted me dead. The awful blankness on his face when I locked him in the heli storage closet.

The fury as we argued in the cave, the way my knife *thunk*ed on the ground between us and he walked away.

My voice cracks as I speak, not sure I know the right things to say, his fingers warm against mine. "I know it doesn't make up for anything that happened before, but you aren't alone anymore, Howl. I don't care about your marks. Neither does June."

"Don't you?" He waits until I look up. "You don't care that I spent a good six years of my life hunting Reds in the forest? That I've killed people? Probably people you know?"

And there it is, underneath. *I almost killed you.*

I almost killed him, too. Both of us, only a hair away from letting the other fall. Of not looking, hoping it didn't happen, but walking away anyway.

When I don't answer, Howl's eyes narrow a fraction, his hand on mine, so still it's as if he's afraid I'm only seconds from exploding and that moving even a centimeter will pull the pressure switch. I can't look away from his eyes, brown and familiar and so deep I'm drowning and I can't—

"Sev, I'm just going to say this and hope you're listening. Bad timing . . . but we might not have that much time left, and I don't want to die quiet." He speaks slowly, every word hanging in the air between us. I sit still as death, everything inside me a blank slate, as if there should be new answers to the questions I've been asking myself for the last couple of months.

"What I did when I first met you was stupid." His hand circles my wrist, and I feel as if I'm made from lead, so heavy I can't move, and I'm not even sure I want to. "I was naive to think I could ever go back to the Mountain. I wanted to be with the people I thought I understood, to *belong*. As if after they tried to hunt me down, I'd be able to step right back into the ranks and salute with the rest of them. Be a part of the army that would finally liberate Yuan Zhiwei's lab rats. I wanted to pretend that somehow you would be okay. But then at one of our meetings, Dr. Yang just said it. That one of us was going to have to die. I'd been lying and trying to convince you to stay and hoping and . . . there it was. The truth."

A tear pricks in my eye, like needles under my skin. I was there. Outside the door, listening. Howl agreed with Dr. Yang. It was that conversation I remembered when Sole told me who Howl really was, words from his own mouth confirming what she said. It was those words that made me run.

Howl leans forward, staring into my eyes as if he can't blink. Or he won't. "Back in the City, I thought I was capable of trading your life for mine." He swallows, speaking more quickly now. "But it only took a few days before I knew I just . . . couldn't. I *wouldn't*, no matter how much I wanted to go home. And then I got to know you, and it wasn't even a matter of not wanting to kill anyone else so much as it was that the thought of you dying wasn't something I could live through. Then Dr. Yang said that one of us dying was the only way and . . . I couldn't pretend it would somehow be okay any longer." His fingers brush up my arm, and I'm not sure what to do. My insides burn with indecision, Howl's hand touching me so softly. Hands that have been slapped down, hands my mother touched. Hands that won't fire a gun anymore for some reason, that pushed me out of the way when the gores came.

Hands that have killed people.

"You know, out there in the forest, I couldn't stop thinking that you were all that was left of Jiang Gui-hua." He leans closer, whispering as if what he's saying is a secret between us. Or maybe he's just trying not to wake June, bundled in a blanket on the other side of him. "Of someone good who was trying to help everyone, not just herself. I was afraid you were all the things that made her weak, that made her fall. But I'm not sure that what she did *was* fall, now. She kept the cure safe. She died for it. For you."

I can't think, everything inside me gummed up, Howl's voice stuck in the gears.

"I want to be more like her. Like you. When you found out Dr. Yang wanted to cut you open, the first thing that occurred to you was to give yourself up. Because if giving up your life meant saving everyone else from SS, you were willing."

Is this what I want? His hand moves from my arm to my shoulder, and then across my collarbone until he's touching my neck, tracing the line just under my jaw. My ribs warm over, my heart pounding so hard it hurts, as if the next beat will break through my ribs.

"When Dr. Yang handed me a gun on my way out of the City, it felt as if it weighed a hundred pounds. That the moment I used it, all I'd ever see again were uniforms instead of the people inside them." He pauses as if he wants me to say something, but I don't know what I should say. "I heard what you said back in the heli. While I was . . . whatever it was that gore bite did to me."

That I don't want Howl to die.

I don't.

It's not even just that. I'm *sorry* for what happened between us. It's not all mine to be sorry for. But I wish . . . There are so many things to wish for, and no one to grant them.

The wanting I've been trying to tamp down uncurls, burning up inside my chest, flooding out to my fingertips and down my spine.

"And, though it seems like sort of a baseline thing to not actively wish someone would die, I feel like maybe that's progress." He so close I can feel the brush of his every breath touching my cheeks. I look up to find him staring at me. "Is letting a gore bite me enough to prove I like you a little bit?"

"I want to trust you," I whisper, because admitting it out loud makes it solid and scary. "I want you to be real."

"I am real. I'm right here." The hand under my jaw coaxes me forward, and he's so close the words could have come from my mouth.

He waits. I could lean forward and forget everything. Reclaim the version of Howl who disintegrated the night I escaped. The only person who ever saw me as an equal, not as a tool or a traitor.

I lick my lips, staring down at his, and then somehow I'm

kissing him. It's soft, like a question, Howl barely moving as if either of us acknowledging what is happening will somehow make it disappear. When I pull back, he stares at me, and I'm not sure what to do next, what he's thinking, just that Howl brushing up against me is like fireworks erupting inside me. He leans forward so quickly I hardly understand what's happening, just that his lips are hard against mine, his hand is in my hair and then pressing into my neck and back. Every part of us touching seems to burn through me until I can't remember anything except right now, Howl in everything around me, not close enough and everywhere at once, his sling an annoying barrier between us.

June groans in her sleep, rolling over to let an arm flop out of her blankets.

I freeze, Howl's lips hot against mine as I catch sight of the scars peeking out from under her sleeves. So many scars, so many dead.

"Wait," I whisper, but he moves to kissing my neck, behind my ear, and I'm not sure I can pull myself out of the fog. "Wait," I say a bit louder, my hand on his shoulder pushing him away.

He does stop, forehead pressed against mine, his eyes closed. "Please, Sev. Why can't we be fixed?"

"I . . ." I look down. When I told Tai-ge things were too complicated, it wasn't just because I knew I didn't want him to kiss me. It would be so easy to just lose myself in Howl right now, to forget everything that came before, but it won't fix anything. "I don't know if this is a good idea."

Howl leans back an inch, our eyes locked together, his hand still on my cheek.

I *want* to think it's a good idea. The moment I saw him lying on the ground under the gore's dead weight, his shoulder torn open and his eyes glassy, I knew that the world without Howl would be a few shades too dark for my liking. But this is how things got so complicated before. Howl kissed me, and I didn't think.

"Everything is too . . . this is . . . *You* are one of the things I wish wasn't so complicated." I stumble over the words, wanting to wipe the awful confusion from Howl's face, but the silver slice of wall clicks, cutting me off.

The door slides open, Luokai's now familiar yellow robe appearing in the gap, a case strapped to his back and one of our packs over his shoulder. "I have some of your things and some food. . . ."

Surprise touches Luokai's features as his eyes trace the line from Howl's shoulder to his hand at my chin to our heads so close together. My heart is still beating so loud he could probably hear it out in the hall, and I'm both angry and relieved he came in. Luokai holds out a bundle of material toward Howl, raising one eyebrow. "I brought you a shirt. If you want it."

Howl lets his hand fall to his lap, clearing his throat. Then he nods and holds the hand out for the shirt.

"Why are you here?" I have to grasp for the words, my head foggy. "I thought Gao Shun was done talking to us."

"Gao Shun is not in charge of me." Luokai hands the shirt over, a smile tugging at the corners of his mouth.

Luokai switches to looking at me, the hint of smile gone. "I came to tell you I know where to find the things your mother left for you. I just can't give them to you."

CHAPTER 52

HOWL MOVES SO WE AREN'T TOUCHING ANYMORE, staring down at the shirt as if he's not sure how to put it on with only one functioning arm. He won't look at me, but the fact that it takes him a moment to speak makes me think he's still rearranging himself inside the way I am, trying to find a way to talk when just a moment ago neither of us was much interested in talking at all.

"What do you mean, you can't give it to us? You want to?" Howl finally asks. "If this is some kind of backhanded attempt at showing me you are my brother, then you can stop. It's clear enough to everyone in this room what's most important to you and the rest of the people in this place."

Luokai turns to force the door shut, ignoring Howl, then pulls the pack from his shoulder. "Most of your possessions were added to our inventory here, but I managed to save some things that I thought you might like to keep." He settles onto the floor in front of us and pushes the pack toward me.

June's smaller bag is there, with the book Howl gave to me back in the Mountain zipped inside it. The story of the sleeping princess.

There are other things he saved for us: a small bag of dried pears and Tai-ge's electric razor. The gore tooth Luokai gave to Howl before he left the Mountain. I guess the pointed end has been rubbed smooth enough that it doesn't constitute a weapon anymore.

"So, you know where the cure is. Were you going to tell us, open the door, and let us get shot down while we looked for it?" Howl awkwardly pulls the shirt over his head, groaning as he puts his good arm through the sleeve. He waves me away when I move to help, pulling the other side of the shirt loosely over his arm in the sling. He takes the tooth from the bag, sliding it open with one hand to find the link still inside. Carefully reassembling the pieces, he loops the leather string around his neck.

Luokai pulls the case from his back, opening the clasps to reveal the erhu I heard him play in Cai Ayi's trees. Light glints off the reptilian scales of the instrument's belly, the two strings slack against its neck. "We have medicine here"—he gestures to Howl's shoulder, the spicy smell still full in my nose—"but nothing for SS. No Mantis. Whatever makes up the ingredients for your mother's cure, I doubt we have the materials or capacity to make it here. We didn't know what it was she brought to us, and she didn't take time to explain."

He folds his legs underneath himself so he's kneeling, balanced on his heels, his back almost unnaturally straight. Setting the round belly of the erhu on his thigh, Luokai twists the tuning pegs until the strings are tight. When he gives one string an experimental pluck, June's eyes jolt open at the sound, making me wonder how long she's been awake, the foreign sound of the erhu finally registering danger. She pushes back from Luokai, crashing into my knees, her breaths coming fast through the iron grate of her mask.

Luokai doesn't look at her, examining his instrument with unbreakable focus until she stills, sitting with her back up against me. Once she's settled, Luokai picks up the erhu's bow, holding it loosely in his hand. "If quarantines fail, Port North will fall." He looks at me. "If we give those Reds the cure, then we sign ourselves over as slaves before they even attempt to set foot on our shores." He gives the erhu another experimental pluck, then twists one of the tuning pegs. "And I'm afraid that if there is a way to shed the manacles I've been bound with for most of my life, I'm not going to turn my head while it sails out the door."

"I thought Speakers made decisions that were best for everyone." I raise an eyebrow, even as hope roars to life inside me. He wants the cure, and Gao Shun is about to give it away. So he came to us.

"I do not think my wants and Port North's needs are mutually exclusive, Jiang Sev." He runs his fingers down the erhu's strings, breathing slow. "Reds will come here eventually whether we give them those papers or not."

Howl glances at me, the air sparking between us with the promise in his words. I lick my lips, choosing each word with care. "Anything we find in those papers, any cure we come up with, we would share with you."

"I'd like to believe you would make a cure and bring it back to me." Luokai's smile presses at his cheeks, his smooth skin bending to either side of his mouth.

Howl leans forward, his eyes going hard. "What do you want, Luokai?"

"I think I've seen proof enough that you're cured." Luokai nods to me. "I should have seen it. Here people are not so afraid of SS as they are in your mountains, but the moment I told you I was contagious, you were frightened for the other people here on the island. For your friend." June curls in on herself even tighter, and I pull her close, wrapping my arms around her, the snarls of her mask pressing into my chest.

"But not frightened for you, Howl." Luokai smiles his humorless smile, as if it can somehow cut the tension between the two of them. "So I assume it's the both of you Jiang Gui-hua cured. But not her." He points to June.

"Just tell us what you're after. We don't need to go into everyone's medical history." Howl's shoulders are starting to sag again, as if sitting up for the last hour or more has taken all the energy he had stored inside him, only the last dregs holding him upright. He blinks, cringing as his uninjured hand cradles his arm in the sling. Guilt lances through me, remembering the way his arm was pressed into my ribs when we were kissing. I probably hurt him. Not that he was complaining. "And while we are bargaining, how much would it be to throw in a dose of Da'ard?" he asks. "Painkillers?"

Luokai's smile warms a degree or two. "I can put something in your tea, but it would make you sleep. You *should* sleep. I'm afraid you probably shouldn't be up and talking quite this much yet. However, I didn't want to make you sleep without asking first."

Howl blinks, as if he's surprised. But then nods. "Thank you."

"So you're willing to help us get Mother's papers in exchange for . . . something." I pull my eyes away from Howl. "Tell us. We don't have time to dance around this."

Luokai's eyes draw away from me, slow like a dribble of water falling from an icicle. "I can't survive on hope, Jiang Sev. I need to know without a doubt you'll come back here, and that you'd bring the cure. For the others afflicted by this disease. Against the chance that SS does spread, leaving us caged underground with no way to escape. But, most especially, I want to know you'll bring back the cure for me. I need there to be a reason for you to come back that both of us believe in." His gaze drips down onto June where she lies against my chest.

Her head comes up, the mask cloudy over her mouth as she stares at me. Green eyes glazed, she gulps down what sounds like a sob.

"You want June . . ." Howl sounds hollow. "June *infected*? Is that what you're saying?"

"That's not an option." I wrap my arms around June, chin on her frizzy head. She doesn't move, her stillness sending flickers of alarm up and down my chest. She twists away from me, her gaze a tight beam of focus on Luokai so intense, it must be only moments before he starts to burn. Her breaths wheeze further and further apart, calm overtaking her as she burrows down inside herself.

Howl inches forward until he's a few inches in front of me, as if he can block June from Luokai. "We won't leave her here."

"If I fall Asleep . . ." June's whisper is rough. "If I stay, you'll give them the cure?"

Luokai inclines his head, sadness etched into the lines of his face. "Yes."

"We aren't going to leave you here. If he won't help us, I know where my mother's papers must be. If Gao Shun means to hand them over to the Reds, she'll have them with her," I cut in.

She pulls away from me, meeting Luokai's eyes. "I would be safe?" The strain in her voice is palpable, even behind the metallic aftertaste of filters.

"We expect helis to start toward us within the next twenty-four hours, so we'll have to move you . . ." He glances at me. ". . . all of you to a safer place. If Gao Shun has to shake the helis from the sky, we don't know exactly what else will shake apart while they're falling. We'd have people take care of you, June. The way they take care of me."

I try to hold back the awful growl building in my throat, as if being so close to the gores Outside left some part of them inside me, waiting to take a bite of any threat, no matter how placid Luokai looks on the outside. There's no one taking care of him now. No one to stop him if SS decides it wants our teeth making pretty lines on the ground.

Howl touches her shoulder with his good hand, looking toward Luokai. "Leaving June is an exchange we can't make. There are other ways we might be able to offer—"

June slaps Howl's hand away, and he breaks off in surprise. Her bright head bows down, blinking wetness from her eyes, the tear tracks gleaming against her pale skin. She reaches up to brush them away.

And rips her mask off instead.

CHAPTER 53

"NO, JUNE!" I GRAPPLE FOR THE MASK, HAMPERED
when June sits back against me, her weight heavy against my chest.
When my fingers finally close around the mask's rigid curls, Howl's
grabbed hold of it too, both of us shoving it toward her face, the
thin plastic feeling as though it might break.

June rolls out of my lap, scrambling to the edge of the room,
with her eyes wide on both me and Howl, as if we were the ones
who took the mask off, not the people trying to put it back on.
The skin around her nose and mouth is lighter, underexposed
after wearing the mask so frequently in the weeks since the new
strain of SS broke loose.

"You get the cure. I'm not your sacrifice." She sucks in a deep
breath and chokes as if she can feel the poison spreading out from
her lungs. "You come back or I'll find you both and kill you."

Howl's grip on the mask drags my hand to the ground when
he lets his arm drop. I wrench it away from him and stand, taking
slow steps toward June. "You don't have to do this. I don't *want*
you to do this. *I'll* stay here if Luokai needs a hostage. It's not

like anyone needs me anymore. You're both better at running . . .
hiding. Howl knows where Sole is. . . ."

Luokai's chin rises in an unexpected lurch at Sole's name that
makes my fists ball. All of us are silent for a moment, watching
the Speaker, as if this moment might be our last, waiting for the
compulsion to come. But he doesn't rise from his seat on the
ground. He only takes a deep breath, then goes back to staring at
the floor.

June's arms fold around my ribs in a hug. I hold her, Howl's
good arm snaking around June's spine, his side nudging into mine
as he presses in close to us, the three of us crushed together like
the night June's father lay dead in the snow, as if somehow we can
hold one another together. I can't let go of the mask, can't let go
of June, wanting to stop each of the deep breaths ballooning in her
chest. To keep SS from going inside her. I promised to take care
of her, promised everything was going to be okay.

But my decisions have all been the ones that made it not okay.
I sent June to signal our getaway in the camp, in clear sight of a
Menghu who almost killed her. I trusted Tai-ge. I fought with
him instead of looking outside the heli window, instead of watching for the people we *knew* were going to come for us. I let Xuan
go, the man who stole her mother.

Xuan. The words trip out of my mouth, eager to escape even
as I'm not sure they're right to say. "June, before Xuan left, he
told me about what must have happened to your mother. That he
was there when they took her away, like you said." She looks up at
me, her eyes wide. "She was probably sent to one of the southern
farms. You can't . . ." I bite my lip. We can't do any of this without June. Even if she weren't family, I don't know how to get back
to the Post without her as a guide. How to find Lihua and Peishan

and the others. The idea of of leaving her here alone sends spirals of anxiety washing down my whole body, as if I'm leaving a child just outside a gore hutch and hoping she'll survive.

But June isn't a child. She made her own decision. And now I have to do my part to make it all right.

"After we get the cure, we're going to find your mother. Find out what happened to her," I whisper into her hair. "I love you, June. You're my sister." My brow feels crinkled, lined forever. How long do we have before she Sleeps? The new strain moves fast. Mei was asleep within an hour when she was infected.

If only I could.

Was there ever anything I could do? Everything inside me is hollow, made of bird bones and rotted grass, the control I thought I had nothing but a shell.

That doesn't mean we've lost, though. I take a deep breath, inhaling June's dirty-hair scent, the rough sandpaper scratch of her clothes, the crinkle of crumbs where she must have hidden something down her shirt. I will make her safe. No matter what it takes.

June buries her head in my stomach, her arms ratcheted so tight around me, my bones creak. "Will you tell me a story?" she asks, the words muffled against my shirt.

"A story?" My brain is full of sick and death and the metal taste of blood. "I . . ."

Howl hugs us both closer. "I will."

Luokai picks up his bow. "I brought this because it often makes me feel calm." He swallows, takes a deep breath, then looks at her, kindness in his eyes that she cannot see with her face pressed into my stomach. "Would you like me to play?"

June doesn't move for a moment, but then she nods.

Howl's hand on June's shoulder tightens as the first notes slip through the air. "My mother used to tell me this story. It's old, older than SS or wars or whatever this country was before. Older than the mountains or the trees. It starts with a girl."

The slow drawl of his voice familiar and comforting. It's like the story he told me about stars and qilin when there was a gore howling at our feet, every word meant to smooth down fear.

"This girl lived under the sky and slept under the stars. No man or woman could touch her because she could leap from shadow to shadow, hiding as if she were darkness itself."

June looks up at him, her eyes narrowed. "Darkness?"

"The people of the Earth feared her because she could flit from the highest of trees down to the ground to shelter under the smallest leaf. She could find food anywhere, shooting it down with her bow. They feared her because she didn't need them. All she needed was the sky and the ground, the trees and their shade, and her bow by her side. She kept company of the wind, made friends of the birds and the rivers, tracked each of the ten suns as they took turns sailing across the sky."

I've never heard this story before, but I can tell Howl is searching for words, either because he's changing them for June or because he can't quite remember. The notes from Luokai's erhu twine together with his voice as if they were born under the same star.

Howl continues, "But one day, the sky grew too hot, burning away the girl's beloved trees, the shade that kept her safe. Instead of one sun at a time, the sky was full of ten all at once. The ten suns, so lonely after years of solo journeys across the sky, decided to stay together. They talked and laughed, their blaze in the sky searing the forest. Each tree was like a matchstick. The village like coals. It was almost as if the suns couldn't see the way the world burned beneath them. Or perhaps they could see, and all they cared about was their own place in the sky."

June's wide eyes flick to Luokai, though the Speaker doesn't pause in pushing and pulling his bow, his eyes closed as he listens. Luokai who wants to find his own place in the sky, alone and ready to do anything to fix it, even if it leaves every corner of the world but his smoldering. Tai-ge's mother, the new General, the Chairman, Dr. Yang. The Menghu. It feels as if our sky has been full of suns for years, and we didn't know why we were burning up.

June looks back to Howl, her eyes wide. "What happened?"

"This fearless hunter came out from her shadows. She climbed the tallest mountain to stand the suns down. 'You must leave!' she shouted up at them, their rays burning at her hair. 'You are destroying my home!'

"'Your home?' one of the suns sneered. 'I've seen the way you hide. The way the others fear you. You have no home.'

"The girl looked around at the world she loved so much, her beloved trees burned to ash, the villages on fire pointing to her in dread almost as much as toward the suns, as if she were the one who brought them. The very ground began to crack under her feet, and she wondered if maybe he was right.

"But as she stared up into the ten suns' fiery depths, she knew someone had to fight, someone had to stand, or everyone would die. The girl took her bow from her shoulder, the wood specially made so it couldn't burn. 'You cannot tell me I'm worthless. You may believe you're stronger and more important than me up there in the sky. You're too high to see any of us for who we are. Too high to know what I'm capable of.' She drew back an arrow and let it fly straight into the sun's heart, and he shattered into a million pieces of fire and glass, raining down in pieces on the earth.

"'I am strong!' the girl yelled up at the suns, 'and I will protect the earth, even if the earth doesn't want me.' And she shot the heart out of each sun threatening her forest, and the villages cradled underneath the trees. The suns had seemed so far away, their glaring lights untouchable, but each shattered at the pierce of her arrows, falling to the ground in a deathly blaze when faced with such strength. The girl shot until there was only one sun left. He hid behind a bank of clouds, and the girl left him be. The villagers needed one sun, one bit of light they could shade themselves against, one bit of light to make her trees grow and to make her shade."

He pauses for a moment, swallows. "We need one sun because the heat brings out the best in us."

"I wish . . . ," June whispers, her eyelids heavy, and I can see her thoughts just where mine were, on the many suns burning down on us, competing for space in the sky, our homes smoldering ashes, all that's left after a fire.

I hold her close, her hair bright as sunlight against my dirty uniform shirt. "You've already shot the first one down, June." Luokai doesn't look up from his strings, though his fingers slow over the notes.

June's head is heavy against my shoulder, her eyes finally closed. I can feel each breath in the press of her ribs against my stomach, long and drawn out at first, and then slowing. Shallow. Almost as if she's full to the brim inside and can't fit another mouthful of air. The long notes of Luokai's song settle like a blanket across us, heavier than the gas mask ever was. When I slip my fingers under June's wrist, her pulse is dying like the sputtering glow of incense as the last bits of ash fall. Howl shifts to her side, wrapping his hand around her other wrist, both of us watching her chest rise and fall. Until it stops.

The new strain moves quickly, the Chairman said. It takes hold and doesn't let go.

I brush June's curls back from her face, trying not to remember when she first came into the cell, panicked. Trapped. Is she awake behind those closed eyes, begging for her arms to move, for her lungs to open?

I pull her closer, confidence injected into my voice more for me than for her. "I love you, June. You're going to be all right. No matter what happens, we will be back for you with a cure."

Luokai's song dwindles to a single sustained note that dies in the cold air of the cell. Silence takes the room, pressing up against me, smothering my mouth and lungs, pushing down hard on June's still form.

He opens his erhu case and pulls back the furry inside to reveal a single sheet of paper, the white of it stained to brown. It's black with my mother's spiky writing.

"You had it here the whole time?" I choke on my tears and the outrage that boils just beneath.

"Most of Jiang Gui-hua's things are in the care of the Speakers. We were worried Gao Shun would destroy it all because she was so angry with her sister. But today she removed a device from the box, a miniature telescreen."

"The Speakers just let her have it?"

"There was no reason not to. She told the Speakers it might scare away the helis gathering like flies before they attempt to mob us." Luokai sighs. "I can't risk going up against her directly, not without the time it would take to convince my fellow Speakers. As it is, I took the paper without my fellows knowing. If Gao Shun realizes they're gone and that I'm missing too . . ." He shrugs. "Tomorrow, though, Gao Shun will be distracted, and she'll be less careful of the device once the Reds tell her they'd rather take it than bargain. You might be able to get it away from her while she's trying to shake the helis from the sky." He turns to Howl. "You have a link in the things I brought you. The one in the tooth. Can you send pictures with it?"

Howl sucks one of his cheeks in. "I think so."

"Do it. I'll take the paper back to the Speakers before anyone notices it's gone." His eyes follow the tooth as Howl pulls it out, his expression hungry. If I remember correctly, Luokai is the one who gave it to Howl in the first place.

Once the little black device is out, Howl hands it to me, awkwardly caving around his bound-up arm. "Will you? I can't with my arm . . . the way it is."

June a dead weight across my legs, I can hardly bring myself to pull my hand from her wrist, as if I keep holding on, her heartbeat will reappear. But I take the link. The paper. Find the command to capture a picture of the graphs and charts and closely knit characters strung together in sentences I don't understand. I catch mentions of chemicals, of measurements and trials. Howl's name is on the paper, and so is mine. At the very end there's a frantically scrawled string of characters that almost looks like a chemical formula.

The cure?

It feels so heavy. This, my answer to the war, like a rock around my neck. But I take the pictures and send them. It's hard to hope when June lies almost dead in my lap.

Luokai pulls the paper out from my grip once the pictures have been taken, then presses it back underneath the lining of his case and stands. He goes to the door and calls for the Baohujia, and they come with a cup of sludgy-looking tea, which Luokai sets in front of Howl.

After shooing the Baohujia away, Luokai bends down in front of me, his arms out. He wants June. To take her now.

My arms curl around her, my fingers pressing into her little arms.

"I need to take her somewhere safe." He gently pulls her away from me. "Once she's situated, I'll come back for you. We need to move you before the morning light breaks. Just in case negotiations go poorly and the helis come."

"If anything happens to her . . . if she doesn't wake up, I'll . . ." Howl's voice is so tired it seems to be coming from a person choking out their last words, garbled and rough.

"If anything happens to her, I'll be the first to mourn. I am not one of your suns, and I will not shatter," Luokai whispers. He stands, June's head lolling back against his arm. "But I am sorry to be the bars on her cell."

CHAPTER 54

THE IDEA OF SLEEP FEELS WRONG, AS IF GIVING IN
to my tired eyes will be some sort of betrayal. That doesn't stop
me from taking the medicine-doused cup of tea Luokai offers and
holding it in front of Howl's face until he succumbs, taking the
cup and drinking. Only a few minutes pass before he lets me help
him back to the pallet, eyes closing as his head touches the pillow.
It reminds me of the time we were together out in the forest. How
he used to fall asleep in the oddest places and times, as if he could
just turn his body off, knowing his next opportunity to rest might
not come for a while.

Except, when we were in the forest, June was with us. After all
those nights of waking up to find her tousled hair, there's nothing
to find. Nothing but a quivering ghost of an image in my mind, a
presence I keep reaching out to touch, only to find it gone.

I huddle next to Howl, my brain slowly losing the fight against
sleep. I keep the link balled in my fist, staring down at the glowing
letters as they scroll across the back of my hand, the light too bright
in the cell to allow me to read them. If Sole answers, I can't see it.

Luokai returns within the half hour, the erhu still strung across his back, but somehow it looks as if it weighs a hundred pounds less, no cure weighing it down. He settles himself down across from me, noting with an approving nod that Howl's eyes are closed. "We'll give him some time to sleep. We are safe here for a few more hours."

I wrap a blanket around me, refusing to answer. Its scratchy fibers seem to have soaked up all the water in the air, leaving me shivering. Luokai folds his hands comfortably in his lap, back straight, closing his eyes. Watching is almost uncomfortable because I keep waiting for movement, wanting to itch and scratch in sympathy as a fly lands on his forehead, crawling down to his cheek and across his lips. Not even a twitch.

Is he asleep? Maybe—just as being able to flop over anywhere and start snoring is part of being a Menghu—pretending to sit at attention and snoring away inside your head is part of being Port Northian.

It's the last thought that twists in my brain before my eyes close.

"You are angry at me." The voice brushes past my ears, not enough to ratchet my eyes open when they seem gummed shut with sleep.

"You just took someone very important to me, Luokai." Howl's voice rasps with sleep, sending prickles down my arms. I keep my eyes closed, not sure I can face Luokai right now.

"I'm sorry about June. But you cannot pretend that is the only reason you are angry."

"You've got everything about me figured out, then? We might share blood, but that doesn't make us the same."

Long pause. "I didn't want to leave at all, much less disappear without even saying good-bye. Every day I've been here I've thought of you there in the Mountain with no one but the dormitory heads and Jiaoyang to take care of you. I wanted to come back."

"But you didn't."

"I couldn't."

Silence.

"I would go back with you now if I could. You're not the little boy I left there, but you're not a young man the way you should be either. There's something hard inside you that I wish I could . . . fix."

"I don't need to be *fixed*." Howl shifts, and I can feel his warmth against my side.

"Maybe not. I'm glad you aren't alone now. I worried that . . . you would be." I can almost feel Luokai's eyes flick past me. "I wish I could be so lucky. The two of you move together. One an extension of the other. Two halves of something yet unfinished."

"Me and Sev?" I can feel them pause; now it's Howl looking down at me and a thread of nervousness sews its way up my spine. "Sev's made it pretty clear that she was done with me a long time ago, and it was only you opening the door earlier that saved me from hearing it out loud. Again." Howl's voice is quiet. "And you know very well that Sole is still sitting in the Mountain waiting for you. More alone than you are here, I think. You could write her a message now, if you wanted. She's on the other end of this link." There's a rattle, the sound of the link inside the gore tooth around Howl's neck. He must have taken it out of my hand and put it back where it belongs.

Now the silence is Luokai's, heavy and thick, tasting of something I can't define. Mourning, perhaps. When the Speaker finally speaks, his voice creaks, as if he's gained a hundred years in only a few moments. "I'm dangerous, Howl. Just because they try to give me a place and a life here doesn't mean it's less of a risk to be in the same room."

"Sounds like an excuse to me. We've had Mantis at the Mountain for years."

For a while I think Luokai isn't going to answer, but when he does, the strain in his voice sends a jolt of surprise down my spine. "There are men and women who protect me from myself, protect others from my sickness. Their life's work is to hold me up when I fall, to make sure no one else falls when I do, like human crutches. They can't change me into someone who isn't infected, though. Mantis might make some people feel safe, but what if it doesn't work? What if I don't take enough or take too much? With so much at risk, how do you make friends, love, *marry*, if at any moment, your mind could decide to hurt the people you care about most? You could only watch yourself do it. Live with the memories that you took away your happiness with your *own* hands."

The image crimps inside me, memories of the darkness of the Sanatorium, the people sequestered from society because they couldn't trust their own hands to obey. The one compulsion I did have is buried deep in my memory, a curtain drawn over it so I don't have to look. The terror, the rot and bile it tracked through my mind, leaving nothing but a wish that I could scrub myself clean from the inside out. It happened right before I left the City, right before it was just me and Howl, before I knew I'd been cured. I worried for him every day, just the way Luokai is saying. Worried I'd wake up one day and he'd be dead next to me. But the reality of that first brush with the sickness curdling in my mind . . . I hardly knew where to draw the line between myself and it.

SS wasn't me. It terrified me. It was inside me, and I couldn't get it out. How many times had Luokai had those same moments of terror, of not realizing until it was too late that he was not himself, and not being able to stop?

I open my eyes, finding the two of them sitting across from each other, sunrise streaming through the window to touch Luokai's lined face. There are threads of gray caught in his hair I didn't notice before.

"How could I come back, knowing I couldn't trust myself to be near you?" Luokai asks. "Couldn't be near her? I'd have had to watch as you played without me, pretend I was happy for her as she fell in love with someone else. I've had nightmares of situations like . . . *this.*" The frustration lacing through Luokai's voice seems to weigh down his shoulders as he gestures to us, the room, him in here with us. "I can't even have guards to protect you, or they might miss their chance at escaping the contagion. Anything could happen in here. I'd never forgive myself if something did." Luokai sighs. "Even in Port North, my life is one of watching from afar. I can help people. Mediate problems, look at crops and decide how they can be grown better. Bring food when it is scarce. Give peace when there is none. But that's all I can do. The only way I can keep from hurting others is by choosing to be alone. I don't think I could make that choice if I were with you."

I close my eyes again as the two of them stare at each other.

"I *was* alone. For a long time. It wasn't a choice."

"But now it is," Luokai says, and once again, I feel them both looking at me.

"It's her choice too," Howl whispers. "You've been worried that you could hurt me or Sole. I did hurt her. She hurt me. We're both . . . You can't take back the worst things you've done unless the other person lets you. But even after everything . . . I think I love her."

My brain goes blank, just trying to fit around those words. *I love her.*

"She's kind when she doesn't have to be." Howl's still talking. "Makes me laugh. Makes me want to do better." He stops, and it takes everything I have to keep my eyes shut. "I would do anything to make her happy. I think she loves me too, and that's what makes it so . . ." He exhales. "*So frustrating.*"

I feel an echo of what he's saying in my chest, as if it's been traced there over and over, suddenly feeling trapped in the tiny space of those words. Maybe it is that control Luokai is talking about that makes my hands start to shake when I think of Howl. If I choose Howl now the way I did back in the Mountain, that means entrusting a tiny bit of control over my fate, my plans, my *life* to another person. Again.

Trying to go against the war machine Dr. Yang is creating is dangerous enough without allowing someone else to have a finger on the self-destruct button. Someone who could have pushed it before. Someone who almost *did*, whether he meant to or not. I let myself be vulnerable for the first time in my life, realized the walls I had built so firmly around myself were a weakness instead of a protection. That I could finally let them come down. And it was a mistake.

And now . . . ? Now what? After everything? I open my eyes again, willing myself to really look at Howl. At the things he's said and done. The things people have said about him versus the things I've seen with my own eyes.

Luokai takes another deep breath, his lungs expanding through his stomach and ribs. I catch myself holding my own breath, waiting for him to exhale. "Hope is something you fight for, Howl." He breathes again, deep. "I would do anything to have that kind of

hope. To be able to control this weakness, the awful base humanness SS imposes on me."

"Humanness?" Howl looks up. "I wouldn't call compulsions
particularly human."

"I disagree." Luokai's voice curls up in a smile. "If humans'
first inclination were to love and trust, then there would be no
war, no starving, no infected. No kidnappings. No slaves. SS
doesn't *create* violence or greed in its victims. It merely removes all
the barriers we impose on ourselves. It's people listening to their
basest instincts who harm others." He sighs. "No, we rise above
the fact that we are human and control ourselves. We ignore the
fact that others are human too, and choose to love them anyway."

He looks at me, catching me with my eyes open. I pinch them back
shut, trying not to think. Trying not to agree with his words because
it hurts. My whole life I've been attempting to do exactly what he is
saying. I thought it was my sickness or traitor blood in my veins that
made me selfish, made me want to think of myself, when I should
be treating people like equals. Like people, not as though they were
objects standing between me and the things I want.

It makes me think of Sole, trying to recompense for her crimes
by sewing up wounds just like the ones she inflicted for so many
years. Of Howl recounting what my mother said about enemies
looking like friends if you are close enough to see. It is not anyone's first inclination to do that. We fight, we are defensive, we
assume. We kill.

I might as well have. I left Howl to die instead of me.

But I can't let it go. "You don't know what happened between
me and Howl. It's not just a matter of being imperfect, something
you can wave away and hope everyone tries to do better tomorrow.
He might have been *killed* because of me. And me because of him."

Howl's swivel to see me awake was almost comically abrupt. Luokai cocks one eyebrow, unsurprised. "On purpose? You tried to kill each other? Guns? Knives? Poison?"

I pull my head up from the floor and sit with my hands in my lap, thinking of the scar at my throat made by Howl's knife when I found him in the heli cargo bay. It was a mistake. An awful, horrendous, horrible sort of mistake, one that makes me question Howl's judgment. But it wasn't on purpose.

Luokai catches my expression, turning it over and over in his mind as though he can discern my thoughts, a picture painted across my eyes and mouth. "Trust is a choice, Jiang Sev. Love is a choice. Choices you should be happy to have . . ." He blinks. Takes a deep breath. Tries again. "No matter which choice you make, it's . . ." His voice squeezes to silence, cutting off mid-sentence.

Luokai's mouth screws down tight, and he takes a deep breath through his nose, the way he did when we were looking out over the underground market, as if he can send all his thoughts flying. He slowly raises a hand, his fingers flexed. His eyes open, but it's almost as if he's looking straight through me. He lowers his hand to the frayed yellow hem of his tunic and pulls out a thread. The concentration bouncing between him and the fiber pulses burns. The hairs on my arms stand up as he takes another thread, carefully placing it on the ground. He does it over and over again, each thread adding to a precisely arranged pile.

"Luokai?" Howl's voice crimps over the word as Luokai pulls each string, his unraveling hem boasting more and more available threads each time he takes one from the dusky yellow fabric.

He can't hear us, the compulsion's grip on his mind blocking out everything but the design. Horror punches through me, pushing me to move between him and Howl, to keep June safe from this uncontrolled compulsion, only to feel as if I've stepped over a cliff into thin air when I remember she isn't here.

The swirls grow to form a design, interlocking circles covering the stone floor in front of him. Luokai's hands are graceful, each movement part of a ritual, a dance. He's in another world, at peace with compulsions, allowing them to take place instead of being controlled by them. The measured movements look like harmony and tranquility personified.

The breaths scrunched down tight behind my throat slowly relax and flow. After a few minutes, Luokai stops, his eyes refocusing. He stares at his hands and then they drop, as if his marionette strings have been cut.

"What you need," Luokai whispers, as if our conversation hadn't broken, "is to stop trying to decide who people are. Look at what they are *doing*. It is actions that make a person, not the ideas you choose to attach to them."

When I look over at Howl, he's looking back, a self-conscious expression quirked at the corners of his mouth, as if I overheard something he wasn't ready to share. "I didn't know you were awake," he says.

I bite my lip. "Do you wish I hadn't been listening?"

He glances at Luokai, but then looks back at me as if he's made some sort of decision. "I wish you'd heard me saying those things to you, not to him."

Electricity seems to spark through my chest, but it's swirled together with indecision, with the fact that Luokai is sitting here watching us.

Luokai looks up at the ceiling, discomfort twitching across his expression. "I'd really rather not be a part of this conversation."

"I'd really rather you weren't too." Howl sort of laughs. "Could you give us a minute?"

The nervous energy sparking through me flares as Luokai gives a slow nod, then rises from the floor, leaning down to pick up the erhu case. I'm not sure I have answers to the questions I'm afraid Howl will ask me.

"You're both awake, so I'd like to move you to a safer place. And then go get the device your mother left." Luokai's eyes weigh on me for a moment before switching to Howl. "I'll go find someone to carry you."

"If anyone tries to carry me, I'll kill them." Howl's head jerks back toward me, his eyes wide. "Figuratively. Without any actual violence." He presses his lips together when I raise an eyebrow at him, then looks up at his brother. "I'm glad to have finally found you after all these years . . . but it's hard."

"I understand. I, too, am guilty of many such moments. Just talking about the Mountain still makes me angry, when I should have long ago let go of what happened." Luokai runs a hand along the case's long neck once, twice. Then opens it and takes the instrument out.

The stone underneath me begins to hum, a loud *crack* echoing through the window and shaking the stone floor. Howl and I look up at the ceiling as a cloud of dust mists down over us, like a stone-made smattering of snow.

"Are the helis here already? You said something about things shaking." Part of it is concern that makes me ask. Part to forestall the moment when I'm in here alone with Howl, because everything is too close to see clearly. I know that what he says is true. I do care about him. A lot. Maybe even love him. But that thought in and of itself is terrifying, even without all the extra baggage weighing us down like cement up to our necks.

"She's . . . at the top . . . the central tower." Luokai's every sentence trails off as if he can't remember that he's speaking, the endings not so important as the beginnings. He doesn't look at me as he speaks, fingering the erhu's long neck.

But then he looks at Howl. Raises the instrument.

Swings it directly at Howl's head.

CHAPTER 55

I DART BETWEEN HOWL AND HIS BROTHER, THE BLOW landing on my upraised arms with a hollow *thunk*. Luokai pulls the instrument back toward himself, fingers grappling with the slippery wood. "Gao Shun," he croaks. "At the top." Luokai's glassy eyes stream tears, hardly able to focus on me. "Your aunt . . ."

He drops the erhu and grabs both of my shoulders, pulling me so close his breath is in my nose, filming my cheeks. His fingers squeeze until I'm afraid I'll hear bones break. Something in his eyes fights, and his lips purse as one word wheezes out from his throat.

"Run."

"Help!" I yell, hoping the guards are listening outside. Luokai's fingers clutch harder and harder as I try to wriggle out from between his hands. Stamping down on one of his feet with my bare heel loosens his grip for a split second, enough for me to take a step away. But his grasping fingers follow me, streaking up toward my face. I duck, kicking him in the knee. No one comes to the door to let us out, to pull Luokai back.

Luokai stumbles back long enough for me to crash down next to Howl, sliding under his uninjured arm to help him up.

"My shoulder . . . ," Howl gasps, his weight too heavy for me to carry up from the ground. He falls to the side, a tear slinking down his cheek, the two of us trapped as Luokai's alien gaze settles on us. He begins crawling toward us, light from the window hesitant and gauzy where it creeps through the window to settle across Luokai's shoulders like mold. Another ripple of shakes erupts underneath us, the sound of an explosion tearing through my ears from outside.

Luokai inches closer, unhurried as he reaches for Howl's foot.

Howl kicks at his brother, catching him under the jaw. Luokai's head jerks back, and Howl and I scuttle along the wall, trying to get away. It isn't a large room, and Luokai only pauses long enough to find his feet and flick his tongue out to lick at the blood trickling down his chin.

"Stay behind me!" Howl rasps, swearing as his hand skids out from under him when it comes down on the bag Luokai brought to us in the pack. The bag with the book inside.

I dart between Howl's crumpled form and Luokai just as he charges at us, snagging the bag. Swinging it by its straps, I smash the book into Luokai's temple, slamming his assault off-kilter. "The pack's by the door, Howl. See if there's anything useful. His last compulsion only lasted a few minutes."

"You know compulsions aren't consistent."

"What other choice do we have? We can't open the door. It's either wait it out or let him do . . . whatever it is he's trying to do." Another echoing *boom* shudders through the stone, almost knocking me off my feet, but I stay upright between Luokai and Howl as the erhu player reaches for his instrument.

I don't know what Howl is doing; his presence just a flutter of movement, and the sound of a zip that means he's gotten to the pack. I can't look away from Luokai, his unblinking stare leveled on me as he crawls closer, the scratch of the erhu's wood against stone as he drags it toward me creeping up my spine. The cold, no-longer-in-control stare sends chills of dread through my core.

He throws the erhu at me, rushes at me as I dodge, the instrument splintering on the wall as it hits. Hardly noticing as I swing the bag into the side of his head again, Luokai crouches low and darts underneath my next swing, his shoulder slamming into my ribs and taking me to the floor. My shoulder hits, slivers of pain slicing through my arm and side, Luokai's heavy weight on top of me. His long fingers, so graceful during their last compulsion, contort as they clutch at my arm, fighting to bring his bared teeth down on my skin.

Before he can bite, something flies through the air to crash into the side of his head, and he recoils with a yelp.

His nails gouge long scratches into my skin as I slam my knee into his ribs, and his grip loosens enough for me to roll away. Howl's sitting over the pack, his whole body curved around his shoulder as he tears through the contents, looking for something else to throw. Heart thumping, I stagger up from the ground and snatch the pack away from him. Holding it up like a shield, I charge at Luokai before he can get up, tripping over whatever it was Howl threw at him before. The stagger launches me forward into Luokai, and using the pack, I slam his body into the wall, his head *thunk*ing hollowly against the stone. Glassy-eyed, Luokai lunges, landing full on top of me and the pack, a bloody stream of saliva dribbling from his cracked-open mouth onto my collarbone. Something spasms through the erhu player, or whatever is left of the man inside this hungry shell, and I clench my eyes shut, bracing myself for the moment his teeth clamp down on my neck.

Instead, his skull hits my shoulder, a ripple of pain shaking me to the bone, his dead weight crushing my lungs flat. I can't breathe, the smell of fear and sweat and dirt from the pack clogging every attempted gasp.

But then, he doesn't move. Silent and still, his blood dripping in warm beads onto my skin.

My arms shaking, I push Luokai and the pack off me, scrambling back from his limp form until my spine hits the wall. Howl hunches over his brother, Tai-ge's electric razor sitting on the floor next to him. Howl's face is gray, red marking the bandage at his shoulder and chest.

He doesn't speak for a moment, the two of us just staring at each other. I take a full breath, and then another, my head feeling so light I'm afraid it will detach. "We need his hand to unlock the door," I whisper.

Howl nods, but he doesn't move for a second, his hand an anchor, keeping me grounded. "I don't think I can drag him. He's not going to stay out for long."

I swallow, then go up on my knees. For some reason, standing seems impossible, as if crawling will somehow be stealthier, won't alert the erhu player that anything in the room is alive, that he needs to come back and tear us to shreds. I force myself to get up, to go to his limp form, and take hold of his arms. Drag him to the door. Shove his palm against the silver strip.

The door clicks and slides open, the hallway outside bare. Has SS has already put the guards who were out there to sleep somewhere? Or perhaps sent them on more frightening sorts of errands?

Howl uses the pack to push himself onto his feet, swaying

until he leans up against the wall. I drag Luokai back into the far-thest corner of the room, then grab the pack and slip the straps over my shoulders. The two of us stand there staring down at Howl's brother.

"I'm sorry," Howl says to Luokai's unconscious form. "But I'm alive. Both Sev and I are, so you don't need to worry."

"We'll be back," I add. "Soon."

Luokai groans.

Pulling Howl's arm over my shoulder, I stagger under his weight when his knees buckle. Luokai rolls over, his eyes open wide and darting across the smooth stone walls until he turns around to level his flat gaze on us. "So hungry," he mumbles, a broken tooth dribbling out of his mouth as he slides over onto his knees, getting ready to spring.

I drop the pack and lug Howl through the door, his feet trip-ping over mine as we stumble out into the hall. Ducking out from under Howl's arm, I pull at the door, stuck in its slot under the silver panel. It won't budge.

Luokai is crawling now, limping toward us with the slither-ing grace of a gore. The bag with the book inside hits my hip as I wheel to face him. I wait until Luokai gets to the doorway, going up on his knees and reaching for the wall to pull himself onto his feet. Before he puts his hand to the stone, I swing the book-heavy bag sideways into the doorjamb, the weight of the book veering around the corner, slamming Luokai's hand against the silver strip on his side of the wall.

Hope like an inky poison in my veins, the two of us stare at each other, time itself paused.

The door snicks shut just as I pull the bag free and clutch it to my chest.

Not waiting to see if Luokai can remember how to open the door while in the grips of a compulsion, I run to Howl where he's huddled on the floor, pull him up, and drag his shuffling steps down the hall. The floor shudders under our feet, stone powder dusting down from the ceiling, a terrible promise that even Port North cannot stand against Reds forever.

CHAPTER 56

HOWL DOESN'T SPEAK AS WE HOBBLE ALONG, HIS good arm draped across my shoulder, the other cradled in his makeshift sling. Neither of us speaks until we're down the hall and out of sight, a frustrated, inhuman scream issuing from the prison cell like an aftertaste in the air. But the door doesn't open again.

I pause for a moment to loop June's bag across my body so I won't drop it by accident. Of all the things we end up with, it would be the gold-embossed lines of the ridiculous book inside, the princess's impossible happy ending mocking us from between its tightly closed pages. The book and . . . "The gore tooth! Howl, do you still have the link to Sole?"

Howl looks down, his bare skin prickled in the cold air. We can both see the necklace is gone. "That little gore hole." He glances back the way we came. But when he looks back there's a shadow of a smile on his face.

"Why would he take it?"

"I told him who was on the other end. He and Sole used to be a thing. A big thing." Howl groans when I start walking again, forcing his feet to follow. "There isn't much help she could give us now, anyway. She has what was on that paper. That's what matters most."

"The central tower is where he said Gao Shun is."

Howl nods. "Then I guess we go up."

We go up a flight of stairs and then rest, Howl on his knees on the stone floor. Everything seems quiet, as if we're in a tomb instead of a city that is supposed to be full of people. The floor doesn't shake anymore while we wait for Howl to catch his breath, the dark seeming to reach out to us from the blank doorways marking the long hall. Once Howl is ready to continue, we walk and walk, up more stairs, down more hallways until Howl's weight is bending me over sideways, one of his feet dragging.

I grit my teeth, muscles screaming and my bones aching, wondering if he'll collapse first or if I will. Will we ever find another person? A glowing arrow with the words GAO SHUN THIS WAY pointing us upward? Luokai said she was at the very top of this place, but not all stairways are going to lead there. And with the stones shaking as if bombs are falling, will Port North fall on our heads before we even come close?

The ground shivers under my feet even as I think about bombs, and something overhead fractures, the terrifying *crack-crack-crack* of stone caving in. Howl stumbles, and I fall under his weight just as a shower of stone chips rains down over our heads. Ceiling and stair groan as if Port North is giving up, ready to fall into the ocean and feed us to the fish that live at the bottom rather than face the onslaught of bombs raining down from above. Chunks of stone crash to the floor just ahead of us, the solid rock over our heads feeling as if it's shifting forward.

I drag Howl toward a blank doorway, the two of us huddling in the braced space as rock rains down. I've only lived for sixteen—almost seventeen—years. I've seen more than anyone should be subjected to, thought I was dead more times than I care to count. We're so close to finding the cure. This would be the stupidest of ends.

But, as the ceiling shivers overhead, the air so clogged with dust that there's none left to breathe, all I can feel is him. His arm over mine, the warmth of his skin, the chalky dust gritty between us. Something in me settles as I pull him closer, as if somehow us being together will protect us from rock and stone.

I don't want to die. But I don't want to live in a world without him either. Is that not answer enough? Howl's heartbeat pounds under my cheek, his arm around my shoulders and mine around his waist, his sling caught between us. The stone raining down around us seems to thunder and strike, only to leave an awful, entombing silence. A tear burns down my cheek, and I keep my eyes clenched shut, waiting for the world to finish crashing down on us.

But it doesn't. It sits, watching. Waiting for us to have hope again.

Something inside me settles.

Howl coughs, his chest heaving as he attempts to free it of the dust roaming through the air. "I think I see . . . light?"

I open my eyes to find a glimmer of light dripping down from the stairwell just in front of us. Coughing, I pull myself up from the floor, pulling my shirt up over my nose to filter out some of the dust. Howl attempts to roll onto his knees but doesn't make it onto his feet until I help him up. Together, we creep over the fallen chunks of stone up the stairs until the trickle of light becomes a thick band, then an actual crumbling circle of light, white-hot and searing into my eyes.

An opening to outside.

Is it possible we could reach Gao Shun from out there?

The opening is the remains of an entrance, the corners all cracked and leaning up against one another, the actual door flapping in a salty breeze. Though the door itself looks as if it might fall to pieces at any moment, the ceiling and the hallway supports seem to be all right. The light filtering through the opening hits a long wooden bench turned on its side. I prop Howl up against the wall, right the bench, then help him to sit, his body seeming almost to fold out from under him, no matter how much he swears at it.

"Sometimes I forget you grew up in the City," Howl says when his back is against the wall, his head lolling to one side. "I mean, anyone could drag me up flights and flights of stairs, but using the pack as a shield back there was pretty cool. And that book thing at the end? I'd say you'd make a good Menghu if I didn't think you'd leave me here out of spite. Without a razor, even, since I'm pretty sure it broke when I threw it at Luokai's head." He tiredly adjusts his arm, pain flicking across his face. "I'd probably die of itchy beard before anyone found me."

"I left it in there with him so, one way or another, I think you're stuck." I smile, sitting down next to him, barely managing to repress a groan at allowing my overtaxed muscles to relax for a moment. "Lucky for you, I like it when you're scruffy."

"You like something about me?" Howl thinks for a second, a flicker of a smile cutting through the strain on his face. "I'm not really sure how to take that. I can *understand*, of course, I just didn't expect—"

Another rumble of an explosion blisters through the stone under our feet, a delayed boom filtering through the opening, accompanied by a warm rush of air. That sounded like a bomb, not whatever weapon Gao Shun is using on the helis.

I look back at Howl. "You should take it exactly the way it sounds." My heart gives an uncomfortable skip, the sweet taste of fear and hope in my mouth. And decision. "I . . . I'm sorry I left you at the Mountain. And tied you up. And was generally awful to you. I didn't trust you enough before." Silence coats the air between us, and though I can feel Howl staring at me, it takes me a second to meet his eyes. "But I think I do now."

"You're leaving me here, aren't you?"

The air outside seems too quiet. Poisonous, as if it has already killed anyone else stupid enough to go out and attempt breathing it. "Yes."

"It's what I would do." He presses his lips together, an expression I've seen on his face so many times I wish I could just see his thoughts written out as they connect rather than having to wonder. "You don't have to do . . . that."

"Leave you?"

"No, you don't have to try to make things better between us. You don't have to say anything. I was being selfish earlier. I want things to be fixed, but nothing is *that* tidy."

"I want to." My stomach twists. "What if this is the last chance I have to say it?"

He smiles, an ironic twist to his mouth. "Both of us have lived an entire lifetime of moments where it might be the last chance to say something."

"I really am sorry for my side of what happened, though. And if this is the last, last chance, I'd rather you knew that than didn't."

"I'm sorry too." He takes a deep breath, all signs of cockiness smothered. "I just don't want you to say anything that isn't true all the way. I don't think I can survive watching you run away from me again, Sev." He stops, shaking his head. "Sorry, that sounds dramatic. But please don't tell me there's a chance here if there isn't. Or if it's *only* a chance. Things *are* complicated. I think I've untangled my side, but if you haven't . . ."

The question he's not quite voicing tingles like an invitation at the tip of my tongue. I lean forward the two inches between us and kiss his cheek. Whispering, because even if I know this is right, it's still hard to say out loud. "If I could take back running away from you, I would."

He pulls away, a crease marking his forehead. "You ran because of what Sole said. I love Sole; she's like my sister. And . . . she knew me before I left the Mountain." He looks down, fiddling with my hand, running his finger down my thumb and along my palm. "There's more you asked about before." He looks at me, my memory of that awful morning under the owl's tree seeming to cloud the air between us. "I couldn't make myself tell you, and it's hard to say it even now. The Menghu—even *Sole*—all think—"

I reach out and cover his mouth. I'm not going to close my eyes and hope whatever it is about Howl that frightened people isn't there. But no matter what other people tell me, I think I've seen pretty clearly who Howl is. And for right now, that's enough. "I know I don't understand. I might not even have the capacity to understand who you were and the things you did before." I let my hand fall, try-ing to find the words. "We've lived very different lives. Had very different choices." And different reactions to them. Like my dreams and flashbacks. Howl doesn't have them. But that doesn't mean he mourns the dead any less. "In the months I've known you, I've never seen you hurt anyone just because you could. I've seen you do the opposite. If you want to tell me about whatever it is that bothers the other Menghu, then you can. But you don't have to right at this very moment. You said you're done with lying. I trust you."

He stares at me, his mouth still open. My heart feels open too, as if I've left it standing in the center of an icy swirl of snow, naked for anyone to see. Hoping I'm right. *Knowing* that I am, but still feeling just how vulnerable it is. I reach out and gently touch his cheek. "I love you, Howl." And kiss him lightly on the mouth.

Howl barely leans into me, and when I draw back, his eyes seem wet. "I love you too." His smile is a little too soft and sad, the light hollowing out the dark circles under his eyes, the sharp edges of his cheekbones and the shadows of his long eyelashes.

"I need to go. Whatever was going on out there, it isn't happening right now."

"Yeah." He blinks a few too many times, but then he nods. "Yes. Go. I'd just slow you down."

"I'll be back. With the cure. I'm not leaving you this time."

"Wait. There's one more thing we need to be clear about." Howl takes a moment to find the words. "I really do want to live in a tree house. So let's not have this be the last chance, okay?"

I can't help but start to laugh, the sound filling me up, filling us both with something other than gravity. He reaches for me then, and even though I can feel exhaustion and pain riding every line of his body, we hold each other up.

CHAPTER 57

EVERY STEP AWAY FROM HOWL SEEMS TO JAR against my feet, the space between us yawning wide like an abyss.

When I step into the light, open air swirls in from outside the cracked door. My heart knocks against my ribs at feeling so exposed, as if the next blast from the towers will tip a building directly onto my head.

I square my shoulders. I don't have the luxury of fear at the moment. June is counting on me. Lihua and Peishan. All the infected in the City, in the Mountain. Howl.

When I look back at Howl, he smiles and gives me a thumbs-up. I do my best to return the smile. Then walk through the door.

Just outside, there are crumbly remnants of a patio, the rock cracked and sunken in what's almost like a crater. Beyond that, a rickety cobbled street winds up what seems to be a mountainside, the path more stairs than pavement. There aren't any soldiers that I can see, so I'm not sure where the blasts were coming from. I step outside and edge around the hole, finally peeling my eyes up from the damage to find uninterrupted gray. The sky and sea fill my whole vision, so large I might as well be a tiny insect perched on the bald face of a cliff with nothing between me and the endless horizon. My stomach drops as if it's already falling the thousands of feet down to sink into the waves below.

I turn from the awful height, setting my feet on the winding path up the island's mountainside. Sharpened bits of rock press into my palms as I use them to help me climb. A heli buzzes overhead, making all the hair on my arms stand up as I wait for a bomb to come screaming toward me, or for the tower, whatever it does to swat it down. Nothing happens, though, the roar of propellers merely sending gusts of air to pull at my hair. Up above where I'm perched, cliffs rise up to form a tall central peak, one to either side a bit lower as if they're bowing. All three are shaped by sweeping lines of tiled roofs clinging to their sharp faces, stairs crawling up and down and between like overgrown centipedes.

My stomach turns at the thought of climbing. Even without any doomed aircraft buzzing overhead, the height reels me side to side until I'm afraid I'm falling even though my feet are still firmly planted on the ground. Alongside each stairway cut into the stone there are chains bolted into the mountain's face, a lifeline of balance for me to grasp as I crawl higher and higher up. The statue I saw from across the water stands placidly below me, a woman with her arm raised. Her hand has been broken off, cracks riddling the lines of her flowing hair and dress. Port North's protector standing up against the storm.

After climbing for a few minutes, I stop to catch my breath. Luokai said Gao Shun would be up at the top, manning one of the towers that peels helis from the sky. Holding tight to the chain, I crane my neck to look up the mountainside, rewarded by the sight of a single red-tile roof tucked into a crack in the stone higher than any of the other buildings. Clay figurines of dragons guard its eaves, a metal-mesh disk of some kind peeking out from behind them.

If I weren't so terrified of the cliffside behind me, I'd be confused. How could something so small protect this place?

By the time I find the right pathway leading up to it, my hands are shaking and every inch of me is coated in sweat. The stairs leading up to the house's open-air balcony are almost a ladder, the chain handrail hanging limp on either side.

No time to be afraid. I swallow, stare hard at the slippery stone under my fingers, and climb. The house feels almost like a pulsing beacon above me, everything I'd hoped to find here hidden away inside.

The cure . . . and my family.

The word just doesn't mean everything I hoped it would. It's all right, though. Mother was mine. June and Howl belong to me too, the same way I belong to them.

Did my mother ever come up to the top of this mountain floating on the sea? Did she look down at these tile roofs and think they were beautiful?

Pushing the stone-hard breaths threatening to clog my lungs, I climb until my muscles burn, the bag with the book in it banging against my hip. A heli drones past, and one of the side towers begins to hum. A high-pitched shriek screams across the sky, and the rock under my hands and feet begins to shake. I grab hold of the chain with both hands, the metal links digging into my neck. Below, I hear something crumble and fall, the frequency catching a piece of Port North and rattling it to bits.

But before the sound can adjust and catch the heli's propellers, something changes, the tone rising to an ear-shattering squeal, like an animal with a knife at its throat, knowing death is about to stab through it. The awful sound cuts off abruptly, and I chance a look out at the tower, only to see the mesh disk at its top, so sturdy and straight only moments ago, teetering over from its perch and falling the hundreds of feet below to tear a cluster of buildings from Port North's steep slope.

I hazard another glance over my shoulder, the whole side of the island like a waterfall of roofs below me, punctured by smoking holes where helis have crashed to the ground, or where the frequency weapons took houses and glass. Looking across at the tower on the other side, I realize there's no dish at the top, the weapon already a dead piece of metal lost below. The heli above me lowers down onto the gray expanse of bridge that connects the island to the mainland, soldiers pouring from its belly like ants from a nest before the craft is even properly settled.

The tower above me is silent.

I felt the island shake before, the rumble and crack of bombs on stone. These aren't the first helis to have gotten by. Somehow, Dr. Yang must have gotten to the two shorter towers.

I turn back to the ladder and climb with a renewed fervor. The house is only twenty feet above me. Ten. Two. Until I pull myself up through the gap in the balcony rail and lie there panting until my arms stop trembling. I roll over onto my knees and crawl toward the door on the other side of the balcony.

The building looms down at me, and I wonder if there are people behind the empty windows, the gaping door, waiting behind gun sights to see if I'm one of the soldiers who steals children, who sends a terrible disease to unfold in their ranks. But no shots come. Something sharp stabs into my palms when I get to the door, but I don't pull myself up from the ground until I'm against one of the long wooden benches just inside, my bag a lump under me, the wooden carving of a dragon and phoenix decorating the back poking into my cheek.

After a moment, I sit up and look around. There's a control panel of some kind with a telescreen displaying waveform. A fan set into the wall, the blades silent. But there's no one here.

Am I too late? Did this tower already fall to whatever venom Dr. Yang has injected into the other two?

Luokai said Gao Shun would be here. That she'd have the device. I pull myself into a crouch, pushing up from the floor onto my feet. Even if Gao Shun is hiding, even if she's *dead*, I am not leaving this place without the last thing my mother left for me in my hand.

Most of the furniture in the room has been upturned in the chaos. The sharp edges and points pressed into my hands and knees are shattered bits of clay, the remnants of broken cups, and what I think may have been a teapot. My boots crush the brown clay shards as I go farther in, splintered remains of wood and torn papers littering the floor. It's a graveyard of picture frames. They couldn't all have been shaken from the walls and still have this building standing upright, could they? It almost looks as if they've been pulled down from the wall and left to gasp their dying breaths on the floor. I pick up the one closest and almost drop it when my mother's clear gaze looks out at me from its crumpled rice paper. Blood from my cut palms leaves an ugly red smear across the bottom of the portrait, as if my touch has killed this memory of her, tainting the cool grays and blacks of the water-color with blood.

Just underneath there's a wider canvas, the frame still mostly intact. A man with storm-filled eyes, a woman with a round face, wings of gray streaking her hair. Next to them, my mother and father sit, a little girl on each of their laps, the high collars of City uniforms brushing their ears. Our ears. Mine and Aya's.

It's in my hands before I even process picking it up. Aya's eyes, her eyelashes so much longer than mine. Her lips and her blunt nose. I thought I'd forgotten her face, but she looks just the way she feels in my heart. Like my sister. I'm so lost in this family that has been gone for so long that when the shards of pottery crack under a boot behind me, I almost don't hear it.

Almost.

I pivot, my fingers digging into the heavy picture frame as I swing it around, the woman who was sneaking up on me dodging back to avoid its sharp corners. But unlike a Menghu or a Red, who probably would have shot me, she freezes, one hand covering her mouth. Her eyes drop down to the painting in my hand, my dead family's faces between us like a shield.

When her eyes meet mine again, a jolt of recognition fizzles through me, my muscles contracting. She's the same woman who came to warn the village to evacuate, who looked as if she could somehow belong to me. And now, closer, it's so obvious she does. Her eyes . . . She looks like my mother. I glance down at the painting too, finding the face of the older woman I assumed was my grandmother between streaks of my blood running down the canvas. It's the same face as the woman before me, only Gao Shun's hair isn't threaded through with gray, her face only touched by lines instead of cut through.

We stand staring at each other, waiting for the other one to say something. My aunt's cheek is marked, the swirl of color under her ear dark against her skin. Like Mother.

Like me.

I set the painting down on the floor, trails of red dripped over my sister's face and trickling around my neck. Now that my hands are empty, though, all I can see is my brand, bloody and red. "I'm surprised you kept this. You don't consider any of us to be family anymore, do you?"

"You're . . . just like . . . You're supposed to be below." Her eyes seem to devour me, taking in my cuts and scrapes, the bruises and lacerations at my neck, the star burned into my hand. This woman, who I was convinced was just a blur of shadow, a voice whispering doubts into my ear, now looks as lost as she made me feel when we spoke earlier.

I hold her gaze, my jaw molded from metal, my words unmoving. "Give me the device Mother left here. I need it."

"How can you be doing this to us?" she whispers.

"Dr. Yang isn't going to negotiate for something he can just take." I can't help but glance out the window, the ant-like crawl of soldiers below hidden by the house's balcony. The sound of propellers spikes through the ceiling, and I can't help but duck. "I thought you were protected here."

"We were supposed to be." Gao Shun points to the control panel behind her. She blinks as the sound of propellers draws nearing, spinning to face a smoky picture that appears on a screen, a heli's double propellers purring across. She swivels the picture with the controls, then presses a button, a high-pitched tone issuing from above us. I cover my ears as the ground trembles under me, eyes wide on the screen as the heli's propellers break apart, the aircraft erupting in flames as it careens offscreen.

Every breath Gao Shun takes seems to break her ribs, pain a heavy filter that colors her face. "I won't let you destroy this one too. This place isn't yours to break." Gao Shun tries to brush the hair from her eyes, her shoulder-length hair standing out at odd angles as her hands shakily push it back from her face. "I should have listened when you warned me."

"Warned you?" I start forward, and she tenses, her arms up. "I have not destroyed anything. I haven't been outside my cell except to climb up here. . . ."

Gao Shun points out the window, the swarm of helis as they drop one by one onto strips wide enough for their propellers. "You told me your friend was here to destroy the towers. Now that we're down to one, and I'm supposed to believe it's just happenstance that brings you here?" She gropes at her side, and my stomach twists when I see a gun's shiny handle sticking like shrapnel from her coat. A tear streaks down her cheek. "I can see your mother inside you. Down to the charred bits that were all she had left of a heart."

"Tai-ge is *dead*, isn't he?"

"You'd kill a Red spy when an invasion looms just over the hill?" She looks out into the blank sky. "If he isn't dead by now, then we're all doomed. The other one must have helped him escape. The First?"

"Do you mean Howl? He can hardly walk."

Gao Shun shakes her head. "So it was you who let him out, then. I can't make myself believe there are traitors here."

"Tai-ge's . . . here somewhere?" Fear prickles down my arms. "If he's alive . . ." I look out at to the blank spot where I saw the dish fall. "Listen to me. Tai-ge wants that device. If you kept him here somehow and he got out . . ."

The words dry up from my mouth as she draws the gun. "Even if you kill me, Baohujia will be up here in a minute. You'll never get out."

"I didn't come here to *kill* you. I came here to *beg*, Gao Shun.

Dr. Yang is going to take everything you have. They'll infect this place and force you to kneel for the cure." My heart pounds, desperately wanting her to belive me. "I can help you. If you give me the device, I'll bring the cure here. I'll make sure the Reds stealing your people don't have access to it until they stop."

A tear spills out from Gao Shun's eye, marking her face with a single line. "You sound just the way she did."

"If they find a way to get in here, they'll take everything you have, Gao Shun. I want to save this place. I want to save the people in farm camps, the people who've been left to die because they can't control themselves anymore. I want to stop the people who have been hurting you." My heart cracks as I say it, thinking of the boy below, a smile untempered on his face. "And this is the only way. *Please* let me have the device."

The gun shivers in Gao Shun's hand. "They wouldn't negotiate when I told them I had it."

"If you give it to me, they'll follow me. They'll leave you alone, at least for a while," I whisper. Like June told Cai Ayi at the Post, only I don't know how to negotiate, don't know how to show her I mean it.

Her shoulders sag as if she's exhausted.

"The man who told the helis to come here is the one who broke the treaty between Port North and the City. He's the one who killed Mother."

The blackness of Gao Shun's irises seems almost deep enough to fall through, as if any hope she's had has been replaced with despair. She lurches forward, and I tense, waiting to feel the sting of a bullet. But the gun clatters to the ground and she grabs for my hands, squeezing them hard between hers.

Pieces of pottery and broken bits of furniture skitter across the floor as she pulls me over to a wide bookcase set into the wall. She throws her weight against its solid frame. "Help me," she grunts.

Together, we push until an inch of empty space blinks out at us from behind it, a passage to the caves below. The bookcase is so heavy, my muscles burn from pushing, the sharp edges of the wood cutting into my shoulder until there's enough room for us to slip through.

"You'll need a way out of here." She says it with a whisper as she pulls something from her coat, a cheery gold fire igniting between her palms. Almost like a quicklight, but brighter. A steep stairway swirls straight down below us, the walls set with windows along one side, the other solid rock.

My chest burns with a sudden flare of hope. "You'll give me the device?"

"We'll keep you below until the worst of it's over." Gao Shun continues with a nod, "They can't come down into the caves . . . or if they manage to, we can take the boats. Spread out. We'll sneak you to the hangar on the mainland." She stops to look at me, and the flames in my chest curl down at the skepticism in her eyes. "Trusting you seems far-fetched at best. But you are right about the soldiers coming out of those helis. They will take everything they can." Her thick brows scrunch together, her mouth following suit. "I want to believe you because I don't see hope in any other direction."

She turns back to the stairs, taking them two at a time. I follow, all of my bruises and cuts and soreness protesting at once, none so loud as the family-shaped hole in my chest. This isn't the moment to wonder about a woman who kept my portrait on the wall for eight years and to try and find the heart inside her.

There will be time for that later. There will be time after I've found Sole. After the cure is in my hand. "You have helis that can take me back to the mountains?"

"We have two. Though one of them is damaged, and there aren't many who can fly . . ." She sucks on her bottom lip, slowing a step." I don't know the state of the quarantine areas, but I think both of our pilots fell sick after going up into the mountains with Luokai." She says something I don't understand in Port Northian, but if I were to guess, it wasn't something polite.

Murky echoes climb up toward us from below, the sounds of feet crunching on stone. The first Baohujia to come into view falls into an aggresive stance, his gun leveled on Gao Shun, though it drops immediately when he recognizes her. Unintelligable words pour from his mouth as about fifteen Baohujia rush past us up the stairs, hardly breaking stride.

More footsteps echo from below.

Gao Shun paws at my arm, pulling something small and black from her coat. She holds it out to me without breaking eye contact with the man as he continues to speak, sounding frantic. "Take it, Jiang Sev."

The thing is some kind of electrical device, the metal still warm from being inside her coat, the screen dark. "This is the device my mother left?"

She frantically pushes me until my hips slam into the window alcove. "Get up there," Gao Shun orders, waiting until I've obeyed to climb up next to me. "Whoever has been breaking our towers is coming for the last one."

The shattered glass slides under my feet as I huddle against the alcove wall, the open drop straight down to the shattered island buildings below rattling through me. Shouts echo up the stairs, but I can't see much hunched in the alcove, Gao Shun pressing me against the wall. Baohujia soldiers take up defensive positions, aiming their weapons down the stairwell.

And then suddenly there's a flood of soldiers from below. I don't see uniforms, insignia, anything but a blur of shadow and gunmetal gray, the blasts from their weapons shattering my ears.

"What is happening?" I scream, pulling at her iron-band grip around my middle, shots screaming past us.

Gao Shun grunts as something slams into her with a meaty *thunk*, twisting her sideways away from me. She falls out of the alcove, onto her knees on the stairs below.

A voice filters through the awful noise of bullets and yells and screams and echoes. My name. "Sevvy?"

Everything seems to slow into a molasses crawl. A figure vaults up into the alcove, his features not matching the Baohujia robes draped across his frame, bruises marking his face. A face I would know anywhere.

Tai-ge.

There's a silver sphere in his hands. I've seen one like it before. In Howl's hands, back when June was beaten up by some Reds, stashed in their tent . . .

The rush of soldiers who came with Tai-ge are falling back, the Baohujia above us on the stairs marking each of them with calm precision. I don't know how they know who to shoot, because they're all wrapped in the same Baohujia robes, only the direction of their guns to point to their loyalties. I reach for the flashbang grenade as if I can somehow stop Tai-ge from throwing it, but it's already in two pieces in the air before I can slam my fist into his arm. Tai-ge pulls me hard against his side, one arm wrapped tight around my skull over my ears, jamming my face against him. "Close your eyes!" he yells.

When the grenade detonates, the sound shakes me straight to my core. My legs collapse under my weight as something pointed jabs into my ribs. Before I can process falling—or the ringing in my ears, or the Baohujia man who stumbles toward the alcove from the stairs above, then crashes through the last of the glass—Tai-ge is up, pulling something away from his face and ears before grabbing my arm and wrenching me up from where I fell.

Tai-ge swears when I try to dig in my heels, grappling for a hold on his loose robes, but I'm no match. Whatever the sound and light did to me leaves me flailing and off-balance, unable to judge where the stairs are and how to walk. Baohujia are strewn across the stairwell, their eyes open in horror, blinking painfully after the flash, echoes of the grenade's concussive blast still pounding away inside my head. Whatever it was Tai-ge did to protect my eyes and ears wasn't quite enough, my balance teetering drunkenly from side to side as I fight him to a stop, his only choices to let go or to fall down the stairs on top of me.

"Why are you up here?" he yells. He must be yelling, but it still feels like a tiny whisper in my head, dampened as if he's screaming into a pillow. "Did they give you the cure?" He sticks a hand into my coat and feels each of my pockets.

"You stay away from me!" I can't keep myself from shouting, wildly searching for the place where my aunt fell, only to find that she's rolled down to just before the stairway curves out of sight. Is she dead? It doesn't look like anyone is still standing, not even the people who were shooting from Tai-ge's side. "How did you do this? Who from the Baohujia would have helped *you*?" All of them are wearing robes, the ones below me bloody and shredded on their owners' backs.

"Mother told me there were Baohujia who were sick of

fighting. She made sure they found me." Tai-ge's eyes follow my unintentional glance toward Gao Shun, and he drops me, haring back down the stairs as if me looking toward my aunt was some kind of tell. Even as I internally scream at my feet to run, to do something other than stand here waiting for Tai-ge to come back, my legs don't listen, crumpling to the floor as my brain tries to recover from the grenade. There's a Baohujia girl collapsed next to me on the stairs. Tugging her shoulders straight, I attempt to help her sit up, but she flops back down, boneless and staring blankly.

I gape down at her, my insides awful and cold, as if I'm the one who is dead. The device my aunt gave to me is lying just inside the windowsill, as if when the blast hit me, I let go of everything, assuming it was the end. Pulling myself up from the stairs isn't as hard as attempting to pick the device up, my fingers sliding over it twice before I can convince them to bend around the black metal. I have to hide it. Have to make sure Tai-ge doesn't find it. . . .

"It's not in her pockets. Wait . . ." Tai-ge's back behind me, hands on my shoulders. No, snaking down my arms until he finds the device clutched between my fingers. He pries it loose and tucks it into his pocket. "Maybe this is something. Even if it isn't, the soldiers can do a better search when they get here. Come on. We have to disable the tower before Kamar gets anyone else to stop us."

"*Us?* Do not touch me. Don't . . ." Everything in my head feels underwater and slow. I try to twist away from him, but I can't shake Tai-ge off as he drags me up the stairs. I jab my hand toward his pocket, meaning to take back the device, but nothing is working the way it should.

Light assaults my eyes as Tai-ge pushes me through the hole behind the bookcase. I stumble to the floor, but he just climbs out over me. He pulls something out from under his stolen tunic and runs to the corner of blinking screens and buttons where Gao Shun controlled the frequency weapon. He yells into his hand—is Tai-ge holding some kind of link?—about weapons and coordinates and extraction before picking up a broken piece of wood and swinging it straight into the dark screen.

"What is *wrong* with you?" The words finally leak from my mouth as I push myself up from the floor, shreds of broken pottery stuck to my cheek.

"This is the right thing to do, Sevvy." He clicks the communicator in his hand—a radio, I realize, as a voice comes through crackling confirmations. "Right for you. For the City. Everyone."

"No." I can't make my tongue work, wanting to scream all the things I've said before. All the things he listened to, then dismissed. Tai-ge swings again, this time decapitating a lever and denting the console, bits of plastic skittering across the ground toward me. I rise up onto my knees, my hands scrabbling for something to fight with, something that will pry Mother's device from his pocket before the Reds come. "What do you think is going to happen to me when the Reds come? What will happen to June once they have the cure? To Lihua? Remember her?"

Tai-ge turns back to look at me, adjusting the wooden plank between his hands. "I'm your link to them, Sevvy. I'll keep you safe. I'll say the things you've been telling me all along."

"Your mother believes this, Tai-ge." I try to hold up the traitor star burned into my hand and almost end up flat on the ground. "This scar is all I am inside those walls. I don't want to live in a world where someone else has to speak for me. I want to speak for myself!"

Tai-ge's eyes dart up as pottery shards grind under boots behind me. My fingers find a long tooth of clay, the edge freshly shattered and sharp. Turning to face the person who walked in makes the room swirl around me, my feet unable to balance when I attempt to stand upright.

It's a man in a Menghu coat, the one I remember from Dazhai wearing Cale's old mask with sharp teeth painted across the filters. The Menghu's tiger snarls up from this man's collar, hungry for blood.

Tai-ge swears. "Don't touch her!" he yells at the Menghu. "Don't come a step closer . . . !"

The ceramic shard in my hand cuts into my fingers because I'm gripping it too tight. Menghu. I know what Menghu can do to me. They'll do it and not care. Tai-ge slides in behind me as if he means to hold me up. Or perhaps shelter behind me.

"Don't touch her?" the Menghu's voice rasps through the filters of his gorish mask as he looks us over. "Didn't you just call for help? Looks like you need it."

"I called *my* people for help!"

"Isn't that what we are now?"

I stab the shard point-first toward his neck, but the Menghu's eyes smile as he bats it out of my hands as easily as swatting a fly. As a second Menghu comes through the door, Tai-ge swings his chunk of wood at the first. The Menghu ducks, slamming the handle of his gun into Tai-ge's arm and then his leg, dropping him to the floor before lifting me onto his own shoulders, just the way Howl did all those months ago. My arms and legs shake, but the effects of the grenade are wearing off. I contort backward to kick at the Menghu's side, and when that doesn't work, at the Menghu standing behind him, my heel catching his mask.

But it does no good. The Menghu walks to the balcony, gripping me tight, as if he means to launch me over the edge.

Howl's waiting for me in a bombed-out hall of stone. June is in a cell underneath this rock somewhere. Lihua is back at the Post counting pills until the day she's sold to some scavenger clan.

My aunt. My own blood lies on the stairs just out of reach.

This can't be my end.

Twisting, I manage to sink my teeth deep into the Menghu's neck, just inside his collar where the tiger snarls. The taste of copper and iron and poisoned humanity bursts across my tongue. He drops me, and I manage to land on my feet, trying not to gag. Pushing away from the sharp sting of his swearing, I pull the clasp of his mask at the back of his head, attempting to wrench the device away from his face, to turn him back from gore to human. Humans I can fight.

"I want to talk to your superior!" Tai-ge's is a voice used to being obeyed. But now he just sounds like a tantruming child. "Give me your radio. Mother promised—"

Other Menghu crowd onto the balcony, the streaming lines of them multiplying like weeds swaying in the water. My stomach twists with nausea as I dodge between two of the soldiers, trying to ignore the way their laughs turn to rust.

A Menghu tackles me to the ground, broken pottery cutting painfully into my back as he straddles me. It's the same one who first picked me up, teeth painted across his filters. He grins at me through the awful mask, his voice tainted with a familiar oily cast. "You always did like making things much harder than they had to be, Jiang Sev. Call this a gift. It'll keep you in one piece."

The handle of his gun streaks down toward my head. A blast of pain, and then all there is to see is black. No Tai-ge. No aunt, no blood, no guns.

Nothing.

CHAPTER 58

MY EYES DON'T OPEN AGAIN UNTIL I SLAM INTO the floor, dropped like a sack of poisoned millet for the rats. My shoulder and hip scream at the impact, nothing responding the way it is supposed to when I attempt to roll away, to run. The man who was carrying me sits down with a sigh, his presence tapping like spider legs up my spine, the promise of a stinging bite to come.

He pulls at his gas mask's straps, adjusting the awful gore grin painted across the filters. The sound of propellers fills my ears and the floor lurches under us, throwing me flat onto my stomach. Underneath me the bag makes a lump, the book's sharp corner digging into my ribs.

"If you hadn't run away before, none of this would have happened." The Menghu's slippery voice is a flood of grease in my ears. He turns to look at me, my brain screaming at me to remember, to link that voice to the person wearing Cale's mask. Cale, who was so close to . . .

Helix. My stomach lurches, and suddenly I'm vomiting onto the heli floor in a projectile stream.

"Rotted Sephdom—!" Helix jerks up from the floor and retreats to a corner to escape the expanding pool of sick, the mask's painted teeth glinting in the dim light as he pulls it tight over his nose and mouth. It's just us in the small room, almost as small as the storage closet on the heli we left by the abandoned village. Bars line one wall, and there's a drain in the floor with barely enough room for me to lie here, an acid taste in my mouth, bile soaking into my shirt.

"Water!" Helix calls through the bars. At first I'm not sure how to react to that. Helix doing something nice? But then he adds, "And a mop."

"Where's Tai-ge?" I croak. But then all I can think are swear words, and I don't even want to share those with Helix.

I know why he did this. I don't know how. But this is fate's way of showing me just how much I was risking when I trusted Tai-ge back on the heli. What the inevitable end was from the moment he chose my side. He had help. Lockpicks, a radio link, contacts on the island . . . orders to destroy their comm towers . . . How could he have hidden all those things from the Baohujia when they brought him onto the island?

Maybe that's why he was so flustered when Xuan disappeared. If Xuan was Tai-ge's connection to the Baohujia who were sick of fighting—who Xuan did not *want* to talk to because getting away from the City meant cutting all ties to anyone who know who he was—then my letting him go would have been a huge obstacle to overcome. But I guess they found him anyway.

I taste the inside of my mouth, the acidic hint of vomit making me gag. Does Tai-ge believe me yet about not asking Reds for help? Dr. Yang probably already has the device in his hands. Something triumphant crows inside me at the thought of the device, lonely and empty, because that wasn't all Mother left. We sent the rest of it to Sole over the link. Maybe that will be enough. We have something. He has something. There's still room to play the game. To win.

Helix jerks me out of my thoughts, toeing my feet aside as he moves out of range of further bouts of sickness.

"Why didn't you just shoot me?" I put a hand to my mouth, wiping away the slick coating of bile dribbling down my chin. "You don't need me anymore. I thought Menghu valued kills. That's why you take trophies. Since when do you save victims to play with later?"

Helix slides down in the corner, arranging himself as far from the pool of vomit as he can, waiting until another Menghu comes with a mop and sort of sloshes it toward the drain until it's a new layer of varnish on the floor rather than a puddle. The soldier hands Helix a waterskin, murmuring something I don't understand before he backs out the door.

When Helix turns back to me, he holds the waterskin out. "You must be thirsty. Can you hold it yourself?"

The water *is* for me? I try to think about moving my cheek from the floor, about moving at all, and reject the idea. He walks and pulls me up by my shoulders, propping me up against the wall. Bile burns up in my throat again, but this time it stays down, just making me choke. A part of me wants to fight Helix, but the promise of water is enough to keep me from flopping back down on the ground.

"I'll get you some clean clothes before we land," he says, not offering the waterskin, as if he knows that's what I want and has chosen to relish in watching my pride break down far enough for me to ask for it.

I narrow my eyes at the Menghu, my mind jarring against the

tiger at his collar. His high cheekbones peek out above the mask, circles shadowing under his eyes. His once-slicked-back hair I remember so perfectly now looks as if it hasn't seen a comb in days, mussed into a greasy chaos of spikes. "What do you want? Did you get . . ." But I shouldn't ask about Howl. What if they don't know if he's down there?

Or worse. What if they saw Howl in his broken state and just ended him?

"Did we get Howl?" Helix asks. For a moment I'm afraid I'll start retching again, that the nothingness in my stomach will continue heaving until I'm inside out. "Dr. Yang told us you would probably be together. The two people who can stop SS just running away into the sunset. Very romantic."

"I can't cure SS. Neither can Howl. It was never about . . ." I start coughing, my rusty throat scraping against each word. "It was that device. . . ."

"Sure. The *device*." Helix nods and looks away, holding out the waterskin again. "What if that device doesn't have everything we need to make a cure, Jiang Sev?"

"Then you're out of luck, because my brain isn't going to do anything for you. Ask the doctor. He knows."

"Dr. Yang specifically asked me to find you. Honestly, I doubt there's anything at all on that device. This whole invasion and Kamar having a cure is just a fairy tale the Firsts swallowed whole. All we really need is you."

"If that were true, I'd already be dead, Helix." I cough, my stomach turning as all the muscles clench. "I would have turned *myself* in."

He gives the waterskin a shake in my direction. "Do you or do you not need help?"

I take the waterskin from him, the water bubbling out to dribble down the front of my shirt. This isn't the Helix I remember. He was all pride and polish before. Until he raised his gun, and then he was empty Menghu, like the hollow-eyed tiger badge they all wear. But now he looks deflated somehow.

The mask catches my attention again, and I point to the toothy filter, meeting his eyes. "Cale didn't wake up?" I ask. "I didn't realize it would matter to you."

He glares at me, his eyes like burning coals over the curls of the mask. "Do you know how many people died because you and that monster ran away? Hundreds of people stuck inside the Mountain wishing they were dead. I always felt a little sorry for you before, but not anymore. And Howl . . . I hope I'm the one who gets to put him down."

Anger builds inside me, the casual reference to killing almost like an item on his to-do list, but it doesn't tamp down the hope that kindles at his words. Howl isn't dead. Not yet. "How can you treat people the way you do? Like targets and animals, as if you're some other kind of creature. Howl doesn't do that, but *he's* the monster?"

"*Howl* doesn't do that? He's still trying to make you believe he's a human?" Helix takes the waterskin back, upsetting the rest of it on the floor to wash away the last remnants of vomit. "I wonder what he wants from you now?"

"Stop talking. Get away from me." I let my ears close, but I can't make my eyes shut him out. Not when he's so close. Once a group of Reds in the Youth Corps of the Liberation Army decided to try their new hunting dog's skills out on me. I couldn't close my eyes then, either. Not when the dog cornered me a street down from my cannery shift. Not as its bared teeth inched closer to my arm. My eyes were pried open by terror, waiting to see if my brain would let the predator disintegrate into the dust of hallucination.

I still don't know if that really happened. The Reds could have called the dogs off. Or it could have all been inside my mind.

But I can't afford to close my eyes and hope Helix will disappear. Even if I don't know how to escape or how I'm going to get the cure back from Dr. Yang, if all I can do is freeze and wait for my problems to disappear, then what am I worth, anyway?

Breathe in. It's hard. I'm almost afraid some of the air I sucked into my lungs was once inside of Helix. But it's a relief. Even if I don't know all the details, I refuse to be stuck.

Another Menghu walks in, and Helix gets up. "Suicide watch," he says. "Dr. Yang needs her alive."

Breathe out. Like I would try to kill myself.

The Menghu nods and settles gracefully to the floor across from me, dark brown hair falling forward across her face. I can feel all the muscles that had been clenching—pushing me as far away from Helix as possible in this small space—start to relax. Even if my new guard would hurt me just as quickly, I think she wouldn't like it. Her round face is a shade lighter than I remember, as if she's been spending time inside, freckles standing out sharp against the skin across her nose.

But Mei doesn't look me in the eyes.

The heli jogs under us, then goes still. Much like the one we stole from the City, this one's underbelly is meant to hold twenty or more. But it's cut into pieces, a labyrinth of cubbyholes ready to stack prisoners, one on top of another. A heli meant for hunting on the outskirts of Port North, where the sound resonance weapon couldn't reach. Slave transport.

When I steal another glance at Mei, she's biting her lip. Her eyes run up and down her hands, fingers interlaced so tightly I can see a white outline forming on her skin. There are bones at her wrist. Six trophies. Six more people dead.

I try not to care. "It's okay," I say. "You've got to do your job."

She glances at me, then returns quickly to her hands. "Are you all right? It looks as if you've had it rough since I saw you last."

"I'm fine." Bruised and cut in so many places I can't even count them. My head still spinning from the stunning grenade and the fact that my friend threw it. My *not*-friend. My former friend, who still somehow believed after *everything* that going back to the Reds would have some other consequences than me in a cell.

Maybe he doesn't care about me in a cell. Then all of this would make so much more sense. But it doesn't really matter anymore. "Look, Mei." I sit forward. "I need to tell you something. Helix seems to think they still need me and Howl in a lab—"

"I really did like you. Back in the Mountain." Mei's voice spins out like a gold thread, continuous and beautiful. Metallic and cold. "But you must know how selfish you are being. Hundreds . . . maybe even thousands from the Mountain are dead because you ran away. We can't wait for the cure anymore."

Selfish. The word sinks past the fury of thoughts ricocheting back and forth through my head. I suppose it is true. I ran from becoming the cure back at the Mountain, ran from saving thousands of people from SS. I thought that saving Mother meant I didn't have to die, and that SS would be cured without my blood.

What would I do now, if my life truly were the price Dr. Yang was asking? Would I be like June, taking off my mask and waiting for death to come? Or would I be like Howl and fight my way out? Do whatever it takes to survive, only to regret it later?

No. I sit up a little straighter. *I make my own decisions. Find my own way.*

"Mei." She was my friend once. Maybe some small part of her will want to listen. "Dr. Yang is the one who set the contagious strain of SS free. He's the one who let you spread it all over the Mountain."

She starts, looking at me with narrowed eyes. "How do you know about me spreading SS?"

"I was there, Mei. He is the one who turned SS into an even more dangerous weapon than it already was."

Mei shakes her head. "Dr. Yang tried to *stop* it. He's the one who told me I could stay, that I could have Mantis. If you'd stayed in the Mountain and let them take the cure, I wouldn't have needed Mantis in the first place. All this fighting would be done. Everyone would be happy."

"Do you really believe that? The fight would just stop when Dr. Yang snaps his fingers?" I inch toward her, trying to hold her gaze as if I can somehow infuse her with the truth she doesn't feel like listening to. "People aren't just fighting over Mantis, Mei. And they aren't going to stop once there is a cure if Dr. Yang is the one who has it. He'll use it as a reward. As a way to control people."

Mei scoots back until she's propped against the opposite wall. "I thought you were so brave, following your mother out to the Mountain. Standing down that gore with Cale on your shoulders. Still fighting when your life had been hell. But I didn't know about the cure then. I was too new. I didn't even know who Howl was." She takes a shaky breath. "You should have told me."

I wait for a second, not sure what she is trying to say. "Because he's really one of you? A Menghu? It's not like he's going to kill you in your sleep for believing he was a First." Never mind the fact that I didn't know either.

Mei finally looks up, something like pity in her eyes. "You really don't know anything, do you? You're not brave, just oblivious." She looks at the door, craning her neck to get a look down the hall, and at first I think it's so she can make sure no one is listening. But it isn't. She's worried about something. Waiting for it to come up the hall to get her.

Is she taking Mantis? Or is this the beginning of some made-up danger starting to take hold of her brain?

But Mei doesn't start compulsing. "They won't tell me if they found him or not." She goes back to her hands, whispering it almost to herself as if she can't bear to admit it out loud. She's frightened. Frightened he's here?

"You're . . . scared of Howl?" The last image I have of Howl, the light from outside clinging to him as he waved me on, is lodged in my brain. I don't need an explanation from Howl as to why the Menghu were so terrified of him. I know *him*, and that's enough. But for some reason, watching Mei go pale and check the door again makes my stomach twist. "How can you possibly be more scared of Howl than of *Helix*? Helix has actually hurt you before." I saw the bruises. All because of a stupid game, too.

She looks at me again. "Howl was brutal. He and Sole—"

"I know about him and Sole. I thought the way they went after Reds would be a reason to respect him for other Menghu. You idolized Cale and her awful bracelet. . . ."

Mei's hand goes to her own bracelet, the finger bones clasped around her wrist. "He didn't just go after Reds, Sev."

It takes a moment for the weight of her words to settle across me. "What do you mean?"

"I mean that Howl didn't always get along with people in the Mountain. And when people went out on missions, sometimes the ones he didn't get along with didn't come back. He was perfect with the generals, with all of Nei-ge, but in the dormitories after the lights went out . . ." She stops, swallowing hard. "To hear Helix tell it, after Howl made captain, the people he didn't care for seemed find themselves right out where the Reds could get them."

A memory flicks across my mind: Cale's face when Howl stood up to block her and the Yizhi men trying to drag me to the hospital. He told her she'd be trapped Outside if she tried again. That he'd make sure she was.

"They saw him hurt people? Kill people?"

"There's no way to prove anything. I guess General Root wouldn't even listen to the reports, saying they were just after Howl because of politics and wanting promotions. He said it was jealousy, because Howl was so good at what he did. But *Howl* never denied any of it. He just waited. Watched. And when you crossed him, you disappeared. Not even a finger left of you to remember." Her bone bracelet rattles as she brushes a clump of hair out of her face.

Howl's face clouds my vision, the broken expression on his face. *The Menghu—even Sole—all think . . .*

But what do I think? Howl won't touch the trigger of a gun.

Mei glances down the hallway again. "I can't shake the feeling that he's in this heli somewhere. Sitting in a cell where I can't see him, but he can see me. Watching all of us. Memorizing our faces. When Dr. Yang gave orders to look for him, they told stories the whole way over. . . ." She shivers.

A few weeks ago, what Mei is saying might have horrified me. But now I have already chosen what I believe. *Who* I believe.

Howl's past doesn't change who he is now. Especially not a past colored in by Menghu who haven't enough morals among them to realize that hurting other people just because you can isn't always the explanation that makes the most sense. Menghu who don't look close enough at their enemies to see that they're people too.

I fight to keep my voice calm. "Mei, listen to me. Please." She goes back to tracing the walls with her eyes, listening to the sounds coming from outside, my words stopped by some invisible barrier. "Dr. Yang doesn't have to kill anyone for the cure. Not me, not Howl. There were hundreds of Firsts who had been cured in the City. Dr. Yang could have taken any of them. He wants you to believe him because it gives him power over you. You believe he'll be able to cure you, so you do what he says."

She doesn't look up.

"I don't want to control you, Mei. My mother died to keep the cure away from him so he couldn't use it. I need your help to get out of here. To get it back . . ."

I trail off as Mei fixes me with a hard stare, all former friendship pushed under a mask of cold. "I really did like you. I hope you die better than this."

CHAPTER 59

WHEN WE LAND, HELIX AND MEI ESCORT ME FROM THE
heli to an open field. The air smells like home. Mountains and trees
and smoke from hundreds of smokestacks blowing away in the mountain wind. The snow forms a hard crust on the ground under my feet.

Mountains rear up all around us, and it's hard to tell where we
could be. We pass four other helis in the field before entering a
cave, other Menghu trailing behind us. I twist around to look for
Tai-ge, but Helix pushes me forward with a careless shove.

Inside, we come to a telescreen, but it's cracked, the door beyond
gaping open. Some outpost of the Mountain, separate from the
main parts that have been overrun by people infected by SS, I would
guess. Past the entrance, the walls are a familiar sort of blue. They
take me to a door.

Behind that door is Dr. Yang.

He sits at a desk, mask trailing down his face like an old man's
beard. His fingers are steepled on top of the book that was in my
bag, the one Howl gave to me all those weeks ago at the Mountain,
a sleeping princess stenciled on the front.

"Please." He gestures to the chair in front of him.

I hesitate, but only for a second. My knees are hardly holding me upright. I sit.

"Mei, Helix. I'll have you take her down to the cells when I'm through. Give us a moment?" He looks pointedly at the door.

"The cells?" Helix glances at Mei and then lowers his voice. "Sir, I don't mean to argue, but I know of at least four in my company whose masks have stopped functioning. Shouldn't she be taken to a lab somewhere as soon as possible?"

"Just . . . give us a moment. Your Menghu will have what they need."

Helix's eyes flick over to Mei, but then he nods and leads her out. Perhaps the transfer of power after General Root died in the invasion isn't going as smoothly as I thought. I file that away.

When the door clicks shut, the doctor's rasping breath fills the empty air, the sound like an unhealthy wheeze. A death rattle. "Jiang Sev. So nice to see you again."

"Is it? Were you hoping to make amends for murdering my mother and trying to murder me?"

"You were the one who gave her that serum, Sev. Howl stole it from my office without asking any questions about what it would do. I fail to see how that is my fault."

I swallow. We didn't have another choice, or so it seemed at the time. All we knew is that it was supposed to wake her up from suspended sleep. A cure for the condition Dr. Yang put her in when she wouldn't give him her notes on how to manufacture the cure to SS. I don't know why I thought she'd get up and walk away after standing there on the Arch with tubes keeping her alive for eight years.

Dr. Yang opens the book, gilt glinting in the overhead lights as it falls on the outline of the sleeping woman on the front. "You know, I almost think it wasn't worth the trouble to bring you here. I knew Gao Shun wouldn't have made it easy, but this book is an answer in and of itself."

"An answer to what?"

"Everything." He closes it and looks at the binding, holding it up to the light as a First would to analyze a glass of wine. "It's a beautiful book. With certain unfortunate parallels to your mother, no?"

It's the story they used to tell in the City, about a princess who sold her soul for some kind of dark magic, putting herself and her whole kingdom to sleep. Kind of like the propaganda that was sung over the City speakers out at least once a year: *Jiang Gui-hua, put to sleep for selling our location to Kamari spies, for killing half of the First Circle* . . . But it was Dr. Yang who killed the Circle. The Chairman and the Circle itself that decided to affix an enemy title to Port North, to change the island into a lurking monster poised to gobble us down, bones and all.

The book isn't the dark, twisted version of the story they told in the City. This version is about hope. About waiting for the day when a wronged girl will wake up and everything will go back to normal.

Mother is not the girl in that story.

Neither am I.

But still, I flinch as Dr. Yang opens the book and tears it in half down the binding, the stitching making an awful popping sound as he destroys it. The torn covers come next, Dr. Yang peeling back the endpaper, scratching his fingernails against the hard cover underneath.

He's breathing hard, a look of pure anger smoldering over

his features. The pages drift away from him in pathetic trails, a waterfall of dead paper. "Is it in the pages? Some kind of code?" He fixes me with a stare that sends knifepoints down my arms. Dr. Yang, murderer of eleven members of the First Circle, murderer of my mother and who knows how many others, with one attempted murder not yet complete. Mine.

"I have no idea what you are talking about." I maintain a calm face despite the fear coursing through me.

He sweeps the book off his desk, swearing as the pages go up in a white storm of destroyed fairy tale all around him. The doctor bats them out of his way, his eyes freezing on me as he brings his hands back down to tent in front of him. "Where is it?"

"I'm sorry, did I bring you the wrong story?" I ask.

"You . . ." He stops himself, staring down at his hands until the outburst has stopped hammering away at the inside of his mouth. "You got the book from Port North, didn't you? You must have. You didn't have it when you woke your mother."

I shake my head. Howl gave it to me from the Mountain library. It was like a sick joke sitting at the bottom of my pack when I left the Mountain, the promised hope of finding my own happy ending hemorrhaging in my chest. I left it with June when I went to wake up Mother.

Dr. Yang sits up straight, smoothing his salt-and-pepper hair. He's no longer wearing a white Yizhi coat with squares at his neck to show his authority. He's dressed in a City Outside patrol uniform, but with all the patches and numbers cut off, no markers on him anywhere to show where his allegiances lie. "It has to be here. You found something on that island—I know you did." His voice is an intense whisper, eyes wide on his hands where they lie on the desk. "I can't be wrong. I'm never wrong."

The contents of Mother's paper are safely in Sole's care. And the device . . . the Menghu took it from Tai-ge. So if Dr. Yang is still looking for the cure, it wasn't on the device. An extra curl of hope unfurls inside me even as my stomach sinks. Maybe what we needed was on the paper all along . . . but could it really be? A whole complicated world-saving cure on a single sheet of paper?

Dr. Yang fixed me with his flatline stare, steeped in ambition and hatred. I jerk back in my chair before I can control myself. It's like gazing into the black eyes of a gore, nothing inside but hunger.

"I'm going to show you something, Jiang Sev." He opens a drawer and pulls out a paper. It's thin and creased into four sections, as if it's been folded up in a book and forgotten until this moment. "You'll have five minutes to tell me everything you know, or there will be consequences." Dr. Yang settles the paper in front of me, the cramped, compact characters looking very much like my own handwriting.

"She told you to go to Port North to get *this*."

My eyes try to focus on my mother's scrawl as if I can somehow memorize it. Did Dr. Yang somehow get the paper we took pictues of, too? But after a moment I realize that it isn't the chemical formula and diagrams I saw before.

It's a passage from a fairy tale.

"What is that?" I ask.

"The device Hong Tai-ge found was the very same one Gui-hua used to catalog data when we were working on Howl."

I lift my chin, concentrating on keeping my face smooth. "And? What does it have to do with my Mother's work?"

"*Our* work." Dr. Yang gives the paper a tight-lipped grimace. "The data device was wiped about nine years ago, most likely when she left it there."

The little flares of hope inside me roar into flame. Sole really does have everything my mother left. It doesn't matter that I'm here, that Tai-ge handed everything we worked for straight to the monster we've been running from.

"This"—Dr. Yang holds up the paper—"was screwed inside the device's casing."

I reach out to touch the paper, the words so, so familiar. A princess asleep. The ending to the same story Dr. Yang just destroyed—only this one is the City's version, where the princess was condemned never to wake. Mother always said that wasn't the end of the story, that things weren't always the way people wrote them down, but she still wouldn't tell us what really happened to that princess. Trying to guess had been such a fun game between Aya and me. A game I could only remember with hollow remorse after they put Mother to Sleep and left her to rot over Traitor's Arch. For the longest time I believed the only change you could make to your future was to accept it. To be happy. Maybe even make fun of it a little. Giving the princess some other fate than death was just as hopeless as pretending my own life could change course.

But my life *did* change course. My destiny is shaped by me, even if others try to force me to take a certain path. I'll always have a choice.

"She made sure you were the one to get the message about where it was. Perhaps it's worded so only you will understand." Dr. Yang watches me, every movement too calm, too smooth, as if he's sitting in the eye of a storm, the back end ready to unleash. "So tell me, Jiang Sev, what am I missing? Where is the cure?"

There's one sentence, one word in particular I don't remember from the many times Mother told me the story of the sleeping princess. At the very end, instead of finishing with the curse, it adds a line: *"Her secrets were now hidden in a place no one else could reach."*

Secrets like Mother, Aya, and I stole when we used to play spy, listening in on conversations, using hand signals like the one Dr. Yang used to make me listen to him that awful day he pulled me off the street in the City.

Hand signals she probably learned in Port North. From her family. Mother always said secrets were no fun if you didn't share. The very memory of her smile as she said it is enough to make my jaw clench. She was the one with secrets, not me.

Except . . . I had one secret from Mother. Me and Aya together. "It's just a story, Dr. Yang."

"Is it?" He transfers his gaze from the paper to me.

Aya and I would sometimes write secret notes—and we had a secret place to hide them, even from Mother. Once we even hid a whole batch of sweet bean buns from her, wanting to keep them all to ourselves. When she asked where they were, we told her it was a place she couldn't reach.

My heart starts to pound.

What if the secret place of two giggling girls wasn't so secret from our mother after all?

"Are you willing to bet your life on this being a worthless piece of paper?" Dr. Yang licks his lips.

I look the doctor straight in his muddy brown eyes. "Whatever it is you think I know, I don't." I don't waver, each word woven from steel and dreams, wistful and hard, unbreakable. "I wish I *could* tell you. Since you let SS out to eat everyone brain-first, even *you* having the cure would be better than letting everyone die this way. How are the Menghu going to feel now that you don't have a cure for them? Or the Firsts who know it was you involved in developing contagious SS?" I reach out to take the paper, but he pulls it away, folding it into his pocket. "There's no miracle end to this story, Dr. Yang, no brilliant solution for you to present to the people following you. Maybe Mother was just a little bit too far gone in the end to know what she was doing."

She wasn't. I can feel it, more true than anything I've ever known. The cure isn't in those pictures we sent to Sole. It isn't on the device. The cure is in the one place no one was supposed to know about besides Aya and me. A place out of reach, where only I can find it.

Dr. Yang stands, his fingers twitching together in an agitated pattern. "She wouldn't have told you to go to Port North and talk to the Baohujia if she hadn't wanted you to find her device."

I shake my head. "She told me to find family. *My* family. You don't think that maybe she just wanted me to be safe from you?" She sent me there to find them. So they'd help me. So it wouldn't just be me against Dr. Yang and the Chairman and the entire mountainside of no-man's-land.

Dr. Yang swears, every word a hot needle in my calm as he sits back down. "No. You know what this means. There's no other explanation."

I shake my head, hope flaring even brighter. "Not all of us are as smart as you, Dr. Yang."

"Every day more masks break, Jiang Sev. Every second you keep it back, people are *dying*. Killing one another because they can't help it. If you won't tell me what you see in this paper, it will be *you* killing them. I can save them with the cure, Jiang Sev. I've spent my whole life trying to *save people*."

"No." I shake my head, thinking back to Mei, let loose in the Mountain, spreading SS to everyone. Of Dr. Root, dead. Of

General Hong, sliced to pieces by slivers of jade. Of my mother, slowly turning to dust. "You've been trying to turn the world into a place where everyone thinks you have all the answers." I remember the conversation I overheard between him and the Chairman. "Where no one can tell you to sit in a corner and ignore you. I can't help you, Dr. Yang, even if I wanted to. You put yourself in this corner. That paper is nothing more than a bit of trash."

He swears again. "I'll give you a month."

"I thought I only had five minutes." Dr. Yang pulls a vial from his desk and holds it up to the light. "Do you know what this is?"

I keep my hands in my lap, danger prickling across my skin. It's just a glass vial, clear so I can see his fingers bulging and distorted by the glass on the other side. "Unless it's going to manipulate my brain into some sort of instant genius, I don't think it will help anything."

"Your mother was Asleep for eight years." He sits forward, tapping the glass vial with one finger. "I did that. With this."

"I've already fallen Asleep and woken up, thank you."

"This isn't SS, Jiang Sev. This is something wholly different. Something *I* created. Suspended Sleep isn't the same disease. It's a medically induced coma that mimics the symptoms of the first stage of SS."

My blood seems to freeze in my veins, a flash of the paralysis swamping my brain, the terror so much worse than being trapped in the box at Port North, worse than gores or Menghu could ever be. Darkness, with no way to move my arms, my legs, no way to even blink . . .

"You can't do that."

"The fate of the people I am responsible for rests on finding the cure. All those people you think you are fighting for? They follow me. Because I can help them. I am a doctor. I created this cure, and your mother stole it."

"That is *not*—!"

"Whoever it is you think you are helping, you are killing them right now. The people in these mountains need a real leader. One who will give them the things they deserve, not hoard it all for themselves."

The doctor walks around the desk, fiddling with the vial. "I wouldn't do this if I didn't have to. Do you really want to go back to Sleep? Because you're afraid I might not cure your friends?"

"If I could fall Asleep again, I would have already." Words start pouring from my mouth as if talking is going to negate what comes next. "I've been exposed enough, haven't I?" He doesn't even look at me, walking past me to open the door. He murmurs something to Helix, who stands just outside.

After a few moments of murmuring, of feet walking away and the awful quiet of no one being here but me and Dr. Yang, Helix returns, handing something that crackles with plastic to the doctor. Dr. Yang lets the door swing closed and goes to lean against the desk directly in front of me.

There's a syringe in his hand, still wrapped in plastic. Glassy, sterile, with a needle in a separate package inside.

"A month Asleep, Jiang Sev." He says it matter-of-factly, as if it's a prescription, a blessing rather than a threat. "I'm interested to see if that will be enough to loosen your tongue."

"You say you want to save people? How many of them will die if you put me out for a month?"

He takes a step toward me, mouth pursed in a thoughtful frown. "You are making this choice, not me. Their deaths will be on your head."

"It *killed* her when I woke her up." I hate the frailty in my voice. What if he's right? What if holding it back kills more than I could possibly save? Who will die because I'm sitting here with my lips sewn shut?

I grit my teeth. The same people who will die if I open them. The people Dr. Yang cares about have Mantis. No one else will see a single drop of the cure.

If I give him the cure, June will die a Seph like her father. Maybe even totally wiped clean with nothing but sickness left inside her brain, like Parhat. Lihua will get thrown from the highest tree branch of Cai Ayi's Post.

If I tell Dr. Yang where the cure is, he'll use it as the new currency of his regime, and none of the people I love will have anything to trade for it. This has to be a bluff, because if I'm his one last link to finding the cure, he isn't going to stab me in the heart. He's just trying to scare me.

I can't help the note of pleading that threads through my voice as he fiddles with the syringe. "Killing me isn't going to get what you want."

When he finally looks at me, my skin goes cold. "Shall we find out?"

CHAPTER 60

MY EARS RING AS HELIX DRAGS ME DOWN THE hallway after Dr. Yang, the empty syringe gripped in the doctor's hand. The compound is silent, an echo of what it's supposed to sound like, deadened by the high-pitched peal in my head. Gray walls and cement floor, numbers in chipped red paint that mark the number of rooms as we pass, counting down until I'm dead. Seven, six, five . . .

Helix's hand on my wrist bites, as if he has teeth instead of fingers. Two other Menghu I don't recognize trail behind us. Dr. Yang stops in front of a door, a blocky 4 stenciled across the heavy metal.

The hinges creak as we go inside, Helix's stranglehold on my wrist relaxing when the doctor asks me to climb up onto the table in the center of the room. This place is a blank, nothing but the table, the walls . . . no restraints, no scalpels, or saws. All Dr. Yang needs is that one syringe.

He slowly pulls the plastic packaging from the tube, fixing a needle to the end of the syringe. Once he injects me, I'll be aware, awake. Paralyzed. Only this time, I won't have a chance of waking up. Not until he lets me.

"Helix?" Dr. Yang stabs the vial without looking up. "Would you go notify Dr. Bai we're ready? We'll need a short-term feeding tube. Catheter. Same supplies for a typical first-stage SS victim."

Helix hesitates. "You don't want me to have them prep the surgery?"

I'd laugh if I weren't so terrified. What will it take for the Menghu to finally figure out that Dr. Yang can't cut my head open and extract the cure to SS with a ladle?

Pulling the needle out of the vial with a muted pop, Dr. Yang hardly glances at the Menghu captain, flicking the syringe with his fingertip. "Did you not hear what I just asked for?"

Helix's eyes flick over me, my clothes torn, feet bare. Still dirty from scaling the walls in an effort to get to Gao Shun and the stone dust from being underground during the attack. I stare back at him, at the dark circles raccooning his eyes, and try to muster a defiant smile. Not willing to let him think I'm frightened of him. That I'm frightened of anything.

Holding Helix's gaze takes so much concentration, I'm not expecting it when the needle punctures my arm, trails of acid and fire swimming up my veins in a suicide sprint. I gasp, pulling away, and earning myself an extra jab from the needle as it pushes to the side.

Dr. Yang withdraws the syringe and holds it out to Helix, finally glancing over at the Menghu. "Do I need to ask one of the others?"

"No, sir." Helix's back almost seems to bend without his permission, giving the doctor a deferential bow. He takes the empty syringe and walks out without another glance at me.

"This is your last chance, Jiang Sev." The doctor finally meets my frantic gaze. The acid in my arm spreads up to my shoulder, across my chest, and out to my other limbs. I bite my lip, fists clenching weakly. I won't let this man see me cry.

My mouth is buttoned closed, so many lives sheltered inside. Sole, who has Mother's research, whatever was in it. Peishan, my old roommate, up in the trees at an old trading post. Lihua, waiting for me to come back with the Mantis that will keep her from hurting the people she loves.

June, Asleep at Port North. *I'm not your sacrifice,* she said. But she *was* the sacrifice, the price we paid to Luokai to get the cure.

Howl. Alone and broken. Left on the Port North steps.

Their faces grow fuzzy and soft, fading into the shadows in my mind as the drug takes hold. But I don't forget them, even as everything about me blurs.

They say power grows from the barrel of a gun. They're wrong. That's not power, it's fear, and fear can be conquered when there's more to stand for than your own life. True power grows from love and family and friendship. They give you the strength to do what is right even when it is impossible.

Power is standing in front of the gun, knowing how powerless you are, and still refusing to move.

The world goes black around me and I let my eyes shut, stop fighting the hold Dr. Yang's virus has on my brain.

Power is my silence.

PRONUNCIATION GUIDE

Baohujia	Bow (rhymes with "cow") hoo-jya
Cai Ayi	Tsie (rhymes with "my") AH-yee
Cale	Cayl (rhymes with "pale")
Dazhai	Dah Jie (rhymes with "my")
Helix	Hee-lix
Hong Tai-ge	Hong (long o, like in "tome") Tie (rhymes with "my") guh
Jiang Gui-hua	Jee-ang GWAY-hwa
Jiang Sev	Jee-ang Sev
Lihua	Lee-hwa
Mei	May
Menghu	Mung (rhymes with "rung") hoo
Peishan	Pay-shan
Sun Howl	Soon Howl
Sun Luokai	Soon Loo-oh-kie (rhymes with "my")
Xuan	Shwen (rhymes with "pen")
Yang He-ping	Yahng (a as in "fawn") Huh-ping
Ze-ming	Zuh-ming

AUTHOR'S NOTE

In the opening and closing paragraphs of the book, Sev is referencing a quote from Chairman Mao Zedong. The real quote is, "Every Communist must grasp the truth; 'Political Power grows out of the barrel of a gun'" ("Problems of War and Strategy," November 6, 1938, Selected Works, Vol. II, p. 224).

The military camp in this book is named for a commune that was held up as the ideal during the Cultural Revolution in China as what communism really meant. Supposedly, self-reliant workers turned the invertile soil of the area into productive land relying solely on hard work, with little oversight or help from the government. Mao said, "In agriculture, learn from Dazhai." Dazhai's methods soon became the standard for all communes regardless of local conditions, which did not turn out well.

The statue on Port North was inspired by Mazu, a sea goddess worshipped in Southeast Asia. Though there isn't any religion actively being practiced in Port North, the City, or the Mountain, hints of what came before the Influenza War are still there.

ACKNOWLEDGMENTS

Acknowledgments are both fabulous and terrible to write. Putting them on paper makes me feel warm and fuzzy about all of the generosity and true friendship in my life and reminds me how lucky I am to know so many lovely people. On the other hand, it makes me anxious because I'm afraid I'll forget some of them. So, if your name isn't here and it should be, know that it's because I was having a selfish, blank sort of moment, not because I don't appreciate you.

First of all, my editor, Sarah McCabe, and her use of all caps and italics and general ANGER at certain members of the *Shatter the Suns* cast, is probably one of my favorite things that has ever happened. It's so nice to have fictional people to hate. Working with an editor in general is such a learning experience, and I count myself lucky to have one who is so smart, who is so quick, and who I actually like. Victoria Wells-Arms is next on my list for believing in me and this series before anyone else did.

David Field and Aaron Limonick gave me the best cover an author could ask for. In fact, the whole team at Simon Pulse is the absolute best to work with, and I can't go without mentioning them: many thanks to Mara Anastas, Chriscynethia Floyd, Liesa Abrams, Jessica Handelman, Michael Rosamilia, Katherine Devendorf, Rebecca Vitkus, Sara Berko, Lauren Hoffman, Caitlin Sweeny, Alissa Negro, Anna Jarzab, Jennifer Wattley, Christina Pecorale and the rest of the Simon & Schuster sales team, Michelle Leo and her team, Nicole Russo, and Samantha Benson. These are the folks who make dreams come true.

Without my fabulous writing group, Kristen, Cameron, and Dan, this book would have never quite started breathing, and Sev would be significantly more prone to sexual innuendo (even if it was unintentional). The Wellies: Rebecca, Elizabeth and Hillary, who muscled through the second draft of this book and didn't even spit in my hair when they saw the word count, and also McKelle George, who did a last-minute read for me when I was in full panic mode. For that, and for all of you, I am forever grateful.

Thanks to the members of the writing community here in the Valley who spend so much time pepping each other up and being the best sort of people to hang out with.

The people most deserving of acknowledgment are, of course, my family members. They put up with me and my books on a daily basis. To my kids, who have already started writing books of their own and disappear into their rooms to have "writing group," I can't wait to see what you do with yourselves. My husband makes writing possible, listens to all of the weird things that come into my head without thinking I've come undone (and is able to tell me when I haven't come quite undone *enough*), and doesn't mind when I get up in the middle of the night to write things down. There aren't enough thanks in the world for such a perfect, wonderful partner in life.

And thank you to all the readers who fell in love with Sev, June, Howl, and Tai-ge and came back for round two to see what kinds of new messes they could get themselves into. It still blows my mind that other people get lost in the world I made up in my head.

TURN THE PAGE FOR A
SNEAK PEEK AT THE
THRILLING FINALE!

CHAPTER 1
Sev

THEY SAY TO FIND A HERO YOU CAN'T LOOK TO the past. Heroes from stories aren't real anyway, and that's what the past is, right? A story told by whoever had the biggest gun. Instead, we're supposed to find heroes around us.

I have nowhere to look, though, because my body *won't* look. It's made of ashes and wind and dead things, nothing but an echo of a heartbeat left inside me. My life has turned into a dream, every moment I'm Asleep making it harder to remember what it was like to be awake. If there was a hero next to me I wouldn't know, because all I can see is the dark side of my eyelids, feel the grainy sheet on the bed underneath me. The only things that change are sounds. Temperature. Right now I'm cold. I can hear the steady *plink, plink, plink* of fluid dripping to my IV.

The door hinge squeaks, and cool air washes over me from the hallway like a breeze from the ocean, vast as a year and deep as the sky. If my body could tense, it would, but instead I'm curled up inside my mind, waiting for whoever it is to poke or prod me. To pick up my dead weight and throw me in a burn pile, mutter ugly things into my dead ears, or touch my dead body because I can't stop them. Whoever it is stays quiet, lurking near my bed.

You are alive, not dead. It's a whisper at the back of my mind, crumpled like a wet sheet of paper. *Just like the princess in our story. Asleep until someone kisses you awake.*

I wish I could grimace, because that's not the only ending I've heard to the sleeping princess's story. Also, I don't want anyone in Dr. Yang's base to kiss me, thank you very much.

The person prowling in my room sits in what I think must be a chair, the legs squeaking under their weight. I hear quick, nervous breaths that are free of a gas mask's rusty tang. The bit of me that's still awake braces for violence or worse. No mask means SS now, and SS is a beast that I don't have the muscles to fight anymore.

"We've done everything you asked." A muffled voice filters through the closed door. *Helix*, my brain supplies. *The Menghu who killed June's father.* The person invading my room bolts up from the chair, footsteps padding to the far side of my bed away from the door. "There isn't enough Mantis to last us much longer." Helix's voice grows louder, though it's still attempting a respectful tone. "You *promised*—"

"Don't argue with me, Captain Lan." That's Dr. Yang. The door opens again, his footsteps tapping in, probably here for my weekly checkup. I think it's weekly. Maybe it's daily, and I've only been lying here for two days. I can't tell.

He pauses inside the room. "Aren't you supposed to be sending orders to Dazhai?" Not speaking to me, because he knows I cannot answer.

The intruder by my bed doesn't move for a good thirty seconds. But then the loud ring of army boots on concrete ring out as they leave my side and walk out the door.

Eight years my mother survived this. Eight years she *listened*, keeping her mind awake so she'd be able to pass on the possibility of curing SS. I'm like her, I guess. Dr. Yang put me to Sleep for knowing the truth too. That the note Mother left me in the device we found at Dazhai wasn't gibberish. It was a clue telling me where to find the cure.

"Medicine is an exact science." The doctor is speaking again, vague amusement at my unauthorized visitor melting away to leave only clinical precision. "You'll have to trust me, Helix. I promised you a cure, but you and your soldiers will have to be patient."

He can't get the cure. Not unless I tell him where Mother hid it. The tiny living part inside me raises her head, listening to Helix's silence. It's heavy. A waiting silence that could end in death or destruction or maybe a cup of tea. It's hard to tell. All I know is Helix doesn't ask any more questions.

CHAPTER 2
Tai-ge

THE COT FEELS LIKE SOME KIND OF CANVAS. ROUGH
grain, stretched tighter than I'd expect. Of course, all the missions
I've participated in with the City up until now required specific
flight plans, an eye on the clouds, and exactly zero cots. Maybe cots
have been this way all along, and I had to sleep on one to know the
way the fabric scratches at my skin.

Voices outside my tent draw my spine straight. Each time I
inhale, it strains through the filters of my mask, so loud I have to
hold my breath to listen. Three voices, coming from the direction
of the Chairman's tent. Female. Two I don't recognize, harsh and
precise as they issue through gas mask filters. The third voice,
however, is familiar as the raw-scrubbed lines of my knuckles even
through the rasp of a mask.

When the voices draw close, the two unfamiliar ones pass by,
leaving a shadow waiting outside the tent flap. I stand, waiting to
see if she'll finally come in. Wanting her to. But not wanting to
face her.

An arm pushes aside the untied tent flap, General Hong's

polished boots all I allow myself to look at once she steps inside. The air between us seems to be filled with nothing but disappointment.

"I have an assignment for you, Son."

I chance raising my eyes past her knees, almost to her belt buckle, the City seal a proud falcon and beaker etched into the metal. Silence is respect. I wait.

"It's a chance to alleviate some of the difficulty in which we find ourselves." She sighs, bending until her face comes into view, forcing me to break the boundary between our stations and look her in the eyes. "I'm proud of what you did, Tai-ge." My chest lifts, some space finally opening inside it, only to turn back to stone when she continues. "It just wasn't enough."

Failure. I got into Kamar when it was supposed to be impossible for a Second. I got the device Sev's mother left behind. And then I let Menghu take it away from me.

"Do we know where they took the cure yet?" I ask, knowing better than to voice the other question that's been burning inside me since Dr. Yang's Menghu flew me from Kamar to Dazhai camp, leaving me on the dead airfield and taking everything of value with them.

It's been two weeks. Two weeks of measuring the gap between my tent and the next. Of eating exactly what I'm rationed and hanging my uniform coat so the wrinkles left from being stuffed under my mother's bed will smooth. Two weeks of disappointed silence.

"No," Mother finally responds. "We don't know where the Menghu took the device you found in Kamar. Dr. Yang has been quite communicative about progress, though." She sighs, her tone a familiar frustrated cadence. "After Jiang Sev killed her mother with anti–Suspended Sleep serum, apparently the setbacks seemed insurmountable. But, now that he has this new data, Dr. Yang is optimistic we have what we need to cure SS."

"Sevvy—Jiang Sev—didn't hurt her mother on purpose. Dr. Yang told her—"

Mother frowns over my slip using Jiang Sev's nickname, but mercifully doesn't comment. "There are other patients in a similar state, and he's had success waking them when using the serum correctly, Tai-ge. That girl never was much for listening. There's a proper procedure. A dosing schedule. You can't give it to a patient all at once. If it wasn't on purpose, then it was incompetency."

I lick my lips, letting her finish. She's right about Sevvy. Rules seemed an annoying itch to my friend as we got older.

"Apparently, Jiang Sev can read the data contained on the device, but she won't cooperate." Mother's eyes narrow. "I have no doubt the obstacles will be worn down soon, though."

Worn down. I keep my eyes focused on Mother, refusing to blink. It doesn't stop the terrible images that crop up in my head, the tingles of pain that streak down my arms and back that make me wish I hadn't been a part of putting Sevvy in a cell. But I push that thought aside. Sevvy should know better than to hold back now. We need the cure. The whole world does. We can't be picky about who is in charge if there's nothing left to be in charge of, but still it sits wrong in my stomach that I'm here in this tent and she's being . . . worn down.

"Is Dr. Yang allowing First and Second involvement?"

"There are Firsts from the Circle, who are being asked to help, but the Chairman won't relay any details. It is my belief that Dr. Yang isn't allowing him to do so. The information you brought me before going to Port North regarding Dr. Yang's true loyalties and Chairman's actions . . . You were correct. He has been compromised somehow by Dr. Yang. We have to forge forward ourselves."

"If Dr. Yang manages to develop a working cure . . ." I pause, not sure how to phrase what we must both be thinking. "How long do we have before he stops pretending to be a loyal City comrade? He'll use the cure to compel Seconds and Thirds to support his Menghu forces."

Mother walks over to my cot and sits down, the frame squeaking. She gestures for me to sit next to her, a smile touching her lips at my automatic hunch. My head higher than hers makes me uncomfortable. "Dr. Yang says he wants to unify us, but I am afraid you are right. He means only to take what we have. I have great admiration for what you were able to accomplish, as I said before. But without the device we need a way to fight. Which brings us to your new assignment."

Fight? I hold the word inside. There was a time when I could say some of what I thought to my mother. When I could tease her and deviate from what she wanted without repercussions. That was when we had beds, pillows, wooden floors beneath our feet. Walls that isolated our family enough to allow us to be mother and son when no one could hear. Now she's stepped into Father's shoes and we live in an open field where every moment we are made from gas masks and metal stars. The fate of the City has slipped from the Chairman's shoulders to settle on Mother's.

The Chairman. Anger churns inside me, my teeth clamping so tight my jaw begins to ache. I've seen him here in the camp, waving, encouraging. Serving the Seconds and Firsts with a stalwart firmness, a determination that's meant to be inspiring. As if rationing isn't a direct result of him handing our supplies to

Dr. Yang. Without Chairman Sun, the Menghu would never have invaded the City. We never would have ended up in this cold-water camp, biting our tongues as he opens the gate and lets gores in one by one.

He and Dr. Yang together have much to answer for. But Mother and I are the only ones who know.

"We need to have another way to fight SS until we can take the cure for our own, Tai-ge." Mother pats the cot next to her again, and this time it's an order, so my knees bend. "Masks break every day, and we have no way to fix them or build new ones. The Mantis stockpiles are growing thin, disappearing into Menghu camps. The moment Dr. Yang has a working cure, it will be loyalty against an empty stomach and compulsions. Our soldiers and workers will become his slaves." She touches my shoulder, pushing my hunched shoulders straight. "You remember the medic we sent with you to Kamar who was so easily swayed into betraying you? I doubt we can expect better from most of our ranks. They are frightened."

My chest clenches over the memory. Xuan tried to kill me. He told Sevvy . . . I don't know what he told Sevvy, exactly. Something that made her set him free and turn me out for the gores . . .

I mean, I do know what he must have said. That I was working with Mother to get the cure. That I meant to take it back to her, to people who could analyze it, reproduce it, and actually use it to save us all from SS. But the way he said it must have cast me as a villain because he didn't care about saving anyone. All Xuan wanted was to escape from his duty. His expertise was supposed to get us into Kamar's main city, onto their island, so I could disable the weapons they used to shoot our helis out of the sky. Instead, he left. Landed us all in Kamari jail cells.

Xuan is the reason I failed Mother. Failed my people. Failed Sevvy.

I blink the thought away before it can take over. I don't owe Sevvy anything. She's the one who wouldn't listen to reason. And excuses are for the weak. For those who refuse to take ownership of themselves and their actions. My failures are mine, no matter who else contributed. It was *my* failing to place trust in Xuan.

Mother leans forward, fingering her mask before letting her hand fall. For a moment I think she means to put a hand on my knee. A comfort. Instead, she stands. "We must be able to protect our people, to give them an alternative to capitulation." She touches my shoulder, her hand perfectly positioned as if she thought out all the angles and pressure before moving. "So I'm sending you back to the City."

I push myself up from the cot. Back to the City? We abandoned the City, its labs, and its factories to SS, the disease spreading too quickly to do anything but run.

Lagging a respectful two steps behind my mother, I square my shoulders and follow her out of the tent. The light seems bright outside, cheery after the two weeks of gloomy waiting for judgment inside my tent. I may have listened to Sevvy during the invasion, dirtied my boots with the spoiled world Outside, then failed at the task Mother set me after I tried to make amends. But now I can make up for it.

All the muscles tensed along my shoulders loosen because I'm back where I belong: two steps behind the General. Whatever it is Mother has for me to do, whether it's in the City, in the camp here, or at the center of the Earth, I will do it if it means she trusts me again.

TO SAVE THE WORLD, YOU NEED AN UNSTOPPABLE GIRL.

BELIEVE IN YOUR SHELF

Visit RivetedLit.com & connect with us on social to:

DISCOVER NEW YA READS

READ BOOKS FOR FREE

DISCUSS YOUR FAVORITES

SHARE YOUR IDEAS

ENTER SWEEPSTAKES FOR THE CHANCE TO WIN BOOKS

Follow @SimonTeen on

to stay up to date with all things Riveted!